Terrible With Raisins

Lynne McVernon

ISBN-13: 978-1492898788

ISBN-10: 1492898783

For my parents, Barbara and Harold McVernon,
who always supported, always believed.

PROLOGUE

CLAIR

Dorothy Parker said it first

Birthdays, eh? Pinnacles of delight until we're twenty-one. After that, they're just annual records, shoved into a concertina file of years.

Stop being cynical. And subjective. Fair point, I suppose. Few of us can deny the fairy tale glee of having our own special celebration day. I can. Could. Did. Given the birthday I faced. The ogre rose menacingly from the calendar, eyeballed me across three short months and grabbed me by the – throat? Ego? Libido? Apologies. I'm an artist; I mix metaphors as well as paint.

My introspection was stimulated by a brilliant writer who, facing the same trauma said: "… there was something, something pretty terrible… Not just plain terrible. This was fancy terrible. This was terrible with raisins in it…". That remarkable, terribly clever woman spoke to me directly across time and an ocean – to me, that knot of self-doubt skulking behind a shed in Aborigine Road, Guildford.

Twilight, early May. As her words dimmed on the page, I sipped whisky from a tea cup and sneaked a risky cigarette. The last cigarette – maybe. The hall light wasn't on, so Jess couldn't be home yet. I'll give it five minutes. Five minutes of solitude to mourn my looks and feel guilty for all the wasted time and opportunities. Five minutes to contemplate making a list of 'things to do' before the Terrible Birthday. And to know I wouldn't make it – or do them.

Her voice stabbed the dusk.

– I knew you'd be down here!

Back indoors my accuser perched on a chair arm. I slumped on the sofa opposite.

– It's a fair cop. Let me have it, I deserve it.

– This is serious.

– Sorry.

– I mean – what kind of an example is it?

– A bad one.

– You said you'd give up before your birthday.

– I will. There's still three months to go.

I pulled rank and turned the spotlight on her AS level revision. History, it seemed, was no longer a candidate for A levels, nor even a topic for discussion.

– But I thought you liked – ?

Jess rose impatiently from the chair arm.

– OK, there's <u>obviously</u> no point in trying to talk to you at the moment, not with your hormones all over the place. Why don't you finish your whisky? You're <u>obviously</u> dying to. Think I'll join you –

– <u>Obviously</u> you think you have me at a moral disadvantage. But <u>emphatically</u> no.

She stalked to the door and made a passable attempt at a withering look.

– Mum – you are so unreasonable at the moment! I'll be glad when your menopause is over!

Game to Jess. She left a grisly silence in the room as the word bore down on me. *Menopause.*

I waited for the bedroom door to slam, then topped up my drink. The real crisis, of course, was reaching fifty. *How do I deal with this appalling slice of life?* Problem you never had to face, Dad. Bless you. I raised my cup to his painting over the mantelpiece, 'Blue Period 1', J Harkin, 1951.

– Here's tae us, wha's like us. Damn few an' they're a' deid!

Well, most of them.

My book had disappeared but I couldn't be bothered looking for it. Dorothy wouldn't have minded. She knew what I was going through.

That night, I was roughly seventeen hundred miles north west of the island and unaware of its role in my next phase. Would I have felt differently if I'd known?

CHAPTER ONE

STILL CLAIR

Terrible times on the way

We made it to the end of AS levels.

June. The imminent weight of great age fell away simply because it was Saturday and sunny. Veering toward the gamin, I plopped a loose denim dress over a tight white T-shirt, scrunched my hair up and finished with wooden bead earrings and red clogs. Jess, sober in jeans and jogging top, was appalled.

– You can't go out like that, Mum! You look like a bloody art teacher.

– I am – was – a bloody art teacher.

I drove her up to Heathrow, despite protestation. But with exams behind and freedom ahead, she abandoned her sulk by the end of the road, enthusing over her solo flight to Scotland. Which liberated me, too.

Imitating art, the M25 truly was 'The Road to Hell'. It was touch and go whether Jess would make check-in but we made it with ten minutes to spare. It meant heading straight for the drop-off zone instead of short-term parking and ruled out hanky waving in Departures. To avoid irritating my spirited daughter, I resisted maternal instructions and advice.

– Have a great time, darling! Give Maggie lots of love and hugs. And Jack and Tatty.

She sauntered into the terminal with no sense of urgency while I sat amidst transient Mercedes and BMWs, immobilised by anxiety in the L reg. Polo. *If she doesn't shift her arse she'll miss…* My mobile rang.

– Mum, go! You'll get a ticket.

– Have you found the right check-in desk?

Stupid question. Invites sarcasm. Which it brought. Inevitably. The leave-taking was ruined and the umbilical cord snapped back like coiled steel. *Sod you, then. Awkward little cow.* I slung my mobile at my bag and headed for Richmond.

Acute pain flagged the thirty-year time lapse since last wearing clogs. I leaned against the wall of the old house dabbing the raw bridges of my feet while I waited for a response from Sonya's entry phone. Probably not up yet. *Or has Brian stayed the night? Should I try again or –?* Sharp treble static cut across my dither –

– Shit – is that the time? Clair? Come in.

Buzz. Not up yet. Clogs in hand, I padded barefoot through the porch and up the wide, carpeted staircase. Her front door was ajar, somewhere a loo was flushing; Sonya's day was just beginning. *Will Jess have taken off, yet?* Sonya appeared clad in a plum satin dressing gown, slightly askew. Her expensive copper hair was a dragon's nest and her face was streaked with last night's make-up. She lit two Dunhills and passed me one.

    — Darling. You're here.

    — Thanks. Are you all right?

    — Fine — for a re-tread of all the bits Cher's had cut off and sucked out.

She took a long drag and shuffled out again.

    — Scrape this gunk off my face. Help yourself to stuff.

I made coffee and took it to the sitting room. The last remnants of haze were lifting from the river making the Vale of Richmond look Turner-esque. *Did she forget I was coming? Will Jess be over Gloucester? Or the Lake District?* Sonya swept back in looking cool in khaki cotton trousers and top, head swathed in a towel.

    — Had Jolyon back here last night for a bit of touchy feely. Kept the telly on for company. Then it felt a bit like dogging so I chucked him out. Couldn't sleep for hours wondering if his red patches were herpes.

Jolyon was a mildly porcine PR client who'd lusted after her for years.

    — Does this mean you and Brian — ?

    — Certainly not. But I can't spend every night alone with a Rampant Rabbit while he's snuggled up to Madame Cellulite.

The last being Brian's wife.

    — This coffee's disgusting. Which jar did you use? Gravy granules?

    — As if you'd possess such a thing.

    — So-o-o-o, Jess got off to a flying start?

I related the flawed farewell then unburdened Jess's recent AS level traumas, the imminence of her sleeping with new boyfriend Raz, of her hitting seventeen, nagging for driving lessons, an iPhone and a tattoo of the Buddha's entrails. And her monumentally annoying fixation with my menopause. Sonya pounced on that.

    — Oh god, the bloody 'm' word. Everyone's obsessed with it! By the way, I'll get her the iPhone — one of my retail accounts. Yep, menopause — menopausal, peri-menopausal, sub-peri-menopausal. I refuse to have a biological crisis just to provide material for Woman's Hour. Drives me bloody tatah!

She paused for breath.

    — Oh my god, Clack, what have you come as? A bloody drama teacher?

Clack – Sonya's pet name for me since teacher training college.

Brian, Sonya's boyfriend, was – possibly still is – financial director for a small film independent. She was joining him on a business trip to LA and, consequently, had urgent clothes shopping to do. She lent me a pair of men's – *Brian's?* – flip-flops and we set off. Flapping along next to her I felt like Goofy.

– Where are you working now, Clack? Not those solicitors, still?

– No. They found that email I sent you calling them a bunch of bloodsucking incompetents. I'm PA to a fourteen-year-old at a software company, now.

I looked at the price tag of a shirt and replaced it like a live grenade. The place was way beyond my extravagance limit.

– I know you hate teaching, but wouldn't it pay more?

– It's all crowd control and no teaching. I thought about marrying for money, but billionaires are so bloody choosy.

– True. Bastards.

Sonya spoke with authority having met more than one.

– Don't you dare go marrying old Gluefeatures –

Howard – and I'm not rising to it.

Sonya lined up a jade silk crossover top with a foxily slit, weasel slim skirt and set off on the hunt for shoes. Emerging back into George Street with a dizzying pair of heels, she had a pang of conscience.

– Come on, Clack, I'm spending for Britain! What d'you fancy? Something floaty? Less galumphing?

We huddled into a fitting room where I struggled into a dusky pink top and trousers and turned to the mirror, expecting the worst.

– Fabulous! I've never seen you in that colour before. You've got great arms, no bingo wings – well, none to speak of.

– The trousers are too tight.

– No, they're not.

– I'm too old.

– Your head is, your bum isn't. You'll be billionaire bait – or at the very least, shaggable –

– But –

– Shut up and get your Play School gear back on. I'm starving and I'm dying for a fag and a pee.

At the bistro, the waiter responded to Sonya's flirting as far as was polite and good business – and then some. She always got her man. With liquid green eyes, gin-sodden voice and spectacular breasts, her sex appeal was not just intact but remarkable, even to gay men and straight women. Much as I loved her, I wished her pheromones would hibernate occasionally. She winked, as the waiter slid away.

– A little bit of 'what if?' does you good. So, how is Gluefeatures? Why aren't you two stuck together this weekend?

Gluefeatures was Howard's old nickname that Sonya had treacherously shared with Jess.

– He's visiting Stepmother Bunce in Dorset.

– No invite yet?

– Thankfully not.

We were back at the flat when Jess rang from Maggie's. She'd left her lunch on the Oban train. It was raining. Mr Scrymgeour was just putting the car away and, yes, Maggie looked fine and sent her love. Demented yapping distracted her.

– Ohhh! Jack! Tatty! Hello-hello-I-love-you-too-got-to-go-'bye-Mum.

– but Jess… ?

There was no point in trying to call her back.

Sonya opened a bottle of Sancerre. Thirty years on, alcohol still played a key role in our friendship. In fact, only the loon pants and platform boots were gone.

– How's Maggie?

– She's fine – amazing, as ever. Seventy-eight last birthday.

– Bugger, I missed it! Give her my love – I'll organise some flowers.

Prompted by the subject of age, Sonya lurched into the familiar list of woes concerning Brian; thirteen years her adulterous lover and still using wife, kids, business, even mother-in-law, as excuses not to move in. I couldn't stomach yet another re-run and tried a lateral approach.

– I'd swap Howard for Brian any day.

You lie through your teeth, Clair Harkin, they're rivals in repulsiveness. Sonya's features melted in sympathy.

– Poor you. Sports car at his age! And the Rab C Nesbitt hair.

What about Brian's beer gut, ear hair and personality by-pass? And your sports car? But Sonya was in heroic mode, her chic sitting room was an amphitheatre and she was the tragic heroine. Which left me the rôle of chorus – as usual. All womankind, she declaimed, well, women of a certain age, were undervalued because of the double standards that still governed society. *Hardly original, Sonn, but I wouldn't dare say so.*

– How many female actors over fifty are still at the top? Playing leads? Judi Dench and – Judi Dench. Yeah, well, all the Dames, Maggie, Diana and Vanessa – Helen Mirren. But – but look at the flabby old middle-aged male newsreaders! Why do the women have to be trim, cute and under forty? What's wrong with being forty-five, fifty, fifty-five and talented? Creative? It threatens men of the same age, that's why. Because they're not in as good shape physically or mentally. Age is a state of mind, other people's minds!

I hunched miserably on the carpet. *Coming up fifty and what have I got to show for it – apart from Jess? Other women become brain surgeons, climb mountains, screw a celebrity – but me... I'm just a big fat mediocre vacuum.* I put a cushion over my face and whined into the kapok.

– I don't want to be fifte-e-e-e-e...

Sonya, safely a year away from the event herself, grimaced with alcoholic compassion.

– OK – OK sweetheart – how about... how about don't be?

– Sorry?

– Don't be fifty – bugger off for your birthday! Go abroad, and when you come back, leave all the crap of the last fifty years there –

– What?

– Go back to Greece –

– Oh yeah, so who am I? Shirley bloody Valentine or an extra in Mamma Mia?

– Why not? Shag a Colin Firth or a Pierce Brosnan! Or a... that Swedish one nobody'd heard of – and go to – Hey, yes! Symi! Remember Symi? Go there – turn the clock back. Take your new pink gear. Find a boy and turn him into a man. What fiftieth birthday?!

That's how the Symi idea started. It was Maggie who made the idea a reality.

MAGGIE

Late June

There was a fire in the grate even though it was officially summer. Evening sun burnished the top field and gilded the window frame, throwing shafts of warm shadow across the room.

– Incidentally, Jessie James, do not, repeat, do not tell your mother that you and I were well down a whisky bottle on your first evening.

– Scout's honour!

Jess had a look of her grandfather, James. But at this moment she bore another resemblance, almost as familiar. I felt a catch at the similarity.

– She's on at me about everything at the moment, anyway. Getting really neurotic about being fifty. Still, I suppose it is incredibly old.

She took another slug of malt with the nonchalance of the young and tactless.

For a while, there were only the sounds of the fire, the ponderous old clock and the occasional cry of a gull winging shoreward. Jess sat on the floor in the front parlour, sifting through the box of photographs, ones that hadn't made it into an album, yet. Probably never would. They told stories of escapades and mystical experiences, days on the loch and by the sea, of Hogmanays and holidays; they transported long dead pets to befriend anew and childhood scrapes to savour. Most of the old, two-inch square, black and white photos had faded to sepia over some sixty years. None from the blue box, though, not yet.

– Is that Granddad James – next to you?

I sat forward in the rocking chair, peering over the rim of my whisky tumbler.

– That's him. You've seen all these before, JJ, surely?

But I was pleased that she wanted to look again, not least because then I could, too.

– Wish I'd known Granddad.

She stretched full length on the rug. She had never expressed the same wish about her father, Clair said. Probably just as well.

Displaced by her movement, both dogs snuggled up again, whimpering in an effort to get as close as they possibly could.

– He was so clever.

I knew from the direction of her gaze that she was looking at James's study of Connie nursing baby Clair. It was atypical of my brother's painting style, showing a softness and fluidity in contrast to the energy of his other work. His rendering of the lone mother and child, however, had proved a chilling prophecy.

– Was it very difficult for Granny after he died? I mean, they didn't like single mothers then, did they?

– People weren't easy on unmarried mothers. But your grandmother was a widow, so she got a lot of sympathy. It was difficult for her, though, because women couldn't earn much, there was no childcare and she didn't have any relatives over here – except for me, and I was at work all day. Her own family didn't want her back.

– That's so not fair – just because she fell in love with my Granddad and he didn't have any money. What a bunch of snobs! Or was it because he wasn't American?

– Who can say?

Jess was thoughtful for a while, attending to Jack's ears and Tatty's tummy.

– This is my other home, isn't it, Maggie?

– It is, lass.

– Good. By the way, could I have driving lessons for my birthday, please?

Tired out from her journey and rather more whisky than she was used to, the we'an fell asleep curled up with Jack and Tatty in front of the fire, still clutching her glass of malt. I watched her until near midnight, musing on how she embodied the past I knew and yet moved into a future that I wouldn't. She had arrived, a seven-pound bundle who brought so many questions and created so much love. And now, being a young woman and so strikingly beautiful, continued in exactly the same vein. Not at all biased, then? Me? I leaned over the slumbering huddle of dogs and girl, gently disengaged the whisky tumbler and stroked the shining black hair.

– Come on, Jessie James, you've had a long day. Time for bed.

As Jess tottered out sleepily, I collected the strewn photographs and dropped them back into the shoebox. The other box, blue, tied with ribbon and hidden in my dressing table, contained my photographs of Julia. But they were for another time.

Later, pulling up the coverlet, I thought about Clair's forthcoming 'big' birthday. Jess and I would talk about it tomorrow.

STILL MAGGIE

Early July

Of course, despite the best of intentions, Jess and I didn't get around to deciding anything about her mother's birthday and she whirled off South again, leaving me to get used to the croft without her voice and chaos filling every cranny. So, the problem of Clair's fiftieth was still filtering through the gravel in my old head. I thought a whiff of sea might help.

Esmeralda was nibbling new grass in the upper field and the water pipe was sunk in the burn. I came back across the low field into the back garden, threw my leather gloves into the lean-to and called Jack and Tatty. They bounded out of the house to the five-bar gate, barking. There was no need for such a mighty barrier across the drive; I should ask Wally Scrymgeour about removing it. Still, it was handy for times like this with Tatty in an inviting condition.

There were pale green candles on the pine tips and the earth burst with scrambling fern. The honeysuckle was strong enough this morning to scent the salt breeze. Marvellous infusion. Senses thrilling to it as ever, I strode down the incline to catch up with the Westies. And, as ever, I found it strange still to be walking down the lane without footsteps alongside mine. Of course, I was missing Jess, that's what all this was about, despite three long phone calls and a couple of emails. I hoped the cheque was enough to buy a few driving lessons, just to get her started off. Later on, she would need some help with funds for an old jalopy. Clair's baby seventeen! Seventeen years since that extraordinary day. And now the baby's taking driving lessons! Baby of the baby. Near fifty years – and no time – since James's telegram: "Am Dad. Mother baby girl well". Not written as he would have but, in those days, the Post Office was strict about content. Now Jess's latest email ran through my mind. We should have discussed her mother's fiftieth birthday properly while she was here. Why hadn't we? It required action.

As I followed the two shaggy white bodies tumbling down the lane, I realised I hadn't sprayed Tatty with repellent. Still, there was nothing likely to get at her on the strand this morning. Besides, this was just a quick outing before kirk. The dogs had disappeared from sight but not hearing. Something on the beach must have excited them. I trekked up the ridge to the crest by the folds of grey rock, looking out towards Oban and Mull. Silvered by the receding tide, the beach mirrored the morning sun, making me blink. They were down by the surf, two dark spots against the light, bouncing with excitement as they scolded something floating in the shallows. A figure moved along the sands from the south. It was Isobel Mudie, walking her husband Archie's dog, Jasper, some sort of cross between Lurcher and Irish Wolfhound. It would be wise to get to Tatty with all speed. No knowing what that combination might produce, even if it were physically possible! Too late, Jasper picked up a scent and caught sight of the distant Westies. I tensed, prepared to defend Tatty's honour. But, unaccountably for a healthy dog with all his equipment intact, Jasper reeled around and lolloped off in the opposite direction. Can't take after his master, I thought. Isobel hailed me as we met on firm ground at the top.

– Good morning, Margaret. It's a fine morning?

– Good morning, Isobel. Beautiful. In charge of Jasper?

Isobel sighed, watching Jasper canter into the distance.

– So I am. Indeed. For the weekend. Archie's across in Aberdeen again.

Archie being 'across in Aberdeen' was an old Kilachlan intrigue. For years, Isobel's husband had headed eastward 'on business'. But he'd been spotted more than once dropping south at Crianlarich instead of joining the A85 to Perth. What was more, Nessie Scrymgeour had seen envelopes addressed to 'Glasgow Parking' as she hoovered his dressing room. The widely-held theory was that while his Range Rover was being clamped in a Glasgow street, Archie was getting clamped nearby. Popular opinion was that if Isobel was aware of Archie's deception, she was surprisingly tolerant; if she wasn't, she was astoundingly dense. And I – knew what I knew.

– Your great-niece will be away by now?

– Jess? Yes, left on Tuesday. Flew from Glasgow.

– Did she, indeed? Well, now!

Isobel reacted as though Jess had simply flapped her arms and taken off. We watched Jasper gallop in a wide loop then stop, scratch an ear and roll off balance, threshing shaggy limbs in the wet.

– You'll be at coffee after the service, Margaret?

– Wouldn't miss my cup of Fairtrade and a flapjack. But I won't stay long. I have an appointment on the internet.

– No indeed, not with the cost of international calls.

Isobel was sublimely ignorant of information technology, too. We stood for a few moments contemplating Jasper wriggling on his back until she, to our mutual relief, terminated the encounter.

– Indeed, well… best be getting back, then.

She chafed her hands pointlessly, it being July and surprisingly mild.

– Mustn't keep the minister waiting!

A single woman living alone is nothing unusual, especially at my age. But I had never been dignified with the title of 'Mrs' and there was also the matter of my 'friendship' some years ago, so Isobel treated me with some awkwardness. Not an uncommon reaction around here. Small coincidence, then, that the last witch executed in Britain met her fate in Dornoch, only a broom's flight away up Loch Ness. While Isobel trailed after Jasper, I strolled to the water's edge where Jack and Tatty worried the remains of a cormorant, tangled in fishing line and gnawed by fish. Poor thing, caught by other fishers then eaten by its own prey.

– Come on, you two, drop! It's time for God and the flapjacks.

Back at the cottage after kirk, there was an email from Jess – it's not just Clair and I who are telepathic – and she gave me just the inspiration I needed for her mum's fiftieth birthday treat. I sent an email to Clair. That sounds very casual. In fact, it followed much cajoling from Julia (she who was innocent by some years of personal computers) to get on with it. I told Clair about 'dimitte diem'. That was our special phrase, Julia's and mine. She would approve of Clair knowing it. Of all people, Clair could put it to good use. Then I wrote a large-ish cheque and took the Westies for a snuffle to the post box. It would catch first post Monday morning.

CLAIR

Maggie takes the sting out of Terrible

Maggie sent me an email:

Dear Clair, What a marvellous idea to spend your unmentionable birthday in Greece. I spent mine on a wet Sunday in Glasgow, although it was more of a dry Sunday really, being before the licensing laws changed. Enough of me. May the retsina – or something less like turps – flow on your birthday. And forget all this Carpe Diem nonsense – don't seize the day but let it go. Dimitte diem. (dimitto = to leave, forgive, send away, abandon etc – 'forgive' might be asking a bit much, I suspect). Sadly, I never follow my own advice.

You are a wonderful woman and deserve the best in all you do. Indeed, you have the best in Jess. I send you much love, many thoughts, all power to your strivings, truth to your hopes and dreams

Maggie

P.S. Early birthday present in the post. You are to bank it!

P.P.S. Esmeralda ate Wally Scrymgeour's Scottish Daily Mail yesterday. Hope she doesn't turn Tory on me.

Maggie is my father's younger sister. Esmeralda is a goat. Sometime after Jess came back from Kilachlan Maggie sent me a cheque, a big one. I worried whether she could afford that much. But after a lecture on the generosity of receiving, Jess filled out my deposit slip and marched me to the bank. Then we went online and booked the holiday. Afterwards, I reread Maggie's email. It left my insides warm with love. Dimitte diem. Let the day go.

The phone interrupted my thoughts and I picked up without thinking. I always forget to monitor calls. Drives Jess demented. It was Howard, my... the person I was seeing. Served me right.

– Hello, Howard. How did the conference go?

He'd tell me anyway. It never occurred to him that my interest in his work might not be genuine. He might have been gibbering in ancient Norse for twenty minutes before he asked dutifully for my news. I delivered it clumsily in anticipation of a hurt reaction. But he took it well, saying that he wasn't familiar with Symi or, for that matter, any of the Greek Islands and weren't they full of students? He pointed out that it was very brief notice and outlined a few other shortcomings in my plans. Was surprised, too, that Jess was coming. *That Jess is 'coming'? Not 'going' – 'coming'? Shit! He thinks he's in on it!* I fell against the wall, winded.

– Howard –

– Just a minute – the twenty-fifth? That means we'll be away for... Oh – I see! You want to be away for the big one! Silly girl. It's not going to hurt that much! I promise you, when I –

– Howard!

– You don't have to explain. It's quite a watershed for a woman, I know.

He made it sound like the onset of incontinence. I had to be blunt. But I wasn't. I improvised, lied, apologised, blamed myself, blamed the travel company, the school summer holidays – a foolish point to make when talking to a Deputy Director of Education – and finally, used Maggie. Maggie's name would put an end to it. He always referred to Maggie as 'redoubtable', largely because he didn't know how to deal with her.

– The holiday's a gift from Maggie – for a mother/daughter bonding jaunt. Exclusively.

Maggie will back me up. I gabbled recklessly, compounding the untruth.

– Besides, I got the last two places.

– I see. Hum. Well... Don't worry, my love, we'll think of something.

Good old Howard, he only compromised when he knew he was beaten.

I put the phone down, exhausted, as Case, one of our two lodgers, bounced down the stairs and swung round the newel post gustily.

– What up, Clair? You sho' bumpin' tonight, real dime, ba-donka-donk. Gotta roll out dis crib now. Bust out de rent a.m., straight?

Or some similar shite. The gangsta slang was a leftover from his last drama school project. Case, of the precise cornrows and devastatingly beautiful body, was a child of Swindon. He also owed a month's rent.

– Peace out ma homie!

He gave me a high five, did a jêté through the front door and escaped. The other lodger, Phee, was away on a storytelling workshop and Jess had already left for work at the restaurant. I was alone in the house. A dimitte diem moment if ever there was one. I sat on the back doorstep with half a tumbler of whisky, chain smoking and dreaming of the Aegean. Hot days and warm nights, wine dark sea, tamarisk trees, hornets the size of vultures… I wrapped the stubs in kitchen foil, stuffed that into a broken eggshell, put the whole lot in an empty baked beans tin, crushed it underfoot, then hid it in the bin under last night's take away cartons and this morning's half-eaten breakfast. Jess's olfactory organ had astonishing range.

Thereafter, Howard dropped the subject of Symi – apart from a few 'I think Clair's trying to tell me something' cracks at the Aborigine Road Neighbourhood Watch barbecue that Saturday – and crooning 'I left my heart on Symi Island' during the routine session of coitus later.

HOWARD

The conference in Nottingham was the usual affair, the usual fare and an unfairly small proportion of the fair! The DfE sent along a very junior junior, a trainee in tedium. Fiona must have known about it when she volunteered me to attend. Coming back, queues on the M1, accident at Lutterworth and had to refuel at Newport Pagnell. Didn't get home 'til gone six. No messages. Had a shower. Rang Guildford. Clair vague as ever. Had booked a holiday on some Greek island to avoid her fiftieth. All very Shirley Valentine – or what's that other one? Full of pop songs? Greek island. Well, suppose I can understand her wanting to escape the birthday. Big one for a woman, something ending, not a lot to look forward to. Unaccountably, she hadn't discussed it with me first. Not only that, it seemed she hadn't considered my involvement at all. You see? Vague. And she was taking the daughter. Invoked the redoubtable aunt, too. No doubt I could sort it out, find a flight etcetera – involve a lot more cost than if she'd thought of it in the first place. Reassured her I'd think of something. Will ask my shared PA, Pat, to sort. Remind her not to mention it around the office. Wouldn't want Dame Fiona to accuse me of misusing staff time.

Went down to Guildford that weekend for some god-awful session with Clair's Neighbourhood Watch group hosted by some Eugène Terre'Blanche lookalike and his pantomime dame wife. Unlike dealing with Dame Fiona, I'd learned with Clair never to explain or to reason, just act. So, I teased her a bit about the Greek holiday – made remarks like "Any other chap might think you were trying to put him off". She looked suitably sheepish. Didn't object to a spot of the old horizontal jogging later on, though. Happily.

MAGGIE

It went down well. I was a wee bit concerned we'd have a tussle about it, knowing how Clair is about accepting gifts. But I have a feeling Jess put her straight on a few points. Anyway, good. They're going to Symi, a Greek island Clair and Sonya visited on one of their jaunts. I have a feeling that was the year Connie's mother died. Yes, in fact it was, because I remember them coming back to the flat in Thirleby Road, both filthy dirty and tired out having flogged up from Victoria coach station with half of Greece in their rucksacks. I still have the evil eye Clair brought back hanging in the back porch. Come to think of it, I still have Sonya's bottle of ouzo at the back of the drinks cabinet. Aways… I remember telling Clair her grandmother had died and that Connie was in Florida attending to matters. Clair never met Emily and wasn't sure how to feel given the negative press Connie had given the old lady. As it was, she didn't get the option of flying over for the funeral. Or the wedding. And the next time she saw her mother, Connie was Mrs Dubrowsky.

CHAPTER TWO

CLAIR

Nothing too Terrible so far

... wine dark sea and a coastline the colour of myth... That familiar headland rises from fabled depths and down every darkening slope, dwellings of ochre, cream, russet and pink tumble in jubilant –

– Hey – I just got a direct tweet from Raz –

... greeting. A last flourish from Helios as he dips below the western hills –

– He says Cancun is awesome –

... beckons me across the waters, their Stygian black silvered by sister Selene's –

– His brother's been grounded for barfing in the pool –

The happy little pastiche of Greek myth racketing round in my head collapsed. So much for fabled depths and tumbling dwellings. Jess, my bid for human perfection, was more interested in a 3 x 2 inch screen than in the blue rapture of the Aegean or the stunning panorama of Symi harbour.

The bovine surge to collect belongings started well before the ferry nudged the quayside. We joined the herd at the back of the boat, sweat settling in every crease. Our bags, of course, were under a mammoth turd of luggage; our carefully ironed holiday clothes would look like the scrapings of Jess's bedroom floor. This was not a propitious start. Even so, shuffling to board the gangway, lungs clogged with body odour and ship's diesel, I still felt the holiday excitement of a child. Of course, I had to think of Jess being parted from her boyfriend and suffering post AS level stress. I wasn't the only one with something difficult to face. We could help each other through these two weeks.

As we stepped onto the stone quay, a green sort of fly's eye on wheels slewed towards us and lurched to a halt, a chunky mermaid and 'Symi Port Harbour Service' stencilled on it. An ample Greek, white shirt straining, emerged from the tiny cab and landed solidly on sandalled feet. I nudged Jess matily.

– Blimey, it's Captain Pugwash!

She reacted with one of those 'you really should take your medication' looks and continued clicking a response to Raz. To be fair, Pugwash was a generation before her time and didn't wear a baseball cap or a Bugs Bunny tie. But I had tossed the ball lightly – it wouldn't have hurt her that much to pat it back.

– Kalispera Mixailis!

Our travel rep, a sociable Scot, hailed Pugwash then turned to us, curving a corporate grin.

– Clair and Jess Harkin? Kalos eelthate stin Symi. Welcome to Symi.

At the airport, with all the world-weariness of her seventeen years, Jess had assessed and rejected the rep's romantic potential in a split second. Peeping humbly through my burkha of desiccating hormones I decided there was no hope for me anyway and so no point in passing comment. He continued, jauntily unaware of our contrasting reactions.

– Aphrodite Apartments, it's no distance – if you'd just follow the folks over there, Pickfords have arrived.

He nodded towards a mule being loaded with cases. Jess glanced up and her eyes bulged with indignation.

– You mean that donkey's got to carry all those bags?

– It's a mule – it's used to it. See you on The Giorgios in the morning?

He winked at Jess and nodded at Pugwash.

– I'll give Mixailis your regards, aye? Unless you'd like his mobile number?

But Jess barely heard, her thumbs skittering across the screen in a blur of interchanging text and icons. So much for animal rights. So much for her loving Greece at first sight. Equine pathos and Hellenic charm were no match for the iPhone and the WIND mobile network.

Metallic geranium and warm sage seduced me with every breath as we journeyed round the harbour. Jess carried on – texting, tweeting or emailing – as our beast of burden clopped up a cobbled slope.

– Come on, JJ, take a look around or you won't know what you're texting about.

She remained impervious. When we reached our accommodation, however, she focused a scowl on the mule driver as she snatched her bag. I called out apologetically as man and beast wound on up.

– Kalinichta – efharisto!

'Parakolo!' resonated back over the clacking hooves.

We hauled our grips up several uneven treads to a small terrace shaded by a large mulberry tree. A plaque over the door read 'Aphrodite One'. The key was in the lock.

– Look, JJ, no need for Neighbourhood Watch on Symi!

– Mmm. Cool.

Inside, it was – cool – wonderfully cool. I flipped the light switch, illuminating white walls, marble floor, simple furniture. We dropped everything, savouring the chill. Jess, though, was still gripped by iPhone fever. How to buck her out of it? By this time, I was hyper on nicotine withdrawal. The opportunities for a sneaky drag since leaving Guildford had been nil. I didn't need a scene on the first night. Inspired by desperation, I started a hectic, clumsy strip, heading for the shower.

– Beat you to it!

Jess finally dropped her newborn to struggle out of her jeans, shrieking.

– Not fair! I need the loo!

– Tough!

– No-ho-o!

She laugh-howled, pushing past – and won. Or thought she did.

Half an hour later, dried and well sprayed with insect repellent, we sat on plastic chairs under the mulberry tree sipping overpriced whisky, late of Gatwick. Far opposite, a plantation of sapling white masts rose over rippling black water that flickered firefly reflections of taverna lights. Jess's face, though, was uplit by her phone. I prodded her.

– No telling Maggie I'm weaning you on whisky.

As if Maggie would deny her – either of us – anything. Jess 'h'mm-ed' and took another sip. Her phone blooped an incoming text. We'd been travelling more than twelve hours so, despite the view and the sensual caress of warm air, bed was irresistible. iPhone at her fingertips, Jess sank swiftly into sleep, limbs spread-eagled carelessly under a single sheet. I lay staring at the vague pattern shed on the wall by the mulberry tree, restless with the heat. Or was it a hot flush? Or night sweats? Wondered if I dare have a sneaky cig outside. Rejected it. I got up at three to check that I'd plugged in the mosquito machine (I had), at three ten, to check that I'd locked the door (I had). Wondered if I dare have a sneaky cig outside. Rejected it. Twenty minutes later I finished my water and crept to the fridge to pour another. I timed the sips, hoping to bore myself to sleep. Rejected sneaky cig before I thought of it. When my tired brain eventually gave way, it toppled into a kaleidoscope of losing Jess, missing planes, failing exams and, as ever, beating my fist on a locked bedroom door, calling for my Daddy.

Daylight poked me awake. Jess had hardly moved. I watched the incredibly beautiful young problem I'd brought into the world and tried to stave off my habitual wave of guilt. As ever, fear seeped into the vacuum. Jess was growing up too fast. Blossoming too soon. Where was that tiny body with pale blue veins tracing delicate ribs? Abandoned to relentless adolescence, that was where. Heading fast into womanhood. There already, probably. Come on, definitely. For Jess, the transition had been easy. Not for her the revulsion I had felt at first menstruation. She announced it to the world – or so it seemed. Wearing a bra was an achievement for Jess, whereas I had squeezed my mother's roll-on girdle over my chest to disguise my swelling breasts. And at seventeen, Jess had male friends, good male friends, as well as boyfriend Raz. To me at that age, young males were another species. Now, I felt protective anger as men turned their heads to watch my daughter. And maybe a touch of envy? 'Indeed, you have the best in Jess…' Maggie had written me. I welled up. Bloody menopause.

Maybe it wasn't working yet. The Greek magic. But then I'd hardly given it a chance. Impatient with myself, I flung off the sheet, slapped barefoot across the marble floor and threw open the door – to a sudden punch of heat and a stunning transformation. The hill opposite glowed, the painted houses shone in bright relief. Far below it, people worked on boats, served customers, strolled along the quayside. And I glimpsed the little Pugwash car wheeling into a narrow street. Symi was awake. I squinted beyond the harbour to where parched rock plunged into cobalt water. Little by little, the blue fused with soft silver that dissolved distantly into the smoky lavender hills of Turkey. And it happened, I found myself fending off the dread of going home. Oh – the relief. It was working. Greece. Symi.

FRASER

To: Annie

From: Fraser

Subject: All right all right all right

Sister of mine, anyone who can make me feel a shit from 2,000 miles away doesn't need to go to university because they have a PhD in emotional blackmail already. OK, THIS is how things are on Symi:

Bill Paterson voice over: Symi – the island that ALTERS LIVES. Then I take over – (Bill's fees make my buttocks clench in terror).

1/ The ships that brought big trouble to the Trojans were built with pine from Symi.

2/ The Greek Gods got stocious on white wine made from Symi grapes and behaved badly ever after.

3/ Same Gods made Prometheus feed his liver to the vultures for fencing the secret of fire, then commuted it to community service on Symi where he either turned into a monkey OR spawned a race of monkeys OR, arguably, both. Understandably, monkeys are a touchy subject on Symi.

4/ Symi's been invaded a few times but the locals always make the best of it. They conned the Turks into funding the sea sponge business and the Italians into building real estate to-die-for. The Germans were a bit trickier – but with a little help from the Allies, the islanders kicked them out. War in the Dodecanese ended at a taverna on the harbour in… SYMI!

Back to Bill: ALTERING LIVES.

Me again: All these interesting facts make Symi A GOOD THING. People come here and find…

Big finish from Bill (blowing my budget entirely): THEIR LIVES ARE TRANSFORMED.

Then there's me in person. Still here. On Symi. Trapped in the grasp of Anatolia. Don't get excited – Anatolia's not a love interest, it's a chunk of Turkey.

How are you, anyway? How's the we'an? F xx

I sort of had this vague feeling it was time to grow up. My wee sister Annie seemed to be on the right road and kept offering me directions. Helpfully. Unasked. Easy for her, being both twenty-three years old and a thousand years clever. Certainly more than her parents – our parents. Definitely more than me, despite eleven years' difference. And a super hero. I would say heroine, but no one could accuse Annie of being that girly. Kick starting her life again the way she did. She's also got a thing for Bill Paterson. The actor. Well, for his voice. Well, his politics. Old enough to be her granddad. Any normal bird her age would have the hots for – I dunno – Ewan McGregor? Maybe even he's too old. Anyhow, me ask Annie about ego mechanics? Stand the indignity of conceding she knows better? I'd rather walk down Argyle Street wi' a feather up ma airse. I love her to wee mint drops though. And Jude. Did I not mention Jude? Annie's we'an. He's just the DB.

It was my third season with Aegis. Tooling along. Mel – my – this bird in Lindos – was near enough, far enough. Sun. Sea. Beer. And the music. Work – just enough to keep me going. The Harkins: Didn't really notice them in that week's intake. Not until we got back to Symi and the bimbette had a strop over the mules carrying cases. All I needed on a transfer day. The mother looked resigned, like she'd been there a million times. Kind of tall, she was. Bizarre hair. Nice eyes. Not unfriendly, but more like she was a spectator than a player. Social work is not in my job description, though. And she was way too old. The Annie-in-my-head said: Too old for what, knobhead? For being a human being?

CLAIR

Not Terrible at all – in fact, quite nice, really

On our first morning in Aphrodite One I made tea and drifted happily into the day. Around nine thirty Jess shambled onto the terrace, frowning at her phone. Whined.

– Why didn't you wake me up? You've had breakfast and – everything.

Just then, a tiny brown lizard with a bright blue tail and immaculate timing scuttled across the dry earth and stopped on a rock, apparently sizing up this fortnight's tenants. Awed, Jess crouched down to photograph it on her iPhone but it made a swift dash for the tree, skirting the trunk and disappearing through a hole in the wall.

– Shit. Would've been so cool to tweet that to everyone.

Despite her missing the shot, the unexpected bonus of a resident reptile eclipsed her tetchy mood. She swung back indoors, ignoring the glorious vista, to start her morning ritual.

The gathering onboard the boat Giorgios was a complimentary introduction to the island. I had promised Jess that if it was tiresome we could leave but suspected she'd take so long getting ready we'd miss it, anyway. To my surprise, she reappeared by five past ten already dressed – in cut offs and a skimpy top. Her long black hair was still wet and slicked back, her white skin a defiant challenge to the Greek sun, eyes a near reflection of the Aegean. All my own work. Well…

– Have you taken your pills, Mum?

My daughter the quack.

– Wild yam root, dong quai, black cohosh, B12, B6, lecithin, calcium with vitamin D – um – ginkco biloba. My short-term memory's improved already.

– Ready then?

We negotiated the treachery of Symi's alleys and stairways, their design – or lack of it – hazardous enough to make Jess put her phone away and concentrate on avoiding broken ankles. Relieved to reach the harbour unscathed, we strolled along making mental notes of bars, a pharmacy, tavernas – and lingered far too long looking at clothes.

An old chap, grinning around four or five teeth, helped us aboard the – blue and white, naturally – Giorgios. Jess hissed at me.

– If this is Symi, are the people here called Symians?

– No.

Twenty or so holidaymakers sat along the cushioned side seats or lounged on the low cabin roof of the wooden vessel. The rep was recapping toilet etiquette to a scattering of self-conscious laughter.

– Greek plumbing isn't quite so robust as you're used to – so don't flush anything you haven't swallowed first –

Jess did a gagging mime.

– Like – gross!

– Ssshh!

He spotted us.

– Hello you two, out clubbing last night were we?

Everyone turned to look. I elbowed Jess before she could make another caustic remark.

– Help yourself to a drink, ladies. There's coffee, fruit juice, wine, ouzo – but take it easy, our captain, Panos, doesn't allow dancing – unless it's with him.

The little audience gurgled with mirth. Panos leered at us from under a black monobrow, sounding like a sixty-a-day man.

– Kalimera. Have anything you want.

'Including me' was the unsubtle implication – aimed at Jess, of course. I wondered if he genuinely believed stale tobacco breath filtered through a clumpy moustache could be seductive to a seventeen-year-old girl. But, true to conditioning, I simpered girly thanks while Jess gave him a toxic glare before sidling along to a space under the central canopy. Following, I spotted that she carried an ouzo and a retsina.

– If you're sick, I'm not holding your head!

– Sshh! Mum, everyone's looking.

Which, of course, they weren't. The rep's talk continued.

– You'll have noticed the Kali Strata stairway by now – I see one or two of you still on oxygen.

Pause for polite titter.

– Kali Strata means 'good steps' and there are three hundred and odd of them leading from Yialos, down here, to Chorio, the old town at the top. What's good about that, I hear you ask? They're the reason the inhabitants of Symi have such shapely calf muscles! There used to be an old yia yia mou – a grandma – waiting halfway up with a cup of water for you. No charge, it was sheer altruism on her part. But if you didn't buy a bundle of her dried herbs you'd be wise to watch your footing on the way down.

Cue laughter.

Jess took a few snaps to tweet back to friends as The Giorgios nosed toward the harbour mouth. The rep – whose name was Fraser Buchanan – pointed out a few shops along the way, advising on souvenirs. Although sponge diving was no longer a regular industry, sea sponges were still a popular souvenir of Symi. Jess was glad to learn they were protected from over-harvesting; it meant she could buy one and keep her eco-conscience clear. I decided not to let on that they were animal, not vegetable. We passed Harani boatyard and Nos beach heading for Nimborio. 'Emborio', from which Nimborio derived, Fraser said, meant commerce, and the commerce on which Emborio thrived in earlier days was piracy. These days, though, on the far side of the bay were the floats and antibiotic tanks of a fish farm.

– Not so much swashbuckling as fish suckling!

I thought he was quite amusing. Jess was busy reapplying factor 30 having either not heard or not understood.

By the time the boat anchored in the middle of Nimborio Bay, a good third of its human cargo were clearly itching for their first plunge. Jess, stripping top and shorts to reveal her new nano bikini, cautioned me to watch her iPhone then was off over the side in a diamond spray. Several others followed her, greeting the water with theatrical yelps. The Aegean in August is not cold. Fraser joined them, diving perfectly from the rail. He had a lean, lightly tanned body. Just on the modest side of handsome, I decided. Preferring a slightly more sedate, less public introduction to the aquatic element of my holiday, I lifted a plastic cup as I watched, realising too late it was Jess's ouzo. Captain Panos was heartily amused by my choking and lifted a coffee cup in toast.

– Yamass!

He tilted his head to pout from beneath his abundant eyebrow in a way he obviously thought sexy.

Like most travel companies, Aegis ran local tours. Amazingly, Jess agreed to a picnic on Sesklia Island.

– Why not? After all, thanks to Maggie we can manage two weeks here, so we need a bit of structure.

I resisted any allusion to her normally anarchic lifestyle and handed over the euros.

– Afraid we can't manage the trip to Turkey, it's a bit too much.

I watched her in the booking queue, pausing from her phone to chat with a youngish blonde woman. The age range of our fellow travellers looked to be late thirties to mid-sixties. Jess must have noticed there was no one near her age but she hadn't complained. More tolerance and sophistication than I gave her credit for.

Back in Yialos, she was desperate to swim again. I hadn't brought my costume. She waved to the far side of the harbour.

– Fraser said to use the hotel. Why don't you get your stuff and meet me there? We can use their umbrellas.

It offered the opportunity for a sly nicotine fix, so I agreed and made my way up a random series of paths and stairways alone, catching Aphrodite One unawares. As I put the key in the door, I saw a flurry of movement and a wisp of blue tail along the wall, but even though I froze, the little git wouldn't show itself again. Just like my bloody memory these days. I lit a cigarette and, six minutes' guilty bliss later, stubbed the butt at the base of the mulberry tree and threw it over the side wall. Brush, gargle, mint. *Just who's the teenage daughter here?* Riffling through hastily offloaded clothing for my swimsuit, a glimpse in the dressing table mirror revealed that I was a woman-soon-to-be… that age – but still fighting the same battles of youth, feeling too deeply, speaking unwisely, giving too recklessly. Or perhaps I've played a trick on time, gone straight from puberty to senility. If only. At least that way I'd escape the bloody, bloody 'm' word. Suddenly reality shifted a gear. I could see Maggie there, Connie, too – and no doubt my father, all in one face. A 'specular' moment! I remembered it from English Lit.. The Brontë girls and Virginia Woolf had them a lot. So did Harry Potter, come to think of it. I concentrated on what there was of Maggie in me. My instant cure for negativity. And I left the wrinkles in the mirror.

I tried another random, bone shattering route back to the harbour, some steps were glassy smooth stone, others rough concrete and all were splattered with ripe figs. Eventually, clinging to walls and sweating more with fright than exertion, I arrived at the back of a refreshment kiosk. The few teenagers lounging under its canopy ignored me as I passed through its shade into the vivid heat of the quayside. 'The Way of Overripe Figs leads to The Shop of Sullen Adolescents.' *There has to be a profundity in there somewhere.* Halfway around the harbour, buying a telephone card, I was waylaid by the shop's cigarette counter. They had Silk Cut, but only in boxes of two hundred – I still had three single ones left. *I will have given up before two hundred.* The alternatives were the amusingly named Assos and the more sophisticated sounding Karelias, both in packets of twenty-five and both of unknown quality. *Risk Analysis: High – Jess discovering them outweighs the questionable benefit of Greek brands.* I remembered Greek cigarettes as comparatively rough and decided to take the middle ground. Twenty Marlboro Lite invaded my shoulder bag flanked by a support squadron of mints.

The answer machine was on in Kilachlan. I left Maggie a message of love, thanks and exhortation to join us. Sonya's Los Angeles flight was today so she'd hardly be up for a chat. I loitered by the bridge, puffing a consolatory Marlboro Lite, alert for any sign of my living conscience. Even though she was easily quarter of a mile away and probably underwater.

– Gliurrrgghh!

I remembered why I didn't like Marlboro, either. The remaining Silk Cut must be saved for times of crisis. *And I will give up before my birthday.* I popped a mint and chased it round my mouth, tooth decay being preferable to the ire of Jess.

There were no free tables outside the Hotel Nireus. I sat on the edge of the quay, dangling my feet in the water, book open, attention elsewhere. Having missed the film of the first book I was, on Jess's insistence, reading Phillip Pullman's His Dark Materials trilogy and was a chapter into The Subtle Knife, already loathe to turn the final page. A few yards out, Jess waved and dived under like a baby seal, popping up inches away, glistening and pulling her nose.

– It's super-salty! You must come in, it's wonderful!

– Where did you leave your things?

– With Mandy and Richard over there!

The blonde woman she'd been chatting to at the meeting waved across.

– Go on, Mum, Mandy's great, she won't mind keeping an eye on yours as well.

– This is based on the many years you've known her?

Jess responded by kicking off backwards, drenching me. I pulled myself up and crossed to Mandy and Richard's table. *'I have the best in Jess?' Best example of a pain in the arse. Sometimes.*

– You must be Clair! Saw you at the meeting.

Vowels well north of Watford and her hard 'g' a Manchester giveaway.

– I'm Mandy – and Rip van Winkle there's Richard.

Mandy indicated the white-haired man at the table, snoozing over his paper.

– Jess says it's a special holiday for you –

I tensed. *Jess promised not to –*

– 'cos you were here before, a long time ago. Gorgeous, isn't it? Sit you down.

Sorry, Jess. Mandy pulled a chair across, causing Richard to stir slightly.

– Don't worry – he sleeps for Britain! Would you like a drink? We're on Mythos beer – Greek – but it's not bad. Or d'you want a swim first?

Mandy was built to demoralise the peri-menopausal woman. Petite, with chin-length natural (I assumed) blonde hair, huge dark brown eyes, cheekbones to die for and a personality the size of the Trafford Centre. Her conversation was funny, self-deprecating. Halfway down my beer I knew that she came from Bolton (*so nearly right*), lived with husband Richard in Leeds, was a PA for an IT software company on Whitehall Riverside business park – and that Richard was a consultant in electronic engineering, working from home…

– My Mum wasn't keen on me marrying an old man – or crossing the Pennines – but she just loves Richard. They get on like toast and dripping. None of this 'mother-in-law' stuff!

Jess arrived, panting, glittering with droplets. Mandy passed her towel.

– Thanks, Mandy. That was brilliant! Aren't you going in, Mum?

– Maybe after lunch.

– I knew we'd forgotten something! Richard! Come on, lover, time for lunch!

Richard jolted reluctantly from some reverie.

– Hmm? Oh – hello, you'll be Clair. I'm Richard.

– Uh – huh – hello…

I was besotted. Instantly, painfully. Simultaneously, I was aware that this was not a problem. He was safe as – *as a married man with a sexy little blonde wife half his age. And about three fifths of mine. Now, Clair, don't get bitter…*

Mandy and Jess led the way while Richard and I sauntered behind. His voice was soft and measured, his eyes kind behind gold-rimmed frames. He was as restrained as his very young wife was outgoing, extracting information as easily as she dispensed it. I heard myself tell him about Guildford, about work, about the house… He ribbed me for living in the affluent South East.

– How can you sleep knowing that you're personally responsible for the unfair distribution of wealth?

I was joyously on form.

– Sleep? I buy it from poor people.

His laughter was intensely gratifying – until he noticed that Mandy and Jess were out of sight. There was a moment of real concern that ended abruptly when we spotted them poring over a menu outside a taverna called, oddly, Catherinettes. Richard noticed a plaque on the wall behind them. It read:

THE SURRENDER
OF THE
DODECANESE TO THE ALLIES
WAS SIGNED
IN THIS HOUSE
ON THE 8TH OF MAY 1945

Jess took several photos on her iPhone. On the strength of its historic importance we decided to eat there. Richard was fascinated by the place and talked about the Greek experience in World War II. It tied in with my sketchy knowledge, based mainly on what I'd read in Captain Corelli's Mandolin. Jess had just started reading it and was agog.

— So, all that's really true?

— Sadly, yes, and a lot more.

He was so sensitive to her naïveté that I fell for him another fathom or two. Mandy was in relentless comic mode.

— So long as the food hasn't got a World War Two use-by date.

Lunch was, though, delightful in venue, menu and company. Jess charmed and was charmed by our new friends, sharing girly chat with Mandy and relating to Richard almost as to — a father figure? It was near four when we left. I'd relaxed into Greece as easily as pulling on a favourite old cardigan. *Even if there isn't the chance of a sly smoke.*

Whether through too much booze, not enough nicotine or the sheer perversity of the Richard/Mandy thing, I slithered into melancholia on the way back up to the apartment. Poor Jess, she's never had a significant male influence in her life. History repeating itself. Jess, however, twittered and prattled alternately about Richard and Mandy and predicted an outstanding holiday. Back at Aphrodite One we showered and dressed then sauntered back down to Yialos to check out the shops, bars and a cyber café Jess had researched on the internet. We sipped cold beers, condensation puddling on the computer desk in the humid evening air. Jess called up her morning email to Maggie, sent from the quayside, so I wouldn't repeat anything.

Kalimera (Good morning) Maggie!

Symi so FAB!!!! Best place ever - Island bUtiful — Mum rocking! Lovely utha people — RU sure U cant cum? — stil time be4 mums bday — flite 2 Rhodes then hydrofoil / fery 2 Symi. PLEASE? (You cdnt bring Jack & Taty or Esmeralda. EU regs or smthg. But Mr Scrmgr cd lk after them.) Just had realy cool boat trip & swim in harbr. Lunch @ WW 2 caf w Mandy & Richard. Tell U more 2moro

Megaluv&hugs Jess

Knowing Maggie would struggle to decipher it I elaborated on the 'join us?' theme in my message.

MAGGIE

Wednesday 25th July

Half past eight and letting the dogs in from the lower field, I thought, 'They'll be on their way – I hope'. They'd be on the plane, I reckoned, waiting to take off. If they weren't delayed. Jess had more or less begged me to go with them. I don't think Clair was party to the invitation. Not that I wasn't welcome, I knew that. Apparently, they're two hours ahead of us in Greece.

Thursday 26th July

I walked down to the shop for a few bits and pieces and missed Clair. She was on the answer phone when I returned. They'd arrived on the little island and it was clear she was happy to be there. I know you shouldn't say it these days – but she did sound as though she was in the next room. And there she was on a baking hot harbourside in the Aegean. Marvellous! Not so marvellous to miss her, though. Received an email later, written by Jess but from the both of them. Full of excitement and holiday happiness, beaches and boats – and more pressure to join them. As if I could. Maybe if I felt 100%.

And you can stop that, Julia. I am quite well. I'll see a doctor if need be.

CLAIR

Turned out nice again

Mandy and Richard were there the next morning, Friday, at the mooring for the Aghia Marina taxi boat. With the queue it was uncertain whether we'd catch the first shuttle. Mandy's blonde hair and size ten – or *even more demoralising*, eight – figure crossed the linguistic barrier. She nodded to Richard who was the last person to hop aboard.

– Thought I'd break him in gently. The book says it's the second beach along and they've got toilets. But they're in the taverna, so we might have to buy a few beers.

Delighted chorus of 'Shame'!

Aghia Marina was the name of the tiny chapel on the island at the centre of a little bay. The taverna, facing it, was more an elegant alfresco trattoria than simple beachside café, with terraces for sun loungers. Jess found four loungers together and was in the water straight away, rejoining us tingling with happiness and insisting on everyone taking a dip. Which we did, one by one, throughout the day. During her brief moments betwixt phone and sea, she became irritated with the course of Captain Corelli.

– She's getting old! It's nothing like the film!

Richard sympathised –

– Hollywood never felt constrained by authenticity.

Then he translated it into simpler English for Jess. Immediately she wanted us all to cast Hollywood versions of our own lives. She picked Keira Knightley as herself and Dev Patel as boyfriend Raz. Mandy had no problem in casting Richard.

– He's a dead ringer for George Clooney.

Yes, I can see where she's coming from. Richard peered over his spectacles, brushing back a lock of white hair.

– Eye test for you when we get back, Toots. By the way, Sophia Loren's playing you.

– But she's at least seventy – nearly eighty! And she's got black hair!

– Allure of the mature woman. Pop on a wig, my love – and I'll finally get to be a toy boy. Please?

I'm fif – forty-nine, my libido volunteered, *does that make me too young for you?* Nobody, including myself, could identify my movie doppelganger. Jess shattered the impasse by casting Homer Simpson as Howard and Marge as me. The cruelty of her accuracy was shocking.

– Don't worry, Mum, he'd only have a small part – if the rumours are true.

– Jess, that's enough!

Where did she get that sharp tongue? *And that information?* Mandy broke the heartbeat of silence.

– You lot carry on – my bladder needs comic relief!

Jess escaped with her to the bar. Richard winked at me and re-immersed himself in le Carré.

I couldn't believe I'd waited until the second day to get into the water. I used to be off the ferry and straight in. Even so, that first moment underwater was still as thrilling, still as familiar. *I'm back.* The sea floor was sandy and bare and there were few fish. It didn't matter. I snorkelled timelessly in my silent, blue world. When I sloshed back, Richard and Mandy had gone to find a table for lunch. As I towelled off, Jess said –

– I looked at the menu, Mum, it's not too expensive – if we just have Greek salad.

That shame again. For all her short life, Jess had had to consider prices. *Yes – millions of kids in this world have it a lot worse. But I should have made it better for mine.*

– Let's spend today in style, JJ. Plenty of time for packed lunches after this.

A party of Italians lounged one terrace up. As we headed for the tables, the men's eyes flickered towards Jess. An older man made a comment to a younger one and they laughed. Bastard! I want to smack his old, bald head! But as I passed him, he smiled and raised a hand in greeting.

– Ciao.

He had the sexiest eyes… *Perhaps I'll let him off.* I half-raised a hand in response, flushing magenta from head to foot, no doubt. *So much for Black Cohosh, then.*

Over lunch we all bantered as though we'd known each other for years. Later, Mandy and Jess swam along the rocky wall of the bay while Richard read and I wrestled with a dilemma: *Do I enjoy this moment with Richard or sneak round the back of the taverna for a Marlboro?* Eventually, I compromised and disappeared up to the loo for half a cigarette. I passed the sexy Italian baldy who, this time, didn't notice me. No sexy young daughter in tow? I returned sucking a mint and tried to concentrate on The Subtle Knife. At one point, Richard and I reached, simultaneously, between the loungers for a drink and the hair on his arm brushed mine. Fffff! If he noticed, he ignored it. Minutes later, Mandy and Jess returned with tales of rainbow fish and abandoned anchors. I smiled, envying the firmness and the lack of cellulite on their two bikini-clad bodies.

Around five, we made our sun-weary journey back to the port. Mandy dragged Richard off into the back streets to scour a few shops before scaling the Kali Strata to their Chorio villa. They planned to visit St Michael's monastery at Panormitis on the following day. Mandy rolled her eyes, as they waved goodbye.

– Just a loada monks wi' mucky habits.

CHAPTER THREE

FRASER

Panos had a virtual orgasm when the Harkin two got on The Giorgios. Imagined himself as the meat in a mother/daughter sandwich no doubt. Some chance. The one too serious, the other too young. It didn't take long for Nikos to stake his interest, though. Nikos is rep for another company but we share an office – and an apartment. Always up for it, Nikos. Why would this week be any different? Not to say he wasn't discerning. Nikos has standards – when there's a choice. And bimbette Jess was a wee stunner... He hit on her on the Saturday morning at his Uncle Nektarios's supermarket unleashing his animal magnetism like a chav unchains a Pitbull. Invited her up to the Saturday night gig at Angelina's Bar in Chorio where I am a musician of sorts and he – isn't. Bimbette says it might not be right for her mother who's older than she looks. And I'm thinking 'If your aged mother heard you say that you'd get your arse kicked from here back to Rhodes airport' – because in truth, her mother was fairly fit for an older woman. So, I made some cheesy remark about bringing her along. Then booted Nikos and his testosterone back to the office and Paid Work. There was an email waiting for me.

To: Fraser

From: Annie

Subject: Re: All right all right all right don't go on.

1/ Does Bill take his holidays there?

2/ Don't believe the bit about Anatolia.

3/ We're fine, Jude, me and R D Laing.

4/ What you doing tonight? (Me – essay & Pinot Grigio) A & J xx

I replied –

Subject: Bill??? – not saying

Anatolia really is not my dusky, full-breasted, clandestine love slave. Look at a map. Glad you, Jude & the Mind-y man are good. Tonight, I'm going to give my golden oldies selection at Angelina's Bar.

Have a glass on me. F xx

CLAIR

Kalimera – Jess?

Saturday was the third full day on the island. I emerged from kinder dreams to see an empty bed. Outside, I found the terrace table laid with a basket of rolls and a cafetière of coffee. But no Jess, just a note saying 'Rest in fridge – JJ x'. The cafetière was lukewarm, so had been made a while ago. I toyed with the thought of a sneaky Marlboro, even got as far as delving through the tear in the lining before chickening out. Consequently, I was fairly annoyed when it was another hour before Jess arrived back with a carrier.

– Yoghourt, feta, tomatoes, peppers, honey and a bottle of red wine.

– But you're not eighteen yet, they shouldn't –

– Oh, Mum – we're in Greece – and I look forty-five!

– No. I look forty-five – nine.

– Fraser said you don't look old enough to – erm – so, er, how was breakfast?

She was usually better at hiding gaffes.

– Lovely, thanks.

There was definitely a whiff of rat. I let it go while we prepared a packed lunch and then headed for the bus to Pedi. Fraser had mentioned a beach a short walk from there. I showed Jess The Way of the Overripe Figs and Shop of the Sullen Adolescents where, today, only one of them manned the kiosk – and she smiled a 'Kalimera'. *Another preconception shattered.* We smiled and said 'Kalimera' back.

Jess sat in the bus shelter, reading. Cheated of nicotine, I paced slowly up and down, checking the harbour for Richard and Mandy. Couldn't see them. Ten minutes later we pitched about as the driver countered precipitous inclines and hairpin bends, mobile phone in one hand, cigarette – *lucky bastard* – in the other. Jess, still frowning over Captain Corelli, snapped –

– Chill out, Mum, he's done this thousands of times.

We got off at a dead end – presumably Pedi terminus – and looked around for signs to Aghia Nikolaos beach. There were a couple of small beachside kafeneions, two tavernas and a small strip of beach with elderly straw-thatched umbrellas held together with wire.

– Nikos said it's about twenty minutes from – here… down to the right.

Jess trailed off realising her blunder. *Nikos?* Rat aroma intensified. I said nothing. We set off down the side of the long bay, passing between the houses and tamarisk trees at the waterside. Festoons of washing and fishing nets made the place look homely until the path met the rocky shore and dwindled to a precarious-looking track. Twenty treacherous minutes later we reached the little beach.

It was a lazy day of sunbathing, snorkelling, eating and drinking. Loos and cold beer at the small taverna plus our packed lunch were enough to keep us in comfort. Jess finished Captain Corelli, annoyed with Louis de Bernières for lousing up the love story and sent copious messages to say so. I started the third of the Pullman trilogy. As we waited for the return taxi boat Jess remarked for the third or fourth time –

– Good day, yesterday, I really like Richard and Mandy.

– Mmm.

– I don't think Mandy wanted to do that monastery. I said she could come with us today, but she wouldn't. Don't know why. They are married after all, they must see enough of each other at home.

Such innocent reasoning.

It being Saturday night we dressed up with no particular place to go. Or so I thought. Jess approved of my recently acquired pink linen extravagance.

– Wow, Mum – you look so cool. Sonya's a good influence on you.

– That's not what your Gran used to say.

From alongside our apartment some wide steps led up to the Kali Strata and Chorio. The small bar we entered there at Jess's casual suggestion was dark and reeked of stale smoke. No EU bullying directives for Symi. Dreading temptation or withdrawal symptoms, I turned to go and walked into the lean, lightly tanned, too-young-for-me, travel rep., Fraser.

– Off so soon? Anything I said? Kalispera, Jess.

– Fraser!

Exhibiting a social ease that I didn't even aspire to, Jess kissed him on both cheeks. A tad familiarly for three days and for her initial value judgement on him, I thought. Was this the rat I'd smelt earlier? And then she'd said, oh so casually: "That bar looks OK – why don't we try it?" Exactly how random was this choice?

Perched on a bar stool in her cheap, high street dress, hair tamed to silky curtains, Jess attracted both open and covert admiration, stirring my usual anxiety. The bar was run by Angelina and patronised tonight by her competitor, a dour Brummie called Nobby who eyed Jess beadily.

– Now young lady, Angelina's got a reputation to maintain here, so don't you go raising the tone.

A shortish Greek woman slapped him playfully round the head –

– Eh! Leave the customers alone, Nobby – lucky I got any 'cos of you!

I offered Fraser a drink, certain that travel reps weren't paid much. Jess wanted white wine. *Mental note: keep count.* For all her seeming sophistication, she hadn't developed much sense about booze. Fraser accepted a mineral water.

– Got to keep my head clear for later.

Jess had almost given up any pretence of coincidence.

– He's playing a set! Nikos said he's really good.

Angelina agreed with her, passing my change.

– Is true, Fraser got better taste in music than friends!

I squeezed Jess's arm.

– You are a mine of information about our travel rep., darling. Thanks to – who did you say? Nikos?

– Mum! I told you, he shares the tour office with Fraser.

I'd been had. *Why do I never see through her?* She prattled on until Nikos joined us – medium height, closely cropped black hair, devastating smile – and Jess went gooey. *OK, Jess, I can relate. I am now a giant, nearly-fifty-year-old gooseberry.* Nikos took my hand.

– You are Jess's mother? You're joking me!

The fusion of colloquial English with his Greek accent gave the platitude charm and originality, I decided. Plus, I have a profound capacity for flattery. He insisted on buying the next round on the grounds that he was related to Angelina and got staff prices. Jess sank her second white wine in half an hour.

– Cheers, Clair!

She beamed at me as she raised her glass, her subtext being: 'You get heavy with me and I'll outdo you'.

Bloody hell, let it go. Just… dimitte diem. That said, I kicked maternal care under the table and joined in the spirit of the evening. Fraser and Nikos topped each other with tourist tales and eccentricities of the locals, most of whom Nikos was related to by blood or marriage.

– It's not strange I'm so handsome, all Symiots are beautiful until they are thirty – then poof! They lose the teeth and hair, the nose comes to the chin and they er – dry up – like an empty pig bladder. And that's the women!

Much laughter.

– It's lucky I have nine years to go!

Groans all round and a hollow fisted gesture from Nobby. I wondered just how inaccurate the claim was. His laughter lines seemed deeper than I'd first noticed and there were one or two white hairs in his chin stubble. *Could I persuade Angelina to grass on him?* Around ten thirty, Fraser disappeared behind the bar. Nikos whispered.

– He is putting on his Elvis Presley suit.

– He so isn't!

Jess enjoyed the tease like a small girl. *Or is it the wine?* But Fraser reappeared unchanged, carrying a Fender 12-string acoustic. I suddenly felt very edgy without any justifiable cause. *What if he's dire?*

– Good evening. I'm Fraser, you're on holiday – and this is for all the poor buggers who aren't.

Coasting the laughter, he went into a strong version of John Sebastian's 'Summer in the City'. OK, he was quite good. In fact, he was – good. He followed with 'Love of the Common People', Robbie Williams' 'Angels' then REM's 'Man on the Moon'. After which, by way of comic reduction, he played 'Obladi Oblada'. With audience participation. He'd gauged the average age and taste of the clientèle about right. Catching my eye, he shrugged – presumably in apology. Suddenly, Nikos grabbed hold and pulled me across to the small platform. And Fraser introduced 'a song from the shows'. *I won't, won't, won't do it! Whatever it is –*

– I can't do this.

– Yes, you can. Here!

Oh brilliant. He knotted a black headscarf under my chin and another on himself in a parody of – whatever it was they called Greek grannies. *I'm playing a pig's bladder. Thanks, Niko.* Jess was gleeful, banging the table and whistling through her fingers. Fraser struck a chord and trilled.

– Biddly diddly diddly diddly deeeee!

Oh no – 'Cabaret' – 'Two Ladies'.

– Und I'm ze only man, jah!

Fraser lisped, camp as Christmas. It was a well-rehearsed interlude designed to feature a hapless member of the audience. Nikos was no slouch in the comic arena, singing both female parts, bumping hips and comparing his false boobs with my genuine if inferior-sized ones. *Did I think you were attractive earlier? You smarmy –*

– Biddly di di dee, we like it –

Nikos trilled, rolled his eyes and towed me round the tables, flirting with the men and remarking on the women's fashion sense. I stumbled stupidly behind as the double entendres bounced off me.

– Oh, for god's sake, Clair – you can do this!

It was Sonya speaking.

– Go on – crack your face – do a shimmy at that old bloke.

Oh, what the hell…

Jess clapped and hollered as I broke away from Nikos and shook my 34A's at an astonished elderly man. Laughter welled through the audience. Encouraged by success, I risked my pink linen trousers, swinging my foot onto a table and lunging, causing the occupants to whisk their drinks away. And when a German's wife pushed me from his lap, I shrugged and waggled my little finger, raising yelps of delight. Even Fraser succumbed, dropping a chord and half a refrain. The bar was on its feet, cheering as I blundered back to the arms of a very tipsy Jess.

– Mum – you're assolutely – really really – 'mazin'!

I shook my hair free of the black headscarf as Nikos flopped next to us fanning himself with his. A beaming Angelina delivered another round of drinks.

– These are – um – 'on the house' – for being such good entertainers.

Fraser had a job to calm the audience and the 'ladies' had to take another bow before he was allowed to introduce the last song of the set. It was 'The White Rose of Athens'. Despite my recent high, I felt my eyes pricking. *When will all this emotional crap leave off?* Nikos put an arm round me and traced a tear, which only made matters worse.

– You are very sad? Why is that, beautiful lady?

I snapped at him, honking into a tissue.

– I'm not beautiful, Jess is beautiful and I'm – just her mother.

– Jings to mickty! I should have such a mother!

The Scots catchphrase turned my tears to laughter just as Fraser returned.

– Hands off, pal, I saw her first. Angelina needs your help at the bar and I need a beer.

I saw her first? Nikos vacated the seat and Fraser sat next to me.

– You have to be the secret love child of Liza Minnelli and Bob Fosse.

A chronological impossibility – but I was suddenly self-conscious. And flushing.

– Ach away! On your bike, pal! Anyway, how about you? Talk about lights and bushels…

I'm talking too fast and too loud. At which point, arch-conspirator Jess slid off her seat, soused. She had her uses.

Only after I insisted that we knew our way home did Fraser reluctantly wave us off. Once alone, though, I couldn't find our short cut back and had to follow the steps down into the middle of Yialos. Jess was spectacularly sick on the Kali Strata, projected a midnight snack to the fish in Yialos harbour and threw up again on the climb to the apartment.

At four that morning the insomnia was less ghoulish than usual as I re-ran the evening like a film, picking up at different points... *the secret love child of Liza Minnelli and Bob Fosse... You are Jess's mother? You're kidding me! Hands off, pal, I saw her first... Applause. Biddly diddly diddly diddly dee!*

FRASER

That night, Bimbette turns up at Angelina's bar with mother in tow. And she's looking, like – amazing. Her Mum – Clair – I mean. They don't look much alike – well, maybe the shape of face. Clair has really curly brownish hair, long, and Jess has straight black hair. We all shared a table until it was time for the set. While I was singing, even though it was dark, I sort of kept catching sight of her. She looked as though she liked what she was hearing. Come the set piece, 'Two Ladies', instead of going for a bloke, Nikos goes for Clair and I thought 'Oh no, this is really going to fall flat on its arse'. But it didn't. I mean, she was a bit surprised at first but she certainly called his bluff. Shimmed up to guys, sat on their laps and shook her boobs. Very nice boobs. Cute bum, too. Everyone loved it. I mean, loved what she did. Very funny. Even Nobby, our po-faced refugee from Cannock Chase, cracked his face. She got to me – I totally lost it. End of the set, I went back and sat with them. Just for a moment, I thought Nikos had decided to take a crack at Clair instead of the bimbette. Which would have been inconvenient because whenever the two of us have hit on the same bird, he's won. Turns out not, though. Bimbette was off her head – Clair and I just caught her before she hit the floor. I offered to walk them home but Clair said no. Probably wanted to give the we'an a roasting. Not without cause. Myself, I was peed off they had to go home so soon.

MAGGIE

Saturday 28th July

Around six that evening in Kilachlan, sunny, humming with insects, I was at the top end of the garden milking Esmeralda. Leaves danced transparent in the light and long fluorescent strands of grass fringed the back lawn behind the wire fence where it was safe from Esmeralda's molars. Jess named her Esmeralda after the cartoon of the Hunchback of Notre Dame. How like my great-niece to have a goat as her familiar. I noticed Jack and Tatty snuffling around in the corner nearest the burn. Something interesting must have passed that way recently. An otter perhaps? Otters.

Wouldn't that be a joy? Unless you were a gamekeeper, of course. But it was probably a rat or a young fox – or maybe a water vole. I'd have to search the dogs for ticks later. Disgusting wee beasts. Esmeralda lunged her head round, nudging me on the shoulder for not paying attention to the job in hand…

– All right, sweetheart, not much longer.

…then resumed chewing, but shifted her dainty back hooves impatiently. Her character rivalled Jack and Tatty together. She'd nuzzle a stranger lovingly for no reason then butt the innocent donor of a titbit. In summer she spent most of the day head down, keeping the lawn in trim. But occasionally she would lift her shapely nose, sniffing delicately, golden eyes fixed on some distant goat ideal then suddenly prance in small circles, back legs flicking out bronco fashion. Jess always fell about. I had a sudden vision of Clair and Jess laughing together; it was dark, there was guitar music. Gone, as soon as it entered my head. But it pleased me. The two of them deserved a special holiday and I had been tempted to join them, but for that feeling of – unwellness – of late.

The phone intruded on mine and Esmeralda's ruminations. The way it kept on ringing meant the answer machine couldn't be on. Ach, what chance it was important or interesting? Ignore it. Unless it was Clair calling from Greece again… I hurried down the slope to the back door, clattering down the pail of milk in the kitchen, and on through to the sitting room. This was the point at which the phone normally stopped. But, whoever was phoning was determined to get hold of me.

– Hello?

– Maggie, it's Connie. What took you so long to pick up?

– I was milking the goat.

– You still do that kinda thing?

Sinking into an armchair, I tried to reconcile the slender young woman in James's mother and child painting with the American matriarch at the other end of the line. I settled in for a long session, holding the ice-cold earpiece as near as I could bear.

Later on, I got onto the internet and sent Clair a message. She really should have rung her mother. It put me in an awkward situation and made for a difficult conversation with Connie. 'No change there, then', Clair would say.

CHAPTER FOUR

STILL MAGGIE

Sunday 29th July

I was in a pleasant waking dream. Italy. Julia and I were in a speedboat heading towards – where? Capri? – the day gold and blue, the boat steering itself. Then we were swimming with Clair and Jess, even though that could never have been. Next, the two of us were alone again, sitting at a table, high above the world, drinking Chianti, the sun in our eyes as it sank to the sea bed. And Julia was about to tell me –

A little whimper and a scratch pulled me back to Kilachlan. Jack and Tatty wanted out. I sat up, swinging my legs from the bed, and felt the blood rush to my head. I clung to the mattress, heart pounding, black and red patterns dancing under my eyelids. After a minute or so, the feeling lifted and I forced myself upright and opened the door. Jack and Tatty raced out, bursting through the dog flap at the back to open air and relief. Maybe my dizziness was a reaction to hearing Connie last night. Connie! I must email Clair and let her know about Joe. I'd never met Joe but I was sorry to hear he was so poorly. I suppose I felt sorry for Connie, too, but she never made it easy to feel anything positive. I went straight to the computer.

CLAIR

Terrible if you're an octopus

Sunday was the Aegis travel company boat trip and picnic. After a quick breakfast and a futile scout around for the lizard, we set off for The Giorgios. Captain Panos rumbled 'Kalimera', squeezing my hand as he helped me aboard. I mumbled back. Scanning the boat for Richard – and Mandy, of course – I was disappointed. Fraser greeted newcomers warmly, briefly, treating us no differently. *Why should he? Because…*

Jess was irritatingly bright, even the rocking of the boat didn't faze her. *Oh, that I still had a liver like that.* We cruised slowly southward to Sesklia Island, stopping en route for swimming and snorkelling from the boat between the sheer cliffs by the chapel of Aghia Giorgios, Saint George. The beach there enjoyed relative exclusivity, Fraser explained, due to the lack of any facilities other than goat droppings. Several goats nosed between a half dozen sunbathers adding credibility to his spiel. I was eager to be in the water. Clutching the snorkel mask, I climbed gingerly down the ladder and plopped in. My hair streamed above me as I sank, bubbles coursing up my body. Jess called unkindly from the deck as I surfaced, choking.

– Aren't you supposed to hold your nose when you do that?

She chucked down the flippers and I thrashed about awkwardly hindered by the Aegean's salty buoyancy, trying to pull them on. Eventually I succeeded, ducked under and flapped off to recover my dignity. As I did, I recalled vaguely a theory about women's body fat and direction of hair growth that linked them to life in the water. *That extra layer of fat under the skin is not flab. I am a dolphin.*

I was suddenly entranced by a vision of light as spellbinding as the first time I saw it many years earlier. From a central point, directly below, soft, silvery gold shafts radiated from a pinpoint in the astounding blue. Such unearthly beauty was surely the inspiration for haloes in Renaissance paintings, for the perfect blue of the Madonna's cloak? Leonardo designed diving gear. *Wonder if he ever used it? Bet Michelangelo never gave it a go.* Of course, the light was not coming from below but from above and it was my body diffusing the transit of light between sun and sea that caused the phenomenon. *Something to do with the Rayleigh effect and why the sky is blue – where did I dredge that from?* I always have to spoil things. But it was definitely a dimitte diem moment, relaxing every tension, dissolving care. I was euphoric. Suspended there physically and emotionally, I could never reach fifty. Too soon, I heard someone calling. It was time to move on. Hauling myself, flippers and mask inelegantly up the metal ladder, I rolled over the side, flopping sodden on the deck. *I can't help it – I am a sea creature out of her element.* Jess passed a beach towel.

– Really cool entrance, Mum.

– One day you'll get stuck with that sneer.

She gave the patronising little smile employed universally by seventeen-year-olds who know better.

We left the main island for Sesklia, past desiccated tawny cliffs fringed by jagged spray and into open water. Fraser came round with a tray of drinks, whistling with admiration as Jess lifted a retsina. Half an hour later, we moored at a typically rough concrete quay jutting from the little beach. Some disembarked while others stayed for a nap in the shade of the canopy. A few smaller craft were anchored in the bay and another leisure boat moored alongside, dark brown with square, orange life belts on the side rigging, looking like a pirate ship from a Disney film. The sun was at its height, I could feel my skin crisping in the heat.

Slippery with lotion and decked with sunhat of sombrero proportions, I sloshed knee deep along the water's edge, reluctant to be parted from it. My old jellies, relics of Brighton beachfront, protected me against the pebbly bottom while shoals of tiny, silvery blue fish performed endless synchronised manoeuvres around my legs. How could I leave any of the crap from the last fifty years on Symi? I was totally in love with the place.

Symi made me see possibilities, not regret the past. *I want to live here, want to be it. Maybe, after Jess's A levels, I could come out here as a travel rep...*

Greed lured me back to The Giorgios where the crew had prepared lunch to eat on board or transport to the beach. Shade seekers dotted the bases of tamarisk trees like fleshy fallen fruit. It was too hot to swim, even. By three thirty, it had cooled enough to attempt a little snorkelling. Jess pootered slowly up and down the bay for a while and returned, disappointed by the modesty of sea life. As she relinquished the snorkelling gear I took over and submerged, anxious to relive my silvery halo. I'd just found the right angle when I heard noises muffled by the water but sounding very much like shouting. I swooshed upright and located yelling coming from the direction of the quay — a female voice screaming abuse — a very familiar female voice. Wallowing to shore, I wrenched off mask and flippers and hobbled along the shingle to the jetty where my daughter harangued a couple of bemused Greeks, the younger of whom held a large, limp octopus.

— Jess! What's going on?

— These — these — fucking bastards! They turned it inside out and —

Her considerable vocabulary was exceeded by the enormity of her outrage. Fraser tried to placate her.

— But Jess, that's what they do in Greece. They always —

Jess screeched, near to tears.

— They turned it inside and they — they...bashed it to death on the fucking concrete!

The years fell away and I saw my tiny girl in one of her frequent tantrums.

— Bastards!

I had to get her away before the tirade descended into physical violence. All of a sudden, I was diving at Jess and half-lifting, half-dragging her past Fraser, the Greeks and The Giorgios. I fought the spitting, swearing activist to the edge and toppled us both into the sea. As we hit the water, Jess went under and came up choking, too shocked to retaliate. I took a few strokes to clear myself from reprisal and waited. Jess recovered enough to slap the water in fury.

— Where's my fucking iPhone?

I turned and swam to my gear on the shore. Jess flailed about diving for a while then followed, trudging angrily up the shingle, past politely averted eyes and lowered speech. She reached me at our bags and clothing and screamed just as a long note signalled departure time.

— My whole life was on that!

– Oh – come on –

It was insured, Sonya had seen to that. And as for mobile numbers and so on, she'd catch up within a couple of days back home.

– I will never – ever – forgive you.

I didn't argue, just dressed over my damp costume and walked back to The Giorgios. The non-octopus-wielding one of the two culprits, grizzled hair, squashy nose and the ever-present needle thin roll-up, spoke to me in Greek as I reached the quay. I guessed at what he was saying and replied with elaborate mime.

– Efharisto, I apologise for my daughter's behaviour. iPhone in the sea.

He cottoned on to the gravity of it.

– Ochi?!

– Neh!

– Gamóto!

I looked back at the lone figure on the beach and recalled a Cornish camping holiday when, apart from lightning breaks for the toilet, fourteen-year-old Jess, abnormally flawless for an adolescent, had refused to leave the tent for three days because of a spot on her forehead which, to be fair, had assumed third eye proportions. Now, as Fraser helped the last of the group on board, she sulked on the beach, just visible beyond a tamarisk tree, compounding her public shame. I was furious with her and ached for her, remembering all my stand-offs with my mother. Pegged to a cable on the prow, the octopus corpse flapped its broken tentacles in a grisly parody of drying washing. It would be painful for Jess to see it and face the all the others on The Giorgios. Knowing that she was being a brat would make it all the harder for her to back down. She was stuck. *Oh, Jess!* The craft's motor started, then above the noise of it came singing. A disgruntled woman with a purplish complexion led the captive assembly in: 'Why Are We Waiting?'. *What a cow!* To make matters worse, passengers on the jokey cartoon boat alongside joined in then jeered and cat-called as their vessel hauled anchor and reversed out to open water. Fraser gave me a sympathetic grin.

– I'm really sorry, Fraser. You should leave us here.

– Ach away. Time for action. No one can resist my Caledonian machismo.

Gesturing 'five minutes' to Panos, he climbed ashore and crunched up the beach to Jess. Panos attempted to mollify me.

– Don't worry, be happy. We have a drink back in Yialos. OK?

You might be in with a chance today, Dog Breath.

In the distance, Fraser was talking to Jess, his words indistinguishable. Almost immediately, he turned and trekked back across the shingle. Two seconds passed – Jess straightened – and followed! Fortunately, Octopus-slayer and partner had unstrung said ex-octopus and retired to the wheelhouse. Climbing aboard, Fraser winked at me and padded along the rows giving brief reassurances. Jess crossed the gangplank wordlessly and suffered Panos' whiskers and halitosis politely before stalking, inscrutably, to where I sat. *Come to me, my difficult child. I don't know which is in a worse state – you or the poor, bloody octopus.* There were a few sour faces and mouthed comments in the immediate area of the purplish woman. But Fraser busied himself with extra liquid rations for all and it was, on the whole, a jolly party that disembarked at Yialos. Helping me ashore, Panos made a small drinking mime and nodded towards the town. I shook my head.

– Efharisto, ochi. I must take my daughter home. She lost her iPhone in the sea.

– Ochi?!

– Neh!

– Gamóto!

Grabbing Jess's hand, I hurried us ashore – even so, I managed to scan the area for Richard – and Mandy – but they were nowhere to be seen. Back on The Giorgios Fraser was looking in our direction. He waved.

An hour later, Jess and I sat on our private plateau, enjoying the evening sun. Jess's hair, caught up loosely, escaped in liquorice skeins. Dark as her father's. My colouring was chalk pastel compared to her Japanese lacquer.

– You were right about the octopus, JJ. And I'm sorry about your iPhone. We'll get you another one in Guildford.

– No worries, it's insured. And I'm sorry, Mum. About today. It'll be better tomorrow.

FRASER

Next day, Panos smarmed Clair and Jess on board The Giorgios for the Sunday picnic outing. You wouldn't have known the we'an had tied one on the night before. Dark glasses but apart from that super-fit. Clair shrugged and smiled when I caught her eye. I spent the first half of the trip wondering what she meant – was it surprise that Jess was upright? Or was she sorry they hadn't stayed longer at Angelina's? Or 'what next'? And why was I bothered, anyway? I was fairly busy, keeping the punters fed and boozed, so I didn't find an answer but I managed a keek when she changed into her bikini. Slightly fuller body than I was used to, but then she was a woman, not a girl. Confess I felt a slight stirring. She was overboard in a moment, though, and my modesty was saved.

After lunch, at Sesklia, a couple of the guys caught an octopus, great old granddaddy of a thing, and despatched it in the time-honoured manner. Not a scene I enjoy particularly but I've learned to look the other way. Next moment, this harpy comes screaming down the jetty. Jess. And the gob on her! If they didn't understand English, they got the gist of it 'cos she was in full flood. Amused them. I tried to calm her down but just made matters worse. Suddenly, Clair swooped down, scooped her up and flung herself and the we'an in the water. Very funny, as it happens, but no one was laughing, specially not Jess. She flailed about, squealing and diving for her phone then gave up and swam to the beach. I had a word with the crew to hide the offending corpse and eventually they did. It was time to go but bimbette was in a huff and refusing to get back on board. Clair did her shrug again, but this time she wasn't smiling. Maybe Jess had been a handful all her life and this wee gesture of Clair's was all she had left. Decided to do the honourable thing. As if I'd know what the hell that was. But I had a boatful of people watching me and some old witch had started singing 'Why are we waiting?'. Closing in on Jess I felt like Garry Cooper in 'High Noon'. Wondered how Annie would approach this. Annie is a very direct kind of person, always finds the right words. If they stab you through the heart it's probably for your own good. As I got closer and closer to Ms Harkin Junior, Hallelujah! Annie spoke through me. Out it pinged. The words just hung between us. I waited for an explosion. Nothing came. I turned and walked. She picked up her bag and followed me back to the boat. Hero or what? Cheers, Annie.

Rest of the trip back, Jess huddled with her Mum. I was liberal with the booze and that seemed to keep everyone happy. Clair carted her off as soon as we docked. Probably just as well 'cos I might have asked them to join me for a drink. Very unprofessional. Besides, I was seeing Mel tomorrow.

CLAIR

Countdown: Monday – Terrible minus five

After the trauma of the Sesklia trip, I passed a febrile night, failing all my O levels by not bothering to revise then standing helpless on the quayside as Mum and Joe smuggled Jess aboard a schooner with square orange life belts, bound for the New World. After which – same locked bedroom door, same no reply from my father. Same sickness, same shame. Through the familiar, anxious early morning doze, Jess materialised, wrapped in a bath towel, watching me.

– Cup of tea, Mum.

Jess made disgusting tea, always put the milk in with the tea bag.

– Thanks, love. Dreamt you'd gone to America on the Triton with Gran and Joe. She was wearing a hip holster.

Jess laughed.

– You have such peculiar dreams – and you remember them. I try but mine just slither away.

– Probably just as well.

I took a sip.

– Mmmm. Lovely.

– I've already had a shower. How do you feel about walking to Nimborio?

She flung herself alongside me. Tea slopped everywhere.

– We can get a water taxi back. I can make lunch – boiled eggs? And feta and tomatoes?

She was trying to atone for yesterday, big time.

We hoisted on rucksacks and bade farewell to the still absent, bastard lizard. As we 'ooh-ed' at the clarity of the water in the harbour and pointed out random fish, I gave in to curiosity.

– Jess…

– Mmm?

– You know yesterday?

Silence.

– I just wondered – well – what did Fraser say to you – when he came to get you?

She sighed deeply…

– He said, "OK – you made a tit of yourself. Get over it".

… then she stood abruptly and walked on. *Don't laugh – don't laugh – don't laugh* – I watched the slim, straight figure striding away. *God – she's got a lot of her father in her.* I caught up to find her chatting with yesterday's diplomat in person. He was sat outside a kafeneion, smarter than usual in chinos and a white T-shirt. Jess outlined our plans as though the octopus incident never happened.

– But we've got to stop off for some water, first.

– The supermarket just behind this place is open, Nikos just popped in for some milk.

Jess was gone, instantly. I sat down and breathed in the aroma of coffee trying to expunge the memory of Jess's tea. Fraser turned to me.

– The we'an seems bright enough today.

He was almost blond. Teeth slightly uneven – but very white against the tan.

– Look, I'm really sorry about – all that. We haven't mentioned the 'O' word today yet.

– 'O' word?

– Eight tentacles, lives in the sea…

I was back in cabaret mode.

– Tuh! Say no more – forgotten.

He lifted his cup, right-handed, guitar-plucker fingernails clicking on the glaze.

– Even so – thanks – I mean – you dealt with it brilliantly, saying – what you said.

– Comes of having a wee sister and shitloads of suave charm.

He tipped his shades and puckered his mouth at me. He was looking on the confident side of handsome. *His face looking down at me, his weight on my belly. What – ?* I croaked, mentally dousing myself in ice water –

– So – is this elevenses or work?

– Waiting for the Rhodes hydrofoil. My girlfriend's coming over; she's a rep in Lindos.

Girlfriend. My stomach – ego? – hit the cobbles. *Crank out some words – any words…* Pause of some hours.

– You're… so lucky working here. The more I see of Symi, the more I… love it.

– Yeah, it does that. Before Symi I was desperate to get back to being an accountant.

– Eh?

– Left off eight years ago with one set of exams to go. Symi was reeling me in.

– Ah.

– Tried to resist. Bummed around in Spain. Earned a bob or two busking. Crewed on a corporate yacht in the Caribbean. Then met a guy who owned a bar on Rhodes – three weeks there and snap! I took the bait – landed gasping on Symi. It forced me to take the rep job. Then lobbed you and Jess at me. Your turn.

Lobbed us?

– But you've really done…

Menopausal aphasia kicked in.

– … stuff. I'm just Jess's mum.

– Drop the humility. What about vamping round Aegean nightclubs? And your hobby as a wing forward? Great flying tackle yesterday, by the way.

My self-worth rose to about knee level.

– Thanks. Only took up rugby because the Pilates classes were full –

Satisfying guffaw from him. Half a breath later – annoyingly – a super vivacious Jess arrived back with Nikos in tow. And Fraser spotted the approaching hydrofoil.

Jess made a self-consciously jokey farewell to Nikos – *I really have to check out how old he is* – and we strolled alongside Fraser as far as the hydrofoil mooring. A casual parting and onward. But as we passed Catherinettes, I couldn't resist a sly glance back. Jess was annoyingly perceptive.

– Having a noss for Fraser's girlfriend, eh?

– No, I was just – just – well just –

– She's probably some blonde bimbo with double D cups. Who cares?

She babbled happily about Nikos, who was studying architecture at Aristotle University in Thessaloniki and working through the summer to pay his way. His older brother had a restaurant in Brisbane and of his three married sisters two were living on Rhodes and one on Samos to the north. His parents lived on Symi but he 'sort of' shared an apartment in Chorio with Fraser. *Sort of? When he needs to entertain, no doubt.*

– … Nikos when you talk about him, Niko when you talk to him – it's a Greek thing.

– I know.

We skirted Hotel Nireus *(no Richard – or Mandy)* then Harani boatyard, where there was a fleet of rotting hulks and a distinct absence of boat building. Already, the sweat tricked down my back as the hot air clamped my clothes to me. Nos beach with sun beds aplenty caused a slight waver of intent but the loud Greek pop music at the taverna drove us on. Up the incline and round the corner of the headland, the heart-jerking blue sea lured us way down on our right. We discussed Jess's options following A levels. I was concerned about the pressure on her after years of unrelenting and seemingly pointless tests and examinations.

– I'd really love you to have a gap year.

She liked the idea enough but was reluctant to incur more expense than I could support.

– I can do it after my degree, when I've earned a bit of money, paid off the student loan. I don't want to scrounge off you forever.

Where did all that guilt and responsibility come from? My mother, I was sure, had some answering to do. God knows what crap she'd drummed into Jess's infant ears on the rare occasions she'd had charge of her.

We continued the debate through reapplying oil to each other's shoulders, during a sitting break to finish the water and while I peed behind a wall. There was a brief pause when we stopped to chat to some swimmers, twenty yards down in the green blue of a small inlet, their voices incredibly clear. Then the wrangling continued until we reached Nimborio at nearly half eleven. We sat outside the taverna for a cold drink and after another half hour of contention, I put a stop to it.

– Right. I'll ask Connie for the money.

– Mum! You wouldn't ask Gran! You absolutely wouldn't!

– If it's the only way you'll do a gap year, I'll swallow my pride and ask her. Then if I choke, it's your fault.

– OK, truce.

We agreed to save it for Aborigine Road.

Connie. Or 'Mum' as I called her to her face. Difficult. Not the moment for her, yet.

After lunch, exhausted by the long argument, soporific through heat and eating, we both snoozed on the beach. Around three, I woke from a pleasant interlude during which Maggie held my snivelling five-year-old self on her knee teasing out my tangled hair with a tail comb.

– Don't cry, darling – I'll be as gentle as Mickey Mouse.

And Julia, sitting on the floor cross-legged, smoking a cigarette, sang the Ying Tong song, making me laugh through my tears. Julia. Maggie's Julia.

Drifting back to Nimborio I saw Jess, hunched on the edge of the small concrete jetty, pointing at something in the water, watched by a man and small girl. It was a perfect composition. I fished out my ageing Canon and managed three shots before the moment was lost. Two minutes later she was back.

– There was a starfish down there but this bloody speed boat farted past and it buried itself in the sand!

– What a pain. Who was the little girl?

– Dunno. Met her paddling. That was her dad. Quite fit for a wrinkly. He's attached, though, unfortunately for you.

That evening, passing Restaurant Tsampikos with its tables set on the brink of the harbour, we decided it would be ideal as a last night extravagance. We sauntered on past ever-open emporia. Jess coveted a plum-coloured shoulder bag but was tormented by the fact that it was leather. A couple of shops further on, I fell for a cotton shirt and Jess for a camisole. But sensibly, frugally, all we bought was a small torch to shine our way back along the unpredictable stairways. It was not yet mealtime, so we popped into Vapori cyber café to check email. There were two for me. Jess displayed uncharacteristic diplomacy.

– OK, I'll get some drinks in while you read the one from Sonya.

I appreciated her tact and sat down to the screen.

Subject: 24 hours and no sign of Pitt or Clooney

Sun, infinity pool, frozen daiquiris, heaven… Is it f**k!!! Not being coy with the asterisks here – the Puritan hotel server might delete the whole email otherwise. The TV pixelates out nipples, even. Still, you know all about that. My beloved's at a ****ing breakfast meeting AND I HAVE 'FLU. CAN YOU BELIEVE IT? Managed 30 seconds on the balcony before sore throat and aching joints. Must have caught it on the plane. Room service never heard of Beechams 'Flu Plus. Be easier ordering cocaine. Hotel fab. Said infinity pool, private jacuzzies and masseurs with edible pecs and buns of steel. Gay, tho' – what a surprise. Room info includes dial-a-colonic-irrigation called Inner Sanctum. Yeah quite. Weather gorgeous, even the airport's laid back – 'LAX'. Enough about me, how about you? Offloaded 50 years of s**t yet? Found a sh*ggable Greek?

Sweaty snotty bug-ridden love to you and sprog - Sonn x

The email was three days old. I rattled one back.

Subject: – and then the sky fell in

Only just got your email – what a pain darling. Hope you're over it and Brian's business meetings don't leave you too much time to misbehave. Re. Greeks, have managed only ageing sea dog Panos – brown teeth – brown breath – irresistible. Might have to sh*g the holi -

At this point, Jess arrived back with two beers, so I pressed 'send' quickly. *Might have to shag the holi… ?*

– How's Sonya?

— Pissed off. She's got 'flu.

— What a pain! C'mon, let's read Maggie's, it's obviously to both of us.

Subject: Re: Kalispera from Symi!!!!!!!!!

Dearest Lasses

Thank you for your email, Jess, and for your phone message, Clair. Symi sounds as wonderful as you remembered. Clair, I'll be thinking of you on Saturday, and wishing you all you would wish yourself — and then some. Connie rang last night because she couldn't get hold of you. She didn't know you were in Greece. Joe isn't too well. Call required. Sorry to have to tell you this. Jack, Tatty and Esmeralda send love. So do I, in great dollops -
Maggie

P.S. Jess, Wally Scrymgeour said you're not to marry one o' they Greek.

Joe ill. Oh no. And Connie doesn't know I'm here — sure I told her — didn't I? Dunno. Probably not.

About Connie. Best taken in small doses:

<O>

The night Sonya and I arrived back from Greece — half a lifetime ago — after we'd cleaned up and had a meal at her Westminster flat, Maggie broke the news. My grandmother, Emily, had died in Florida. Connie was over there now, making funeral arrangements. I'd never met Grandma Emily and knew only that she and my mother hadn't spoken since Mum left America. I wondered how Connie would take the bereavement and whether I should feel sympathy or relief for her. And I wondered how I would react to the news of Connie's death? Maggie was solicitous.

— Are you all right, Clair?

— Mmm - yeah. D'you think Mum wants me to fly out?

— I don't know, pet. She hasn't said…

Sonya and I talked it over in bed.

— Isn't your grandmother incredibly rich?

— I think so. But she and Mum really hated each other. She'll probably leave it to a dogs' home.

— You never know. She might have gone senile and forgotten she hated your Mum.

— Fat chance.

As it happened, Grandma Emily had, in fact, left the lot to her only daughter. There were significant investments in several blue-chip companies, a high-rise in Chicago, several oil wells in Oklahoma and the local newspaper in Emily's Massachusetts hometown. My mother was loaded. But she couldn't get her hands on the money instantly to pay for a flight for me – she said. So, I stayed in England. After the funeral, she told me she had to remain in Florida to 'settle your grandmother's affairs'. More to the point she was embarking on one of her own with a millionaire called Joe Dubrowsky. But I didn't discover that until much later. All I knew, when she returned, was that Connie's perpetually defensive air had been replaced by one of assurance. And she had some very expensive clothes. And a new husband.

<O>

At Vapori cybercafé we stared at the screen, nursing sweating glasses.

– Poor Joe.

Jess was fond of her step-grandfather. I had a slightly edgier relationship with him.

– Mmm.

– You said you were going to ring Gran before we left home.

– I know.

– Why didn't you?

She knew why. Even from six thousand miles away Connie's displeasure could freeze sunshine.

– They're seven hours behind us in Florida. I'll ring her after dinner.

I drained my drink and stood while Jess logged out.

– Let's go and find that taverna we saw near the bag shop.

– Can we have a carafe of wine?

– I think we both need it.

Heading inland one layer, we found a crowded taverna and sat outside.

– Look at this – 'cheese pi'.

– I fancy the 'stuffed sweat peppers'.

After floating a meal on local red wine, we lingered over coffee and braved a metaxa. Any caution over Jess's alcoholic intake had evaporated. I staved off the moment of ringing Connie. The urge to have a cigarette was really strong and I toyed with begging Jess's indulgence, it still being some five and a bit days before my birthday. Even went as far as reaching for my bag when I noticed a welcome face. After all, if Mandy's there, can Richard be far behind?

— Look who it is, Jess!

With whoop of joy, Jess ran across to Mandy and they both disappeared, reappearing two minutes later with the very man.

Over another carafe of red, Mandy admitted that the monastery at Panormitis had been — marginally — more interesting than she'd thought.

— They've got all these bottles there and little boats with prayers rolled up in them — and they just arrive in the sea — from all over the world. And then all the monks pray for you and the Archangel Michael grants your wish. I've got an empty bottle but I can't decide whether to ask for world peace — or a nose job.

She elbowed Richard, who had said nothing.

— Shut up, you —

Jess, herself, brought up the octopus incident. She told a good story with an excellent sense of timing. Something else she'd inherited from her father — or Sonya. Magically soon, it was near midnight and we were the last four. And I was a bit pissed. All right, a lot pissed.

— Oh shit, I forgot to ring Connie!

— In that case, I plead the Fifth Amendment!

Jess knew it had something to do with the American Constitution, if not precisely what. Even so, it got a laugh.

— No, seriously — I seriously must! Most serious.

I could hear myself slurring. Mandy came to my aid.

— Well — if it's that serious, Richard had better help you find a phone.

Obediently, Richard led me away from the taverna.

— I'm pretty sure there are a couple of phones along here.

I don't think there are, but never mind, I'm holding Richard's hand.

We found a telephone by the tobacco kiosk on the bridge. Richard helped me use my credit card because, he said, the local telephone card would expire after about a minute to the States. He refrained from saying 'besides which you are completely rat arsed'. Then he waited outside. The long single note of the ringing tone repeated several times and I was about to hang up when I heard my mother. During all her years in Britain, Connie's American accent had not softened and she relished the comment it provoked. And now she sounded like she'd never set foot outside Florida.

— Hello, Mum, it's me, Clair.

Who else would I be? I'm your only child.

– I was wondering when I'd hear from you. How come you're in Greece, anyway? What's wrong with Florida? And you don't have hotel bills here.

Because you're so sodding super-critical I become fourteen years-old again as soon as I get off the plane.

– How's Joe?

– He's sitting up, now. Has to stay in bed for the next four days. The doctor's coming twice a day.

– Did he have a heart attack?

– Well, he didn't slip on a banana skin. It was Friday. Who told you? Maggie?

Who else would know to tell me?

– Yes.

– So, you rang her?

– Yes – well, no – she emailed me – us.

Joe's frail voice came on the extension.

– Hi, Jess?

– No, Joe, it's me, Clair. How are you feeling?

– I thought it was Jess. I'm OK. Jess with you?

Connie's voice cut in.

– Too busy having a good time. You tell her Joe'd like to hear from her next time.

Joe, conscious supporter and unconscious imitator of George 'Dubya' Bush, wheezed back in.

– Don't let her go getting hitched to any of them Grecians.

Christ! Jess again! Is nobody worried about me catching a Greek? Or is that just too ridiculous to contemplate?

– Oh dear! My card's running out – I'll have to ring you another time. Bye Mum – Bye Joe – Bye!

I slammed the phone down, too depressed to feel remorse for the lie, and delved recklessly into my bag for the Silk Cut. I reeled at the first pull of unspeakably divine tar. Through the smoky Perspex hood, I could see Richard leaning on a bollard. *Richard – my bitch of a mother and her decrepit zillionaire husband have just managed to demoralise me from across the Atlantic. And I'm going to be fifty on Saturday and I don't want to be. This is the part, Richard, where you put your arms round me and say, "Darling Clair, Mandy's my wife in name only. I married her to save her from –"* What? *The white slave trade? Doing A levels? Being a bimbo?* I left the booth unsteadily, flapping to clear the smoke and gobbling a mint. I managed to reach Richard without incident. Deep breath.

— Duty done!

— Jolly good. Let's get back then.

I don't remember much of the way back – except he told me he wasn't keen on next Saturday's day trip to Turkey but Mandy wanted to see the market – and I fell over a litter bin. As he picked me up I said –

— If you don't want to go to Datça, I know Jess would like to.

There's something on, next Saturday – something… can't remember.

Back at the taverna, I announced to Jess, with the all the enthusiastic generosity of the seriously drunk, that she might enjoy the Datça trip with Mandy. Her face was a study. Mandy thought it was a good idea.

— Yeah – come on, Jess, it'll be fab. Richard doesn't like poking round markets.

Realisation hit. *Next Saturday is my fiftieth birthday… Jess! Don't say anything…* But Jess was impeccably gracious.

— Mandy – that's really sweet of you. But I came on holiday with Mum because we don't spend enough quality time together at home. It's kind of missing the point if I go away for a whole day.

By her look I knew I was in big trouble. Mandy sighed.

— Ah – isn't she lovely? You must be so proud of her, Clair.

— Yesh.

After the goodnights, Jess steamed ahead of me. She was on the terrace when I arrived. There were two whiskies on the table. I started to say –

— Oh no, I don't think I could –

Then I saw the tears, silent and profuse, glistening on her face in the light from the doorway. So, I sat and lifted the other glass.

— I'm sorry, darling. On the way back from the phone, Richard said about not being keen on going to Turkey and I – I just didn't think. I didn't connect Saturday – with birthday. You dealt with it so well. I'm very proud of you, you know. I don't tell you often enough.

Jess snuffled and wiped her nose angrily with her wrist. Her voice was shaky and she spoke in fragments.

— Saying I could go to Turkey on your birthday – do you know how hurtful that was? It was like… stopping me from being generous – from giving you a great day –

— Darling, it wasn't like –

– Yes, it was like that! You always do it – always have to give people more than they give you – like it's a competition – like your life depends on it. Presents – time – affection – to anyone – everyone. And no one's allowed to give back. You've even offered to pay for presents I've given you! When I was a kid – can't remember how old I was – I saw this butterfly hair slide in the little post office at Maggie's – and I had enough pocket money to buy it for you – so I did. And do you know what you said? You said it was lovely, but you asked me how much it was so you could give me the money. Do you know how – how – shitty that was? Like a big wet towel – smack in the face!

– I'm sorry, I didn't know I –

– You do it to me, you do it to Maggie – Christ – you were even going send back the money for this holiday! Do you know how much that would have hurt her? She bloody loves you so much – and you were going to spoil that really generous thing. And I worked out why you do it! I worked it out. It's because if you give more than you get back – you don't ever owe anything. And you kid yourself it's being generous – and that's the sickest bit. Even when we haven't got enough to buy our favourite stuff in Sainsbury's, you still buy ridiculous presents for people! And you don't even like Howard. You shag him – but you don't even like him! That's why you buy him such expensive presents!

It was bound to come round to Howard. Jess had lost the thread of her argument. But she found it again.

– People always owe each other stuff – that's what it's about, it's what glues us all together – we all owe little things or big things all over the place. It's like you don't trust anyone enough to owe them anything – even me – and I'm your fucking daughter!

It's too big to take in tonight. I'm pissed, battered, and crazy for sleep.

– You've said a lot that I need to think about, Jess. We will talk, but not now. You're upset, I'm tired.

– When, then?

– I don't know. Maybe tomorrow – let's see how it goes.

– Before we leave Symi?

– Before we leave Symi.

I gave her some space before following her to bed. My night was spent largely awake, the dreams fragmentary, realistic and fantastic by turn, Connie moving back to Aborigine Road while I, still in school uniform, watched helplessly. Maggie floated on a raft from which she tried to save a drowning Tatty – or was it Jess – or was it me? And, of course, the knocking on the door routine.

CHAPTER FIVE

FRASER

Mel. New Zealander, from Auckland. Doing the world trip and stopped in Rhodes. Not a great meeting of minds. From the first night, it was always very physical. And my problem was? Didn't have one – not to start with. She did, though. Why couldn't I be more laid back? More entrepreneurial? Less into music? More into sport? More into clothes? Prefer wine to beer? Less political? More like her? Or just – different? With so many guys to choose from, I couldn't work out why she didn't pick some hunk instead of me, who obviously fell so far short of her ideal. And then go to all the bother of changing me. Especially since it was such a hike to get from Lindos to Rhodes Town before even getting the hydrofoil to Symi. Why? Had a nasty feeling it was something to do with her biological clock. Made me feel like the last chance stud. However, next morning there I was, having a coffee and waiting for the hydrofoil that carried Mel and her ageing eggs. When along come the Harkin duo. The we'an disappeared to the supermarket and Clair joined me to wait. One egg hatched and the rest hard-boiled by now, so no danger. Can't believe I said that! She looked good. Very good. Sun had just touched her skin. Slight creases at her eyes, made her look interesting – and kind. She was worried about yesterday – about the Jess/octopus incident. I'd mostly forgotten, having spent all night devising reproduction avoidance tactics. But I remembered Clair's flying tackle into the sea with considerable relish. Found myself almost flirting with her. Did she turn a bit pinker or was it my imagination? Next, I was giving her a rundown of my CV. Just to encourage her to talk about herself, you know. But not probing. Like, maybe, was there a man? I turned up the humour. And she turned it back on me. Then the hydrofoil, the bloody hydrofoil containing said Kiwi fertility goddess hove into view.

Brilliant. Perfect timing. Chummed Clair and we'an along the harbour. They went on – walking to Nimborio. Wished I was, too. But Mel was first off. Tall, skinny, blonde hair, brown skin, magnificent diddies. And a face like twisted gut. What day off? After a quick peck I suggested we take a walk up to Chorio, but she wanted to look at Aris's leather shop and a couple of jewellery shops then go for lunch at the top end of the harbour. Pointed out that Chorio was a better bet – Yialos would be heaving when the tourist boats came in. Might as well have boaked into the wind for all the response I got.

One leather jacket, a handbag and two pairs of shoes later Mel had finished with leather and hauled me to the far side of the harbour to the classy gold shop. My mind should have been concentrating on survival but it strayed to Nimborio, so when Mel eventually swam back into vision everything turned cold. She was trying on a sparkler. Always thought vampires couldn't come out in the sun, but this woman wanted my blood for sure, smiled showing every tooth and said

– Have you got anything to say to me, Fraser?

Or 'Fry-zuh' as she said it. Too late to consult Annie. Couldn't think of a vampire gag but I was quick under the circumstances.

– Now, Gollum, put the ring down.

My crass attempt at humour inspired by Mel's New Zealand origin and the 'Lord of the Rings' connection did not raise much of a laugh. It was never going to end happily. And it didn't. Global warming was bound to soar the day I dumped Mel. The screaming match in the shop spilled out along the harbour and as far as Nos beach where I turned back and managed to lose her in the crowd getting off a tourist ferry.

I hid in a kafeneion in Chorio until the hydrofoil came and went again. Afterwards, I retired to Nobby's. She'd been going to stop the night but I was fairly sure she wouldn't bother. Even so, I stayed at Nobby's until he threw me out. Took the long way home. Threw rocks at the bloody window until Nikos came out and promised she wasn't there. Stayed up strumming 'til he told me to shut it. No trips the next day.

CLAIR

Connie and Aborigine Road

<O>

The day of Eleven Plus exam results, we were let out of school to tell our parents the news. I ran all the way. Wanting to surprise Connie, I slipped down the side of the house instead of ringing the bell at the front. The back door wasn't locked, so Mum must be in. I moved quietly through the rooms, anticipating her cry of delight when I told her. She wasn't downstairs, so I crept upstairs, stepping carefully at the edge of each tread so as not to make them creak. Upstairs, it was quiet. Where was she? Her bedroom door was shut, but she wasn't in any of the other rooms so she must be in there. I stood on the landing uncertainly, battling with my conditioning, knowing that under no circumstances was I allowed to enter without knocking first. Would it be so wrong just to go in? With such good news? *Perhaps she isn't in, just forgot to lock the back door? And if she is in her bedroom – well, she won't mind because this is special. She won't mind. She'll be pleased. She'll tell me I'm really clever. She'll let me ring Maggie at work. And Maggie will be really, really pleased.* Heart full of expectation, I stepped forward. As I touched the handle, a small noise came from the room. It sounded like a gasp. Was Mum all right? I snatched my hand away, uncertain, afraid, even.

– Mummy? Mummy – it's me. Clair.

There was a flurry of movement from inside and whispering, like there were two people. I moved away, foreboding overcoming my earlier excitement. The door whipped open six inches and Connie's irate face appeared.

– What the hell are you doing home?!

I couldn't speak, so intense was her annoyance. The door closed for a moment and reopened as she burst through, slamming it shut again and pulling her dressing gown to her. She grabbed my arm hard.

– Listen, young lady, you'd better be sick or you're in big trouble! Are you sick?

– No, Mummy, I –

– Then what have you come back for? How many times have I told you, you should –

She shook me hard. My legs buckled and I sat on the floor, Connie still gripping my forearm. Through sobs, I tried to explain my reason for coming home.

– What? What?

She yanked me to my feet.

– Quit yowling, I can't understand you!

Somehow, I choked out my wonderful news. Connie let go.

– Oh. OK. That's good… They shouldn't have sent you home, though – um – hold on – ah – what say you go down to the kitchen and help yourself to a cookie? And I'll – er – be with you.

I plodded downstairs, insides writhing with misery and disappointment, my moment of glory torn to shreds and ground underfoot for good measure. I sat in the kitchen unable to swallow the crumbled biscuit in my mouth, throat tight, face drying stickily. I wished myself far away from the house and longed for Maggie and Julia, imagined telling them I'd passed, lost myself in a warm vision of their delight and praise. Connie came in, now dressed in sweater and trousers, feet bare.

– You've done very well, honey. Here – that's for being a clever girl.

She passed me a ten-pound note. I let it drop on the table.

– Don't you want it?

Suddenly I was on my feet heading for the back door.

– I hate you! I hate you! I really hate you! I wish Maggie was my mum!

And I was out, running back to school, liberated by the outburst but fearing, already, the retribution. Swerving through the side gate to the pavement, I noticed his car parked a little further up the road. There weren't so many cars about, then, and his was particularly distinctive – large, black and expensive looking. But I'd missed it in my earlier euphoric rush. As my breath gave out I slowed to a walk, wondering why I hadn't seen Ben in the house and whether his car was there every day while I was at school.

<O>

STILL CLAIR

Tuesday – Terrible minus four

Jess and I skirted carefully around each other the next morning, she, exhausted by anger and hurt, I through deference to it. She settled on the terrace, slumped in one plastic chair, feet crossed lazily on another, her eyes shaded as she read. Her angry words still filtered through my mind, the essence of truth distilling into a sizeable pool. Gritty from insomnia, I decided on a day around the apartment, maybe pop out to pick up a few postcards, come back and write them. My vitamins were laid out on the table as usual. *Is this pill ritual Jess trying to keep up with my bullying generosity?* I took them slowly, keen to show appreciation, then excused myself to slip down to the town for the postcards. Jess sanctioned it with a neutral – 'Cool'. She was reading 'Pride and Prejudice' for the fourth time. *I should warn her that not all good looking, arrogant, rich men have a heart of gold and a mind for monogamy.*

I wandered down the stairways, heading nowhere particular in the alien heat, bought an indiscriminate selection of cards then headed for the cybercafé. Over a coffee and iced water I lit a Marlboro and logged onto email. Three new messages, two junk and the third from Sonya –

Subject: Dumped!

Brian has flown home. Why? His bl**dy mother-in-law has a slight cold or something. He'd finished his meetings and the last few days were going to be our little holiday. Maybe this is IT Clack! Fortunately, met a riveting film director (through S***head) who has a place in West Hollywood and I'm crashing there for a few days. Before you get sniffy, it's a she. Staying with a local means I get to see a lot more of the real LA.

Who's the 'holi' person you might have to shag? An Orthodox Priest? (Is Orthodox the same as Missionary?)

Big love - Sonn x

Perhaps Brian really had gone too far, this time. I was glad to hear Sonya had, as usual, landed on her feet. I decided to ignore the cracks about orthodox sex.

Subject: Re: Dumped!

Sonn – Kalimera – Really sorry to hear about Brian. Hope you are keeping that suntanned chin at least horizontal. Sounds as though you've turned it into something positive, though. Have a ball, if only to serve him right. Who's your director friend? What's she done? Thinking of you, pal.

Jess and I on shaky ground. Lurve has reared its ugly head at her. Connie's discontent blights glorious summer with news of Joe's heart attack. He's stable and I'm in the doghouse for being here. Plus the Terrible Day looms. Otherwise Symi bliss. Downing sufficient alcohol to float Odyssey – Yamass! Stay brave and enjoy the Californian sun. Heaps – Clack

I logged off and found a table outside to write a couple of postcards. The first, to Maggie, with a picture of Nimborio. Enthusiasm had waned by card number two – Pedi Bay to Howard. I gave up, slipped Maggie's card into a post box and meandered through the stone lanes of boutiques, bakeries and mini supermarkets. Then I saw it. Jess's shoulder bag, plum-coloured, cut simply to sling diagonally from shoulder to opposite hip. But as the impulse spurred me to buy, I remembered: "You give everything – presents – time – emotions – to anyone – everyone". *Is Jess right? Am I afraid of obligation? No, that's absurd. I don't feel obligated to Jess, I enjoy giving her little presents… but that's her point – that I should let other people enjoy giving to me – isn't it? Can't I be generous to my little girl any more?*

The salesman prowled around the counter.

– Deutsch?

– English.

– Ah – English, very good. You enjoy Symi?

– Oh yes, we love it.

– You like this bag? Very good leather, you see? And this –

He held out the shoulder strap,

– Better for the – er –

He made a vague crossways mime. *Tits? Tai Chi? Genuflection technique?*

– You know? Ladies, always too much in the bag!

Much shared laughter. And so the conversation continued until I found myself in the alley with the bag in a plastic carrier and foreboding gathering around the solar plexus. *Bugger! I've done it again! I can't give it to her after what she said. Can't take it back —*

— Clair — hello! How's your head after last night? Mine feels like I'm talking in a bucket.

It was Mandy. She didn't wait for a reply.

— Been spending money you haven't got? Come on — let's have a look!

— Oh, it's just a —

What the hell? I handed over the package.

— Ooh — it's lovely— gorgeous colour!

Richard was up at the apartment reading, not her idea of holiday. She suggested a coffee. Her understanding smile on my refusal was too quick.

— I could go a cold drink, though.

We sat at the table Fraser had occupied the previous morning. *Wonder how it went with girlfriend from Lindos, yesterday?* Mandy's chat covered sunburn, insect repellent, Greek food, the monastery at Panormitis, Greek icons, triptychs, Jess…

— She's really great, so mature. I can see why she's so lovely. It's you — no, it is — you've brought her up really well. And on your own. Sorry, that sounds patronising. I mean it's just the way you — well, you know, the way you both get on.

There's irony.

— I think it's down to Jess's nature more than my nurture.

— Or because there wasn't a man to mess things up?

Mandy snatched back the edge of bitterness instantly, leaned back and laughed

— Now my mum — well, sometimes even the Pennines aren't big enough to hide behind!

I felt disoriented, liking her, envying her for having Richard and disapproving of myself for it. The conversation switched to Symi and Mandy focused on Fraser. I told her about the girlfriend from Lindos. She winked.

— Very easy on the eyeballs, Fraser, and his voice is dead sexy. Shame he's got a squeeze!

— And you a married woman — I'm shocked, shocked I tell you!

She laughed and nudged me matily.

— Don't tell me you haven't noticed?! Or are you pining for — what did Jess call him? Oh, yes —

– 'Gluefeatures'? His name's Howard. She's not that keen on him.

I tried to minimise our differences over my… over Howard.

– Can't blame her. I'm not that knocked out, either.

Mandy's snort of amusement encouraged me to confess my nicotine addiction, too. She stayed chatting the length of a cigarette then reached for her bag.

– I'll get this. Time I was getting back to Einstein. Jess'll be wondering where you are, too.

More likely hoping I've fallen down a hole.

As Mandy headed back to Richard, I noticed it was nearly twelve. The time had slipped by easily. *How can I entertain improper thoughts about her husband? What improper thoughts? The subliminal ones. But there haven't been any. So, why do I feel like I do when I see him? How do I feel when I see him? Lonelier than normal.*

– You look like you're mentally restructuring the European Agricultural policy. Crack your face – you're on your holidays.

I felt my face stretch to a smile. It was Fraser in tired singlet, disreputable shorts and old leather sandals. He looked weary.

– Where's the we'an?

– Having a strop.

– Funny that. My ex-girlfriend's doing the same thing back in Lindos. Beer, then?

Ex? I felt oddly, OK, very pleased by this news. As we walked back toward the taxi boats and continued inland he pointed out the maritime museum.

– Come in and take a look, it's amazing.

Inside the small gallery was an old, copper diving helmet, various nautical bits and pieces and many photographs labelled mainly in Greek text. He pointed to some circular stones, roughly half a metre across, with a hole in the middle.

– See these? Skalopetra – diving weights. Each diver made his own. They dived for sponges for centuries around here – and from Halki, Tilos, Kalymnos. The sponge fleets went all over the Mediterranean, as far down as Libya. It was all skin diving, you know – breath control. Then the compressed air system was invented along with a diving suit, the skafandro, and the industry really took off. Good and bad news, really. The merchants made a lot of money, but thousands of divers were killed or crippled. You've heard of the bends?

– I know divers get it but I've never been sure what it was.

– Caused by nitrogen. When divers go down deep, the nitrogen in their bloodstream compresses with the pressure of the water but if they surface too quickly, the nitrogen expands too fast for the blood to absorb it. It's like having fizzy water in your veins… Back then, when divers came up, they used to light a cigarette so their mates could smell them exhaling. There was a tell-tale odour.

– What could they do if they smelt it?

– Not much. They'd rub their joints to help ease the pain. Poor buggers died quickly if they were lucky. Or they'd leave them on a beach with a buddy. Theory was to cover him in sand in the sun to keep him warm. More like the captain didn't want to hold up business.

Socialist outrage – tinged with bitterness at being dumped? I was doing him an injustice.

– The women in Kalymnos got together and petitioned the Turkish Caliph to ban the skafandro. Must have taken some bottle, given the status of women then. And they got their way – he banned it. But he didn't put it in writing, so the skafandro crept back in, and so did the deaths and the injuries. Symi was the first of the islands to ban the skafandro altogether. Quite a move given they depended on sponge diving. A lot of Symiots emigrated to Australia for the pearl diving or Florida to dive for sponges. Maybe it was better regulated there.

Silence as we contemplated the old injustice, broken by Fraser.

– C'mon, history lesson over. Let's get that drink.

We walked past the thick-buttressed walls of the old ice storage house, now a hairdresser's. Guilty, perhaps, for introducing such gloom, he told me a few more tourist disasters, including the loss of a chest expander, seven pairs of false teeth and a toupee.

– Probably went through a goat's bowels. You'd have to be desperate to put it on your head again. I just recommended factor fifty for his bald spot. Here we are.

The taverna was stylish with wooden tables and chairs, instead of the usual plastic or metal, under large green canopies. Surrounding them were shoulder high urns filled with succulents, broad-leafed bamboo and maidenhair fern, obviously tended by some dedicated gardener to survive in the Symi heat. The menu was simple but all meat or fish-based which, I commented, made it a no-go area for my vegetarian offspring.

– Hence the octopus incident? Still – I'm sure they'd whip her something up. You eat fish, though? Their garlic prawns are to die for and the sea bass with capers is pretty mean. Mind you, it's pricey, even by Symi standards. Do you have anything to celebrate as an excuse to lay out a few quid?

– No, no celebrations. Just being here is enough.

Liar, liar. We ordered beers. Silence. I wondered if I ought to ask about his girlfriend. Did I really want to hear about her? Not a lot. What else? I asked how long he'd known Nikos. He studied me, amused.

– Do you mean 'have I known him long?' or 'do I think he has honourable intentions towards your daughter?'. Sorry. I've known him about four years. He's OK. And yes, he's a good looking guy. But she's a wee stunner, so why wouldn't they fancy each other? Sure, he's fancied other birds. Expect Jess has had her eye on a few guys by now.

– I suppose so.

– Not easy, eh? Your wee girl all grown up? Mothers are more tolerant than fathers, though. My sister, Annie – she had a desperate time with my Dad – I mean how many guys have to collect their girlfriends from the front door these days? Drove her berserk.

– Did she kick up?

– Big time. Disappeared for a while, came back pregnant and moved to a flat in Easterhouse. The wee boy's magic. Coming up five. Jude.

– How did your parents take it?

– My mother's OK about it, but the old man's really turned around. He lives and dies at Annie's, decorating, putting up shelves, teaching Jude the offside rule. Mum never sees him. Annie's going into her second year at university – Strathclyde. Doing pretty well, too.

– Good for her. I'm glad it's worked out.

We drank in self-conscious silence, which he broke. What did I think of Symi? I mentioned my earlier visit. He covered his face.

– And you let me drone on about the history like a complete tool –

– I wasn't into that at nineteen. What do I like about it now? The ruggedness, being only yards from the sea, Yialos, Chorio, the food, the smallness of it when the sightseeing boats leave at three, Pedi, the sea again, looking at Turkey, goats –

– You haven't mentioned the holiday rep.

Just a twitch of smile. *Is he flirting with me?*

– You mean the dropout accountant who picks up tourists in the street?

– Aye.

– They say he stands his round in the taverna – plays a mean guitar.

– So he meets with requirements?

– Whose?

– Your glass is empty.

The place filled for lunch without my noticing as we downed our second beer. I was about to suggest another round when it occurred to me that disappearing for the entire morning would not have improved matters with Jess. I said so, fishing for my purse.

– Put your money away. I stand my round in the taverna.

We stood awkwardly. Shaking hands would be too formal, a social air kiss too posey. Fraser shrugged.

– Look – I'm off to Rhodes tomorrow, see this week's group to the airport and pick up the next one, so I'll be tied up for a couple of days. Enjoy Symi.

He touched my arm.

The shoulder bag was tucked back in the carrier, but I needn't have bothered. Outside Aphrodite One, an empty wine bottle sat on the table. Next to it lolled Jess, breathing shallowly, anaesthetised from further strife. Mr D'Arcy and Co. lay abandoned, face down in the Symi dust, the Aphrodite lizard straddling their collective spine. Having been away nearer four hours than one, I was relieved not to have another confrontation. I crept into the bedroom, and flopped down with a finger of whisky. The plum shoulder bag lay in the bottom drawer. A small voice pierced the late afternoon stillness.

– Mum?

Bruised by the trauma of the previous night, we were gentle with one other.

Waiting for pizzas that evening at the harbour top taverna, Jess told me Nikos was at a Pan Aegean company event. *Hence I'm not getting earache about being somewhere or doing something else.* I wondered aloud about his age. She shrugged. I conjectured on how Raz was enjoying Mexico. Another shrug. As the pizzas arrived I tried a third gambit.

– I bumped into Mandy today. She thinks we have a great relationship. I don't think she likes her own mother much.

– I don't think she liked her father, either. When I said I'd never had a dad around, she said 'That's not necessarily such a bad thing'.

And she said "Or because there wasn't a man to mess things up?", this morning. Obviously a sensitive point. But it wasn't the time to talk about fathers or lack of them. I tried gossip.

– Oh – and just after I left Mandy I met Fraser. He split up with his girlfriend and he needed some company, so we had a beer.

Jess clicked her tongue.

– Picking up stray men and binge drinking – you'll get a reputation.

– That's supposed to be my line to you.

– Sad, isn't it?

The banter was back on track, at least.

After eating, we wandered along the harbour. Moored down to the left was a large, shiny black cruiser with even the windows blacked out, flying the Stars and Stripes alongside the Greek flag. It must belong to a rock star, we decided. We eyed it up trying to spot a celebrity and look nonchalant at the same time. It was named 'Hilarium'.

– Hilarium – hilarious? Someone rich and funny, then… Michael Palin? Steve Martin?

– Gran?

– Not that kind of funny.

Next, we hit the shops. Jess toyed with the idea of looking for the shoulder bag she'd liked so much. I remained guiltily silent while she argued herself out of it. But when she reopened the debate on the Greek cotton tops, I conceded, we went back to our favourite clothes shop and both splashed out. Jess went for the camisole. Instead of the shirt, I chose a modest button-down tunic. Nothing could crown this extravagance, so we returned to base and bed without even a nightcap, both sleeping soon and, in Jess's case, deeply.

FRASER

Had to check a few details for the Wednesday arrivals and sort the invites for some kind of a party on Saturday at Hotel Acropolis. Wasn't dressed for the office but I didn't care. Nikos was pretty busy so I left early and went to Panos's brother Stelios's kafeneion, looking for fellow comfort. But everyone was busy. Then who daunders past but Clair, looking down. I made some inane comment and got a smile back that changed my day. Was I onto something, here? Invited her for a beer. Thought I'd take her to Mel's favourite taverna – cleanse the place with a new woman? Was I thinking that way already? Passed the museum on the way. Took her in and showed off a bit. Fascinating story, Symi and the sponge diving. Called to my socialist roots. Started a song about it one time – hadn't got it right, yet.

We had a couple of beers. Not the sort of place you normally go just for a beer – but I got the odd perk for pointing punters in their direction. Ashamed to say I pitched it to Clair, but she said she didn't have anything particular to celebrate. Ended up telling her more about me than I found out about her. Second time in two days. How come? Still didn't know if there was a man. She wanted to know about Nikos as far as bimbette was concerned. Not without good cause, it has to be said. Didn't say that, of course. I went on a lot about Annie, too. More than I ever told Mel. She –

Clair – wanted to pay for the beers but I insisted on laying out the euros. Me buy a punter a drink? That should have warned me. Then off she went to check on the we'an. And, you know, part of me was – jealous.

Watched her until she turned the corner, tall bird with a neat arse. Waiting for another beer, it occurred to me that she and Jess were the only ones not to get white envelopes – the invites to the surprise 'do' on Saturday up at Hotel Acropolis. Maybe they had something else on, but she'd said earlier they had nothing to celebrate? Be a shame if she – if they – didn't come. I was booked to play at it. Not that I wanted to impress her particularly. Strange thing. Even though it was the right result, I'd been feeling pretty bad about the Mel thing up until she walked past. And now I felt considerably better.

– So there's no particular reason for the change that you can think of?

I told the wee sister in my head to shut it. Life felt rosier. Definitely. For no particular reason, Annie! One problem – I'd probably bump into Mel at the airport next day.

HOWARD

Dame Fiona was at the House of Commons with a gaggle of other Directors of Education, meeting the current incumbent, leaving me to get on with the real work of running the place. All the work, I should say, ever since she was appointed Director over my head. Well done her! And three bloody cheers for positive bloody discrimination. How else would she have got the job? Anyhow, with her away and not popping brightly in and out of my office – my *glass cubicle* – with ever more absurd initiatives, I was able to get the Symi project off the ground.

My shared PA, Pat, ignoring the thinning hair and piano legs, is something of a gem. She suggested I might make my appearance on Symi a surprise, and organise the birthday bash to end all. She even offered to do the organising. Not pukka on Education Authority time strictly speaking but hey, I deserve a bit of a break and I'm hardly a hedge fund profiteer. As it happened, Pat was able to book me with Aegis, the company Clair used. She let it slip at the ghastly barbecue affair. Odd that she thought she'd got the last space. Still, I was going a week later, which could explain the availability. Pat also ascertained that the hotel I was booked into could handle a function and provide entertainment – dancers and a musician of who knows what standard. But Clair would probably find it all very 'ethnic'.

CLAIR

Wednesday – Terrible minus three

— We'll have been here a whole week by this evening.

We were having breakfast on the terrace – nonchalant, now, about the view. Jess continued, contemplative.

— You know, it's really odd about holidays. You're having a good time and you think 'I want it always to be this moment'. And you try to hang onto it but it goes racing away and you suddenly find yourself in another moment on a wet day in October remembering the moment you were trying to hang onto. Except we're here, now, and it's holiday and it's wonderful!

She wiped a dribble of Symi honey from her chin and squinted out across the harbour.

— Shall we go somewhere else today? Oh – d'you mind if I go for a drink with Nikos tonight?

The last was tacked on so casually it was difficult to object. I wondered how long the assignation had been on her agenda. *They met at the supermarket while I was talking to Fraser on Monday – before we went to Nimborio! Sly little...* At least the arch manipulator was being deferential. I OK'd it.

As we waited for the next Nanou boat I squinted around the harbour for Richard's white hair. Or Mandy's blonde. Failed on both. When the boat arrived we headed for the prow to avoid the exhaust of the engine and the tobacco fumes of the two-man crew. Jess hissed in my ear.

— Look – there's that woman with the purple face, you know, the one who was so arsey on the boat coming back from Sesklia.

I glanced round instantly catching the woman's narrow eye. She stood with a little man who looked spookily like Charles Hawtrey. I pointed him out to Jess.

— Who's Charles Hawtrey?

On the boat, we played a 'Who would we least like to meet here?' game. Number of points dependent on level of undesirability. Howard was Jess's opening gambit, for which she claimed a thousand points. I vetoed it as too predictable. After a tussle over rules Jess conceded, provided that Connie and Joe were also excluded. Play recommenced with Brenda next door in Aborigine Road, for fifty points. And so it continued with teachers, ex-employers, sometime friends and foes. I hurled in Jess's contemporary, Sharn (sic) Fellowes, for twenty-five points. Sharn had dressed like a hooker since age nine and spoke to her elders as though they were dung beetles.

— But Sharn's a good laugh!

I wouldn't budge. Counter attacking, Jess threw in Harry Whelkin, self-appointed convener of Aborigine Road Neighbourhood Watch and right-wing bigot. I had to admit it was an excellent call, boosting her score to three hundred.

— So why do you suck up to him, Mum?

— I don't. I've been to a couple of meetings because we have been broken into twice.

— So why did you go to his barbecue? You said it would be like a white supercilious convention.

— White supremacist. I couldn't think what else to do with Howard.

Oh tits. Played right into her hands. Jess looked at me solemnly.

— Are you that lonely, Mum? That you have to be with him?

— No, I'm not lonely, darling. It's like that old song, 'If you can't be with the one you love, love the one you're with'. Except there's no one I love that I can't be with. But I may as well be with someone when it suits. So — Howard.

— I so don't understand you!

She could have asked now if I had loved her father. It perplexed me that she'd never wanted to know about him. In her position I'd have been eaten up with curiosity. Maybe she was waiting for me to say. Or maybe she was intuitive. Or perhaps she realised that his role wasn't important — well, not important to our relationship. It was all getting too serious. I played an ace.

— Rita Whelkin!

Jess was caught off guard but delighted.

— Oh yes — no! Bleeurrrghhh! Vomit, vomit! Ten million trillion points — and a zillion for her wig and her dog!

— I win, then?

— I'm a slaughtered daughter! Look — my guts are splattered all over the boat and my bum hole's landed on Arsey Purple!

At Nanou Jess went straight to the taverna and ferried two beers back to the shade of our parasol.

— Here's to everyone we don't want here! Long may they be somewhere else!

— Yamass!

At that moment, three goats barged in amongst the taverna tables through the gate that Jess, no doubt, had left open. The owner — who looked suspiciously like the captain of the last taxi boat — grabbed each one by the horns and propelled them out again yelling 'Souvlaki!' after the invaders. Jess bawled at him, unable to bear the thought of a living creature being reduced to a kebab.

– No! Um – um – ochi!

But the goat slayer returned to the kitchen, gratified and laughing.

She was keen to finish 'Pride and Prejudice' so I checked out the snorkelling. There were the usual rainbow fish, what looked like a tiny John Dory, shoal upon shoal of silver blue fish, almost the length of my hand, and several long thin fish, motionless apart from delicate finning. Pipe fish? Or the needlefish I'd heard Fraser talking about? I forgot time, suspended in heaven. But sloshing back through the shallows the sun hit my skin directly and I realised I'd been snorkelling too long. I checked my watch – I'd been gone over an hour. I should have worn an old T-shirt. Thirty odd years ago in Kos, Sonya had been knocked out for three days for that very reason. I would get hell from Jess.

The telling off was delivered and accepted, the aftersun lotion lathered on, strictures regarding alcohol laid down and relegation to the shade ordered. I could only pick at the packed lunch, wincing as my seared flesh brushed the umbrella pole. The raw back wouldn't even allow an afternoon nap, so I had to watch Jess snoozing happily. Despite my skin slurping in aftersun like a sponge, it felt tight and sticky. The years rolled back. Maggie making a paste of baking soda – plastering it on – and my burning skin setting it instantly into white peaks like icing on a Christmas cake. Going to bed, crying with soreness – and the killer icing shattering into razors inside my pyjamas, stabbing and scraping all night long. Then Maggie, hugging me, bathing it off, saying sorry, sorry, sorry for hurting her special girl. Where had Connie been then?

Crunching of feet on pebbles alerted Jess to the time.

– Shit! Mum – it's the last boat!

We packed in a panic and ran. As we queued for the boat my head started to thump, I felt nauseous and as if my legs weren't connected to my body. Suddenly my toes swum into vision, then somehow collided with the sky. It was all very far away. *Mouth's burning – feeling very bad – aah – no – yes!* Someone yelled –

– Oh, no! She's being sick!

That's better. A lot better. Next thing I knew was voices. We were back in Yialos.

– Hello, I am Dr Mavrakakou. What is the patient's name?

– Clair Harkin. She's my mother.

– Hello, Clair.

I felt something being shoved under my tongue and each eyelid yanked open.

– How old is she?

– Forty-nine – nearly fifty.

That was unnecessary. Some burbling. Following which I took my first mule ride, sprawled sideways across its back. Fortunately, being unconscious by then, I didn't suffer the indignity first hand. That came later when Jess hissed the information at me.

CHAPTER SIX

STILL CLAIR

There have been worse times...

<O>

I am slumped on the landing, distraught at my loss, too weak to move further. The phone rings but I can't answer it. One of the lodgers, returning to the house in the small hours, falls over me in the dark. Voices, an ambulance, a light shining in my eyes, being forced to drink something. A strange bed. Shivering, vomiting and diarrhoea. Then Sonya is there and, finally, blessedly, Maggie. Glad to see her but regretting being alive. I submit to Maggie's voice, to her touch, gradually tell her why.

On the pill for years, so gave my body a rest, left contraception to him. Didn't realise I was pregnant until the miscarriage. After seven years together, Adam left me for 'tricking him' into making me pregnant. I hadn't tricked him. But he had his excuse to leave. So he left. I was very scared I wasn't going to die. So I did something about it. Then sorry, sorry, sorry. Sorry for all the –

– Hush, there, there –

Maggie soothing me.

Summer, no work. As soon as I was ready, a day out here, a day there. Lunch in London at a place Maggie knew.

– Your mother worked here for a while, when you were little.

A tall, white-haired man approached, kissed Maggie. Looked at me. A flicker of mutual recognition, suppressed. Maggie said –

– This is my niece, Clair, the little girl you met on the Terrace all those years ago.

He joined us for coffee. Maggie gave him an edited version of my illness. I could hardly look at him in case I gave myself away, gave him away. Ben. No longer an MP. And no longer my mother's lover. The white hair did not age him, those astonishing eyes had not dimmed. He wished us a safe trip up to Kilachlan. Asked me to ring him on my return. He would take me to lunch, help with anything I might... and, by the way, how was my mother?

– In America? Remarried?

As if he didn't know.

I spent September in Kilachlan with Maggie and Monsieur Hulot, the West Highland Terrier. Strength gradually returned, but my spirits were low, despite long sunny days, silver-blue sea and magically light evenings. Sonya joined us for a fortnight bringing extravagant gifts to delight, wicked tales of the big city to make us laugh and friendship solid enough to coax me back south, convincing enough for Maggie to let me go. Drove down through the Lake District, the Welsh Borders, cutting across the Cotswolds in Sonya's little MG. Stayed overnight in village pubs to the chagrin of local girls who were left in the shadow of the small, sexy one and the tall, beautiful one. Me. Then back to Guildford, back to school, part-time. And the news from York. Adam getting married. To a childhood sweetheart. So, I rang the only other man I really knew. He recognised me as soon as he heard my voice.

– Clair. My little girl with the silly hair. When can we meet?

He came to the house, still had a key but politely did not use it. Brought flowers and champagne, in celebration of finding me again. I felt love radiate from me. He was all I had ever missed or needed. Setting aside complexity, propriety, we buried ourselves in one another. His mind fascinated, his experience taught, his power protected me. And for him? He had, he said, my beauty, my gift of laughter and my talent for loving. I feared the immensity of my feelings for this could not last nor ever be equalled. As it was, it was outshone. I must have conceived her the first time we made love. Once I knew, once I was sure, I unravelled our bonds, gently, gently, keeping the love inside me. Jess. And how could she be wrong?

<O>

Now in Symi, she slept a yard away. Throughout a painful night I woke and dreamt in starts – dreamt of Jess being born, except she assisted at her own birth until a midwife slopped her, howling, into a bucket. *Bring my baby back! Bring her back!!! If I can just get this – barbed wire coat off… Who are those people? At the end of the tunnel in the hot sun? Why are they wearing those old-fashioned clothes? Nineteen fifties. Who's that? Sitting on a ledge, playing his guitar. Smiling at me. Is it Daddy? No, it's Adam, but he's turned into… You know who, Clair. Do I?*

FRASER

Did a tour of the Aegis accommodation in the afternoon, leaving notes and making sure the outgoing punters knew departure time – hellishly early next morning. Back at the office there was a note from Ali Mavrakakou, the GP in Yialos and Chorio. Clair was ill, heatstroke. My first instinct was to bolt for Aphrodite One, but the note went on to say that she should sleep it off and I wasn't to worry, everything was under control. I rang Ali and she picked up straight away.

– Yatrou Mavrakakou. Neh?

– Hi Ali, Fraser – about Clair –

– I said in my note she's OK. She'll be asleep now. Call on her tomorrow when you get back from Rhodes.

– But Jess is only –

– The daughter is capable of looking after her. I'm on call, Fraser, I can't chat.

She cut me off. I was tempted to call in anyway, but the doctor had spoken. I made a note in the day book then locked the office and went back to the apartment. Spent an hour or so on the diving song. Got a few chords right. Went to Nobby's and played flip-the-beer-mat until the Italian bird Nikos was smooching decided to hang onto her virtue. Joined him in another couple of beers then the two of us made our way home, bouncing off a few walls on the way. He promised he'd check on the Harkins while I was off but I doubted he'd remember.

My head hardly hit the pillow before I was up to take one boatload to Rhodes airport and bring the next one back to Symi. Clair was at the back of my mind as I checked, instructed, herded and despatched punters to the various airlines. I didn't even – well almost didn't think about Mel. As it happened, she never turned up. Relief. Not like her to duck an issue. The day dragged interminably. I rang Nikos a few times to check on Clair but his phone went to voicemail. That evening, as the ferry slowed, I went through the main cabin psyching up the new punters. They were easy to spot. 100% British, middle class, and 90% middle-aged. I'd already identified the PITAs (Pain in the arse-s) for this week – a couple off the Gatwick flight who looked like those wee budgie toys that spring up every time they're knocked over. Weebles. Came from some Toy Town place on the south coast – West Wittering? And they'd been to Symi before. Any advice on walks, restaurants, beaches – their fellow Aegis travellers had only to ask them. They were more or less saying 'ignore the knob with the Aegis badge, he's just here for the ride'. Wondered how long I could resist testing their Weeble-ability to bounce back. They promised to be not just PITAs but Profound PITAs. There was also a baldy guy who'd ignored the blue sea and sky on the trip across from Mandraki and was still hunched behind yesterday's Times. Potentially a mega-PITA. I wondered if I'd taken the right line in refusing the information he wanted, particularly under the circumstances. Was I pursuing Aegis company policy or self-interest? Company policy, I decided, and tough on the bad-tempered bald bastard.

The quayside radiated back the day's heat. Symiots and resident holidaymakers strolled, enjoyed a cool beer, or simply stood around. Found myself looking about for a tall bird with fuzzy hair. Fruitlessly. Got most of the Aegis luggage swaying up and away on mule-back, but the baldy guy grouched by his bags tapping his foot. I spent more time than absolutely necessary matching the last few couples and muleteers to avoid eye contact with him. Finally, there was no escape. Despite being allocated a room at the hotel, Bald Bastard had chosen not to occupy it just yet. I waved off the last mule and confronted the steaming shite.

    – Is there a problem with your hotel, Mr Bunce?

He would have a name like that. Bunce. Bald Bastard Bunce.

    – I have no idea whether or not there is a problem with my hotel. First, I want to go to Aegis' company office and make a call to your employers!

He had metal studs of sweat on his forehead.

    – I have come out here especially to surprise my partner, Ms Harkin, and you deliberately deny me access to her. Indeed, it is I who has commissioned the surprise party booked for her birthday next Saturday at the Hotel Acropolis. You are aware of it?

My stomach lurched with pity for Clair and growing loathing for the dollop of rancid lard in front of me.

    – Someone at your office is, undoubtedly, aware. So, either you drop this Boy Scout charade and behave like a responsible adult or I will see to it that you face disciplinary action.

He was sorely in need of a Glasgow kiss.

    –I'm not allowed to disclose client names and addresses, Mr Bunce. Company policy –

    – Company policy? Take me to your office and let's check with them, eh?

My next riposte was particularly sweet.

    – It might be different if she'd mentioned you were joining her –

He trembled till his bald patch turned scarlet.

    – That – is because I have come to surprise her!

    –… or even that she had a partner – but she hasn't. And rules are rules, Mr Bunce.

How sweet to trot out that little cliché to a fud like him. I'd learned to ignore raging punters and keep smiling, but something was beginning to overload. Transfers were one long arse-clench of a day. But mostly – if I wasn't too destroyed – there would be a beer at Nobby's before bed. Unless I got a real treat like this outsize fuckwit –

    – Fraser!

It was Nikos. Unfortunately, with a gob the size of Pedi Bay.

    – I just heard from Jess –

    – Shut up, Niko!

– She said Clair is –

Bald Bastard was on the case like a fly on shite.

– Jess – Clair – Clair Harkin? What's the matter?

– You know Clair?

Nikos was in Reuters mode.

– She has heatstroke. Jess is very upset, but –

– Right, you!

Bald Bastard, dropped a case and grabbed my shirt.

– You tell me where she is or so help me, I'll –

Nikos dragged him off.

– What is the problem?

Bald Bastard yelled, spraying Nikos with spit.

– I am Clair Harkin's partner!

Nikos wiped his face – then started laughing.

– No–o–o… you are Gluefeatures?

I love Nikos. I do.

Forty-five minutes later, Bald Bastard Bunce slammed the office door. Without so much as a baby fart of information. He turned down my half-hearted offer of help and lugged both suitcases, cabin bag bouncing off his flabby backside, to the hotel. Then we legged it up to Aphrodite One. Nikos gave me an update on Clair on the way. She had indeed got heatstroke and bad sunburn and all the unpleasant symptoms that went with it. Clair was sleeping when we got there and Jess was relieved to see us. I swung into paternal if somewhat duplicitous gear.

– Is there anyone you'd like me to contact? A partner or something?

Nikos narrowed his eyes at me. Why? I was right to ask. Disingenuous, but right. Jess was relatively cool.

– No thanks. There's something you could do, though. I'm out of booze.

The we'an had her priorities. Nikos gallantly undertook the mission on the grounds that he could probably get better prices.

Sitting there on her own, Jess looked very young and vulnerable. I had a sudden image of Clair cradling her, breast feeding… and felt instantly, infinitely ashamed of myself. To shock myself out of it I told her Bald Bastard was on the island. Jess was appalled.

– Oh shitting, shitting, shitting, shitting fuck.

– Fair comment.

– We came all this way to escape him!

She thumped the table making a glass bounce. I caught it.

– I mean, just who does he think he is? Mum's worth so much more than him.

– Based on the evidence, I'd have to agree.

– Is he coming up here?

I reassured her, somewhat smugly, that I hadn't told him their whereabouts.

– Aegis company policy. It's up to – your Mum, whether…

– Thank fuck for that! He's such a sack of shit.

Jess combined the looks of a fairy princess with the language of a trucker. She'd get on with Annie.

Across the harbour was Hotel Acropolis, where Bald Bastard Bunce sat – or slept – or, with a bit of luck, shoved his head up his own arse. I wondered about revealing the festivities planned for Saturday. Would it be altruism or transparently childish revenge on Bunce? I was suddenly shocked out of my musing.

– Mum only puts up with him 'cos she's nearly fifty and –

– She's what?

– Oh, for…! I don't believe myself! It's meant to be a secret. She's fifty on Saturday. We came here so she could leave the shit of the last fifty years behind. She doesn't want to celebrate, just forget. You won't tell anyone?

– Fifty? Clair, fifty?

Saturday. The white envelopes. Bald Bastard. It ricocheted round my head like the after effects of a heavy metal concert. Jess was still talking.

– I mean, you're really not so bad as – oh god! I'm trying to say something nice but it's coming out wrong.

– What?

– OK… well, I know that poncey stuff isn't you, like, it's work. I mean, you're really amazing on guitar. Really.

My mind was a meat pudding of tiredness – and loathing for Bunce. The shift of conversation was completely beyond me.

– How flattering. Look, I have to crash. My mobile number's in the information book if you need it. The welcome meeting's on The Giorgios tomorrow, as usual. Hope Clair – your Mum – is feeling better in the morning.

And I left.

The last few days' events featured: Mel's pyrotechnic display of disappointed hormones and subsequent departure from my life, a new and foxy woman who stirred my loins and made me laugh at the same time, Gamma male arriving to claim her and <u>then</u> the discovery that the object of my latest lust was fifty. Fifty! Like, half a century! My life clicked and swivelled like a transformer toy. Except it didn't end up as anything recognisable. I blocked a torrent of Annie. Getting horizontal and staying very still seemed a good idea. Hauling up to Chorio, I passed Nikos descending with several bottles.

– All yours, Niko, just go easy on Jess – she's very young.

– Fraser – what do you think of me?

A few macho exchanges and we continued in opposite directions.

HOWARD

You certainly get what you pay for. The flight to Rhodes was late, the seats packed obscenely tightly. I was wedged knee to coccyx for four hours next to an obese matron who sported a selection of badly executed tattoos and an alarming case of body odour. I didn't recall such inconvenience on my one other package foray. Norway with Saga. Different type of client.

At the airport, once we had passed the surly passport control employees and reclaimed our baggage in the foetid arrivals hall, we were greeted by the Aegis company rep waving a banner at us and led ignominiously to a coach. At the harbour, we hung about for a humid hour or two before setting off for the island. When I broached the travel rep regarding the cause of the delay he smirked and said 'Greece'. Decided to ignore the patronisation for the while and mentioned my need to contact Clair. He seemed startled by this, muttered something incomprehensible and slunk off. Then there was a disorganised sort of shamble aboard the ferry where I had to find my own seat. The sea journey took about forty minutes, during which I impressed on the rep my particular requirements regarding Clair, but he was dismissive to the point of being rude. Said he couldn't reveal the whereabouts of clients without their express permission. Wouldn't give anything away – typical Scot! I had no intention of letting some half-baked beach boy tell me what was data protection and what wasn't. Decided to front him on the island once the other travellers had departed for their accommodation.

We landed. Bloody hot. Odorous. (That could have been me.) I waited until the coast was clear and tackled the rep. Even my considerable ability to hector didn't move the irritating jobsworth. I felt like taking a swing at him. I kept my cool, though, and cited his responsibilities. Then one of his cohorts – a local by the look of him – butted in and let drop that Clair was ill. That was it. It was my right as her partner to know where she was and what was wrong with her. That was when my temper broke and I actually grabbed the yob. Then I heard it: 'Gluefeatures', the daughter's word for me – she thought I didn't know. Enough! Decided to go to the hotel and, ignoring his facetious offers of help, made off on my own. Had to ask a few people but found it after a while.

I had been awake for nineteen hours, eaten too much but too poorly, drunk not enough but too unwisely, felt hot, grubby, tired, frustrated and was, I have to admit, not at my most fragrant. By the time I reached the hotel, the last few conditions were exacerbated by a factor of at least two. Having checked in and discovered the room was a twin, not the double I had booked, I lost the will to fight any more and made for the shower. The water pressure was almost non-existent and I stood under a trickle of tepid water swigging a Gatwick Gin.

At least Pat's fax had arrived and Saturday was organised.

CHAPTER SEVEN

CLAIR

Second Thursday – Terrible minus two

— White rabbits, white rabbits, white rabbits!

— Mmmm?

— First of August, Mum! Say it.

— Wh – rabbs... wh–whi– rabbiss.

— Well done! I've brought you some tea.

Oh no.

— How are you feeling? You've got a lot of sleep in your eyes. Do you want some wet cotton wool? And your T-shirt's stuck to you – look, the bed's all wet.

The blisters on my back had burst and epoxy-ed the T-shirt to raw flesh. Jess was as gentle as she knew how, dampening the gummy cotton and peeling it away by the millimetre. Agonising for us both. I tried to lie on my front. Pain throbbed and receded. Wavering between wakefulness and dreaming, I heard voices from outside but had no recollection of where 'outside' was. A male figure appeared in the doorway and I said:

— Daddy?

A voice I recognised replied.

— Sorry, my friend, I'm not your Dad. I'm Richard. Remember? Of Mandy and Richard?

It was enough to wake me up. He sat for a while, talking gently, soothing. When he left, Jess appreciated my embarrassment. Up to a point.

— Mum, Richard didn't give a toss, so can we drop it, now?

— But you don't understand –

— What's not to understand? You made a tit of yourself. Get over it.

It could have been worse. I might have called him 'Darling'. Whichever way, the whole incident was ghastly. It was also illogical. I remembered my father from photographs as a young man with dark, wavy hair. Richard was about sixty with straight snowy hair – ah – OK, there is that aspect...

— Here's some more grape juice, Mum. Lots of liquid Doctor Makaraka said.

— I'm sure that's not her name.

— Whatever. Drink. How are you feeling? Apart from tit-like, I mean?

– Better. Less woozie. I think I'd like to have a wash.

– OK. But I'd better help you in case you keel over. You mustn't have any more shocks.

Jess was doing the full Nightingale.

Richard returned later with lunch – and Mandy. He was uncompromisingly firm over my embarrassment. No cause for it. And equally firm that they need not stay if I wasn't up to company. But there was humiliation anew in Mandy's flood of sympathy.

– No, you're not stupid. It's very easy to do. I've burnt the tops of me feet before now – like having balloons at the bottoms of me legs – and agony! D'you remember, Richard? That time in Albufeira?

While they demolished a superb combination of tuna (Jess demurred), eggs, feta and all sorts of greenery, I surprised myself by managing half a plate of salad washed down with mineral water. It was enough to flatten me, though. Richard told Jess they'd be happy to stay with me if she fancied getting out for a couple of hours. She frisked off like an unleashed terrier while I, at their insistence, retired indoors.

FRASER

Next morning, before the welcome meeting, Panos and I were drinking spine-straightening Greek coffee at his cousin's kafeneion. He shifted a black kitten from under the table with his foot and lit an Assos. Held the smoke in his lungs for a horrible time. Spoke through the outgoing tar cloud.

– You and Mel have a fight – why? Sexy blonde woman. You are lucky. I cannot have sexy blonde woman because my wife.

– That's very unsporting of Marina.

– Wives – tuh! Blonde womans make my balls ache!

He threw his head back and laughed himself into a coughing fit.

– Damn cat hair!

– Glad it's not the cigarettes, Panos.

– No, no – serious. Get you a woman. Last week, your people, young girl come with her mama – long black hair – beautiful little buds –

He winked, tweaking the front of his shirt in case I missed his meaning.

– You have her – I have the mama! Eh? Bravo!

– No, Panos. Not a good idea.

– OK – I have her – you have the mama! Yes? Yes?!

He punched me to seal the deal.

— Eh — you give all the letters in the white — eh — ?

— Envelopes.

— Yes, from Theo's hotel? Big secret, yes? What do they say?

As if his son, Theo, assistant manager at the Acropolis, would keep anything from him. The juxtaposition of topics, Clair and the envelopes, was hardly coincidental.

— You know exactly what they say, Panos, you devious old bugger.

Panos gave his pantomime hurt look and tapped his clenched teeth.

— Herkos odonton!

The Greek metaphor — no, cliché — for secrecy.

— Eh — Theo says you no want play guitar at the hotel, Saturday. You no want see Mama and Beautiful Buds?

Delivered with a painful elbow to my ribcage.

Bald Bastard stayed out of my way on The Giorgios morning trip until I finished the tour bookings. Feeling perverse, I extended the meeting twenty minutes beyond normal, even laughing and chatting with the globular PITAs from Wittering. But the moment arrived when I had to face him.

— I saw Jess last night, Mr Bunce, and I told her you would like to make contact. She has my number, but she hasn't called.

Bald Bastard's blood pressure rose perceptibly.

— In that case, I am not leaving your side until you get that call. Do you understand?

— Perfectly, Mr Bunce.

I hoped I sounded steely.

Back in Yialos he followed me to the office where I counted euros and travellers cheques and entered them on a spreadsheet, went to the bank and paid them in, engaging the teller in conversation, asking after the health of all her family members. Next, I climbed the Kali Strata up to the square and back for no reason except to make Bald Bastard follow me. I returned to the office and sat back at the computer. I'm a two-finger typist, so the essential communication took a considerable time. Then I printed it off and ran it round to Nobby who was deep in the sports section of last Monday's Daily Mail.

— 'Morning, Nobby. These are the preliminary dimensions for the Yialos/Panormitis by-pass and funicular railway that you wanted. Head Office is very keen that you should cast an eye over and give your assessment of the probable viability before going forward.

– I'll read it later.

– It is – urgent.

Nobby opened it slowly, giving me a bloodshot stare before looking down, skimming through it then peering over my shoulder and back to the sheet. It read:

'Nobby – behind me is the biggest PITA of them all. Please look as though you're thinking hard then ask me to recheck the figures. Do this for me and I promise to play the Country and Western song of your choice every night for a week.'

Whereupon Nobby, who is a Kenny Rogers fan, put on a painful performance. He scratched his chin, wrote down a few figures, looked at the ceiling, and shook his head – until I had to snarl at him.

– That's enough, Nobby!

He glared at me dangerously and a teeth-grinding while later, announced in mega decibels –

– Sorry, pal, going to have to ask you to check your figures again. And tell Mr Rogers I look forward to hearing from him.

I set off up the Kali Strata once more with Bunce behind me panting, sweating and at last, giving me the evil eye from the chair opposite when we arrived back at the office. I wrote a longish email to Annie bringing her up to speed with banalities like the weather and Nobby's new aftershave, asking after Jude's T'ai Chi progress and wishing them a happy day out in Largs next week. Come one o'clock, my strategy to push Bald Bastard to the limit had neared its zenith. I was nauseatingly polite.

– Mr Bunce, this is my lunch break. I'm going home to do my washing. You're welcome to give me a hand with my smalls –

It worked. He steamed off past the Customs House while I went back to Nobby's.

HOWARD

The Thursday morning, I suffered an excursion on a barely seaworthy old tub being patronised by the rep and bored stiff by my travelling companions who included a tedious couple from West Wittering. Passed on a sea dip and suffered a few draughts of appalling Greek liquor. Not having found my sea legs, I chose not to tackle our yob of a host in front of the assembled crew. Back on land, he was so offensive that I bearded him in the Aegis office. However, following two or more hours of being led round half the island not to mention up the garden path by the heathen Scot, I was no nearer contact with Clair than the night before. Rather than share in his domestic chores, I resolved to front him when the office reopened at four. I returned to Hotel Acropolis enraged, frustrated and not a little dyspeptic, picked up the Times Education Supplement and a packet of Rennies then went to the nearest taverna and ordered lunch. I was at a shaded table, but the brightness of the day made me squint through my reading glasses. Reaching for my clip-on shades I realised that I'd left them on the bedside table. I just had time before my 'musiroym omelet' arrived to acquire a peaked cap with a leaf design on the front from the shop next door. It made reading more comfortable. And it hid my receding hairline.

I was back at the Aegis office by four precisely. It was locked and with no sign of industry. I waited five minutes then recorded the time of the fellow's absence in my notebook. I also wrote a note pointing out his tardiness and put it in the letterbox. There being nothing better to do, I retraced my steps to the waterfront, where I sat at a bar with a glass of indifferent white wine. It felt odd not wearing socks, but I had dressed appropriately for meeting Clair who, for some reason, detested the wearing of socks with sandals. Back at the Aborigine Road Neighbourhood Watch barbecue I had overheard her express derision for men who did so and felt a barb of chagrin as I squinted at my feet. Now, just for an instant, sitting behind the TES in Symi, I experienced uncertainty. She'd told me that the holiday company had no more places – and yet Pat had been able to book. Yes, a week later but... was Clair, perhaps, trying to put space between us? No. Why would she jeopardise our companionship? After all, she was practically fifty. And she must realise that I could easily attract a younger woman. No. I was reading too much into everything. Self-esteem restored, I turned to the article on behaviour, knocked back my last drop of wine and ordered another. It was twenty to five. I decided to give the bloody Scot until five, and then – then...

As absorbed as I was I would not have noticed anything had not a woman with a purplish complexion at the next table remarked:

– Timothy! There's that awkward young madam who swore and held the boat up that day at Sesklia. You know! And her mother had to be nursed all the way back from Nanou yesterday? Drunk! Well, the daughter's drunk today by the looks of her. Disgusting. Makes you ashamed to be British.

I looked up and spotted a female figure very much like Jess weaving its way out of town. "Her mother had to be nursed yesterday..."? Instantly, I made the connection. Slapping a few euros on the table I made off at a trot until the distance between us had lessened enough to be certain. It was Jess all right and she looked as though she'd had a skinful. I called. She looked back and quickened her pace. Obviously hadn't recognised me. Suddenly, she turned off into an alley.

Reaching it, I discovered there to be another damned flight of steps and that she'd vanished round a corner. I made my way up. To the right, another alley sloped downhill; to the left were the two other sets of steps. I was confounded by her disappearance and called again, but to no avail. Calves, knee joints and hamstrings screaming, I peered up the first flight. Other than a stray cat, there was no sign of life. At the second flight I encountered an elderly couple descending. I asked them if they'd seen a young girl in jeans running that way. They smiled and shook their heads then replied in what sounded like German. I strained to dredge up some of my schoolboy vocabulary.

– Ah. Danke schoen.

Obviously, my accent had convinced them I was a fellow countryman because they beamed at me and rattled off a barrage of the Deutsch. I panicked.

– Ja. Au revoir.

Felt a total idiot but escaped upwards, leaving them looking disappointed. At the top, blood pounding in my temples, I had to concede that Jess was gone – and I needed to get back to the hotel and have a shower.

FRASER

No one was interested in the hell I'd been through. Nikos was riding a bar stool while Nobby rested his gut on the bar, both glued to the Sports Channel. Nobby passed me a slip of paper.

– 'Ere's yer playlist.

Seven Kenny Rogers classics. My mood sank even lower. But I was no match for the beautiful game. It wasn't until my third beer and another victory for Aris Thessaloniki that I caught their interest.

– Yer mean the fooker followed yer all morning?

By my fifth beer, both Nobby and Nikos were loyally outraged by my tale of affliction.

– He's one ugly mother. How a beautiful lady like Clair can –

I gave my erstwhile friend my best-honed ugly look. Nikos blinked. Obviously, it wasn't just the bald guy upsetting me, he said, I must be missing Mel.

– Mel's got nothing to do with this!

He just hadn't got the point.

– You jealous of me and Jess?

– Christ on a bike!

– You don't mind? Good. Because I think she loves me.

– Yeah, well, congratulations. Here's to your modesty.

I grabbed his beer, downed the remainder and left. He never had time to unhook his feet from the barstool.

Three days' worth of washing-up leered at me from the sink and the breath of Hades wafted out from the bin underneath. The folks next door were out so I dumped our black bag in their wheelie bin. Then I actually washed up – that's how demoralised I was. Fridge-wise, there was an empty vodka bottle, an antique pot of yoghourt and something greenish. Went to the nearest mini market and argued down half a dozen bottles of Amstel. I'd just settled with a beer and lifted the guitar when my mobile rang. It was Jess, calling on Nikos's mobile from Nobby's bar. Richard and wife were up at Aphrodite One. Clair a lot better, but she hadn't been able to tell her about –

– Look sweetheart, stop waiting for the right moment and just tell your mother the bald bastard's here – 'cos I'm about to commit murder.

Gave her the number of Hotel Acropolis. Out of my hands. If Bald Bastard turned up at the office later I could tell him to…

I strummed a few bars of 'Bye Bye Love' before realising the subconscious input.

– Get tae –!

Downed more beer while trying to remember the lyrics of 'Ruby don't take your love to town', then another bottle while struggling with my complex emotional situation. Fell asleep. Next thing, Doc Ali's shaking me awake. Time to get back to work. Like it's any of her business where I should be. And walking into the apartment like that – I could have been doing anything. Still, don't suppose much can shock her, given her job. She'd be an attractive bird but for that. You couldn't get it on with anyone who was checking you for signs of constipation or erectile dysfunction. Plus, she knew better than God about everything and she was pointing it out at that moment. I was irresponsible, should be looking after my guests not ruining their holidays and, most importantly, I had to put Bald Bastard in touch with Clair. I'd rather have snogged Nobby, but she didn't give me that option. I was back in the office in fifteen minutes. Nikos wheedled.

– Sorry, Fraser – I know what Ali's like.

She'd delivered at least three members of his family into the world and certified another couple out of it. I wondered occasionally if he'd taken a crack at her himself. Never asked, though. She'd called in earlier to drop off Clair's bill and given him a tongue lashing for smelling of alcohol in the office. So, he'd told her the story of Gluefeatures to throw her off the scent?

I mean, like Bald Bastard was an excuse for <u>him</u> to get wasted? Anyhow, that's how come Doc Ali dropped by mine. Just as well, I suppose. I could have slept for Scotland. I rang Hotel Acropolis with no result, so took off, searching all the bars and tavernas between Aris's leather shop and Nos Beach. Crossed back over the bridge and toured the lanes of shops and boutiques with no luck. Rang the hotel again. This time, my mood bottomed out. Bald Bastard was sitting down for dinner. I went over, caught him mid-beef stifado and imparted the terrible truth. Then it was a race between Bald Bastard and me for Aphrodite One.

I don't know how we made it at the same time. God's truth, I can't imagine. Jess wasn't that pleased to see either of us. A great amount of unpleasantness took place involving free use of Anglo Saxon followed by Bald Bastard storming into the apartment and flinging open a door. What we saw plus several more strong words from Jess convinced both of us to leave Clair in peace. Vowed to get even with Bunce.

CLAIR

Company in recuperation

I rejoined Richard and Mandy on the terrace about an hour after Jess had gone. They were both reading. Mandy greeted me.

– It's great up here, lovely view and you get the shade of the tree. It's good to take a break from all them beaches.

It was a kind thing to say and I felt the more grateful for their company. But she went one better.

– Go on – you must be dying for a fag. We won't tell!

Richard winked agreement. I lit a Marlboro. It did not taste good – I stubbed it out and tossed it over the wall.

By four o'clock, Mandy was glancing surreptitiously at her watch. Jess wasn't back, but I felt well enough to be left and persuaded them I would be all right. Padded by pillows, I lay on my tummy and tried to read. But it made me feel rough again and I sat up, fighting down the nausea. I remained upright for what seemed like hours, not sure which way the latest wave of illness would go. A huge cramp hit my stomach as Jess appeared at the gate.

– Mum! You're really going to hate this but guess who was following – hey you look awful!

– Think I've got to go and sit in the loo for a while.

– Can you just – just – I'm bursting!

Jess fled into the apartment while I levered myself up, clinging onto the table as another spasm crippled me.

– I can't hold on long, Jess!

I'd been sitting on the ill-fitting plastic loo seat for some time, hours perhaps, exhausted by the expulsion of my lunch at both ends. My back felt tight and itchy, despite frequent applications of lotion, and my wretchedness was compounded by guilt for being so stupid and ruining the holiday, for being a rotten mother, a rotten daughter, for exploiting Maggie and… Connie's voice sliced through my injured brain.

– You made your own bed!

I could always rely on my mother to make a bad situation worse. Snapshots of the holiday so far clicked rapidly through my consciousness – it had been a pretty intense trip up to this point. No wonder my life was flashing past my eyes. Crush on a married man, rapture of the deep, disporting myself in bars, a titanic dose of the squits and the landscape of a toilet door impressed forever on my memory. What next?

The answer came quickly. Voices outside – Jess and a man – two men? Footsteps – Jess shrieking 'No!' – then the door flew open… Just as well I was sitting down already. The sight of Howard framed in the doorway would have made me keel over. And close behind the nightmare of Howard came – excruciating super-humiliation – Fraser. Then a blur of movement involving Howard, Fraser, Jess and a lot of shouting – a slam and muffled argument. I focused on the toilet door again, clutching my skull, trying to hold my head together. *I'm hallucinating. This isn't happening. It's my head, it's my gut, it's my back. It isn't real. Yes it is. Howard's really here. He's outside on the terrace, arguing with Jess. This is not an hallucination.*

All the relaxation, the freedom, was gone. Howard was on Symi.

FRASER

After the incident at Aphrodite One, I returned to the apartment and finished the beer, a shaken man. Sometime after eight I clumped down the steps to my virtual snoggee's bar cursing Nikos for being naturally amoral, Doc Ali for being my conscience, Jess for being seventeen and mouthy, and Bald Bastard for being alive at all. As for Clair – now why would I resent Clair? Annie's take on it rang round my head.

– 'Cos you fancy her and she's old – not a dolly you can just hang off your arm. I can see your problem; how can you cope with anything less than perfection in a woman – what with you being the perfect man?

I was vulnerable to her psycho-barbs even in my imagination. I pitied her tutors trying to find anything she hadn't worked out for herself already. Despite which, I missed her a lot. It would be after six at home; she'd be giving Jude his bath.

Nikos was in deep discussion with a few compatriots, the passion of their argument meant the topic was either politics or football. Didn't notice me, despite my entering with all the tragic drama of a vanquished Viking. Nobby did, though. Put down his 'I love the Baggies' mug and leaned across the bar, pumping Paco Rabanne and BO in equal amounts.

– Yer must've found the bastard – yer've gorra a face like a scrotum.

Life owes any enchantment to such characters as Nobby.

– Nobby – d'you feel like helping me get disgustingly drunk?

Nobby pulled my head towards him and for one horrible moment I thought the snogging gag was about to come true. But he just gave me a wet smacker on the forehead, then slapped a beer on the bar.

– Gerrit downyer, babe!

Some hours later, I had a fleeting sensation of climbing steps, lovingly supported on either side.

MAGGIE

Thursday 2nd August

It was eleven. I sat up in bed surrounded by distractions to induce sleep: a book, remote control for the TV, crochet, my diary; but I was still wide-awake. Jack and Tatty curled together, flaunting their easy slumber, one or other of them snoring gently. Although the curtains were drawn, just knowing there was light outside, childlike, I could not surrender. When we lived in the old house, on midsummer nights James and I would crawl through the attic skylight in the early hours, giggling with the fear of being caught and of the lethal drop awaiting should a foot falter on the slate tiles. We would crouch like baboons on the glimmering slope, concentrating on catching a sliver of brightness at the horizon. Then shivering with relief and arguing in whispers over who saw it first, we would drop quietly back into the attic and tiptoe back to our rooms. Astonishingly, we were never caught. Years later, when I brought Julia on her first trip north of the border; I envied her the novelty and wonder of her first night of near daylight. Now, propped against pillows and desperately wakeful, I felt remote, distanced from life by miles and time. About two thousand miles from Clair and Jess and nearly twenty-eight years from Julia.

At least turning fifty will not be for Clair what it was for me. For her, it will be a beginning, not an end. The dogs dreamed on.

I must have slept for I woke at daybreak as usual. Half five, now. I'd been dreaming of Julia – or was it Clair? They fused strangely in my mind, one with dark hair, glossy as molasses, eyes of velvet brown and cream freckled skin, the other a tousled head of light brown curls, pale blue eyes and china doll complexion. Beloved both, they entered my life on the same day, fifty years ago. Fifty years ago, today. Except, I didn't know about Clair's arrival until James' telegram, the following morning. I knew about Julia's within minutes.

<O>

It was the beginning of the long summer break. The party was an au revoir from The Right Honourable Major Hugo and Mrs Felicity Benfleet to those acquaintances who had not already departed for the French Riviera, Tuscany or the family pile. They, themselves, were off to Cap Ferrat on Tuesday when I would take the train to Oban. But tonight, loyal secretary that I was – PA's had yet to be invented – I was on duty. Staff at the Sussex house were down with a virus and the agency staff, bussed in from Brighton for the evening, needed supervision. I cut in as Hugo turned his charm on an impossibly young waitress who giggled and rattled her tray of sherry nervously.

– Excuse me, Major Benfleet. Mrs Benfleet thought you'd like to know that Nanny is putting Adrian to bed.

– Oh God. Isn't Nanny capable of putting him to bed on her own? Pay her enough!

– No bloodshed please, Major. I'm only the messenger.

My employer tilted his head and narrowed those remarkable blue-green eyes at me.

– Oh, you're so much more than that, Maggie. Or you could be…

Sexual harassment hadn't been given a name, then, or even identified.

– Bedtime story, Major.

– My, my, Maggie. How very – forward of you.

– A bedtime story for Adrian, I mean.

– Ah. Adrian. Of course. Thank you for reminding me.

– You're welcome.

– If only.

– Major – go and see to your son.

It sounds worse than it was. It was a sort of game, for him, anyway. He wasn't used to rejection and that made me desirable. But even he would have recognised that it might make life a little awkward to take matters further. Having an affair with one's secretary was so unoriginal. Also, I was a very good – and discreet – secretary and, if matters went awry, I would be difficult to replace. For myself, I recognised that he was a very attractive man but didn't feel the attraction myself. I assumed it was a combination of my Scots Presbyterian morality and witnessing his succession of women.

That night, as he smoothed his already immaculate black hair and made for the oak carved staircase, I was aware of a young woman, highly amused. I dealt with the slopped Tio Pepe and pointed the waitress towards a gaggle of deserted wives then looked back, but the shimmer of merriment had dissolved into the air. Feeling oddly disappointed, I escaped to the kitchen for a cigarette and a strong black coffee. There was a copy of the Daily Sketch, I remember, lying open on the kitchen table; I was looking at the crossword. The door opened. I turned. I turned and there was Julia. There was Julia. It was as simple as that.

When I say it was simple, for me, in that moment, it was.

<O>

CLAIR

Second Friday – Terrible minus one

Following a ghoulish night, I was up and washed by seven – the horror movie effect on my back ruled out showering. I managed dry bread and coffee at the table outside, facing the Hotel Acropolis almost directly opposite. Where Howard was staying. Howard. Something I had to deal with. I reviewed the scrawled note that had appeared under the toilet door the night before. 'Clair – The surprise has been turned into a fiasco. Hope you're better by the morning. Jess has my number at the hotel. H.' Not 'love' or a row of x's. Just 'H'. I'd come all this way to leave the crap behind and what happened? The pile I left in England got on a plane and followed me. *Am I being ungrateful? Or should I be angry with him for stalking me and invading my time away with Jess?* Resentment rippled through me alternating with the image of a paunchy, red-faced man in shorts and a baseball cap. *Is there a side of him I'm overlooking? No, he's an arrogant pillock.*

All the holiday, apart from the Saturday night, I hadn't bothered with make-up. But the face needed some help today. *I do not have to go to all this trouble for Howard. On the other hand, never know whom else I might meet.* The big question hanging over me was: could I expunge from Fraser's mind the vision of me sitting on the loo looking like death? I fluffed my hair and approximated some make-up, put on loose linen pants and the new Greek cotton tunic. A coolie hat would have finished off the Vietnamese look, but I had only the faithful old sombrero. It could stay off until absolutely necessary. The Marlboro Lights and one remaining Silk Cut nestled in the ancient straw bag. I woke Jess who pulled the pillow over her face and agreed, in grunts, to meet me at the taverna with the green awning at one. I departed to face my nemesis – or Howard's.

How could a place change so much? Symi's whitewashed walls looked grubbier, stray cats mangier, shops tackier, boats shabbier. I could smell the drains and stale, cooked food, see the oil slick on the harbour water. It felt as though the holiday was over. The urge to ring Maggie for her lateral view of the situation was very strong. But Maggie would then know that the marvellous gift of a holiday had gone awry. And using her for emotional support was selfish. *Who supports Maggie all on her own up in Kilachlan? Who was there for her when she lost the person she loved? I wasn't, not really. I didn't understand.*

It was just nine as I crossed the bridge and turned down past Giannis's Fish Restaurant. Standing by the water's edge, inhaling the last Silk Cut, I looked up to Aphrodite One but it was indistinguishable amongst the other houses. Higher up, the windmills topping the ridge were a straggle of squat guardian angels looking over Jess. *Something to get used to, Jess alone, lost to sight and contact.*

The cigarette made me want a coffee, so I stopped at Catherinettes where the coffee made me want another cigarette. It was near ten when I arrived at the hotel. Howard was sitting at an outside table, engrossed in a book resting at the crook between stomach and crossed legs. In dark cotton trousers, short sleeved shirt and deck shoes – surprisingly without socks – he looked better today. *Is it wrong of me to be so critical of him? His behaviour's only a symptom of his condition. Heterosexual men of his era usually need a woman around to act as a conduit to their emotions. And who in his anally retentive Hitchin clique would tell him when he's behaving like a berk?*

– Howard…

He stood, forgetting the umbrella over the table, had to duck out. We kissed chastely, stood awkwardly. He ordered more coffee. I wondered if, following such a bizarre jolt, our relationship might achieve a natural balance. But after a few sips he lapsed into old ways and spent two hours moaning about the previous thirty-six. Then he announced that he'd booked a double room at the hotel and that Jess could have Aphrodite apartment to herself for the rest of the holiday. Yes. He did. I could liken my reaction to a significant force of nature but it's simpler to say I put him straight. Suitably stunned, he retracted meekly. I was astonished. *If only I'd done it before, been this terrible. Where would I be now? Where would he be now? Not on Symi.*

We were early to meet Jess at the taverna but she was there already, drinking beer.

– How're you feeling, Mum?

Said with quizzically raised eyebrow.

– Fine, darling.

Howard shooed a few cats away, oblivious to the exchange.

– I'll leave you two together, then, I'm meeting Mandy.

She pushed the key across and left. I made do with bread and olives. By this time, Howard had recovered sufficiently to order a substantial lunch accompanied by a run-down of last week's activities at the Local Education Authority. He slowed in the middle of a disciplinary hearing, still chewing moussaka.

– I'm sorry, Clair, this isn't the moment. Let's get into a holiday mood. It'll keep.

I'll look forward to that. We sat in self-conscious silence while around us happy, suntanned people ate, drank and laughed. As my desperation peaked, Howard dabbed his mouth, set down his napkin and looked at me intently.

– Why don't we stroll back to your place? Spend some quiet time together?

Because my flesh crawls when you touch me.

– Howard, I don't really feel well enough to –

– Dear girl, I'm not intending to ravage you. But you would feel more comfortable at your apartment, wouldn't you? I'm not trying to worm my way in – I've got the message about separate establishments.

I was flagging, so agreed to a brief supermarket raid before making a slow climb, Howard gallantly carrying all the shopping. I quite enjoyed the cosseting that incapacity attracted, now I was well enough to appreciate it. To anyone passing we looked like a long-established couple. We spent the afternoon on the terrace, Howard reading the biography of Len Hutton and sipping wine while I dozed, fully clothed, face down on the lounger.

<O>

My mother was waiting at the school gates as usual, but carrying the little suitcase that meant I'd be staying with Maggie tonight. I ran the last few yards, excited at the thought of travelling up to London. She gave me a brief peck on the cheek and said:

– Better hurry, honey, or we'll miss the train.

I skipped along beside her to the bus stop, enjoying the springiness of my new red sandals. It was two months before my seventh birthday and the weather was warm, the days getting longer. I hoped there would be time after tea to go to the park or watch the guards at Buckingham Palace. On the bus, my mother tried to catch my mass of curls back into the bunches tied so firmly with ribbon that morning. It wasn't until we were on the train from Guildford that the first tears of impatience pricked my eyes and she gave up on my defiant Harkin hair. We changed at Clapham Junction for Victoria. I jumped down from the wooden step between carriage and platform and my mother swung the heavy green door shut. I loved the smell of trains, even if they were dirty and smoky. They meant going somewhere else, somewhere that wasn't the big old house where we lived. I adored staying with Maggie, especially when Julia was there. It felt more like home should feel. Maggie was waiting at Victoria Station, arms held out for me to jump up and be swung round. My mother waited until she put me down.

– Maggie, hi. I wasn't expecting you to meet us.

Maggie smoothed a tendril of hair behind my ear.

– I'm off work early so I thought I'd enjoy the walk. You'll come back for a cup of tea?

My mother refused and there was an awkward pause while she looked uncertainly at the departures board. There was a train due out in five minutes. She passed over the little suitcase and cupped my face in her hands.

– 'Bye honey. Be a good girl for Aunt Maggie, now.

– Yes, Mummy. Can we come and wave 'bye 'bye?

– No – no – you go now. I'll come by first thing, Maggie.

She hurried off into the rush hour crowds, towards the Guildford train. Maggie squeezed my hand and watched her for a moment before saying –

– Well, Muddle Top, shall we go to the park? I've brought some bread for the ducks. Then what about sausage and mash for our tea?

And off we went, stopping at the humpty man's kiosk for a forbidden pre-dinner ice cream cone, then up Buckingham Palace Road, chattering away, to feed the ducks. The pelicans sailed sombrely down the opposite side of the pond in St James' Park, ignoring the bread, while the ducks squabbled up to the small railing.

– Will Julia be there when we get back?

– Only if we don't walk on the cracks in the pavement. Careful, now!

Sufficient logic for a six-year-old. Woman and child, we hopped and sidestepped home, ignoring the odd looks and occasional smiles of passers-by. Up in the tiny lift to the third floor where I reached for the porcelain bell push. *Is she there, is she there, is she there?* A long wait, then whoosh! The door swept open and there was Julia, still in her airhostess uniform.

— Miss Clair Harkin! Welcome onboard Harkin and Blumenberg Airways flight one hundred to New York and San Francisco! Please make your way to the sitting room where a package awaits!

I pelted in, past Julia, and swung round the doorframe. There it was on the sofa — I couldn't believe it! Peeking through the cellophane of a brightly coloured box was a Barbie Doll! I'd be the first of all my friends to have one!

— Happy birthday, dear Muddle Top —

Maggie and Julia from the door.

— But it's not my birthday yet!

— Good heavens! Isn't it?

Julia was too innocent to sound truthful, even to me. Maggie laughed.

— Ach well, we'll just have to do something a wee bit special on the day.

<O>

I woke in a panic.

— Howard! You haven't arranged anything special for my — for tomorrow, have you?

— No. I took the hint. But I'm allowed to say 'Happy Birthday' at least?

— Only if you say it very quietly.

— That's a deal.

— I'm glad you came.

Why did I say that? Not as pissed off as I thought, perhaps... ? Maybe a couple of hours of relaxation in the shade of the mulberry tree had mellowed me. He smiled back.

— So am I — despite... 'you know'.

Jess was equally mellow when she returned after an afternoon of sun, sea and larcenous goats. She and Mandy had escaped mugging by livestock, but the couple next to them had lost half a beach shoe and a cheese roll. Richard's afternoon of literary solitude at the villa meant he'd missed the fun. Jess was seeing Nikos that evening but agreed, unenthusiastically, to joining Howard and me for supper first. My special holiday had fled her mind, it seemed.

I felt groggy from snoozing. Getting ready for an evening out wasn't high on my want-to list. But my slept-in tunic and trousers were significantly beyond holiday tousled. While Jess showered away the salt and sun lotion, I put on a dowdy Indian skirt — *Why did I bring it?* — a white T-shirt and swathed my sarong over my shoulders. It was far too warm for a wrap, but my frazzled skin couldn't cope with bra straps and Howard might be susceptible

99

to my breasts jiggling about like two boiled eggs in a pillowcase. I apologised to him for the shabby chic.

— You look fine to me.

Coming from Howard, the remark was more deflating than reassuring.

I led my dining companions to the taverna where Fraser and I had shared a beer, only now, live piano music drifted from the interior. It was already filling with customers, drenched with sun and dressed for pleasure. Howard salivated over the notion of a seafood salad for two but opted graciously for the Sea Bass while I leant apologetically towards the blander scallops in white wine sauce on a bed of rice. Jess decided grumpily on a selection of vegetables. When, after half an hour of artificial bonhomie, the food came, it was abundant and delicious, bearing out Fraser's claims for the place. However, the preparation time had tried my daughter's patience; Nikos was waiting. She picked disdainfully at her food, downed two glasses of wine then sat back, arms folded, responding only cursorily to conversation. I tiptoed through the minefield instead of blitzing the enemy.

— Don't let us keep you, Jess.

— Are you telling me to piss off?

Jess had inherited her father's imperious inclination. She had romped through adolescence without significant physical blemish but the hormonal roller coaster had intensified the character flaw. I hoped that independence would be a good teacher, that the disapproval of others might lead her to use diplomacy, as it had her father, instead of sarcasm and contempt. At the moment, however, she was behaving brattishly and I wasn't up to confrontation. She remained slouched in her chair fiddling with her fingernails. Howard continued stolidly with the Sea Bass, finishing before me. Unable to bear the scrutiny of being a lone diner, I downed tools. Jess muttered from the farthest rim of civility.

— If you've both finished, perhaps I can be excused?

And then, mercifully, left. Howard smiled at me over a malt whisky,

— Now, old thing, before you say anything, I'm not going to refer to —

He whistled four notes of 'Happy Birthday to you' then mimed zipping his mouth.

— I only ask how you would best like to be diverted.

— I don't mind.

I didn't. He walked me home and plonked a brief wet kiss on my mouth before setting off rakishly back into town in search of, he said, 'inspiration for the morrow'. I watched him dip below the bank of geraniums, feeling as though 'the morrow' was my first day back at work.

Fifty. Although I'm not that yet, not for another – um – it's ten fifteen now, born at three forty-five a.m. – five and a half hours – or seven and a half really because we're two hours ahead. At least when I wake up it will all be over.

I furtled down the lining of my bag. There they were – my little sticks of sin. *Odd – I don't remember leaving the cellophane on the packet.* I pulled it out. Silk Cut – and round it, secured with a hair scrunchy, was a note in Jess's writing. 'If you're going to cheat – you may as well smoke something you like.' *Sod it – I don't care – I'm going to have one.* Tearing at the packaging, craving that exciting whiff of fresh tobacco, I lit my first and sank to a chair, holding the smoke in my lungs briefly before letting out a long plume. I'd survived a day of Jess at her worst and Howard being himself. That deserved at least three.

Jess arrived back in the early hours and spent a while in the living room before coming to bed. Writing my card for the morning? Nearer sleep than waking, I settled further under the sheet, facing the wall waiting for another harrowing night to usher in my sixth decade.

FRASER

Friday was walking day. Woke up with a mouth like a welder's crotch and a head to match. Nikos nursed me in the agreed routine: black coffee, aspirin and water appearing simultaneously, nil food, zero dialogue. Despite being late, I didn't hurry – on account of the Sumo wrestler stamping round my skull. The walking party, mostly this week's intake, was waiting outside the Leftéris café at the top of the Kali Strata, beaming faces turned expectantly for my cheery 'Kalimera!'. Richard from the previous week was there too, without his foxy wife. I swung into some kind of manic Baden Powell routine to overcome the pain, and had everyone checking their water bottles and snacks like a bunch of nine-year-olds on a picnic. Then I lurched off trying to remember where the fuck the Mihail Perivliótis monastery was with the mature crocodile trudging behind me. To make life just that bit sweeter, the two Witterings who'd been to Symi before were conducting some kind of tour guide booby trap, picking me up on everything. They had matching sunhats, baggy singlets and shorts and lobster pink sunburn. They also had Virgin Atlantic plastic rucksacks – to show they knew everything about the bloody USA as well, no doubt. I tried to remember a convenient ravine to kick them in, but my poisoned brain was in sleep mode. What had gone on at Nobby's last night? Then the word 'cocktail' floated past at the very periphery of consciousness – and I felt my coffee pitch inside. Nobby's Blaster. A seismic beverage combining triple sec, metaxa and absinthe that had been known to topple the most hardened of Symi's waterfront lowlife. That would be it, then.

Richard, the beardy guy with the totty wife, appeared from Heaven and annexed the gobby blobbies. Walked along beside me.

– You feeling all right, my friend?

– If you ever come across a place called Nobby's Bar – let it remain a Greek myth.

– Wrath of the gods? I'll try to keep them off you.

A guide shouldn't moan to the clients, and especially not <u>about</u> the clients, but it was a relief to have a rational, objective person to unburden to. I threw caution into the incinerator. Richard laughed about PITA's and listened sympathetically to the history of Bald Bastard. Even in my weakened state, though, I was careful to edit out my personal stance re. Clair. Whatever my stance was. The conversation turned to the clandestine nature of the white envelopes. Richard frowned.

– So, this Bunce chap is the anonymous host and Clair is the unwitting subject of the celebration?

– She's going to hate it. Jess says she's paranoid about being fifty.

– Poor Clair. We sat with her yesterday, just to give Jess a little break. She's a very nice woman. I'm sorry her holiday's been spoiled by this heatstroke business. It's a great shame if this chap of hers forces an unwanted festivity on her, too.

It made me flinch, 'this chap of hers'. At least he'd said it in a fairly negative way.

Richard's wee wife was waiting at the Leftéris Cafe when we got back.

– There she is.

He said it like he'd been holding his breath all morning and could suddenly breathe again. She looked really young, in a pink kind of top and a baseball cap. I had a sudden image of another pink top – and jeans with that bag hiding half her arse… How sad was I? Lusting after a middle-aged single mother with a dorky boyfriend? Richard nudged me and I remembered the little gang of hikers, loitering expectantly around me.

– OK, everyone. We'll meet back here at three, those of us who want to, for a gentle stroll down to Pedi Beach. Hope you've enjoyed your morning.

There was a general murmur of thanks and a smatter of applause – god knows what for, I'd been talking shite all morning and taken two wrong turns. The Witterings stood apart from the crowd having got on everyone's nerves with their constant corrections and unsolicited explanations. They could find their own bloody way to Pedi Beach.

– Hello, Fraser – you look a bit rough, love.

– That's my wife for you, Fraser, nothing if not direct.

Richard put an arm round her.

– However, correctly deduced, my lovely. Due to that bar called Nobby's we've passed.

– I said it should have a health warning by the look of it. Do you need an Alka Seltzer? We've got some at the villa. Come on back and I'll sort you out.

– Thanks, but I –

Suddenly she flailed her arms and shot a sonic bolt through my head.

– Jess! Over here!

Jess and Richard started lunch together while wee wifey took me back to their villa a few minutes away and sat me on the sofa. The room smelt of woman-y things – shampoo and perfume. And everything was tidy. It was a fair while since I'd been in such civilised, such – feminine surroundings? The brief intrusion on Aphrodite One hardly counted. What with seeing Clair on the throne and all the rest of it I hadn't noticed much else. Felt myself being pulled back and a cool, damp cloth laid on my forehead. Heard her chatting away but surrendered to stillness, comfort and relief. The seat cushion sank slightly as she sat next to me, offering incredibly loud fizzy medicine.

– Och, dinnae make me drink it, Mammy.

– Daft bugger. Sit up, shut up and sup up.

A couple of little raps on my bare knee, then her hand stayed there. Nerve endings tingled up and down my thigh, the fizz kept fizzing, and her hand was still there. It was all too much. I sat up, drank up, then stood up – rather too quickly, as it happened.

The afternoon passed in a heat haze. Back at Nobby's that night, I sat weighing up the situation with Clair. Was it a dilemma? A dilemma was a choice between two things. So, in one way it was a dilemma. To do or not to do? But that wasn't the only question. Do what? There again, if I had many more nights like last night I wouldn't have a brain left, so questions would be irrelevant.

CLAIR

Not so Terrible as Dorothy's

I dreamt I was on a sailing ship. My body was the sail and I gasped for breath in the wind as my flesh billowed out propelling the ship. A sailor with white hair was at the wheel, but the ship zigzagged crazily while my bulging white torso flapped and cracked. Then I broke loose, flying up and away from the ship until my feet touched firm ground in a landscape the colour of a bruise with a jaundice yellow sky. From a kiosk, Howard demanded my passport. I held up the queue, trying to explain why I didn't have one. I wondered why I was going to all this trouble when I didn't want to be there. At the same time, I knew that there wasn't anywhere else. Then I was at a café on the waterfront waiting for Jess to arrive. Maggie, much younger, stood alone on the far side of the harbour, hands deep in her coat pockets. We looked at one another for a long time and I felt sure she knew about Jess.

Rising guilt broke through the membrane of sleep and I sat up, reaching for my watch. Greyish light filtered into the room but it was still too dim to see the time – or was it my eyes? Optician's when I get back. Back. My chaotic lodger Case was still resident at Aborigine Road, assisting on the drama school's summer programme. What state would the house be in? Then I noticed Jess's sleeping form. Why did I never hate her for taking my freedom away? For being difficult when she needn't be? For making my life so complicated? Why don't I resent her for being seventeen when I'm fifty? It was the first recognition. *I am fifty years old.*

I got up, pulled on the crumpled tunic and went outside to watch the Terrible Day take shape. Already the sky was light blue. A sliver of orange sun blistered the claw of Turkey that clutched at Symi. The crest at the top end of the harbour ignited then, swiftly, the collage of cliff, brick and foliage caught light and came to life. With life came warmth, a new day… and the inescapable fiftieth anniversary of my birth.

CHAPTER EIGHT

MAGGIE

3rd August

Fifty years on, I stood at the top end of the garden in my nightdress and toasted Clair's half century with a mug of Fairtrade tea laced with Jura malt, my feet bare in the dewy morning grass.

The phone rang at about ten. I knew who it was. So did the dogs, who yapped their own chorus of greeting. Clair, of course. It didn't sound like her. Too modulated, controlled. She denied any problem – but there was one. I know Clair. Had Connie upset her? Or someone – some*thing* else – other than it being her fiftieth birthday? After she rang off, I went and poured myself another nip of Jura, toasted the birthday girl again and gave the dogs a chew each in recognition of the event. Julia! Our wee lass is fifty!

<O>

I didn't go to Kilachlan that Tuesday after the Benfleets' party fifty summers ago. The telegram arrived at eight in the morning, before I left. I rushed to the nursing home in Clapham to welcome my new niece to the world. I didn't travel to Kilachlan the next day, either. Instead, I cooked dinner in my small flat off Baker Street. In two years, Julia was my first guest there. She brought a bottle of wine, very extravagant for those days, and we sat drinking and smoking after dessert, watching the light fade over the rooftops towards Hyde Park. Frank Sinatra sang 'Three Coins in the Fountain' on the Dansette and we talked until the sky turned from cobalt to jet and the last train to Sussex had long departed. Julia refused to deprive me of my bed. So she slept on the sofa.

Shuffling into the kitchenette in my dressing gown next morning, I was embarrassed to see that Julia had done the washing up. She scolded me for objecting.

– Don't be such a prune! Last night was fun. Next time, you must come to me.

We stood awkwardly at the front door for a moment then Julia pecked me on the cheek.

– Have a lovely time in Scotland. I'll send you a postcard from Sennen Cove.

I felt a vacuum forming in my chest as I watched her glossy dark hair bob down the stairs and out of sight. I wondered how far Sennen Cove was from Kilachlan and whether I would ever see Julia again.

<O>

Listening to shore sounds on a summer evening so many years distant, I recalled the first time I cradled a tiny, scowling, mop-haired Clair. And I felt contented knowing that I had, on numberless occasions, seen Julia again. And though I knew a permanent hollowness now, I had learned to live with it.

CLAIR

Terrible with raisins in it... ain't it the truth?

Being away from home on a birthday involves initiating contact with nearest and/or dearest to enable offers of good wishes. I wanted to ring Maggie, to hear her voice. The other duty call was less compelling. It was five days since I'd rung Mum and Joe; I anticipated a critical reception. The thought occupied me until Jess enfolded me from behind, kissing my ear.

– Happy Saturday, Mum.

I reached up and held my lovely girl's arms.

– Terrible Saturday. Thank you, JJ.

Jess moved round and we sat together.

– Did you have a good time with Nikos last night?

– Yeah. Met quite a few of his mates, and two of his cousins.

– Sounds like things are getting serious.

Jess assessed my back as rare steak coloured, but definitely on the mend, so I braved a careful shower. Later, clearing away the breakfast plates, I wondered if she really was going to ignore my birthday. *Hypocrite. You were the one who didn't want a fuss.* Jess, of course, would do what she wanted when it came to cards and presents. At that moment, she emerged from the bedroom carrying a large, flat package and emitting decibels worthy of Ethel Merman.

– Happy Ordinary Day to you, Happy Ordinary Day to you, Happy Ordinary Day dear – Clair-Constance-Harkin-who-isn't-any-particular-age-today, Happy Ordinary Day to you!

– Too – hoo yooooooooou – uh!

An unsteady and deeply unwelcome baritone echoed from outside followed by the appearance of a profusion of lilies wired into a formal arrangement that climbed the steps towards us on solid white legs. As it reached the terrace, Howard's head popped up from behind, beaming. Simultaneously, his free hand swung out bearing a bottle of Perrier Jouët champagne. He set them both on the table, then lifted my hand, kissed it and whispered.

– Happy Birthday. See? I promised I'd say it very quietly.

Nearly an hour later, down by the harbour, I listened to a ringing tone. *She mustn't be out, not on my birthday.* The phone was caught up and dropped, barked at hysterically and knocked against several hard surfaces before I heard Maggie's voice.

– Clair! Happy Birthday, darling –

Maggie and I were telepathic.

   – Are you having a marvellous time? Tatty – wheesht!

– Just perfect! At the harbour and just about to take a boat to a beach.

– Something's wrong. Has Connie upset you?

– No. Nothing's the matter.

Bugger! How does she know? How does she always know?

   – There's something. Promise you'll tell me when you get home?

   – Maggie, there really –

   – Promise!

   – I promise.

   – I knew it.

As I left the booth, I had a feeling of being outmanoeuvred. There was something wrong in Kilachlan, I just knew it, and my wily Maggie had diverted conversation away from her. Although she'd sounded bright as ever.

Howard suggested taking a boat trip. It sounded gentle, so Jess and I had put a few things together and traipsed off with him. Now, I saw the boat for Aghios Nikolaos was boarding and hurried towards it. Howard and Jess stood a couple of yards apart, her attitude contradicting her promise to be pleasant. Howard pointed to a smallish boat, brightly painted but not, apparently, touting for business.

   – I prefer that one.

He headed towards it, Jess and I followed at a distance, exchanging wordless communication. Howard balanced on the stern, holding out his hand.

   – Step aboard, ma'am. Your birthday. My treat!

   – No – you can't pay for Jess and me, it's –

I heard Jess clearing her throat. *Yup, that's me, turning down someone else's generosity.* I took his hand. Jess followed, stepping heavily onto the deck and demanding ungraciously –

   – Where's the crew? You're not driving it, are you?

Howard reassured her and led us to the prow. Laid out on the low roof of the cabin was a patterned rug and a large cool box containing a selection of drinks. Mindful of the earlier champagne intake, I opted for fruit juice. But Jess dived happily into a rum and coke while Howard opened a bottle of Amstel. We were just clinking glasses as our captain peered out from the 'bridge' making Jess slop her drink down her new camisole. *Oh shit.* It was the octopus basher from Sesklia. Seeing Jess, he made a jokey gesture of terror and ducked back in. With supreme self-restraint, she brushed the drops from her front and refilled her beaker with almost neat rum. Captain Octopus Basher (alias Phanes, nephew of Captain Panos of the Giorgios) came with an assistant distinguished by tattoos and mouse brown dreadlocks. Howard surveyed her with distaste while she returned his scrutiny coolly. Meanwhile, Phanes started the engine and headed for open sea.

Howard had come equipped with a walker's map of Symi from which he attempted to identify our navigation. Jess's expression spoke volumes but she stayed politely silent.

– Ah, he's following the hydrofoil route towards Tilos and Kos.

And shortly later –

– Yes, you see, now we're cutting through the Diapori Straits, that's Nimos Island to our right. We'll round the headland and head southwest, down the far side of the island.

As we turned into the wind, the sea was suddenly choppy and the little boat bucked. We clung to the rails, clutching cups and hooking our bags with our feet while Phanes and Mousey Dreadlocks casually entwined limbs in the cockpit. *It could be worse; the sky could open and spit Connie down on us – Connie! I didn't ring!* The wind dropped from terrifying to invigorating. After about forty minutes we passed between two small outcrops – Pidima and Yi Piros – intoned Howard, and headed towards Vasiliou Bay, anchoring there in a couple of feet of water. The men helped the unbirthday girl ashore by bandy chair. Phanes uncovered a gas-fired grill hidden under a tarpaulin amongst the rocks. The girls transported beach umbrellas and the box of booze then went off for a swim, Mousey Dreadlocks au naturel and Jess in her marginally more modest scraps of swimwear. Howard's eyes swivelled round and back guiltily as he helped Phanes with barbecue duties.

I took out Jess's birthday present: a watercolour sketch block, some soft pencils and putty eraser, a set of chalk pastels, a small box of watercolours and several sable brushes in their own little parcel. 'Show us what you can do' said the gift tag. In the scant shade of the umbrellas I started sketching, trying to catch the colours of sea, sky and rock. Frustratingly, line and tone didn't obey my intentions. It had been some years since I'd committed to anything more than a doodle. Even so, as my fingers reacquainted with the rough texture of the paper, the chalky smudging of pastels, Burnt Siena, Titanium White, Cobalt, Cerulean Blue, I became absorbed. Vasiliou Beach and the first positive action of my fifty-first year. Not a bad start.

There was a deep cleft in the cliff face backing the beach into which, early on, the two men excused themselves in turn. By the time the girls emerged from the sea, I knew I had to utilise that facility.

– JJ – I need a pee – can you sort of distract everyone while I –

– How? Point at the sea and say 'Over there!' like sixty million times?

– It's my fiftieth birthday. I'm having a trauma. Indulge me.

– Cool. Go and have a slash.

A treacherous slope compounded the incompatibility of female anatomy with alfresco peeing. As I returned, dignity asunder, my four companions on the beach cheered and let off party poppers. Howard produced another bottle of champagne and we drank from plastic cups amidst laughter and toasting – in honour of my birthday I hoped and not my recent toilet antics. Phanes gave a gracious and completely incomprehensible little speech. He may have said: "We all saw you peeing and you have the arse of a rhino". But the food was ready and I was past caring. Being young, veggie and a waterbaby, Mousey Dreadlocks appeared to have a lot in common with Jess – apart, of course, from her attitude towards Phanes. In her near transparent sarong, she relished the barbie, quaffed the amber nectar and contributed only her nasal upward inflections to the lunch. Howard directed a look of concern at beer levels.

After eating, with the sun high, everyone lolled under umbrellas. Jess chatted with Mousey, studying her tattoos with interest. Fiddling with my pad and pastels I failed to notice them strolling off until Howard remarked that they had been gone quite a while.

– P'raps they've gone for a long walk.

– Jess? Exercise?

He laughed, peering over his clip-on sunglasses. He had a point. When they did return, arms linked and giggling, they walked without breaking stride straight into the sea, sat down and laid back, thrashing and whooping. Howard was riveted by the exhibition.

– What's going on?

– They're young, they're on holiday and I suspect they're a bit pissed.

– Not surprised – Dame Edna put away enough Amstel.

The girls staggered from the water and polished off what was left of lunch. *The munchies! Are they stoned?* If they were, Mousey Dreadlocks had to be the supplier and if she was, I decided she could make me a small gift in return for gate-crashing my birthday.

Jess and Mousey snuggled under an umbrella while Howard snored gently over his book. Around three, Phanes started clearing away the barbecue. *Nice bum. Perhaps I'll give him a hand.*

– No – is OK.

– Yes – is OK.

Don't be a spoilsport. Between us we had everything sorted by the time the others roused.

Next, the little boat headed out of the bay, southeast. To our left, Howard informed, was the monastery at Panormitis.

– Taxiarchis Mihail Panormitis – it means –

– I know, Howard – some friends of ours visited. We should go – Monday, perhaps.

I'll put a prayer in a bottle and ask for Richard on a plate. Wonder if he liked the market at Datça today? And Mandy – hope she's… enjoying the shopping.

Howard resumed his amateur navigation. The sea was calm and, before four, we approached Nanou Bay. I took control. It was my birthday, after all.

– We'll stop here.

I cornered the girls in the loo at the taverna.

– OK. I know. What was it you two had back at the beach? Skunk? Lebanese Black?

Their eyes went Betty Boop, but that could have been the dope. Jess knew that voice. Feigning innocence was pointless. Mousey, real name Yolanda – Yo for short – sensing trouble, started –

– Hey, cool it, me and Phanes –

– I'm very cool. Tell me. And have you got any left or can you score back in Yialos?

Sharp as a commodities trader, Yolanda swung into business mode and the deal was struck. Mutual satisfaction. *Have I risen or sunk in Jess's estimation? Do I care at the moment?* I joined Howard at a table.

– Sod it – I'm going to have a beer.

– Do you think? – I mean –

But he, too, knew that voice.

Howard walked with Jess and me along Yialos harbour, invited us to meet him at the hotel at seven forty-five. I was about to argue, then thought better of it. It had been an easy day and dinner at the hotel would be a pleasant way to round it off. *Plenty of time for Yolanda's treat after – or before, even, if she's successful.* Jess was still in a state of either shock or stunned admiration following the interlude in the ladies' at Nanou. I took care to emphasise that this was a holiday aberration and not for repetition at Aborigine Road.

MAGGIE

4th August

What to do on Clair's birthday? After we'd spoken and I'd teased out of her that things were less than perfect on Symi, I had a struggle settling so, when Wally Scrymgeour wanted to meet his granddaughter off the Kerrera ferry at Gallanach, I offered him the use of the car in return for a ride down to Oban myself. I had a few bits and pieces to pick up, not least of which was a fresh supply of Jura malt.

I'm a reluctant driver. Landing my father's Austin Healey in a ditch on my first attempt (aged ten) coloured my dealings with the combustion engine ever after. Father deemed the egg-sized lump on my forehead retribution enough for his tomboy daughter. But James got a tanning for daring me. We were confined to our rooms for the rest of the day and our housekeeper, Mrs Fynnie, had to bring us our meals on trays.

Messages done, I popped into a café on George Street before meeting Wally. Usually there was a grand view of Kerrera and on to the horizon, but today the har, the sea mist, rolled a damp blanket across the island and into the town. I would have preferred to nurse a malt over a pub lunch, but the idea of entering a pub alone still sat awkwardly. Back in the late seventies Clair, on a jaunt up here, walked into a pub alone and was asked to sit behind a screen because, the barman explained, they had no ladies' toilets. "So, the screen is to hide me peeing on the floor, is it?" demanded my egalitarian niece – as a consequence of which she ended up outside in the snow. Things are surprisingly different now. Every corner in Glasgow, for instance, has some kind of bar or bistro with a neon sign outside and crowds of young women inside and out, drinking and enjoying themselves. Male company seems to be incidental. As it should be. And there have been other changes. Nowadays bottles of malt vinegar sit unashamedly on café tables. It wasn't so long since abstemious Scottish diners sprinkled 'undistilled condiment' on their battered haddock. On our first meal in a Glasgow restaurant, Julia piped up in her very clear voice.

– Undistilled condiment? What on earth's that?

I whispered to keep her voice down.

– Spirit of John Knox, I'll explain later.

I wasn't sure if I was annoyed with her for not knowing or with myself for being so conditioned to the narrow-mindedness of it all.

As I waited for the bill, I took the Celtic silver earrings from their little box and imagined Clair's face at Christmas. Then, somehow, the har rolled from the sea into the café… or was I looking through tears? Or the wrong side of a magnifying glass? Voices were distant – from a radio in another room? I felt separate from my body, as though it were all happening to someone else. As reality crept back, I found myself lying on the floor, my head resting against the hard bosom of a waitress. There was a deal of fuss and someone was holding my wrist then feeling a vein in my neck. And someone said: "She's the spit o' thon actress fra' 'Brief Encounter'.

Nessie Scrymgeour was waiting at the front door when we pulled into the drive. Wally ushered me into the house. Jack and Tatty, out at the back, barked frantically at the sound of my voice. I appreciated Wally and Nessie's kindness and allowed their attentions, but stopped short of being put to bed. I would have tea in the parlour where I could look out into the front garden. Agnes clucked, but Wally chivvied her into the kitchen to brew up while he let in the terriers. The dogs raced round the room with joy, flinging themselves at me with little yelps. Nessie came in with a tray of tea and homemade scones, trying to mask her disapproval of dogs on the furniture.

– Oh, by the by, Mrs Mudie rang the now, said she'd be by later.

– Thank you, Nessie. Were there any other messages?

– Not that I know. Were you expecting anyone?

Nessie paused, weighing up discretion against common sense.

– Miss Harkin – I really think we should get in touch with your niece.

– I know you do, Nessie. Thank you for your concern, but I definitely don't want that to happen.

– As you wish, Miss Harkin.

After making sure that I had everything I needed, The Scrymgeours left, promising to call in later that evening. I was content with Jack and Tatty's little white bodies snuggled either side of me. I flipped on the television to some afternoon film and drifted into a light doze.

Dr Sharma came the next morning, recommended bed rest for a few days and arranged for a scan at Lorn and Islands Hospital. The numbness in my right arm, the headache, the blurred vision indicated a mini stroke. Recovery could be good, he said. However, there was no guarantee that it wouldn't happen again and I was to take things gently for a while, at least. Gently? If

I took things any more gently I'd turn into rice pudd'n. As Dr Sharma drove off, Nessie moved in with her stovies, her broth and her shortbread. After a few days of Nessie's feeding, I'd look like a pudd'n anyway. But I could resist her nagging to contact Clair and Jess. Dragging them back from Greece was absolutely unnecessary. When would they get another holiday like that? I tucked my Tobermory shawl tighter. Look at me, Julia, I'm an old woman. What would you tell me to do? I wondered about asking Nessie to fetch the blue shoebox but was distracted from the notion when she next appeared with a large bouquet from Interflora.

– Beautiful! Just beautiful. You've some admirer, Miss Harkin.

She waited expectantly. I opened the card; it read 'A'. Let Nessie try to work that one out.

CLAIR

Highly Terrible

What follows is part memory, part forensic reconstruction… We were already changed for dinner when Yo arrived with the goods and some streetwise advice.

– You need to be uber cool – they're well heavy on dope in Greece.

She'd made up a spliff as a birthday present. The three of us sat around the living area, door closed, and shared it. Aware that Jess had already reached the heights today, I rationed her to a few pulls.

– And before you say anything about smoking – this doesn't count.

– No, Mum. Actually, this is really funny – 'cos when I said you weren't looking forward to your birthday – and what would he do on a really awful birthday – Raz said 'get stoned' and I said…

She trailed off, realising that she might have let a large feral cat out of the bag.

Playtime over, we wrapped the evidence in a panty liner, sealed that in a plastic bag, poured the last of the milk into a glass and stuffed the bag into the empty carton, squashed it flat and tied into another plastic bag. The precision of these manoeuvres prompted a look of recognition between Jess and me. It all seemed very funny. Yo thought so too, but she managed to say –

– Well smart. You get life for dealing here.

Somehow, that struck us as even more hilarious.

After that I remember, vaguely, an interesting debate on the blancmange-nish of marble floors. As we lit a second or third spliff, we switched to the absence of a 'use by' date on the little plastic bag the dope came in, deciding to assess it by seeing who could whistle the loudest. Strangely, none of us could whistle at all. We were experimenting with substitute bodily noises when there was a loud rap at the door. Silence descended on the den. We tried to focus on one another through dilated pupils and decided it must be… someone. Pffffbb!

The next bit's wholly reconstruction. The person at the door was Nikos who started switching on fans and making black coffee while he shouted at us a lot. He was taking us out, he said, but not until we were feeling more sensible. He rang Phanes to come and help him and, somehow, the two guys managed to herd we three dope fiends down to the harbour, into a taxi and up to Howard's hotel. Jess and I hung on to Nikos as he walked into the courtyard. The shame I inflicted on all concerned I wrested from another – other – parties. It goes thus:

Howard came straight up to me, barging through a troupe of Greek dancers, in a fit of concern and annoyance. I was very affectionate by return but instantly distracted by the dancers and insisted on demonstrating my own expertise. It was, I can now reveal, based largely on a sketchy memory of Anthony Quinn's performance in Zorba the Greek fused with Morris dancing. Oblivious of my nihilistic impact on the dance display, I tried to engage Nikos in a quasi-eurhythmic version of line dancing. Arsey Purple, an accidental guest along with the Witterings, was vocal in her outrage and insisted that I should be ejected for ruining someone else's party. Ho ho.

Fraser arrived at this point and came to Nikos' rescue, relieving him of me, while Richard and Mandy helped Dr Mavrakakou with Jess and Yo. However, I was too slippery for Fraser, sprinted across the courtyard and disappeared into the hotel. Pursued by Fraser, Nikos and Howard.

Then the hotel manager decided to wheel in the birthday cake, decked with fifty blazing bloody candles. It was Mandy's presence of mind that saved the show. She pushed Richard to the centre of the courtyard and led everyone in Happy Birthday. When the chorus reached 'Happy Birthday dear…' there was a bit of fudging, especially since a banner with the Greek lettering 'ΚΛΕΡ' festooned the trolley. However, Mandy managed to swipe it away before any enlightened holidaymaker realised that it approximated 'Clair'. Amidst cheers and the odd private comment regarding the unkind toll of years, Richard accepted congratulations on his half-century. Mandy, the gracious hostess, urged everyone to eat and drink, mollified the dancers with food, wine and euros and persuaded them to continue. By the time Fraser returned the party had started for real.

The event was, of course, my big surprise birthday bash, courtesy of Howard. Before my overdue arrival he had already insulted some and threatened physical violence to others of his guests. When I did appear, in what was becoming a habit, I made a tit of myself. Apparently. And was put to bed in a hotel bedroom. How long it had taken Howard – or his secretary – to organise a birthday party I didn't want is a matter for her and Dame Fiona.

CHAPTER NINE

FRASER

By Saturday, the incoming Wednesday group had usually settled into sedate hedonism and rarely bothered me. But this Saturday I'd had to exterminate an invasion of ants, call Ali Mavrakakou to deal with a bout of Symi squits and advise on a discreet source of condoms. What makes tourists leave their grey matter in the departure lounge? Half the fun of bumming around the world is finding out things for yourself. Annie has a take on the male chronic inability to ask for help, illustrated by a family outing to the Highlands when Dad's refusal to stop and ask for directions, despite having passed the same ruined bothy three times, had reduced us all to the brink of distraction. Annie's conclusion was typically lateral.

– It's a well-known male anxiety that the genitals contract every time their owner asks the road. Navigation's a sexist issue. Know how you tell a really good navigator? Vagina!

My thought train was interrupted by Doc Ali who plonked down on the opposite seat in the afternoon fug of the bar.

– You look happy, Fraser.

– It's the weekend, I'm allowed.

– I was making a joke.

– Ha ha. So, Doc, patient cured?

– Of course.

– Drink?

It was the least I could do.

– Of course.

There were a few regulars – a couple of old fishermen, landed years ago, several lads involved in grey commerce around the port area and an English ex-pat whose wife ran their gift shop while he boozed away the slender profits. Nobby was on the Datça run today, which meant an honesty box for regulars and random service for the few tourists who stumbled in. One of them, a short bird with pale brown dreadlocks, tooled in just then and headed for the younger guys. Dicey though it was, people still tried to score dope around the harbour. There was no regular place. Nobby would be furious. Made a mental note of the guys, one or two I hadn't seen before. Paid for a Campari and soda for Ali and another beer for myself. We toasted.

– Yamass!

– So, you are playing here tonight? Not at the hotel?

– It's not exactly the best idea – me playing at Bald Bastard's party for his…

I didn't know how to finish the sentence so I just took another drink.

– You should go to the party. I am unexpectedly free tonight. I'll come with you.

I was about to say 'That's kind, but I don't need… etcetera' when something about the way she'd said it persuaded me not to. Doc Ali? It wasn't that I didn't like her. I hoped I'd misread the situation. Couldn't embarrass her, though. Even if it meant getting into another awkward situation. Another dilemma. We arranged to meet. What else could I do?

Couldn't tap into the Annie in my head. Actually swallowed my pride and rang her. She'd just put Jude to bed and was having a glass of wine with a student friend. Told me I'd have to go to the party anyway for the sake of being professional, with or without the doctor. And since the doctor had invited herself along, I'd have to make sure she knew it was just friends. Except my big wee sister didn't give me a bloody clue how to put that one across, just put the phone down and went back to her friend.

The accompaniment to all this, of course, was 'Clair's fifty today'. Round and round, like a chorus to everything I thought or said or heard. All day long. 'Clair's fifty'. Wondered how she was feeling.

Met Doc Ali back at Nobby's. She'd washed her hair or something and put on a long dress. We walked round the harbour catching up on island gossip. Didn't know whether to string out the time with Doc Ali or get to the party. Wanted to see Clair but not her douche bag of a boyfriend and delaying it meant tiptoeing through minefields with the Symi physician. I mean how much fun can a Saturday night get? Had my guitar with me to look more business-like. With a bit of luck, Bunce would sling me out, anyway. Or would Clair let him?

As we walked into the Acropolis courtyard, the party wasn't so much building as unravelling. Clair was there and Nikos was hanging onto her like she was a kangaroo on a lead. She broke loose as I got there and sort of leap-frogged through the guests and into the back door of the hotel. Nikos and I legged it after her. Bald Bastard tagged along, the original haemorrhoid at a curry-fest. After tanking round the corridors forever, Nikos found the birthday girl in the beauty salon where she seemed to be praying to a hair dryer. We got her across the corridor to the health spa and into a shower cubicle before Bald Bastard caught up and blundered past. I never had any kind of aspiration to be a comedy actor and now I was in the middle of a farce my opinion hadn't changed, but I enjoyed the buzz of getting one over on Bunce. It got better, though. Ms Harkin had lapsed into a conveniently foetal state. There was an old dumb waiter in the bowels of the hotel into which we managed to deposit and transport her to upper regions. While Nikos negotiated a room at the desk, I stood on guard ready to unload the cargo. The signal came and I hauled her out of the void. I could hear Nikos instructing Jess and the Oz backpacker. Perhaps I had a future with MI6, evacuating matrons from Greek holiday islands? Rejected the notion. This was not just a middle-aged punter, but Clair – someone I… what?

Back in the courtyard of fun Theo, for some reason deep within the Greek psyche, had chosen the moment Clair lolloped off to halt the dance tape, lower the lights, truck in the flaming birthday cake and lead everyone in 'Happy Birthday to you'. We could hear all this wafting down. Turned out later that Richard's foxy little wife pushed him forward to accept congratulations on his half-century. By the time I returned, alone, it was a typical Greek dance evening. My guitar stayed in its case and, hallelujah, Bunce stayed away. Unfortunately, so did Clair, but Nikos assured me that Bald Bastard couldn't get at her. Had a few drinks, danced with Ali a bit but didn't stay too late because it was the Aegis picnic the next morning.

CLAIR

Strangely Terrible (plus one)

I woke on the second day of my fifty-first year remembering, glumly, that I hadn't rung Connie yesterday and consequently, didn't notice straightaway that I was in a strange room. Not only that, but alone in a strange room. The moment I did, I sat up, apprehension welling. It was a hotel, that much was obvious from the furnishings. And no Jess. *Am I hungover?* I tried getting out of bed. Head fuggy but no whirlies, so that was a good start. And still in top and knickers, so nobody got lucky. Peering round the blind I saw a white courtyard where a waiter was clearing tables. But from breakfast or lunch? A leatherette folder on the dressing table contained the greeting 'Welcome to Hotel Acropolis. Some informations for your benefits'.

Hotel Acropolis – where Howard was staying. That was bad. I lifted the bedside phone and asked to be put through to Mr Bunce's room, hoping they wouldn't tell me I was ringing from it.

– Certainly, Mrs Harkin.

Not his room. But they knew me. *Hmmm.* Ringing. Receiver scraped from cradle. A female voice.

– Yeah? Who's – ?

Suddenly the receiver slammed down. I rang reception again, told them I'd been put through to the wrong room. The voice at the other end was impassive.

– My apologies, Mrs Harkin. Let me try again for you.

After a pause, the receptionist came back.

– There is no reply. I will keep trying for you and call you back.

I was in the bathroom when Howard rang, his voice thick and gruff.

– Clair. How are you?

Better than him by the sound of things.

– Fine, thanks.

– Can you – remember anything about last night?

He sounded wary.

– Not really. Not at all, actually. Why? Did I – ?

– I assume you know that Greek chap – friend of the travel rep – took Jess back to your apartment last night?

– Nikos?

The worst. *Cunning bastard…*

<O>

At teacher's training college, while everyone else was revelling in sexual freedom, I lagged behind, a victim of my mother's double standards. Somehow, Connie had managed to convince me that her own oddly conducted relationship was above reproach. Sonya's libidinous anarchy did something to erode my primness, but it wasn't until the second term of my second year that I relinquished virginity.

Lloyd Barnard was a young lecturer in Fine Art at the university and gave a couple of lectures a term at the teacher training college. He was dark-haired, habitually unshaven, wore gold-rimmed glasses and a full-length military coat. A number of my contemporaries lusted after him and the front rows of his lectures were usually full well before the start. Sonya, specialising in English and Drama and therefore uninvolved, was dismissive.

– He's such a poser. I mean, he looks like a throwback to Sgt Pepper. You don't fancy him?

– I never said I did. I said everyone else does.

– And Arctic Harkin doesn't?

Disastrously, I missed the bus and was late for his next lecture. My attempt at sneaking in unnoticed was abysmally ill timed, casting a flood of winter sunshine into the darkened lecture theatre where he had just commenced a slide show. He looked up with irritation.

— Whoever that philistine is, I hope the night of grubby fumbling was worth it.

I sunk into the darkness, surrounded by snorts of laughter. When the lights came up I kept my head down, scribbling, for fear of catching his eye and at the end of the lecture, filed out with my head down. But as I queued at the coffee machine in the corridor, a hand fell on my shoulder.

— Well, was it?

It was Lloyd Barnard. I mumbled, feeling the heat in my cheeks again.

— Sorry? What?

— Was interrupting my lecture worth your night of sexual excess?

I muttered something about sharing a bathroom and bus timetables. He leaned forward and whispered.

— It's OK. I don't bite unless I'm invited.

His face was very close and I saw something besides sternness in it. Excitement wriggled though me.

— Perhaps you'd care to discuss your punctuality problem? I'll be at — (he mentioned a pub the other side of the station, not a favourite with students) — eight-ish.

Pushing his spectacles up, he paced away, black coat flapping around his ankles.

Slightly shocked, mainly excited, I related the encounter as coolly as possible to Sonya.

— Dirty old git. Shags a different student every week. Probably the single most effective cause of rising syphilis in the Students Union — be careful, Clack.

These were pre-AIDS days. Sonya could have been telling the truth or, more likely, felt upstaged. Sexual profligacy was her territory.

— You gotta lose it, Clack, but he's not the best one to lose it to.

Suspended between two viewpoints, Sonya's that virginity was a burden and my mother's that it was a valuable commodity, I simply let go and floated off into a void of chance. This involved lengthy and painstaking preparation and many changes of clothes to achieve the ubiquitous unstructured look.

I arrived at the pub seven minutes past eight so as not to look too keen. It was a stockyard of noise, foetid with smoke and grimy as the railway arch opposite. He wasn't there of course so I squirmed through the assault course of pint glasses and elbows to order a drink. This was the seventies and gender rendered me invisible to the bar staff for a considerable time even though, it has to be said, I was fairly peachy. Eventually, I slopped a half of lager and lime back the hazardous route to a barely upholstered stool and sat for a gut churning half hour, wondering if I'd got the right place or whether he was punishing me for being late to his lecture. Then I saw him push through the doors on the far side. He was deep in conversation with a tall, thin guy with very long hair and a knitted hat whom I recognised vaguely. I ducked behind Private Eye, bought to serve both as an intellectual accessory for his benefit and a reasonably absorbing camouflage should he not turn up.

– Looking for me in Pseuds Corner?

He was standing right next to me.

– We're at the bar when you're ready.

He flicked the paper and headed away. I rolled Eye into my bum length felt shoulder bag and followed, taking advantage of the swathe he cut through the competing testosterone.

Lloyd Barnard lifted a waiting pint and introduced his longhaired companion, Harry, a Fine Art PhD student, then turned to me, quizzically. He didn't know my name. Not a hopeful beginning. I spoke straight to Harry. Introductions completed, Barnard and Harry talked departmental politics to one another while I stood outside their conversation, trying to look interested. By quarter past nine I had eked out my lager and lime to the last drop and spoken no other word. It was time to go, and I interrupted apologetically to say so. Barnard seemed put out.

– Really? Are you sure?

I wittered about a teaching dissertation and left, weighed low with humiliation. But as I waited to cross the road, he caught up with me.

– I neglected you. Sorry. Harry's got – a few hang-ups. Needed company tonight. Let me apologise?

He took me to another pub, sat me in a booth with a whisky and coke and questioned me assiduously about my life and aspirations. The evening looked up and, as he brought back more whiskies and cokes, I told him anything he wanted to know, grateful to be found interesting, to have his undivided attention. Then we were laughing – he uproariously at anything I said, I was so astonishingly, profoundly witty. I showed him my trick with beer mats and he was delighted, flipped several inexpertly and conceded my genius, then, as I careened off a couple of tables on my way back from the ladies whispered –

– Tell you what, Beauty – let's get you a coffee.

Leaving a half empty glass, I let him lead me by the hand into the night drizzle. Frazzled sodium suns hovered unsteadily in an oily sky as I lurched, giggling, against him until we reached a flight of steps that reared from the slick pavement. I took up his challenge and mounted them yelling 'Onward and upward!' while he caught me, pushed me then finally pulled me through the front door at the top. I leaned against a wall in the dry whiteness of the entrance hall improvising, unaccountably, on the Andy Williams song 'We're Almost There'. Then the light and space changed and I was in a darkish, untidy room, sitting on a lumpy seat and he was unbuttoning my coat. I was lying back and he was kneeling on the floor, leaning over me. The stubble on his face was very black, and I noticed that his teeth were rather horsey and stained. His tongue was in my mouth. Beer and tobacco. His hand was on my breast. My bare breast. How did that happen? He squeezed my nipple, making me gasp. But I didn't mind, it felt quite nice. And he said –

– Are you sure, Clair? Are you sure this is what you want?

– Yes.

I wasn't sure what he meant by 'Are you sure this is what you want?'. It didn't matter. It was quite a surprise, though, to feel his hand between my legs and – no – no – I don't want that – I wriggled a little, but didn't like to tell him to stop. Then I felt his fingers inside me, could even feel his fingernails and wondered, with some imbalance of priorities, whether he'd washed his hands. He was quite rough and I heard little noises coming from my own throat.

– You like that, don't you?

No – I don't like it. He stopped. Was it over? Was that it? What was he doing? He'd taken his coat off – he was standing with his back to me. His trousers were round his ankles – I could see his white buttocks, there were a few black hairs on them, then he turned round.

I had seen an erect penis once before during a petting session in my first year. It had looked so clumsy and pink and, well, so silly with that little dribble of white that I'd laughed. The boy, a third year, was understandably affronted although game to resume the session. But I found it impossible to continue. His revenge was to dub me 'Arctic Harkin', a nickname that lingered around the college long after he'd departed to teach at a primary school in Theydon Bois.

This time, though, it was different. The penis was thick and slightly curved, rearing above a surprisingly long, dark scrotum – then I couldn't see any more because he was lying on top of me, bending my legs up either side of him. I felt him, hard and warm pushing, pushing at my vagina. He couldn't find the way into me at first – so he kept pushing, pushing, pushing –

– Come on, Beauty, help me – uhhh!

And he was in me. It was so uncomfortable I thought he'd caught on my labia and pushed them inside, too. So, this is it? I am – full – and – uncomfortable and – A spring dug into my back as he moved harder and faster. My insides were sore. This wasn't what Sonya had described. His breath came and went as his head bobbed up and down in my vision. His hair needed washing – it smelt musty and slightly rank – and he had a thin patch on top. If only it would be over – because I was feeling slightly sick. He gave a great groan and stopped, slumping forward onto me, his unshaven chin scratchy on my shoulder. After a few moments he said –

– Did you come?

I didn't know whether I had or not, so told him 'yes'. He seemed quite pleased and slapped my thigh a couple of times. But I was feeling less and less well and had to say –

– Excuse me, but where's the loo?

He shifted off me and mumbled directions. Eventually I found the right room by the light from a street lamp filtering through the ribbed glass. The toilet seat was up and there were black hairs on the rim of the bowl. I was feeling too ill to care and leaned on it, my hair brushing the porcelain. I wonder how many people associate Twyford with losing their virginity? I don't know how long I stayed there, waves of nausea pulsing slowly. But I couldn't be sick. Gradually, as the feeling faded, I realised how cold I was and how sore between my legs. I helped myself up by the wall and blotted the sticky liquid that dribbled down my thighs, then felt my way unsteadily to the bathroom and found the light switch. Only the cold tap worked and, in the spotted mirror, I saw that my mascara had run across my temples. I must have cried as I lay beneath him. After sluicing in cold water and drying on a hard, damp towel I went back to the bedroom where he was snoring, lying face down on the bed. I found my clothes and dressed quickly, quietly, then let myself out of the flat, running all the way home through the wet Midland streets. I felt stupid, more than anything.

Sonya was angry on my behalf.

– But Clack – that's virtually rape!

– I don't know. I mean, I did go back with him. He must have thought –

– You were pissed. He shouldn't have taken advantage.

But again, it was the seventies. We all thought rape only happened with a stranger. If it was someone you knew, it was probably your own fault. Next time I saw him, he winked as he passed.

– All right, Beauty?

By then I'd found out he called them – us – all, 'Beauty'.

<O>

STILL CLAIR

Anticipating the worst

On the way round the harbour I had a nagging feeling that I should call Maggie. In my haste to get back to Aphrodite One, I dismissed it as confused guilt over ringing Connie.

Jess was sunbathing. There was no sign of Nikos or his having been at Aphrodite One.

– Hi, Mum! Enjoy your night of luxury?

– Fine, thanks. Were you all right... on your own?

– Fine. I've put your pills out on the coffee table.

Checkmate. A quick summary of the facts: I didn't know if Nikos had stayed the night and I had no idea what had happened at the hotel before I ended up in the room. Had I disgraced myself? If I had, who had witnessed it? I swallowed the pills and went to change, realising dismally that there was nothing clean left. It might be Sunday, it might be the second day of official middle age, but it was washing day. No washing machine but there was half a packet of detergent left by the previous guests. Ten minutes later in the shower room, I groped desperately for scenes from the night before as I trod a greyish bowlful of clothes. Laundering by foot was useless as an aide memoire, though, as I scoured my stubborn memory for clues. Jess was fascinated by the washing process.

– Can I have a go?

– What state are your feet in?

– It's OK. Stamping on the clothes will clean them.

By lunchtime the mulberry tree blossomed with dripping holiday gear and the washerwomen sat at the table beside it, me with a towel draped over my shoulders.

– I think I'm well enough for alcohol, now.

– You didn't have a huge a problem with it yesterday.

– It was my birthday.

— You remember that much?

I hoped my look implied total recall of everything I'd done — and everything I suspected she had. In the fridge were two unfamiliar bottles of white wine. Asking how they got there risked recriminations. So I just poured. We clinked and made small talk like slight acquaintances. There were some deductions to be made from this:

If I'd done something gross she'd be crowing about it.

If Howard had, she'd be even more triumphant.

Therefore, whatever she was skirting around had to be about her.

There was little doubt that whatever it was involved Nikos.

If she'd had a night of innocent fun last night, she'd be prattling on about it.

Jess was avoiding something.

— Nikos stayed here last night, didn't he?

It was out and I couldn't snatch it back. Jess's smile froze and she had the grace to turn a little pink.

— Jess, did you sleep with him?

Jess averted her eyes. Her reply was barely audible.

— That's none of your business.

— What?!

What had started as concern over a first sexual experience degenerated to a clash of temperament. The storm hit and crashed against the walls. Flash!

— Treat me as an adult!

Crack!

— That kind of behaviour's not adult, it's cheap!

Flare!

— How come it's not cheap when you do it?!

Boom!

— I have a responsible relationship with no risk of AIDS and other infections!

Splinter!

— So you're calling me irresponsible?

Crash!

— After all our talks and promises, that's what it looks like!

And so it went, rolling around old territory, raging on until we wore each other out and put between us the greatest possible distance the apartment allowed. Sometime after four, I dashed cold water over my face, too drained to offer comforting words or a caress of forgiveness to Jess who lay on the far side of the darkened bedroom. *It's only because of my disappointing experience I've given her a hard time about Nikos. But – but… her experience with him must have been a happier one, with all the makings of a pleasant memory – eventually.* And I released the guilt, the revulsion and indignity of that squalid night in the seventies. *Dimitte diem. Let it go.*

Instantly the jagged recollection of the duty phone call to be made leapt into the vacuum. I scribbled a note and left. *'Sorry, Jess'* was in my head. But I couldn't quite write it.

FRASER

It was a peaceful day at Sesklia Island, devoid of octopus bashing and dramatic dousings. The Witterings hadn't turned up and Panos' quieter brother, Vassilis, was captain for the day, so there wasn't even the usual joshing to respond to. We turned the headland into port and the communal 'aah' went up as the harbour came into view. The water was a perfect mirror and the picture just too kitsch to be true. Richard and foxy wife had come along for the second time and were the last to disembark.

– Fancy a drink, Fraser?

It was foxy wife. I started making a polite refusal but Richard cut in.

– What a good idea! After a day of sun and sea, we need something a little shadier. Take us to this dive of yours, Fraser. The one with the lethal cocktails. What's it called? Noddy's?

– Nobby's. Can't guarantee that Nobby can handle a rush, though.

If Richard had been on his own I wouldn't have minded. He backtracked, though.

– Sorry, old chap. You don't get much time to yourself, do you? Then the punters stalk you in your hideout.

Couldn't do anything but stick on a grin and lead the way. As they headed for a booth Nobby remarked –

– 'F I'd known yer were bringing aristocracy, I'd've biked a fooking cike.

Just then, Phanes slouched in moodily. Nobby beckoned me closer.

– Oz hippy girl been knocking about wi' Phanes. In here a few times. That Bald Bastard o' yourn – had her in his room last night – she got the hydrofoil to Kos this afternoon. Owze about that? By the way – gorra few hooky watches in Datça yesterday if anyone's interested.

I took the drinks over in a state somewhere between elation and numbness. Foxy was mid-chuckle.

– The look on your face when everyone sang 'Happy Birthday'!

Richard smiled and sighed.

– I hope Clair's all right. She's had quite a holiday, one way and another

– Her boyfriend will be looking after her, I expect.

There was a brief silence while we reflected variously on the implications. My mobile rang. It was Jess in a phone booth in Chorio, sounding upset. She was looking for Nikos who wasn't picking up. I had no idea where he was. I moved away from the others to speak.

– Where's your Mum? Is she at the hotel?

– Yes – no – I don't know.

– I'm at Nobby's with Richard and Mandy. Why don't you join us?

She must have covered the Kali Strata at a hell of a lick because she arrived at Nobby's in under ten minutes. After a couple of drinks I bowed out. Richard and Foxy said they'd take Jess for a meal and see her home. Job done. After a few minutes walking, though, I did a double take. Instead of being well up the Kali Strata on the way home, I was halfway along the harbour. I could cut up a random flight of steps. Or I could drop by to see if Clair was in.

CLAIR

Facing up to Connie (synonym for Terrible)

Standing in my, by now, habitual booth, credit card poised in slot, I ran through the inevitable conversation, rehearsing my excuses for not having called on my birthday. I dialled.

– Hi, Mum, how are you? How's Joe? Sorry I couldn't call yesterday, I had a bug – on my birthday! And Jess has gone down with it today.

That should have covered everything.

– Why didn't Jess call us yesterday? Let us know?

– She was looking after me.

– Glad to know someone puts their Mom first.

Game to Connie. The remainder of the conversation was a replica of the last one. Joe was no better no worse. She didn't even wish me a belated happy birthday. Maybe she would have done if my credit hadn't run out. *Damn! Meant to ring Maggie! Must get another card.*

I left the booth unutterably depressed, not knowing what to do or where to go. *Do I want to be alone, or do I want company?* I bought a two-day-old Daily Telegraph to occupy my mind and wandered towards the water's edge. The day-trippers had gone and the moorings on the far side of the harbour were empty. A few boats had returned from the beaches and the fishing vessels were all in. The hillsides threw their patchwork reflection in the mercury smooth water. I could just make out the steps up to Hotel Acropolis opposite and felt a pang of guilt over Howard. *What the hell happened last night?* My will flagged. Reluctant to return to the hotel, I fished out a euro and rang him from the familiar Perspex hood. *Not a good idea. I have only negative conversations on this phone.* He was in the hotel bar and our stilted exchange lasted only a few minutes, one not wishing and the other not able to recall the events of the previous night. We agreed to defer our conversation to the morning. I plodded to the supermarket, then home. *Fifty for a day and already I've alienated my daughter and my – and Howard. It's all downhill from here.*

Nearing the apartment, I realised I'd forgotten to buy another phone card to ring Maggie. Aphrodite One was empty, my note screwed into a ball on the floor. *Best to have some space, probably. If she'd gone off to Nikos, well, the damage had already been done.* I unloaded the shopping, poured myself a glass of wine and went out to the terrace with a book, drugging my mind with alcohol and someone else's visions. The drawing block lay inside, its blank pages infiltrating my conscience until I could ignore it no longer. I don't know how long it was, but daylight had faded as I sketched by the light from the open door.

– Clair?

It was Fraser. He'd come to tell me that Jess was having dinner with Richard and Mandy. *He's embarrassed. Oh, god, they all wanted Jess out of the way so that he could tell me the awful truth. Time I found out, I suppose. Shit, I didn't pounce on him or anything yesterday, did I?* I decided that it would be civilised to endure his revelations over a glass of wine. He accepted. *He's like a hen on a hot griddle – I'm really going to hate what's coming. What a shame. Well, if he's seen Jess he'll know all about the row, no doubt.* I was so angst ridden about what he was going to say and aware, at the same time, of sitting so close to him that I didn't really pay attention until I heard him saying something about a seedy episode, Jess telling everyone at Nobby's bar – and then taking the hydrofoil to Kos.

– Kos?! You said she was having dinner with Richard – and Mandy!

– What? No! Jess is having dinner. She's gone to Kos.

– Who's she?

– The Australian bird! Dreadlocks! Backpack! <u>She's</u> gone to Kos! Not Jess!

– Whoa – stop – stop – can we have a rewind?

My brain felt as turgid as it had that morning.

– I've been talking about Jess and me having a row over Nikos – what have you been talking about? And what did you hear in Nobby's bar?

– Oh shit! Look – I'm really sorry – I –

– What did you hear in Nobby's bar? About me?

– It was more about – your – Bunce – chap. And the – er – Yolanda.

Suddenly, I rung up the jackpot and thousands of pennies dropped. The female voice on the phone that morning – the phone slammed down… Had Howard shagged Mousey Dreadlocks?

– He did – didn't he? Shag the Ozzie backpacker?

– It would appear so.

Relief, no release, flooded through me. Exhilaration, in fact. *Haaa! No more Mr Deputy Director of Education – no more bleak bonking – no more kidding myself –*

– Oh no – don't cry. Please – look, I'm really sorry. Clair?

But I was laughing, until it converted to a fit of hiccupping. Fraser was terrified. Shoved water at me. Brought me loo roll. I honked and started again – the thought of Mr Sensible and the hairy backpacker. I forced Fraser to fill in the details of the night before, listening with shock and awe. *I'm a true rock 'n' roller! Stoned on my fiftieth. Wait 'til I tell Sonya.* Yes, Fraser was my source of received memory. Despite feeling mortified, I couldn't help being entertained by my own shenanigans – and those, apparently, of Richard and Mandy. He spoke quietly, avoiding eye contact.

– You really don't mind about – about Howard and… ?

I didn't mind and gave him a brief, sanitised version of why. He was thoughtful.

– Can I ask you something?

– Sure, go ahead.

– Would you mind if I… ? Oh, for – come here.

And then he kissed me…

Resisting was not an option and I didn't care who saw. Breath and tongues and the flavour of wine, murmurs and fingertips all colluded until it threatened to get marvellously out of hand. We pulled back, both wanting to take it further and stupidly unsure of how to.

– Wow…

– Yeah…

– Can't leave it at that –

– No!

There was a problem. *How? Where? And what about Jess?* Fraser made a decision.

– You know upstairs – Aphrodite Two? Been empty since you arrived – last minute cancellation. We could listen out for the we'an from there.

I left a note under a wineglass and the key by the mulberry tree.

FRASER

She was sitting outside, hair up, a heap of curls touched by light from the open door. Looked like she was drawing or something, reading glasses perched on the tip of her nose. Glass of white wine, held against her cheek. Completely absorbed. I didn't want to move, to disturb her. Neither did I want her to discover me ogling.

– Clair?

She started.

– Who's that?

– Me – Fraser. Came to see how you are.

She was a bit cool – or embarrassed?

– Fine – fine, thanks.

– Glad to hear it. OK – well I'll be on my – Oh! Jess has gone for a meal with Richard and – um – Mandy.

– Ah.

– Good – well, so long as… er…

Stood there like the tool I was. She smiled – pity?

– Still against company rules for you to have a drink?

– Um – actually, it's my day off tomorrow, so – I suppose I could bend them.

– Would you like to come up – or drink it there?

I climbed the last three steps and sat in the other chair while she went inside. I looked at what she'd been drawing. It was Jess – coloured pencil or something. Didn't know she was an artist. She arrived back with two glasses.

– That Jess you're drawing? It's good.

– Oh I was just – um… Hope you drink white wine – it's all we have.

– Sure – great. Yamass!

– Yamass!

It was possibly the best location in Symi. Not the most luxurious of accommodation, but more than adequate. The lights of Hotel Acropolis shimmered across the harbour in the warmth. I wondered if she knew what had gone on there last night? I wanted her to like me. No, not just like me – I wanted her to fancy me. Why did it feel different, knowing Bald Bastard had cheated on her? Why wasn't fifty a barrier any more? She was wearing that pink top again, the one she wore the day we had a beer. We were doing that contemplating the wineglass routine. Felt her looking at me. I coughed a bit.

– We were on the weekly picnic today, down at Sesklia Island.

– Ah. Anything interesting happen?

– No. No sea life incidents.

I wanted to touch her hair, trace her collarbone.

– And you? What did you do today?

– Oh, indulged in a little domestic turmoil. Suppose you've heard all about it.

So she knew about Bald Bastard and his grubby shag? I felt a rush of sympathy for her.

– Sorry. That must be tough to take.

– Oh – I've got used to it. Goes with the territory.

– It's happened before?

The bloody, bloody Bald Bastard! What was the etiquette of these situations?

– Sorry, that's none of my business.

I blundered on, anyway, trying to be Annie.

– If it's any use, Clair, I know what you're feeling. It's not an easy place to be. And the worst part is the loss – of someone you thought you knew. But it turns out you didn't, so even that's taken from you.

– Fraser, that's very kind of you. But hormones play a large part in it – we all know that.

Hormones? A bit over generous, not to mention too much information.

– I think you're being very charitable. It was a pretty seedy episode.

– What on earth did she say to you?

Spoken very sharply. I'd gone too far. Shit!

– I didn't speak to her. I just – heard about it.

– You heard about it? Where?

– I'm afraid I heard it in Nobby's Bar.

– Nobby's Bar?! Christ! I'll kill her!

Things had got a bit out of control. What to do?

– No – no, she didn't say anything. She's gone. Took the hydrofoil for Kos.

Clair was on her feet.

– Kos?! You said she was having dinner with Richard – and Mandy!

I'd just stepped into a parallel universe.

It took a gut-churning lifetime to sort. I prayed for a convenient hole in the ground, but no tectonic plates were forthcoming. I had to reveal the sordid affair of Bald Bastard and the backpacker. The last few words came out with a gap of centuries in between. After which a millennium of a pause. Then she covered her face with her hands, her shoulders shaking.

– Oh no – don't cry. Please – look, I'm really sorry.

Come, kindly rogue state, and drop a nuclear bomb on my head. Zeus, chain me to a rock with Kenny Rogers playing to eternity. Phanes – turn me inside out and bash me to death on a concrete jetty. My torture was interrupted by a loud snort.

– Clair?

She was laughing. Laughing! There were tears, yes, but… she was rocking. She also squeaked, snuffled, guffawed – almost yodelled at one point. OK, so we'd been talking at some hell of a cross-purpose. But her partner had just been fairly publicly unfaithful. Wasn't she even slightly upset?

Eventually, she slowed down but went off again, then started hiccupping. I was sniggering by now, without knowing why. I fetched her some water. After a while she was able to sprawl, exhausted, across the table, groaning slightly. I wanted in on the joke. She sniffed terrifically. I fetched the toilet roll.

– Now tell me.

– H – H – Howard and…

Another whine started cranking up into a laugh. I made her breathe in. She tried again.

– Howard screwed Mousey Dreadlocks? Oh god – poor bugger. He must hate himself today!

Between us, we pieced together the previous evening, some of it based on educated guessing. Her fiftieth birthday was no longer a lost day. Clair Harkin was the Dope Queen of Symi.

– No need to be embarrassed, you really were very funny. Jess and the Oz bird were just giggly. Then after your gymnastic display, Theo found you a spare room and the two girls put you to bed. Richard had a helluva fiftieth birthday party on your behalf.

We fell comfortably silent this time. I had to know, though.

– So you really don't mind about – about your – him – and... ?

She leaned her head back and frowned then straightened.

– Nope. It's a relief. That liaison's been going nowhere. He's a... a nice enough man, but we're not really – I don't know, 'of a kind'. I'd no idea he was planning on coming here so I was shell-shocked when he turned up. And resentful, too – it was just so presumptuous. Maybe I gave him some sort of signals that made him think it was OK. I don't know.

She shrugged and downed half the glass of wine. I decided it was time to go for it. I pulled her face to me like they do in the movies. She didn't resist. Somehow we ended up in bed. Upstairs, in Aphrodite Two. Just kissing. Then she said –

– So, it's your day off tomorrow?

– It is, and one thing I intend doing is making love to you properly.

– Oh. I was sort of hoping you'd shag me to within an inch of my life.

My kind of woman.

CHAPTER TEN

CLAIR

Time for sweet, juicy raisins

I asked Maggie and Julia many times how they met and when they first *knew*. Their accounts were unwavering and almost identical – although it was Maggie's, the less embroidered of the two, I always remembered.

– I turned and there was Julia. It was as simple as that.

Would it ever be that simple for me?

I couldn't tell how long I'd been awake. I watched Fraser sleeping, allowing myself the luxury of living in the moment. He really was beautiful in repose, gingery gold stubble on his cheek and his mouth relaxed in sleep. His eyelashes were long, dark at the base, fair at the tips. *They'd be spectacular with mascara.* His skin was smooth and tanned, arms lightly muscled, hands strong. His nose and cheeks were dotted with faint freckles I'd never noticed before. *Last night...* I relived the hours of stroking, kissing, talk and laughter, all low in respect for Jess who had arrived at Aphrodite One, below, around midnight. *Sonya, you'd be very, very proud of me – and not a little envious. I'd forgotten what it feels like. Didn't think it would ever happen again. What do I mean by 'it'? Not just sex.* When his eyes flickered I closed mine, fraudulently, so he wouldn't know I'd been conscious for so long. He brushed my arm.

– Good morning. Sleep?

I shammed a fluttery awakening.

– Mmmm.

– Don't go away.

He nuzzled my hair, kissed my ear then rose from the bed, padding naked to the loo. I watched him all the way across, loving the shape and movement of his limbs, mentally caressing his shoulders, buttocks, thighs, impatient to see his return. It was even good to hear him peeing. We'd gone beyond that modesty barrier. Re-emerging, he saw me watching and stopped, on the verge of self-consciousness, then spread his arms –

– Well, it doesn't get better than this. You have three seconds to change your mind. One – two – three – that's it! You're stuck with me for the rest of the day.

I tensed, several wires pulling taut inside. *Only 'the rest of the day'? Is that all? But that kiss, all the talking last night. Is this really just a holiday fling? Grow up, Clair, of course it is. Get real you sad, fifty-year-old!* He stretched out beside me again.

– I can't believe you're here.

– Why?

– Because – because it – no, you – you are so unexpected. There I was, sitting on my Greek island, strumming my guitar, minding my own business and suddenly this stunning lady appears who just – I don't know – turns me upside down. You do, Clair. I don't know which way up I am. I normally talk through my arse, by the way, so you can imagine how unusual this is for me.

It made me laugh. I held out my arms, which he, quite correctly, took as an invitation to pull me close. As we kissed, I felt his arousal. He nuzzled in my ear.

– You see what I mean about upside down? That used to be my elbow.

The view from Aphrodite Two was even more spectacular. Instead of a terrace, the apartment had a balcony. We stood gazing out and drinking Aegis' complimentary coffee. After clearing his throat a couple of times he said, awkwardly –

– Look, Clair, there's something serious I meant to say to you – I hope you won't take it the wrong way –

Here it comes – he's married – no – got back together with the girlfriend – no – doesn't mind a bit of snogging but couldn't possibly take this –

– It's about the dope. You have to promise me you won't do that again, not on Symi.

I was defensive.

– It's not a habit of mine, just a one-off for a terrible birthday.

– I'm not preaching. You can get life over here just for using.

God – who was it said that before? Life? That's why Nikos came back with Jess that night, to make sure there wasn't anything lying around. We arranged to meet later at 'our' taverna, the one we went to the day he'd split up with the Rhodes girlfriend.

Back in Aphrodite One, neither Jess nor I referred to my nightlong absence. My note of ten hours earlier lay on the draining board: 'JJ – We both need some space. I am staying upstairs in Aphrodite Two tonight. Sleep well. Love Mum x'. She planned to spend the day with Mandy at Nimborio while Richard explored the smaller churches around the island. As she stepped onto the terrace, I called her back.

– JJ – I'm sorry for yesterday. It was wrong of me. I just wanted your first time to be perfect –

She didn't react.

– and I realise that Nikos had an honourable motive in coming here to check that the place was clear. He put himself at risk. It was a generous thing to do. I know you both fancy each other like crazy. I don't know I could have resisted if I…

And in fact, I only resisted it technically last night. Oh, the hypocrisy! Jess accepted the apology with a nod and agreed that she understood the seriousness of drug possession in Greece.

– There was nothing here, anyway, we dumped the skins in a bin on the way to the hotel.

– What?

– Yup. By the Customs House. You thought it was very funny. No one saw us – and the bins are emptied every day, so any evidence had gone.

She shrugged and disappeared on her way to Nimborio. I was staggered, firstly at how rash I'd been and secondly by having made the apology of the century on apparently false premises. There had been no need for Nikos to come back to check an already 'clean' studio.

It was a 'dimitte diem' moment. Yo's gone to Kos – could be anywhere by now. And I have more pleasant things to think about. My back was just about resilient enough to stand a bra, so I decided on a T-shirt and jeans. *Youth! Youth's the thing for a fling!*

Although tobacco-free since Saturday, I wasn't confident enough to venture forth without a nicotine safety net. Taking full possession of the plum leather shoulder bag, I dropped in Jess's gift of Silk Cut. The sideways mirror-view of my bulge of tum tarnished the moment. *That's easy, I just won't stand sideways.* One aspect of the last fifty years, permanent fear of bodily imperfection, fell away – for that moment. Crossing the terrace, I took an exultant breath of morning air and said goodbye to the absent lizard before stepping down through the geraniums – and hitting a big, sweating brick wall. Howard.

– Clair, I think we need to talk.

I know what I did on Saturday night – but does he know I know? And does he know I know what he did? And do I let him know I know? Or do I let him think I don't know and see how long it takes him to confess? And can I be bothered? Dimitte diem –

– Talk about what? Your sordid little tryst with the Rasta from Oz? Excuse me, please.

Perspiration deckled Howard's face. His remaining hair from ear level down drooped in wetly curling strands. His mouth hung open and his jowls sagged, immobilised by contrition. Even his nose hair was inert. He seemed incapable of movement. *What would Sonya say? 'Fuck off and decompose, you rancid sack of shit'? Probably.*

– Howard!

– Oh – oh, sorry.

He shuffled aside then stumbled at my heels as I picked down familiar stairways with the assurance of a Symi goat. Breathily, he attempted his manager-to-emotional-member-of-staff voice, low, calm, reasonable. *Did they teach them that on the Cranfield MBA course?*

– I know you're upset, I can see that. I sympathise. It was an unfortunate episode that I hope we can put behind us. Naturally, with your injured back, you wouldn't feel able to express yourself in – that – way. But, although it doesn't excuse what I did, I'll admit that I was beginning to feel… and – and –

If he says 'a man has needs' I'll lamp him! I turned away from the harbour and up towards the town square without slackening pace. He followed, his face even redder and wetter, sweat flowering his shirt at armpits and chest. *Sonya, why did I ever resent your objectivity? You're right. He is a major sack of lard.*

– and I truly believe that in time, if the will is there –

I could see the green canopies and focused on the shade underneath. Howard didn't pause.

– it could even strengthen our –

Leaning back, right hand on a glass of beer, sat Fraser. I was a dozen paces away when he saw me. Howard was panting.

– Oh lord, it's that travel rep chap, let's go somewhere else.

I turned my back to Howard and pulled a horror mask to Fraser.

– Hi Fraser, sorry I'm late. Got held up.

– No problem.

Fraser remained seated but was otherwise impeccably civil.

– Good morning, Mr Bunce,

Howard dithered between fury and incomprehension.

– Clair? Are you – ? I mean, with – ?

– Yes.

– I see. Well, in that case I'll – er –

– OK, Howard, thanks for popping round.

I turned to Fraser again. He was cool, hand still curled around his glass, index finger tracing a small parabola in the condensation. A few moments later, the hand gave a thumb up. Howard had gone. Fraser whistled.

– Just for a moment there, I thought it was going to be deodorant sprays at dawn.

Laughter was easy, eye contact taut. He touched my hand as I sat, streaking it with moisture from his glass.

– Hello, hen, how're you doing?

– Gai fair, pal.

– Ah – the Kilachlan connection coming to the fore.

– When did I – ? Oh, last night. What else did I tell you?

– This and that. I want to meet Maggie, she sounds wonderful. Might need a shot of Dutch courage for Sonya, though.

As he spoke, I saw Dr Mavrakakou approaching. She greeted us both coolly, enquired after my back and then asked if I had recovered from my experience on Saturday night. A million, million nerve endings alternated hot and cold.

– You were there?

She smiled, a little thinly it seemed, and glanced at Fraser, who had got to his feet.

– You gave Ms Harkin my bill?

– Ach, sorry, forgot. I will. Sorry Clair, Ali –

Dr Mavrakakou excused herself abruptly. For a moment, I thought Fraser was going to follow her. *She was about as friendly as a lap dancer with cystitis. Does she know I was stoned? Or does she have a history with Fraser? Or both?* But he sat down, lifting his beer, and apologised for not passing on the bill. I dismissed it. Other questions stood between us, some practical, like where to go today, others less easy to articulate but more urgent. We had to start somewhere. He went first.

– What would you like to do today?

– You're the local around here. What would you suggest?

Did that sound laid back enough?

– Do you want an honest opinion?

Only if it's the one I want to hear.

– Only if it's the one I want to hear.

The suggestion was to take a car up to the centre of the island where there was something he wanted to show me. We indulged in a little ribald banter and departed in chummy, adolescent excitement, the chummy, adolescent part largely mine, to be honest. Twenty minutes later, my knees shot up, hitting the dashboard. Not impromptu sex but unexpected braking.

– Shit, it's Richard. I'd better stop. Stay there.

Then I saw him. We had just passed a small, walled chapel. Fraser got out and walked back. I heard the two men greet one another and strained unsuccessfully to hear their conversation. I was glued to the passenger seat having one of my conversations with Sonya. *Just my bloody luck! Richard! Bugger! – Why? You've found yourself a man who is available and who, apparently, wants to roger you senseless. Why should it matter about Richard? – Because.*

– What a gem of a bloke!

– Eh?

Fraser swung back into the driver's seat and started the engine.

– Asked him if he wanted a lift. But he's hired a scooter. He's great, a really nice guy. Just occasionally there's a punter who stands out. I'll miss him when he goes.

Will you feel the same about me?

We jolted on in the heat as the road became too rugged for easy speech. Some ten minutes' spinal torture further, we came to a magnificent view of the Aegean to the southwest. Fraser pulled the little 4x4 some way into the trees and stopped. Dust billowed gently along the road as the aroma of sage closed around us. Dark green pine trees stood in sharp relief against the bright blue of the sky. It was very hot and crickets shrilled incessantly. We got out and crossed the road. Far below was a glittering mesh of tiny ripples. Away to the left was the monastery of the Archangel Michael Panormitis, majestic in its enclosed bay. Fraser wrapped his arm casually around me, touching my left hip and I leaned in towards him, focusing lazily on the horizon. *Why does this feel so comfortable? It's too soon. This might be the only time we stand together like this. Forty-eight hours from now I'll be at Rhodes airport. Seventy-two hours and I'll be in Guildford, sitting behind a pile of bills – Stop! Stop it! Dimitte diem – no – carpe diem!* Feeling anything but confident, I kissed his cheek gently.

– Thank you for bringing me here.

– I have to confess to an ulterior motive.

– What's that?

– Come with me.

He led me back across the road to the car, collected a rucksack and headed through the trees up a narrow, scrubby track almost hidden by dried yellow grass. Reaching a small crest of pines, he took my hand as I stepped up a couple of feet to join him.

– Nearly there.

He continued through the trees, disappearing momentarily from sight. As I caught up I saw a tiny chapel and, beside it, a small whitewashed building framed by a few olive trees. He was already unlocking the blue door.

– Welcome to Bluebeard's Castle.

I froze. *A bloody shag shack. Does he seriously expect… ?* It was Sonya in my head. Fraser had already gone in. I didn't move. He reappeared at the door.

– Don't go all matronly on me. I've seen your bare arse – now get it in here, Harkin.

He's got a point. I trod carefully down the last few yards, ducked down and stepped into a sea shell, the walls smooth and rounded as the inside of a conch. Even the stove had a smooth, fluted chimney and the floor was pink marble that reflected onto the white walls. There was a small table and chair, a single bed, a chest of drawers on which rested a pitcher and bowl and beyond that, not much else.

– It's lovely. Whose is it?

– Belongs to a woman who does art courses on the special interest holidays. I look after it for her.

– And this art teacher, does she mind you using it as your – lair?

– I don't suppose she would, if I ever did. It's not exactly convenient. Except for today.

I don't know about this. It's just – too business-like. I've got it all wrong. This isn't what I want. This isn't the way I want him to think of me. Or the way I want to think of myself. And if Jess ever –

– Clair – if you meant everything you said last night and you believe everything I said, why don't you just drop the suspicion – and the fear of disrespect?

I couldn't answer.

– I want to make love with you. You made me believe that's what you want, too. I have never brought anyone here because I've never been in this situation – ever. Oh, and the painting lady, for your information, is in her eighties –

He slapped his head theatrically.

– Not that I have a problem with older women!

The man had style. I pushed away from the cool stone and into his arms. This time, he kissed me firmly and I responded, tracing his lips and teeth with my tongue, exploring his mouth, holding him close. He gave a small breath out. As we pulled apart, his voice was unsteady.

– C'mon – let's get these off.

He peeled my t-shirt over my head then turned me round and unfastened hooks and eyes gently, trying not to hurt my back. As my bra fell to the floor, he clasped my breasts and nuzzled my neck, making the nerves in my arms and back shiver with pleasure. I relaxed into the luxury of being wanted, resting against his chest then moving slowly around, helping him off with his shirt, unfastening his belt buckle as he unzipped my jeans. Shedding trousers and knickers was as awkward as I ever remembered and we joked, despite the urgency to press flesh full length. Once on the bed, we lay just holding and looking, finding it incredible that the moment was here. I adored studying the almost familiar, firm body that lacked the imperfection of mine. I didn't want him to look at me, see my sagging breasts, my convex belly, the small blue threads on my legs and the veins standing out on my hands.

– God, you're so beautiful…

He has to say that on the point of shagging me. It's only polite.

– You don't have to say that.

– It's a habit of mine, stating the obvious.

Good answer. He stroked my nipple until it contracted to a bead that he took into his mouth, sucking gently, then harder just to the point of pain before moving to kiss me again, more intensely than before, his hand skimming down my body to my thigh then back to grasp my breast.

– Clair, I can't hold on too long the first time…

The first time? Oh, yes!!!

– Good. Nor can I.

He moved his hand across my stomach, down and further down – and grinned.

– So you can't. Can your bad back stand me on top or do you want to be a cowgirl?

It was the sort of lovemaking to rewrite my future expectations – well, hopes.

CHAPTER ELEVEN

STILL CLAIR

Terrible for a friend

We were in the 4x4 on the way back when his mobile rang and he pulled over to answer. Driving one-handed on these roads was not so much foolish as impossible for anyone except a Greek bus driver. He told the caller he was on his way and pulled back onto the road. I knew something bad had happened.

– That was Ali – Dr Mavrakakou. Richard's had an accident on his scooter. We'll have to get him to Rhodes tomorrow, she thinks.

Our parting in Chorio was casual for the benefit of any onlookers. I walked down into Yialos while Fraser headed for their villa. I would visit later, we agreed, concocting a brief camouflage of having met by chance and heard the news. Passing through the town, I decided to grab the opportunity to ring Maggie but found I didn't have my debit card with me. I needed to let her know I was all right and make sure she was, too. Foremost in my mind, though, was concern for Richard's pain, Mandy's distress and a bad end to their holiday.

There was no sign of Jess. She should have been back from Nimborio by now but I wasn't concerned, Symi was such a safe place. I dressed in my Symi shirt and the pink trousers bought a lifetime ago in Richmond, and left to visit Richard and Mandy. I found the lemon walls and brown shutters of their villa after a lung-searing climb. Mandy came to the door in a flowered cotton kimono and insisted I came in to see the invalid, who rested on a couch.

– My, you're looking glamorous tonight, Clair. You seem to have made a spectacular recovery.

How like him to mention me first. They were travelling to the hospital in Rhodes in the morning. With this abrupt end to their holiday a new dynamic had entered their relationship, Richard dependent, Mandy in control. There was another knock and a young woman delivered several covered platters of food. I wished them bon appétit, a safe journey the next day and onward home, hugged Mandy and planted a kiss on Richard's forehead. In benediction. Mandy saw me to the door.

– I've already swapped email and stuff with Jess, said. Be nice to keep in touch.

We hugged again and I turned down the Kali Strata towards 'our' taverna. On the way, I made a brief detour to Vaporis. To gloat to Sonya. In the purple shoulder bag was a packet of Silk Cut, just in case. Half an hour later I pressed 'send' on my email to Sonya and skipped out of Vaporis cyber café, purple shoulder bag slapping against my bottom, and down to the town square to meet my lover. *I must ring Maggie.* But I hadn't foreseen encountering Jess sitting with the – *octopodicide?* – Phanes outside a bar. Until then, I'd felt fairly sanguine about letting her cope independently for an evening. But seeing her hanging around the harbour, still dressed in a bikini top and mini sarong, with another young Greek tried my tolerance. She pre-empted me, fortunately –

– Nice bag, Mum. By the way, you locked me out and took the key.

Oh shit. Hence Jess hanging about with Phanes who had been kind enough to buy her a drink and keep her company. That, compounded by the shoulder bag gaffe, left me sheepish with remorse. I handed over the key and we agreed to 'see you later', the 'where and when' left unspecified. 'When' turned out to be a couple of hours and 'where' was Giannis Fish Restaurant where Jess, the rigid vegetarian, would not normally have set foot. Fraser and I had been finishing the meal at 'our' taverna when a wave of peculiarly dissonant pop music assaulted our ears. He whooped.

– The Turks are at Giannis's place! C'mon, let's pay and go!

– I have to ring Maggie on the –

But there was no time to lose. The mass destruction of crockery was not to be missed! As we hurried round the harbour, Fraser warned that due to EU Health and Safety regulations, such ethnically therapeutic evenings could be numbered. Giannis, in expansive mood, ushered us to the only two seats left. The other two at the table were taken by – Jess and Nikos. Et voilá. Le coincidence. Each couple, unenthused by the appearance of the other, decided to make the most of it by knocking back a round of complimentary ouzos and ordering a couple of bottles of wine. Any residual rancour dissolved as we joined in drinking, dancing, clapping, hurling plates and laughing. A lot.

Our hilarity was heightened by the sudden appearance of Arsey Purple, irate again and trailing her inoffensive little husband and their new friends, the Witterings. In a manner harking back to the days of overwhelmingly pink-coloured maps and tones resonant of Ealing Comedies, Arsey Purple confronted Giannis, who stood mesmerised, mouth open in mid-shimmy.

– … dare you pollute the environment with this cacophony! It may suit the likes of Faliraki – but on Symi it is entirely –

She wagged a forefinger, gestured excitedly and even stamped a sensibly sandalled foot, provoking fury in a few Turks, but laughter in the rest of us. Arsey's supporting delegation shuffled uncomfortably, probably wishing they were in Faliraki or Corfu – or Bracknell – anywhere, in fact, but behind

Arsey Purple outside Giannis's Fish Restaurant on Symi Harbour. Giannis's solution was both Machiavellian in its cunning and Socratic in its elegant simplicity: Invite them in for a drink! As her wretched spouse and doubtful comrades submitted to the charm offensive and sidled inside, Arsey was left alone and ignored at the door. And the music went on as she strode off, scraggy calf muscles flexing with fury, unaware of the coup she had just achieved. For clasped to Giannis's bosom were two overweight vipers who knew all about plate-smashing. They had, they explained at length to a table of exasperated Turks, done it before. We decided it was time to go.

Parting from Giannis affectionately we ambled off. I looked at my watch; it was too late to ring Maggie. The musicians from a Symi Festival concert were packing up as we reached the town square. Nikos and Fraser recognised friends from the previous year. Great joy in reunion and a desire for alcohol led us all to Nobby's. Stamos, a great, bearded, Poseidon of a man with a voice straight from the bottom of the Aegean, restarted the evening's music with an unaccompanied song. Magically, carefully packed instruments reappeared and crept in as the song progressed. Fraser and Nikos joined in harmonising as each musician led a folk song while the clientèle formed a disorderly Greek dance around the cramped bar. After a while, Panos wandered in carrying a guitar case, Fraser's. Fraser seemed cool about Panos delivering it and greeted the 12-string tenderly, smoothing its grain, caressing the strings. *No wonder he knows how to stroke a woman's body.* I felt myself blush all over. Fraser played a chord and nodded. Nikos left Jess and joined him, said a few words in Greek. Applause, then hush fell on the bar. It began gently, a rise and fall of notes then a chord – Nikos led and Fraser harmonised, then they switched as Fraser sang a verse and chorus in English:

They left him lying in the sun

On some far Egyptian island

Lived his life upon the sea

Roaming wide and diving deep

As he lay dying in the sun

Ebbing by a tideless ocean

I heard him call my name

I heard him call my name

No stone weighing down his soul

His spirit rose to Helios, forever

Poseidon set him free, he set him free

Funny way to live your life

No giant stride, no thinking twice

Take your chance and pay the price

The price of luxury

Beauty doesn't count the cost

The loneliness when love is lost

On Symi, Halki, Kalymnos

So far across the sea

The price of luxury

The song of a diver's wife, recalling her husband's death from the bends while his colleagues sailed away at the command of their captain. From our conversation at the museum, I knew it was Fraser's writing. The potency of his words told me more about him, his poetry, his soul. As the last note reverberated to silence the applause was slow, respectful, gradually swelling until the walls of the small bar bulged. In that company, I could neither touch him nor tell him how the song moved me. But catching his eye for a moment, I hoped he knew.

After that, the music continued, an Anglo-Hellenic jam session until Nobby's desperation for sleep overcame his love of profit.

– Ow right yer scummy gits – sod off!

It was around four.

Nikos and Fraser walked us back to Aphrodite One, the younger contingent lagging further and further behind. At last, I could tell him.

– I know you wrote that song, Fraser – the diver's song.

– Co-wrote. Nikos had a hand. My Greek isn't that good.

– It was your idea, though – and it's beautiful. I saw him, lying there – felt her loss.

He squeezed my hand. The small action was enough for me to feel impending loss overwhelming me. *I must hold on, don't want to embarrass him – or ruin the evening.* We walked on in silence. But as we reached the slope leading to Aphrodite One, he led me on, past the taverna, towards the harbour mouth. The street lighting was ineffectual against the darkness I felt approaching. He stopped and rested the guitar. We touched.

– It's been one hell of a holiday for you, this?

His fingers entwined my hair.

– Mmm.

– Been a fairly memorable one for me, too.

We held one another for a long time.

Reluctantly, we turned towards the apartment and bid a quiet goodnight in the lane. I climbed the steps through the geraniums, strands of music still weaving in my ears. Jess arrived shortly after, mascara smudged and hair awry. As we undressed, I tried to dispel any inference she might make – especially the right one – about Fraser and me arriving at Giannis's together.

– Look, Mum, I definitely heard voices from upstairs last night.

– OK… It was Fraser.

Let's hope she buys this.

– Poor love was going out of his head over splitting up with his girlfriend. He asked me up to Aphrodite Two and poured his heart out. That's why I met him this evening – as his counsellor. I'm years older than him. Anything else would be ridiculous.

That last bit was over the top. Jess accepted the fabrication with unflattering ease.

– Nikos said he thought Fraser'd got over her pretty quickly. You must be a good listener, Mum.

Relieved, I left it there.

For our last day, Nikos had organised a trip that started at an unholy hour, so it was wise to get our heads down. In the few hours left for sleep, I relived the couple of hours in the artist's hut, over and over. And over.

FRASER

We stayed the whole night at Aphrodite Two. To put it delicately, since neither of us was prepared, nothing major occurred – but something definitely happened. In the morning we arranged to meet at the taverna, top of the harbour. She arrived with Bald Bastard two steps behind looking like a soggy bloodhound. Clair gurned for my benefit. I was Dirty Harry cool and he slunk off. Result! But after the pain in the arse came the headache. Doc Ali turned up. Asked if Clair was 'better' in a tight-arsed sort of way. Reminded me about her bill. Definite frost in the air. So what? I'd mapped out the day in my imagination. Ms Harkin was lovely putty in my hands.

Got a Suzuki 4x4 at a good rate – freebie, actually, rep's perk – headed for the hills and Marjorie's pad with my tantalising cargo. Marjorie's an artist, eighty plus I'd think, runs painting holidays for Aegis. Likes to start and finish the season in Symi, so she bought this small villa – hut, really. I kept an eye on it for her. Anyhow, on the way there, we spot Richard at a chapel. Had to stop. He'd hired a scooter and wanted to explore the island. What a great guy. No sign of foxy wife. Wondered what the story was there. Didn't wonder too long – I had a story of my own waiting to happen.

Drove on for the view of Panormitis. Got close to Ms H drinking it all in. Waited a while then led her up to Marjorie's. She went all leery on me for a bit. Coaxed her in, though. Explained about Marjorie and swore I'd never taken advantage of the space before (Mel didn't count). Efharisto Glaucus, efharisto Prometheus and especially efharisto Marjorie. I was not disappointed. After a little coaxing Ms Harkin convinced me, without doubt, she was an artist and a talented one. Definitely my kind of woman.

We were on the way back, feeling the sort of liquid way you do after really good sex, when Doc Ali rang. Richard had been in an accident.

Clair went down into Yialos. She seemed really upset by the news. Promised I'd be in touch as soon as I knew. The villa was a couple of streets away from the apartment in Chorio. Richard was stretched out on the sofa with his right arm in a sling and his left arm and one knee bandaged, but apart from that fine, more than fine. Foxy sat next to him, holding his cup, stroking his hair and making goo goo eyes at him. He was even quieter than usual, shock maybe, but said they'd like to go to Rhodes in the morning and straight on to the hospital. I said I'd book the hydrofoil and taxis for them and a hotel in Rhodes Town for Tuesday night. A nice one, said Richard – and winked. Too much information. I walked down to Mylonos Taverna and ordered a meal to be delivered to them. Shame it had to happen to Richard. Rotten end to a holiday. Why not Bald Bastard, instead?

Went back to organise things and found a snotty note from the landlord of Aphrodite Two. Someone had slept in there last night. Did I know anything about it? Clair's bill from Doc Ali was on the desk. I picked it up and legged it home for a shower before meeting said lady.

She looked edible and sexy, proving that the two go hand in hand – or tongue in cheek – or mouth – or… Went to 'our' taverna – it really was the best on Symi. Treated her to dinner. Trouble with being a Scot is you have to spend money like water to prove you're not mean. Not so necessary, maybe, with Ms Harkin, what with her being a good half Caledonian. I was beginning to tot up the burn hole in my next payslip when it happened. The sound wave. The Turks were at Giannis's place! Ergo a display of plate hurling that made bulls in china shops look like bunnies in clover. Giannis was rocking. Grabbed us and hauled us in to the last table – where sat another man. Nikos. With the we'an. Shit. Nonetheless, after a bit of poutiness from the we'an, alcohol got the better of us all and a good evening was had. Regarding Clair and me, I thought the cat was more or less out of the bag and heading for the hills. Still, we refrained from having sex across the table. Star turn of the evening was a wee grasshopper of a guy, one of my charges, who tossed plates and downed ouzo with the best of Turk and Greek. Clair and Jess were wetting themselves. The Witterings turned up, too, advising on the correct trajectory for plate hurling, but retreated after few near misses from the Turkish quarter. Why had I never thought of threatening behaviour?

CLAIR

Second Tuesday – Terrible plus three and last full day on Symi

– Fraser's face when the two fat people turned up, last night!

Jess sprang ahead while I lurched up a stony track on our guided tour.

– Remarkably like your reaction to a bowl of washing up.

– Oh ha ha. What did he call them, the fat people? The – Clitterings or something –

– Witterings.

– Oh yeah. Wonder where Howard is?

– Dunno. Bar at the Acropolis, probably.

She glanced at me to check I was as unconcerned as I sounded. Which I was.

The excursion to see the Byzantine wine presses and Panormitis monastery was a challenging way of spending quality time together on our last day. Lagging at the back of a perspiring crocodile of tourists, we atoned for two weeks of indolent lolling. Our Swiss guide, Helge, was married to Nikos's uncle Savvas. She almost skipped over the assault course of slippery pine needles, tree roots and small boulders. *All right for her, she's half bloody mountain goat.* We stopped at St Constantine's monastery where, ignoring the fading frescoes Jess focused on the 'favours', trinkets, baubles and costlier pieces of jewellery offered to the Madonna to secure healing, fertility and other blessings.

– They don't seriously believe all that? It's like putting out mince pies for Father Christmas!

Not heeding Helge's frown, she compounded her indiscretion. An ornate screen shielded the holiest area of the church, behind which only men were allowed to venture. Sexist and divisive, pronounced Jess. Glancing sideways at my little atheist, Helge told us about St Constantine's Day when coffee and dumplings were served to locals in the church courtyard, adding 'Only for believers'. Jess had clearly blown her invitation.

Outside again we were, however, offered searingly sweet Greek coffee, fresh figs and spring water. A slightly overripe pair of lovers, he bare-chested, she in bikini top and low-waisted mini skirt, stood aside, their spray-on tans and designer denim setting them apart. He was exaggeratedly macho, straight out of a Superhero comic with an impressive six-pack, well-defined pecs and biceps. *Firm little bum, too.* She looked much older than him with stretch marks, a slack midriff and a jaded air of experience. *Do I look that obvious with Fraser? And why is he with her when he could attract – ? Hang on – this is the exact attitude I despise in other people.* Jess passed me a glass of water.

– Stop ogling, Mum. He's taken.

– One day, JJ, your raging hormones will recede into the darkest corners of your memory and you will discover that there is more to this life than sex.

– Yeah, right. You were still ogling.

Our party set off again, following Helga to the wine presses, a group of large cylindrical stone basins.

– This is where Symiots used to tread the grapes, the gaps in the acid-bleached stones, were plugged with porcelain and sand. Symi, was famed for its white wine –

– God, look at them, now!

Jess indicated Craggy and Saggy now in a clinch of cinematic proportion. Oblivious, Helga went on about Eudoros and the Knights of St John.

– They'll be dogging in a minute.

– Don't look, JJ, it's rude!

– I think what they're doing's a lot ruder.

Helge frowned at the muttering and continued.

–… until piracy destroyed the trade. Then, in the 1960's, for reasons best known to himself, the mayor of Symi ordered all the vines to be uprooted.

At the next little chapel, a bell hung in a tree, engraved with 'Plaia de los Cristianos'.

– A donation by sailors from Tenerife.

Helge opened the door of the small white building while the shameless couple connected under the pines. The rest of us ducked under an arch decorated with blue pentacles into a tiny room with a tiled floor.

– With a bit of luck, they'll climax soon and we can all carry on with the walk.

– Shut up, Jess!

Ignoring us, Helge said the shepherd's wife who looked after the chapel found it difficult to clean so had the richly decorated pebble mosaic tiled over. After wondering at such domestic vandalism, there being nothing else to delay the moment, we ventured out. To our communal relief, the serial sex act had vanished.

– Probably doing disgusting things behind a rock.

– Ssshh!

We all kept our eyes firmly on the ground for a while as we sweated on.

Next came an open-air slaughter house, a makeshift affair comprising a wooden arch the size of a junior football goal, a couple of wooden blocks and a goat pen. Jess stood aside weakly, while we listened to the gruesome details of the bloody origins of souvlaki. The mating pair sauntered up looking as sullen as they had all morning. *Post coitus monotonous?* On we stumbled and slithered past a goat skull talisman to frighten off snakes. Snakes were a good reason to make sure all food was put away, Helge added; her family cats had caught seven in the past year. Jess, scoured the ground around her feet trying to levitate herself. Helge continued happily.

– In our garden. They leave them in the porch as a gift.

We all trod super-carefully until we emerged from tree cover into scorching sunlight. The rich scent of herbs surrounded us, once more.

– That is sage you can smell. Made into a tea, it is very good for sore throats.

Then Helge smiled at me.

– It is also a remedy for menopausal flushes and osteoporosis.

Cow.

We picked our way downhill to the road and boarded a minibus. On the last ridge before descending towards Marathounda, I saw the lay-by where Fraser had parked yesterday. The artist's hut could be only yards away but wasn't visible from the road. I wilted with insecurity. *Perhaps I shouldn't have done it. I criticised Jess for it. Did I carpe when I should have dimitte-ed? But my situation is very different; I'm looking at a – liaison – from a very different perspective. Or am I just a hypocrite?*

The minibus dropped us at the top of a rough path that led down to Marathounda beach. Moored out in the bay was the dear old Giorgios. We all headed straight for the jetty where an inflatable dinghy waited to ferry us out to it. Much to everyone's relief, the unsociable lovers rejected the last leg of the trip, trudging past the jetty to collar a couple of sun beds. It was a relaxed and jollier crew that sailed on round to Panormitis. Panos was mightily pleased to see us and attended personally to our rations of alcohol.

Breathing his unspeakable tobacco breath over us, he related the astounding incidence of messages and prayers that arrived at Panormitis in supplication to the Archangel Michael. From all over the world, bottles and small boats arrived miraculously. A famous actress in Crete had once sent a bottle that bobbed right into the bay! I'd never heard of her but she and her message in a bottle clearly impressed Panos. How could it be but for divine intervention? Once, he continued, it was discovered that a thief had been at work in the chapel. Minutes after the discovery was made, a day trip boat ran aground on its way out of the bay and on board they found the thief, his pockets full of silver. Proof of the Archangel at work!

It was a calm sea and we ate lunch before rounding the southern end of the island and passing the headland into the bay, surely the greenest part of the island. The white monastery set at the water's edge against a backdrop of lush pine was an impressive sight. Once ashore, Jess didn't want to 'do' another monastery, so sat outside on a wooden bench, greedy for sunlight. As the others headed for the café, I went on alone, grateful for some time to think. The chapel was surprisingly small, its interior obscured by scaffolding erected for the cleaning of frescoes blackened by years of votive candle smoke. The inevitable collection of favours, so tangled as to be indistinguishable from one another, were strung before the Madonna and Child. Ducking back out, I headed for the folk museum, passing some euros at the doorway to two women who were more intent on bouncing a baby. Was there a guidebook?

– Ochi.

I went to the gift shop.

– Guide book?

– Ochi.

OK, I'll just guess. There were few other visitors. Deep in the cool interior I passed an old still before entering a room full of earthenware vats sunk into concrete. There was no explanation anywhere. *Good, I don't have to be interested, then. I can think about Fraser. About whether he's a good idea. About whether I've achieved the point of this holiday and left the crap behind. Maybe the crap's just fallen away.*

I wandered past some fog lamps and a sundial and on to the next room in which was an old typewriter, a radio and a wind-up telephone. *Where is he? At the office? At Nobby's? At home with the 12-string? Maybe he's having a beer at our taverna. With Dr Mavrakakou? Wherever he is, is he thinking about me? About last night?* A photograph of a frieze took my attention, depicting men in WWII German helmets pointing rifles at several non-military men including a Greek Orthodox priest. It was labelled in Greek. Greek resistance and German retribution, perhaps? *Richard knows about Greece during the war. Wonder what he made of all this? And did Mandy show any interest? It seems a lifetime ago she was complaining about coming here but it was – what? Ten days ago? Less?* Something significant had happened between the two of them since then. I had seen it the night before. She seemed almost maternal, he seemed vulnerable. He needed her and she enjoyed being needed. I wondered again what their story was and how they got together. They were so unlike. And yet, it looked as though it worked. Or would work.

Meandering on, I passed a glass case of sailors' knots and entered a traditional bedroom with brightly woven bedspread and a rug, crucifix and icon on the wall. It recalled St Constantine's monastery that we'd visited earlier. Jess had been too strident and Helge was obviously offended – some of the others, too, probably. *Have I encouraged her to be too outspoken? Or is it simply her nature? Does she take after Connie? Or her father? Do I have to let her make her own mistakes, now? Is that 'leaving the crap behind'? Letting go of responsibilities? Should I tell her about her father? Or would that be me offloading the burden onto her?* Opposite the Symi bedroom was a sitting room with colourful woollen rugs and an ornate oil lamp embellished with a rippling dragon, then a display of sewing machines, two Singers, another made by Rex and a fourth unidentified plus an old loom. The only information in English to any of the exhibits was 'Do not touch'. *Good advice. Stay solitary. You don't get hurt that way. That's what I've done since Adam. No – not since Adam, since… Jess happened. Poor old Howard. He never stood a chance of getting anywhere near.*

The folk museum had nothing else to offer. The sea-borne boats and bottles were in the religious museum on the other side of the chapel. Here there were English translations: 'In this room are exhibited many boats, boxes and bottles offered to Archangel Michael, many of which have arrived by the grace of the Archangel'. *Many of which? Not all? Some by DHL, perhaps? Is sarcasm the sort of crap I should leave behind? Am I who Jess gets it from?*

My first impression of the collection was disappointing. Instead of a tasteful array of green tinted bottles, the type despatched from desert islands by ragged castaways, there was a motley collection of containers. Amongst them Coca Cola, Seven Up and water bottles, all plastic, a very old Beefeater Gin bottle full of rusty looking water, and various other spirit bottles including Jack Daniels, Johnny Walker Black Label and Remy Martin. There were also coffee jars, olive jars and other unidentifiable glass pots. *All this reverence in all this rubbish.* But there was also the display of model boats that Panos had mentioned, beautifully designed, painted and cast adrift for the same purpose. Mounted high above the door was a pale blue caïque, about a metre long, with a red strip along the side. The craftsmanship was exquisite. The inscription read:

THIS BOAT IS COMING ALONE IN PORT OF PANORMITIS FROM THE TWELVE ISLANDS LIPSI AT 1998 AND INSIDE HAS 5 KG OF OIL, 3 KG CANDLES, ESSENCE AND NAMES FOR PRAY.

Ingredients for divine approval? It must be very comforting to have that kind of faith. And fulfilling to be able to offer your creative talent to an uncritical god. Is that why I dropped painting? Fear of criticism – criticism by rejection?

In the main museum there were religious paintings and glass cases containing richly embroidered vestments. But one contained hundreds of marvellously defined human figures carved from a whole elephant tusk. *Glad Jess didn't see this.* In another was a collection of weaponry, offerings to Archangel Michael, shown on an icon, holding a sword. In a long low case in the farthest room was an extraordinary gold cloth depicting the lament around the grave of Jesus. Seven figures stood out in relief around the body of Christ, the embroidery gold, silver and jewel colours on cloth of gold. In a corner of it, Judas counted his thirty pieces of silver.

Outside, Jess was sitting in the courtyard, leaning back with her eyes closed. I took a few moments to absorb the dramatic contrast of scarlet hibiscus and magenta bougainvillea against white stone, the paving of black and white pebbled chevrons. To the left, at the side of the chapel was a small room recessed into the monastery wall where prayer candles burned innocuously, sparing the frescoes another coating of soot. I nudged Jess and we climbed to the balcony surrounding chapel and courtyard to look down on the scene.

– This time tomorrow –

– Don't.

Descending by the spiral staircase, we noticed hundreds of pencil squiggles on the pale stone walls. The effect wasn't particularly decorative. A rough guide for a painted design, who could tell? Passing under the archway to the open, we looked up at a cherub hovering in an azure sky embellished with gold pentacles. The contrast between it and the pencil scrawls echoed the difference between the plastic bottles and the beautiful model boats. *Room for it all, the shoddy and the crafted, the base and the divine.*

Jess was getting bored. Without consultation, she had invited Nikos and Fraser by text to share our last night meal at Restaurant Tsampikos. I, unashamed charlatan, sighed acceptance of a fait accompli. Now she whined about wasting time when she wanted to get back and beautify.

– Don't wish away the time here, JJ.

I suggested a walk along the waterfront. After a few yards in silence, Jess stopped.

– So when are we going to have that talk, Mum?

The one about me being a generosity bully? Or the other one?

– Now?

– OK.

She sat down on harbour's edge, dangling her feet in the transparent water.

– Look, I'm sorry I made such a big deal about Turkey that night – I know you were pissed and you didn't really mean it about me going with Mandy on your birthday

It's the generosity one. I joined her, trying to organise what needed to be said.

– No, love, I didn't. But I've been thinking about what you said, JJ, and you're right, I do hide behind generosity. Except it's not really generosity. You're very perceptive. It is partly a way of shielding myself from obligation, just like you said. But it's not wholly that. It's also because – I suppose, I feel if I don't give all the time... I don't exist.

Where did that come from? It's right, though. Maybe that's something I have to leave behind, too. Why oh why do I never know anything until I say it?

– What do you mean, you don't exist? This is scary, Mum.

– Sorry, no. I mean I don't know what or who I am. Giving is like a drug – it makes me feel good, makes me forget that I'm – not where I want to be in life. I'm your mother, that's my greatest achievement and I'm proud of it, of you. But otherwise, I'm a sometime teacher, a sometime painter, an office dogsbody – and it's not enough. So I make myself 'Clair the Giver'. I'm sorry, darling, I'm just so used to doing it that I do it indiscriminately.

– Oh, Mum –

She put her arm round me –

– You are very special and really important. Not just my mother. You don't need to do all that giving.

– I'll try not to, JJ, I promise.

– But you can make an exception in my case.

We laughed. I leant my head against hers and we sat, sloshing the water with our toes. No more talk.

As it neared four, we decided to walk as far as the gate across the road into the harbour – there to keep goats out – then back to The Giorgios. We came to a larger version of the frieze I'd seen in the museum. It was clear that there had been some kind of atrocity. Jess was stunned by it; what she'd learned from Richard and what she'd read became real for her.

Back at the jetty, we passed Panos deep in conversation with a plump priest in tortoiseshell glasses. He caught us up along the jetty before we reached the boat.

– Excuse me, I talk to Father Andreas. My nephew – um – his daughter is baptise here, Sunday.

We chatted with Panos on the way back. We were right about the frieze. The abbot of the monastery, he explained, had kept a secret radio and the Germans discovered it. As there was no secure way to imprison the abbot and his assistants, they decided to march them to Symi town. But on the way, one of the assistants tried to escape into the mountains and, as a punishment, the Germans shot them all, including the abbot. Jess was appalled. Panos put a somewhat less than paternal arm around her.

– You don't worry, Panos look after you!

And he aimed his cigarette at an imaginary foe, firing off a few shots.

Back in Yialos I wanted to ring Maggie, but Jess convinced me that I shouldn't be seen in my current state and that we'd ring her after we'd changed and come back down.

That evening the barrier was obligingly open for anyone who cared to ignore the traffic ban. The harbourside was in constant, noisy motion. Jess and I were, of course, late, which left no time to ring Maggie. Around eight, we four lovers, two overt, two discreet, arrived at Tsampikos Restaurant. Owner and Head Chef, Tsampikos himself, took our order. Fraser had had a diverting day; one of his tourists, none other than Arsey Purple's spouse the Charles Hawtrey clone, had gone missing – kidnapped last night from Giannis's fish restaurant by two vengeful Turks and taken to Datça. It meant hiring Phanes – who was making a killing out of Aegis clients this week – to take Fraser and Arsey to Datça on the Turkish mainland to bring back her hungover and decidedly reluctant husband. Our day seemed very dull by comparison but Jess gave a graphic account of the sexy couple on the trip. I avoided Fraser's eye and hoped she wouldn't dwell on the age difference too long. Tsampikos's delicious mezes and seafood got less attention than they deserved. Returning from a mother-daughter bonding trip to the loo, Jess turned my blood to ice as she flopped and said casually:

– Hey Fraser, Mum told me all about your night in Aphrodite Two. She's so great at that sort of thing – sorted out a few of my mates who were having a hard time.

Fraser cleared his throat, glanced at me with raised eyebrows.

– I never suspected your mother to be so spectacular – or liberal.

Later, we shared a clandestine, steamy moment. I didn't waste it by explaining.

Inevitably, it was back to Aphrodite One for Jess and me, hearts sinking at the thought of the coming day. We lay in bed trying to eke out the last few minutes.

– Mum? What are you going to do about Howard?

– I don't know, darling. What are you going to do about Raz?

– I dunno. He's so young compared to Nikos – I don't think I can see him any more.

– Try and be gentle when you tell him.

A small silence. On the verge of sleep she reached for my hand.

– Thanks, Mum – you really do understand, don't you?

– I try to.

– Sorry if I've been a pain in the arse this holiday. I didn't mean to be. I hope it isn't too horrible being fifty.

– It's been a great holiday. Thank you. But as for being fifty, I don't think it's hit me just yet.

And I still haven't worked out what I want to leave behind or keep with me. And I STILL haven't rung Maggie!

CHAPTER TWELVE

FRASER

The day after the Turks at Giannis's place, Tuesday, I had the mother of a problem. One of my tourists was missing. Aegis didn't like losing tourists – bad for business. When Mrs Stone, or Arsey Purple as Clair and Jess called her, rang the emergency mobile at six a.m. to report her skinny wee husband's absence, my first reaction was 'And who can blame him?'. Not that I said it; I had to take it seriously. If there was no sign of him the situation could take a sober turn. He could have fallen in the harbour, be lying unconscious or worse in one of the many ruins… or he might have taken a look at his life and headed off for a better one. I knew Arsey had caused a scene about the music outside the fish restaurant and went off leaving him and the Witterings behind. I called Giannis. He hadn't seen any of them leave.

The police took my report moderately seriously, although nothing much of a sinister nature happened on Symi these days. Nikos hit on an intriguing but plausible theory: the brothers Orhan and Metin Meldüz had stuck close by him all night, it was possible that Mr Stone had gone with the Turks. After all, they'd seen off the Witterings last night.

The brothers from Datça were frequent visitors to Yialos and known for their alcoholic capacity and congenital disregard for authority. Mr Stone would have been an irresistible trophy and abducting him would have the added satisfaction of annoying his sour-faced spouse. A couple of phone calls confirmed it. Timothy Stone was in Datça and hadn't sobered up from last night, yet. Relief all round, then "How do we get him back"? It would mean chartering a boat. If they had to kidnap anyone, why couldn't they have picked the Witterings? I knew the answer to that.

Phanes was available and, by half past three, we were on board his little caïque and speeding past the fish farm at Nimborio. Nikos, moody in dark glasses, refused the jaunt across the straits. It was a nuisance, because being a native Symiot he had no problem communicating with the Turks. Nor did Phanes, of course, but it wouldn't be the same. The crossing took nearly an hour in the little boat. Mrs Stone sat on the bench behind the wheelhouse, flinty as her name, sunhat firmly lashed under a chin of granite.

I grudged every mile taking me further from Symi and Clair. Or was it Symi and an interesting sexual dalliance? My mind free of the Stone crisis for a while, I concocted plans of remarkable cunning to repeat the happy meeting of flesh before Wednesday morning. But they were all about as likely as a Bollywood plot. Landing at the jetty, we showed passports and I took Mrs Stone into the town, leaving Phanes to prowl the waterfront dives of Datça. Plodding along next to silicone woman, I wondered how Clair and

Jess were enjoying their day and calculated how long it would be before I would see them. I'd had no problem keeping my hands off Clair in front of her daughter. Discretion had surfaced when, with shrinking loins, I'd seen Jess and Nikos at the table last night. Admittedly, a few furtive exchanges had satisfied me that the frustration was mutual. Jess and Nikos, on the other hand, had displayed no such inhibitions, snuggling up to one another, dancing close and twining arms to drink ouzo. They wouldn't have noticed if we'd shagged across the fish tank. The very thought produced a small rush of painful pleasure. I was a teenager all over again. What was it with the lady? And would we ever make love again?

Orhan appeared instantly from the back as we reached the Meldüz carpet shop, lured by the joyful sound of feet crossing his doorway. To do him credit, his grin didn't flicker when he saw us and any hope of another sale evaporated. I have these moments of naïvety. He showed us through to back room where wee Mr Stone, looking like a comatose ET, lay on a silk rug snoring gently. Oh, let him sleep, I thought, don't bring him back to the cruel world of Arsey Purple. But this was not a fairy tale and Mr Stone was not about to be woken with a kiss.

– Timothy!

Mr Stone shifted slightly then resumed the light rasp. As Mrs Stone gathered herself for a second attempt, Orhan put a finger to her lips and gave her a smile of such intensity that her knees weakened audibly. He summoned Metin. The two brothers had a brief conversation and turned to me.

– We do this. You take us to Phanes.

While I rang Phanes, they rolled Mr Stone in the silk rug and lifted it onto their shoulders. Arsey simpered horribly as Orhan gave her a slow wink and the brothers, with their precious cargo, walked out of the shop. I was both appalled by the latent sexuality surfacing in Arsey Purple and impressed by Orhan's talent for cynical manipulation. On the way to the dock, the kidnappers reminisced pleasantly if obscenely on last night's excesses in a mixture of Turkish, Greek and English that went over Mrs Stone's head – except for one element of annoyance –

– West Wittering?

– Piss off home!

And they both spat copiously.

A brief word with a customs officer, who checked passports and peered down the tube of carpet, and we were waved through. Mr Stone was deposited, still sleeping, on the deck of Phanes' boat then the brothers helped a flushed Arsey aboard, each kissing a clenched little claw. Her face distorted into a rictus that may have been a smile but it was too remote from human expression to be certain. Mr Stone, Metin muttered to me, could keep the rug since it was his, anyway. Bought for a fair price, grinned Orhan as Phanes started the motor. Revenge on Arsey was all the sweeter for being lucrative. I filed away the snippet of intelligence and joined her in waving farewell to the carpet floggers.

Back in Yialos, it took considerable effort to rouse Timothy and set him in motion. Nikos was on The Giorgios, chatting to Panos but didn't come over to lend a hand. Phanes wasn't too keen on helping out either and disappeared into Yialos. Arsey and I had to monkey walk Timothy plus carpet along the quayside. At The Giorgios mooring, Nikos expressed surprise at seeing us and took over from Arsey. By six thirty, the increasingly hungover Timothy Stone was back in his accommodation. The rug was a beauty. It must have cost him an arm and a leg – or would do when his wife found out.

On the way back to change, I challenged Nikos, who was still sporting his hooky Ray Bans from Nobby.

– You bloody knew we were there, you bastard. Why didn't you come over? And what's with the shades?

Maybe even his liver was no match for a Turkish night at Giannis's place. Come to think of it, though, he was wearing them there, too.

Dinner at Restaurant Tsampikos. My next payslip would be a euro collapse all of its own. The day's escapade to Datça received a generous airing, lubricated by plenty of the house wine. Jess told us about some disgustingly libidinous couple on the walking trip, too old, she judged, to be even capable of sex. I think there was some kicking going on under the table because Jess stopped in mid-sentence to enthuse about the wine. When Clair and Jess reeled off to the ladies, Nikos went for the jugular.

– Come on, Fraser, something is going on between you and Clair, eh?

– In your head. And are your intentions honourable? Or is the stable door hanging off its hinges?

It was beyond even his considerable grasp of English but I skipped explaining it as Jess flopped into the chair beside him, demanding more wine. For odd moments, while Jess and Nikos were distracted, Clair and I exchanged salacious looks that had me shifting in my seat. A surprise revelation of the we'an's was Clair's intimate relationship with the adolescent population of Guildford. Clair was inscrutable. Maybe I misheard.

The evening ended at ten thirty. Tomorrow would be a very long day. Nikos had no such restriction to think of and, after seeing Clair and Jess to the apartment, joined Nobby for a nightcap while I went home to bed. Alone. On the way Theo, manager of the Acropolis Hotel, called with the next episode in the saga of Bald Bastard; what he told me was very interesting. Clair couldn't have known. I considered how much mileage I could extract from it.

CLAIR

Wednesday again – Terrible plus four

We had to be at the ferry by eight. Rising to the rapid bleeping of the travel alarm at half six, Jess and I moved like automatons through showering, dressing and packing last items and found ourselves heavy-hearted and ready absurdly early. The suitcases had been transported by an unfortunate mule the night before so there was only hand luggage to carry down. I pulled the door to for the last time. As we crossed the terrace we saw the little brown lizard sitting on the plastic table, immobile but for his twitching tail. *No doubt hoping the next lot will be less liberal with the insect repellent and not chase off his dinner.* Jess took a last forlorn glimpse through the geraniums.

– 'Bye Aphrodite One.

– Might be back, you never know.

Jess didn't reply. We followed the now familiar pathway, her seventeen-year-old heart and my fifty-year-old one in our respective boots. But as we reached the slope down to the harbour a dark figure approached us and Jess, forgetting her stiff upper lip, cried out. Nikos embraced her, bag and baggage in a convincing show of affection. *Is this a good thing or a bad thing? Is it better for Jess to have a holiday romance and get over it or find the real thing and moon over someone nearly two thousand miles away when she should be working for her A levels?*

Nikos still wore dark glasses. He gave me a hug then shouldered our bags. On the way down to the ferry, holding hands with Jess, he tried to make light conversation. The sea was calm today; it should be a good journey to Rhodes. What time was our flight? What time would we arrive in London? Would it take us long to get home from the airport? Jess was mute with emotion, so I returned the pleasantries. When were his next visitors arriving? Would he be busy for much longer in the season? When did his next university term start? The ferry *Panormitis* was already boarding. I could just see Fraser beyond the bulk of the Witterings and felt a flutter of – something. Jess and Nikos clung. A familiar face and aroma appeared at my side.

– You think you can leave without you give Panos a kiss for goodbye?

The question was rhetorical because Panos, breath and bristles competing for most obnoxious, cupped my face and kissed me firmly on both cheeks then full on the mouth.

– Now you want come back for more Panos kisses, eh? Andio, sweetheart!

And he waved us goodbye passing the Shop of the Sullen Adolescents on the way to his favourite kafeneion. Wiping my mouth, I went ahead and found seats. Jess hung onto Nikos until he gently disengaged her and handed her aboard. She stumbled down the aisle and into the seat next to me, tugging her baseball cap as far over her face as possible. Straining neck tendons confirmed that she was in the emotional pits. There was nothing to do. A touch or a sympathetic word would only make it worse. Knowing it was some hours away from my own significant parting, I was settling back to a last view of the harbour through the salt-flecked window when it struck me. *Where's Howard?*

It was shocking how easily I had erased him from my thoughts, even after Jess's reminder last night. And significant. I couldn't see Fraser on board, so slid round my grieving child and struggled past the oncoming passengers. He was on the dockside, chatting to Nikos. The fat couple stood nearby looking anxiously around. But my attempt to cross the metal gangway was barred by a crew member who stubbornly refused to understand English. I had to yell to attract Fraser's attention. He waved and motioned 'five minutes'. The ship's engine changed tone, throbbing louder, and I could smell the heavy diesel vapour. Panic set in. I had to let him know about Howard. He seemed completely relaxed, so he couldn't be aware. *Or could he? He ticked people off against his list.* The conclusion was inescapable. *Shit! He knows Howard's not here! And he's leaving anyway!* The last passenger was aboard. Fraser clapped Nikos on the arm in casual farewell and hopped onto the gangplank, sidestepping the Wittering Two, who tried to grab his arm. As he boarded, I pounced on him with my deduction. He was irritatingly calm.

– Sure, we can leave him. He's a big boy, now. As I just told Tinky Winky and La La down there.

The engines shifted from throb to roar, drowning the shouts of the Witterings and reducing their angst to comic semaphore. Realising their efforts were futile, they turned on Nikos who responded with an elaborate chicken mime that he kept up, pursued by said Witterings, as far as the pharmacy where he broke into a run. I couldn't help grinning while Fraser hooted with laughter. It shed a different light on him. If Howard was a big boy, Fraser was behaving like a small one. Loath to cause a confrontation during this last precious time, I decided to do a dimitte. Fraser recovered, shaking his head and wiping his face with his palms, assuming a 'straight' mask.

— Sorry about that.

The ferry moved away from the dock.

As Symi slid from view, I envied Fraser. *He'll be back here tonight and I'll be in Aborigine Road.* I felt as though part of me was snagged on the island and I was unravelling inside. Fraser caught my look and swung me round to face him.

— By the way, what's all this Jess says about you 'sorting out' her mates?

— A small but essential service I provide to the deprived adolescents of Guildford.

— Fair enough… In that case, touch me up, doll.

— What? No…

— Why not?

— People might see.

— They won't, go on.

— I am bottling out on the grounds of checking my stricken daughter.

Have I done this to him? Uncovered this outrageous streak? When what I want to say is — what?

Jess was an intractable knot of misery; there was no point in staying with her. I retraced my steps, still perplexed by Fraser's casual attitude to Howard, who was probably scarlet with anger back in Yialos and looking for someone to take it out on. On deck, Fraser was leaning against the rail, hands in pockets, eyes closed, almost smirking. We passed metres from the Turkish coast, no longer lavender hills but light ochre rock plunging into impossibly — *wine dark sea.* Fraser pulled me backward into his arms, singing softly into my hair, 'Ne me quitte pas'. *Don't do this.* But I let him, couldn't do otherwise, and relaxed against this person I did and didn't know, not wanting to leave and knowing I must. After a few minutes gazing at sea and sky, I felt him tense.

— Look – dolphins!

In the middle distance was a pod of half a dozen or so bottlenose dolphins, leaping in shallow arcs, parallel with the ship.

— I should tell Jess!

— No time —

Fraser put fingers to mouth and whistled.

— Jess Harkin! Up at the back!

Jess appeared a few seconds later, panicked that there was a problem.

– See? Dolphins!

Hanging over the rail between Jess and Fraser, I could almost feel her unhappiness lift at the sight of such joyous creatures, a sign, for sure, that we would all be back in Greece together. *Oh yeah? Dream on. Shut up! We will!* Jess was an instant captive of the magic. Long after the pod had skimmed off to charm other romantics she remained by the open doorway recovering her poise and even chatting with a few other young travellers. Fraser wandered dutifully amongst the Aegis passengers, checking that all were confident with the ongoing travel arrangements. In an impossibly short time, we were pulling into Mandraki harbour in Rhodes. Our flight wasn't until four, so there was time to wander around Rhodes Town. Fraser had to go out to the airport to check in passengers on the Manchester flight and promised to give our love to Richard and Mandy. He nodded to a small taverna on the sea front.

– I'll be at yon bar around twelve thirty if you fancy a beer.

Of course we did.

I wondered about ringing Maggie, but with the two-hour time difference it might still be a bit early, so Jess and I headed for the Castle of the Knights of St John to soak up a bit of history. We took a couple of photographs of the cannons and stone cannon balls but ducked a visit to the museum. The day's heat was intense and we didn't want to miss a moment of it. Emerging into the light, we headed into the old town for a nose round. But already, practically, bravely, we were talking about home, work and school. Jess suddenly realised that Howard hadn't been on the ferry. I shrugged, told her neither Fraser nor I was bothered.

– Dimitte diem.

– Dimitte ditto!

Her mood lightened even more. I suspected she'd heard about his indiscretion with Yo. *She must have.*

More shops, more temptation and barely any funds. Jess stopped outside a henna tattoo booth.

– Oh, come on, Mum! It'd be really cool!

Why not? Thirty minutes later we emerged into the sunlight, a leaping dolphin on my left arm, Jess with an octopus on hers – the result of long deliberation during which I nearly gave up and walked out. I looked at the dark blue design with some disbelief. We both took care not to brush against anything as if we'd had painful injections.

I found a booth to ring Maggie and squandered a few euros rather than buying a phone card that I wouldn't be able to use again. I got through but only to that irritating "The person at the other end knows you're waiting". My money ran out before Maggie came on the line. It was nearly twelve thirty so we went on to the bar. I would call from the airport. Fraser whistled at our body art. I assured him they'd wear off in a couple of weeks.

– That's what they tell you in the booth. Sometimes it's six months.

He and Jess enjoyed my gullible horror. He ordered the beers.

– I like to stand my round in the taverna.

He caught my eye. We clinked bottles and drank.

Richard had been checked over at the hospital had his arm X-rayed and set. He and Mandy were safely on the Manchester flight with Richard transported, protesting, in a wheelchair and on a hydraulic lift to the plane. At one fifteen, Fraser excused himself to greet the incoming flight. Another hitch added to the knot in my stomach. He cuffed Jess's chin and touched my hand.

– See you there, you tattooed hoi polloi.

I watched his sun-bright figure disappear down the quayside and into the town. By the time we finished our beers it was time to catch the airport coach. We Harkins were silent on the journey, taking in the last of Greece for a while. From the check-in queue I looked for Fraser then suddenly remembered Howard, but there was no sign of either. He really must have been left behind. I did, however, spot Arsey Purple in the line and received a look to poison the Aegean. I flashed back a smile that was intercepted by her tiny spouse who stood behind, a rolled rug resting on his suitcase. He beamed amiably, probably for the first time since Datça. We all shuffled forward, trolleys bumping into heels; sly fellow passengers shoving their cases ahead round the outside. This really was it. Despite the four-hour flight to come, this was down to earth again. Why did holidays always have to end so drearily? Was airport trauma deliberate schlock therapy to prepare us for the return to Britain? Just as we reached the desk, I spotted Fraser talking to a blonde, tanned woman dressed in a rep's uniform of shirt and pencil skirt. *It's his ex, Mel.* Their body language told tales on them. Insecurity added another granny knot to my intestines. *Perhaps they'll get back together, once I've gone. Perhaps I have been just a* – I felt a sharp nudge. It was our turn.

Once we'd checked in, I loitered, riffling through contents of hand luggage, reading boarding passes, repositioning straps, refastening buckles. Jess was impatient.

– Come on, Mum, or we won't get a seat in Departures! You can ring Maggie from there.

I dithered, mumbled and excused, then finally moved slowly towards Passport Control. He wasn't going to say goodbye. But just as I held out my passport, I heard his voice, breathless –

– Sorry, sorry – a coach broke down and I was sorting out another one.

Mel run a coach company, does she? All three of us stood awkwardly. He was almost shy.

– Look… you've been great to have around, the two of you. I'll miss you.

He kissed Jess on both cheeks, then me, but squeezed my arms tightly as he did.

– Love you, doll.

It was brief, murmured. Jess couldn't have heard. He stood back.

– I've got to go. Let's keep in touch.

He blew another kiss to us and left quickly. *Love you, doll?* As I craned to watch him disappearing through the holiday crowds, I saw Howard join the check-in queue.

FRASER

Early morning and the ferry Panormitis was about to sail. Nikos, still wearing the dodgy Ray Bans, had roused himself to see the we'an off. Tearful parting achieved, she disappeared into the bowels of the ship. I was left on the dock with Nikos (who was in on the Bunce stunt I'd planned), Mixailis leaning on his three-wheeler, and the Witterings – wittering. Bald Bastard nowhere to be seen. Unless, of course one had incredibly good eyesight and could spot whichever dive on Rhodes he was wallowing in – because he'd taken the hydrofoil south two nights ago. The Witterings, for once not in possession of crucial information, flapped with curiosity. And, by the way she was hanging over the side flailing her arms at me, it was obvious that Clair still didn't know. Decided to let them all steam for a while. I mimed 'five minutes' to her and turned my back on Ferry Panormitis, raising my voice to Nikos for the benefit of the stressed Witterings.

–… so I've given the problem over to Interpol. They're currently scouring the Aegean for him.

The Witterings were agog.

– Is this Howard – Mr Bunce you're talking about? Is he in trouble with Interpol?

The truth was this: Theo, assistant manager up at the Acropolis, never one to miss an opportunity, suggested to Bunce that he might be happier in a boutique hotel on Rhodes that happened to be run by a distant cousin of his. Bunce took the next hydrofoil. Result all round with profit for said distant cousin, commission for Theo plus a sizeable tip, no doubt, from Bald Bastard. Hence he wasn't there to miss the ferry on account of living it up in the fleshpots of Rhodes. At great expense of every kind I hoped.

One of the Panormitis crew swore at me amiably from the gang. It was time to go. I made my escape, leaving Nikos with the Witterings who tried to grab me with one last witter. On board, Clair collared me.

– Where's Howard? He's not on board – you can't leave him behind!

Back on the dock, Nikos was doing his 'me no spik English' performance. Even Clair cracked her face. It was hilarious beyond words. Managed to calm down a bit. And saw Clair looking sad. Call me unprofessional, but I had to kiss the woman. So I did. Then remembered what Jess had said last night, about sorting out her wee friends. To be honest, I couldn't tell whether it was true or not, this amazing female was so full of surprises. She escaped off to the lounge to comfort said daughter who was in an advanced state of post-Nikos blues.

When she came back out, I decided to make the most of the last few hours, went for a clinch and a long cuddle. Got over romantic, possibly. Saw a pod of dolphins and dragged the we'an out. Soon as she saw them, complete transformation. They have that effect on most people, even lovesick bimbettes. The three of us stood at the rail watching until Flipper and Co got bored of the Panormitis and veered off southwest, towards Halki. Decided I'd better be a bit professional and share myself with a few others of the Aegis crowd.

Once we docked at Rhodes I went into blue arsed fly mode. I hated Wednesdays. This one more than most, I realised. Clair and Jess had a daunder around the old town and I promised to get back in time to have a beer. When I met them later, they'd both had henna tattoos. Ach well, better now they were on their way home. Updated on Richard and foxy wife. Ordered a round of Mythos for the benefit of Clair. Got a jokey reaction from her. Bless. Half an hour then I had to get back to meet the incoming planeload. As I walked to the taxi rank, my knees turned to custard. Perhaps it was the thought of incinerating half the week after next's wages on taxis to and from the airport – and all for a bird.

That's where Mel and I met, at the airport, that's how it started; she has great legs and caught me giving them the once over. She'd managed to miss the transfer last week but I doubted she'd be able to swing it twice? The answer was, 'no'. Fortunately, she'd decided to maintain a distance and just not see me. All went well until about an hour before the Gatwick flight. I heard this voice behind me.

– Hi, Fry-zuh. Um – I've got a bit of a problem.

My balls froze – she's pregnant.

– How can I help?

– One of my coaches has broken down. I wondered if you could persuade one of your drivers to take my party down to Lindos? After you've taken yours to Mandraki?

Believe me, I was so relieved I could have kissed her.

– Sure. I'll see what I can do.

It took several phone calls, a little shuffling and some fairly significant sweeteners but the deal was done. I pushed it through as fast as I could. Clair would be at the airport by now and checking in. I didn't want to miss her. I was only just in time – she was going through passport control. She and Jess looked as miserable as kids being evacuated. I tried explaining – needlessly. Whole pile of shite came out my gob. Gave them both a wee hug. Slightly bigger hug for the lady and – I heard myself saying it… 'Love you, doll'. ?????? Legged it before I made a total knobhead of myself.

CHAPTER THIRTEEN

CLAIR

Flash forward – Terrible plus nine months

As the plane took off from Heathrow, I remembered I'd left my American Express Platinum Card and spare glasses on the dressing table – then had a blissful dimitte diem moment. *Can't do anything about it, so let it go.* Why couldn't I be more laid back all the time? Maybe I would be, now. There was only one more ordeal, really. Meeting Fraser again. A lurch there. Pit of stomach or loins? Those few centimetres make all the difference. Either way, definitely a hurdle. More. I felt the angst of a teenager.

It was May and I was on my way to Samos, under a year beyond Terrible. The Fraser problem aside, everything was working its way from Terrible to Satisfactory. That's rather too glib. Life had gone from Terrible to more Terrible, then less, then more… Our arrival back from Symi last August was definitely more –

STILL CLAIR

Back to Terrible plus four. Guildford. Very late.

Midnight, in fact. All the lights were on and loud rock music strafed us from the back garden. We dumped cases in the hall and went straight through the catastrophe that used to be our kitchen. A burst of whooping and yelping came from the garden followed by furious knocking at the front door. It was my next-door neighbour, Brenda. Despite travel weariness and trauma, I got the first word in.

– Brenda, we've just got back from the airport. I'm dealing with it.

– Only this noise has been going on all the time you were away and you know Gabriel has ADHD, he's very easily –

Brenda was determined to deliver her prepared speech. I endured it then despatched her back to her well of self-pity in roughly the same time it took Jess to get her own message across to the revellers in the garden. The decibels collapsed leaving my ears in shock. Case bounced into the hall.

– Yo, Clair! You look just so – fan–tast–ique!

He knew he was up to his ears in it. I was immune to the charm. He and his eleven party guests wrapped the evening. Then Jess and I fell unwashed into our unmade beds of two weeks since. I lay awake for the mandatory hours, then –

Fraser laughed at me as I tried to start the motor scooter. He was moving further and further away in the 4x4 and I couldn't see who was in the seat beside him. The harder I tried to start the scooter, the more it slipped down the dusty hillside. The poet's hut was at the bottom and, eventually, I ended up next to it. So I knocked and knocked on the door, but I still couldn't make Daddy hear me. In the end Jess, four years old, tugged my hand and started crying so I had to take her home.

I woke in my own bed in Guildford staring at the pile of boxes on top of the wardrobe. *Why couldn't I hang on to Symi a bit longer?*

STILL CLAIR

Terrible plus five

It took a while to bend my mind around to the day and situation I faced. Depressingly, flecks of white skin were lifting from my tanned arms, despite slathering on lotion to counteract the drying effect of air travel. By dint of angling cabinet mirror to wall mirror I saw for the first time the damage to my back. It was a mess of shiny pink skin where the blisters had been and blotchy brown where they hadn't. *I'll never wear a backless ball gown again.* I showered, carefully avoiding the little dolphin tattoo, put on an office shirt and second-best jeans then dialled Maggie's number from the bedroom. It was engaged. I hadn't managed to get through at all on the way back from Symi. I was worried that she would be worried. *Don't be stupid, Maggie's far cooler than that.*

I gave Case as much time as possible to clear the kitchen before I went downstairs. Two weeks' post, including what were clearly birthday cards, junk mail and bills, lay heaped to the side of the front door. I scooped up a few brochures and flyers, dumping them on the hall table where they sloped off floorward towards last night's abandoned luggage. I riffled through them for the one with US stamps. Yep. From Connie. A drugstore birthday card. Not mentioning my milestone age – thank you for that, Mum – a brief inscription 'love Mom & Joe' and a cheque. Very modest and in dollars. Simultaneously, the morning post arrived. A credit card bill, an offer for a new credit card, leaflets for take away pizza, water softeners, house insurance – and Saga Magazine. Addressed to me. Unsolicited by me. I slung it the length of the hall.

The kitchen could not be put off any longer. The kitchen door, I noticed for the millionth time, needed stripping and repainting. Above the Gothic sized keyhole, was a genuine Bakelite handle. I turned it, foreboding welling in my stomach. A small step for me – and a giant setback for Case's future as a lodger.

Nothing had been done since last night, nothing since we'd gone on holiday by the look of it. A tower of crockery and pans tottered in the sink. Laden ashtrays, empty beer cans, dirty glasses and the remains of an ageing pizza littered the table. The back door was open, which meant it probably had been all night. The swing bin disgorged organic and inorganic rubbish and my soles made schlocking sounds on the filthy floor. In the garden were more beer cans, alcopop and vodka bottles, here a half glass of wine with several dead wasps in it, there a – *no, please…!* A swarm of cigarette butts and roach ends infested the lawn. And from the dustbin came a gut-churning smell that told me it hadn't been put out for collection all fortnight. Hadn't Phee been around? Surely, she was more responsible than this? Then I remembered that Phee was away Morris dancing on Teesside. A sound came from behind me. It was Jess, clutching her old pink dressing gown round her, swollen eyes surveying the squalor. And the sound she made was:

– Shit.

She agreed grudgingly to help with clearing up when she was dressed but miscalculated the size of the task and arrived downstairs with plenty still to do. The squalid business of filling bin bags – some for recycling, others so putrid they needed a second skin – drew a line under the holiday. Life had gone on without us in Guildford.

Jess, terrifyingly out of practice, drove us to the dump. I wondered if Case would cut his losses and just not come back so I was surprised, on our miraculously unscathed return, to see him doing a workout in the garden. His radar vis à vis avoiding domestic labour was obviously keener than Jess's. He beamed at us.

– Ladies! You sho' is lookin' gar – juss!

I let Jess take over. For once, she wasn't going to take his part. It was payback time.

– Cut the crap, Case! We've been clearing up your shit all morning. Great welcome back from a holiday!

He looked genuinely hurt and dropped the lingo.

– What's up, Jess? The place looks great.

I left the two of them to slug it out. Jess could say the things I wanted to say but felt, as a landlady, were too close to personal insult. Case huffed to the far end of the garden, turned and ranted, hung his head and even, at one point, forced a few tears. Good training for an actor – the little opportunist. But Jess was unmoved and managed to crack his denial. He sidled in shamefaced and apologised. There was, however, no mention of the rent. When I brought it up, he faltered a little. It was just an oversight; he'd give me a cheque that very afternoon. No, interrupted Jess, this time it would be cash and, if anything like this ever happened again, he would also pay the deposit that was originally waived on account of him being a penniless drama student. The conversation was taking a perilous turn for Case. Forgetting his training, he neglected to breathe and in a high-pitched voice offered his gold choker as surety. There was a silence. Case's choker was more than cash equivalent; it was his talisman, his guardian and, of course, his status. Case without his choker was like Roman Abramovich taking the bus, unthinkable. The three of us meditated on the awesome nature of the proposition. Clearly the gesture was symbolic, a metaphor for his integrity. So I was startled when Jess said:

– Cool.

… and held out her hand. In a daze, Case surrendered his joy and Jess fastened it around her own neck. He closed his eyes, breathed hard and spun out of the room. She shrugged at me and sauntered off, fingering the gold. I had a brief mental picture of it as a python, strangling her.

Once victor and vanquished had parted, I tried Maggie's number again, but it was still engaged. Disappointed, I tried Sonya's office but she'd stayed on in LA an extra couple of days and wouldn't be in until Monday. *Atta girl, Sonn.* Nonetheless, postponing the gratification of discussing a conquest with my best friend was frustrating. The day remained resolutely at the bottom of the hill. I unpacked a few things, loaded the washing machine and sat down to the bills. Raz rang the landline a couple of times, but Jess wasn't within calling distance or, if she was, chose not to hear. Was everything all right, he asked?

– She lost her mobile in Greece, Raz. Everything's fine, though.

I lied knowing the poor sod had a hard time coming,

– We had a great holiday. How was Mexico?

– Really cool.

Trauma between Jess and Raz was inevitable. If Jess, fuelled by heartache for Nikos, could be hard on Case, why not on Raz? Despite my counsel? I went back to the bills. There would be precious little left in the current account after this lot. It was time to sort next week's work. Before I'd left for Symi, it was fairly certain that the software company would have me back at the end of the holiday – *unless the replacement temp is twenty-three with huge norks.* My call to the employment agency was inconclusive; they would check and call me back.

MAGGIE

Wednesday 8th August

I put the phone down with some frustration. It was very kind of everyone to ring, but I really wanted to speak to Clair this morning. I dialled Guildford and got the answer phone.

– Hello, darlings, it's your mad auld aunt from the frozen North. Jack and Tatty and I say 'welcome home' and send all our love. Hope you had a good journey home. Speak to you soon.

I opened the blue box. On top was a photo of Clair in summer dress and Clarks buckle shoes sitting with Julia on that monster of a sofa, both grinning up at the photographer, me. I didn't remember taking that one, particularly, but it must have been me. I had a flash of recall. Thirleby Road.

<O>

– I met Maggie before you did!

Julia taunts Clair, Clair huffs back:

– She was my aunty before she was your friend!

Not strictly accurate, by some hours. More arguing, then, despite the age gap, pokings of tongues and chasings up and down the hall, in and out of the five rooms, me pelting them with cushions as they pass. It ends in a shrieking tickle fight on the sofa with Julia rolling onto the floor in fake submission. Later, Clair, lolling in the armchair sips a glass of Tizer, face pink and eyes sparkling, feet sticking straight out from the seat. I lie on the hearthrug, drinking coffee and smoking, flicking ash into the alabaster ashtray. Julia sits, trousered and typically cross-legged, chattering non-stop, pinning her hair up into a lopsided chignon, invariably missing the ashtray and letting her coffee go cold.

<O>

CLAIR

Terribly far away

I checked the distance to Symi on Google; Fraser was approximately seventeen hundred miles away. And a cigarette was not the answer. Strange how the – *Fling? Affair? One-afternoon stand?* – had eased the withdrawal from nicotine on Symi. *Vanity – I didn't want to taste like the sixth of November.* I felt trapped by the house, had to get out. What to do? Food shopping, for one. How about the photos? *That would be novel, getting the photos printed within six months of the holiday.* (I had not progressed to a colour printer.) I ransacked my old shoulder bag of holiday ephemera; a couple of bills for cotton tops, a few more for soap, sponges and loofahs, flyers for a few bars and tavernas, the last being Nobby's. *Thank you for that.* The camera was at the bottom. To cheer myself up, I unearthed my new bag from a suitcase and shouldered it, admiring its diagonal hang as I passed the hall mirror.

I circled the supermarket car park to the point of distraction before queue jumping into a space. Wanting to relive Symi as soon as possible I chose the one-hour, top price option when I dropped in the memory card. As usual, I had neither shopping list nor any aptitude for prioritising and fought the dysfunctional trolley up and down the aisles, slinging random goods in until my photos would be ready and I could bulldoze my way to the check out. The conveyor belt was laden with my purchases when I recognised what that dragging feeling meant. *Oh Misery! You have taken me from Symi, away from a blissful union and back to domestic squalor, static supermarket queues and… oncoming menstruation.* Welcome in one way, I suppose. But at fifty! A reluctant young male assistant was dispatched for sanitary towels and tampons.

The bill seemed reasonable until I remembered it was in pounds; it would have to go on plastic. Times are hairy when you have to put the food shopping on credit. The photos came in a glossy folder, making my heart lift and putting extra stress on the card. I slipped them into the purple bag and manhandled the trolley to the car. There was a sharp screech of brakes and a blast of horn. I leapt out of the way, as a white BMW sped towards the exit.

– Did you see that?!

I yelled to anyone who'd listen. The frustration, exhilaration and passion of the last two weeks swirled into a vortex of fury. I ran at the car, calling to a startled employee corralling shopping trolleys.

– That car just tried to run me down, get the number! Get the number!

– Now, now, madam, you're blocking the road.

I lurched to where the white BMW was queuing to exit and banged on the driver's window.

– How dare you drive at me, pedestrians have the right of way, you know!

The driver, heavily made up, with short, lacquered hair, large gold ear studs and letterbox narrow designer glasses, opened the window an inch.

– You need help. It's a very difficult time, the menopause.

About to respond, I saw the driver's face close up. What at first glance had seemed to be a woman of late middle age was undoubtedly a man, a transvestite.

– At least I've got the equipment for it!

Even though I yelled it at the departing car, I impressed myself with the relatively instant comeback.

I was back by three and staunching the bloody flow, but only after it had seeped through the second-best jeans. Sloughing them, I changed into an old black skirt. Jess's music throbbed across the landing. I yelled at her to come and unpack the rest of her suitcase. No response. In the kitchen I dumped knickers and jeans in cold water and yelled at Jess again to help put away the groceries. The phone interrupted. I hoped it was Maggie. It was Connie.

— Joe's had another attack. He's real bad. You better get over here.

CHAPTER FOURTEEN

MAGGIE

Thursday 9th August

Isobel Mudie was sipping tea at the croft when Clair rang with the news of Joe; she excused herself discreetly 'to the cloakroom' while I was speaking but I could see her feet silhouetted in the gap under the parlour door. As the conversation seemed to be closing, she skipped to the loo and flushed it, re-entering the room as I was saying goodbye.

– Everything all right, Margaret?

– Fine thanks, Isobel. My niece, Clair, inviting me to stay. I'll go down tomorrow.

Isobel's too-innocent eyes opened wider.

– Indeed?

From what she must have overheard, her mental cogs would be grinding to the conclusion that I was not being entirely frank. Archie probably had many phone conversations that were not what they seemed. She'd had plenty of practice at letting it wash over. But Nessie Scrymgeour would, I predicted, have plenty to say to Wally as they drove away from Harkin Croft that night – along the lines of 'That's the Harkin family for you, headstrong. And what comes of living alone, too; set ideas, no matter what sense other folk talk'. Wally would have stared hard at the road, knowing better than to respond.

FRASER

The welcome meeting next day on The Giorgios was a giant pill. Not as awkward as the one with Bald Bastard the week before. But the hecklers from West Wittering turned up, even though they had already been on the island for a week. I knew I'd have no peace until I put their obsessive minds at rest about Bunce's whereabouts, which I did. Even so, as I described the trips they commented loudly on their value for money and entertainment as if I wasn't there. They even stole my punch line about the old lady and her herbs on the Kali Strata. Panos came to my rescue, standing behind them and making a strangling action. The punters who saw it applauded, having been equally pissed off with the constant interruptions. The Weebles joined in with the laughter, unaware that they were the butt of the joke. Managed to keep a straight face; openly ridiculing a customer is unprofessional, even if they deserved garrotting.

Back at the office, I finished the paperwork, counted the euros and banked them. It was about one. It would be eleven in England. She'd probably just be waking. Would she think of me? 'Course she would. I was thinking of her, wasn't I? But 'Love you, doll' – where had that come from? Unless I really was – no – unthinkable. Nobby launched into a Bob Marley remix as I entered, managing a slight shimmy of his considerable paunch.

– Nah wooman, nah croy-ah! Nah wooman, nah croy.

– Stuck yer dick in the mangle, Nobby?

Nikos had taken his shades off, forgetting perhaps that they were there to hide a shiner. Even in the grimy light of Nobby's I could see it was a beauty. Nobby saw me looking.

– Caught Phanes with 'is Lady Lurve. Shame he ent got Phanes's aim.

Nikos gave Nobby a look dark as his contusion.

– He was bothering Jess. You should not allow him in here.

He glowered at Phanes who sat at the other end of the bar, already over the Dreadlock Oz bird and Jess and making moon-eyes at a young Swedish tourist. She was sitting with her parents who showed remarkable tolerance and liberality towards her sexual development. Just then, Phanes disappeared to the gents. Nikos slid along the bar intent on the Nordic beauty but was halted by a squirt of soda, ministered by Nobby.

– Yer kin zip yer ego back in yer pants! Not 'avin' my bar trashed in a totty contest!

Then our venerable host produced an old guitar from somewhere whereupon I improvised so repetitively round the theme of departed women it was taken off me again. Sadly, Nikos and I failed to drink ourselves into oblivion that evening. Neither of us mentioned the Harkin women again. Well not that night.

CLAIR

Friday – Terrible plus six

After finding a flight on the internet, frenzied packing and another sleep-free night, I parted from Jess early and took the Gatwick Express. This time I was bound for Fort Myers, Florida, via Philadelphia – a journey time of some thirteen hours, then another forty minutes south to Naples, where my mother and Joe lived. I sank heavily into the scratchy train seat, every minute taking me further from Symi and Fraser. How different from the excited journey of just over two weeks ago when Jess and I bobbed, helium filled, against the carriage roof. I touched the plum-coloured bag, evidence that Symi was all real. In it were my vitamins and herbal supplements, replenished by Jess. I imagined scenes of search and interrogation at US customs. "Clair Constance Harkin, I am arresting you for the illegal possession of Wild Yam Root. You have the right to remain silent, but..." Snap, click! On would go the handcuffs.

Only a month since, Maggie's cheque had arrived and made the dream of Symi come true. Now, I was in a different, heart-sinking reality. Not only that but lurching into debt again, even though Connie would cover this fare. Without Jess around to make me put on a brave face I sank into desolation. At least I'd managed to contact Maggie before the mad dash. She would come down to be with Jess while I was away. I knew that one would look after the other.

The doors were open at Gatwick when I woke and already closing as I blundered through clunking the wheelie suitcase. As the train pulled out, I checked my belongings frantically. They were all there: suitcase, shoulder bag, passport and wallet. And in my best jeans pocket a badge saying 'Blessed are the cracked, for they let in the light', a gift from Jess. While my heartbeat evened out, I pinned it to my shirt. I had to find a loo, and soon; the first twenty-four hours were always the worst. I needed paracetamol, too.

Airports had certainly pulled their socks up security-wise since 9/11. It was a three-hour check-in and a mile-long queue. I cursed my stupidity for wearing jeans. It always meant getting stopped and searched. Still, at least on this side of the pond you could enjoy the odd quip with security staff. The 'Blessed are the Cracked' badge set off the alarm. The young woman who body searched me was jovial.

– Good motto, that. Maybe not for an airline, though!

Another cheery young woman riffled through the still-damp clothing in my case.

– Leave in a hurry, did we, madam?

I had 'The Amber Spyglass' with me and only two chapters to go. I bought an airport dreadful and caught sight of a Berlitz Guide to the Greek Islands. *Stop it! Right now!*

I have always been absurdly excited by flying, whatever the circumstances. Even the purpose of this journey plus the period from hell and the cramped aircraft toilet couldn't take the edge off. I dotted between the choice of movies, flight information and snatches of the chunk of fiction from Gatwick, unable to settle to anything. The flight curved over the North Atlantic and followed the eastern seaboard, tracing the coastline of Long Island. New York was actually recognisable from the air. I couldn't see any distinguishable man-made landmark, but that hazy metropolis could be nowhere else. Shortly after cutting inland we were descending for Philadelphia.

Because it was first point of disembarkation in the States, I had to collect my suitcase and go through Immigration and Customs. Connie had once suggested the US status of 'sponsored family preference' for me after she married Joe. It would have made me a legal alien and my travel a lot easier, even if I didn't want to live in Florida. But because I didn't jump at the chance she took umbrage and never offered again. It was a source of great frustration to Jess that we always entered the States as a potential foreign menace. The officials in Immigration did their best to make my nineteenth or twentieth entry to the States disagreeable as usual. I knew of old not to react, one step out of line and you were on the next plane home. I submitted to their questions, their sidelong looks at my appearance and their backs, turned in order to confer on me. And then the bag search. *Must buy a floral frock and an Alice band for going home – in black if Joe doesn't improve. That's ghoulish. Still, Connie's probably chosen the funeral canapés by now.* By the time Customs and Immigration had finished with me, the four-hour wait had been reduced to under one and a half.

Despite the dreariness of the airport lounge, it was a buffer zone. I could go to the bar and pretend I was someone else on a completely different mission. First, I rang Connie to check on Joe and give a journey update. Antonia, Mum's housekeeper – 'maid' in Naples parlance – greeted me with such warmth I felt hugged.

– Your Mommy's at the hospital, Mr Dubrowsky has made a slight improvement. Don't you worry, now, Clair. Ain't nothing gonna happen 'fore you get here.

I told her I was looking forward to seeing her. In the rest room I sorted myself out: jacket off, hair damped, tumbled and re-clipped, mascara scraped from under eyes and reapplied to lashes, lipstick on, shirt bloused and collar up, 'Blessed are the Cracked' badge back in pocket. Then I headed for alcohol. It was four hours since the last paracetamol so there shouldn't be any risk of a clash. *Wonder can Sonya sense I'm on the same continent? And can Fraser imagine how far away I am? And how I feel?*

I reached the bar. *Perch on a bar stool or hide in a booth?* I opted for perching. No one, but no one could ever mistake me for a hooker, not in my state, although I did sport, I fancied, an arty charm. A barmaid wearing a tooth brace took my order straight away. One thing I like about American bars is the service. I ordered a large Jack Daniels, most unladylike, and watched with pleasure as it arrived, sock-full of ice, with a swirler and a dinky little paper mat. And you didn't even have to pay up front! Dangerous. Not that dangerous, though. I kept a fluctuating stash of dollars at home that diminished at times of domestic crisis when I took George Washington for a trip to the nearest Bureau de Change. Today, I had about twenty in my purse – or bankbook, given my current location. 'The Amber Spyglass' rested on the bar next to the bourbon, last two chapters unread, still. Knowing how distraught Jess was at the ending, I'd decided today was not the best day to read it. The airport dreadful, some female coming of age tract, remained untouched, hidden discreetly beneath the Pullman. I took my first sip.

   – Ma'am, I hope you wouldn't think I was being too forward if I offered to buy you another of those?

How long is it since I heard a question like that? Am I suddenly more attractive because I've had a shag? Still, who's arguing? I swung the stool around, preparing a jokey put down. It wasn't needed. The paunchy businessman on the next stool was talking to a woman on his other side. She was in her early thirties, perhaps, skimpily dressed with orange tan, stringy hair, drooping breasts and thighs pockled with cellulite. *How can I compete with that?* I moved to a booth and decided to tackle the last two chapters of 'The Amber Spyglass'. Consequently, after a classic dilemma of duty versus love, I answered the flight call choking back the tears. *Bugger! Bugger, bugger, bugger!*

As the plane skirted the Carolinas and Georgia I tried to immerse myself in the new book. But my concentration threshold was as low as the plane was high. After midnight, British time, we crossed the east coast of Florida heading southwest. I gave in and adjusted my watch to the five-hour time difference. The onward journey was smooth. Connie and Joe had an account with a car hire company so there was an air-conditioned limo to meet me at Fort Myers. It was dark by the time I reached the wealthy haven of Naples. I was rigid with the familiar tension as the electric gates opened. Would my mother be acid, aloof or neutral? I decided to set the terms of engagement. As the limo pulled up, Connie's squarish silhouette at the open front door gave nothing away. Dropping my hand luggage on the top step, I took Connie's face in my hands and kissed her cheek, then put my arms around her in a close embrace.

   – Hello, Mum.

Connie endured the contact, motionless in the thick, balmy air.

   – So, Jess couldn't make it?

MAGGIE

Friday 10th August

   The Scrymgeours drove me down to Glasgow. Nessie wouldn't pass up the chance of a free keek at the shops. To her, Buchanan Street was the height of sophistication and Sauchiehall Street the depth of worldliness; wild horses wouldn't keep her away. No sooner had my train pulled out than Nessie would drag Wally off for a day of unbridled window-shopping.

I gazed through the train window until well after Cambuslang trying to take my mind off leaving the dogs, though I knew the Scrymgeours would take good care of them. But though the jumble of city, suburbs and industry absorbed me, it reminded me that I spent my life in a rarefied atmosphere, cushioned by greenery, sea and gentle, if idiosyncratic, manners. Was I missing out by shunning urban dwelling? It wasn't all pollution and mugging. When, for God's sake, had I last been to a restaurant or to the theatre? I felt uncomfortable, guilty, for abandoning the vivid and sometimes darker colours of life. Julia would be appalled. But Julia wasn't with me to criticise or argue, to scold or ignore, not with me to listen to an amusing titbit on the radio or in the paper, to talk over the day's trivia, to share a cigarette or a Crunchie bar or a kiss. And she hadn't been there to soften the reminder of mortality delivered by the recent incident in Oban, nor to give me a cuddle and say "Don't worry, Margi, I'll look after you". She was in my heart and mind all the time. Not the same, though.

I wondered whether I should defy Dr Sharma and have a snifter but erred uncharacteristically on the side of caution and instead went to the buffet car for lunch. We arrived in London on time and a young woman with a child helped me with my case. Jess was not there to meet me as promised. She'd probably gone to the wrong station. Time would tell. I didn't panic. I had my mobile phone with me but it was packed in the case. Clair and Jess would fizz with exasperation.

Sitting there on my suitcase, I felt like a parcel with no address on it. After a while, I decided to treat location, opinion and medical advice with the contempt they deserved and knocked back a slug of Whyte and Mackay from my hip flask. As if conjured up by the distillery fairy, Jess dashed past and then back in the opposite direction. I waved and called, but her frenetic rush was completely without focus. Just like her mother. There was a young Asian man at my side in a white kurta and trousers.

– Excuse me, would you be kind enough to tell that young woman in jeans and a pale blue top that her aunt is sitting here?

I smiled my kindly old lady smile. He smiled back and said, "My pleasure, madam," and set off in Jess's direction. He belonged to a culture of respect for the elderly. And I was, devastating to admit, elderly. Jess was tumultuous in greeting and apology.

Emerging from the taxi at Waterloo, I was quite dizzy with Symi and grateful that the Guildford train was due to leave in seven minutes. As we pulled out, Jess was still brimming with tales of the Aegean. I struggled to maintain interest.

– So when will Nikos qualify?

– Oh, he still has two years to go, but part of that is a sort of work experience thingy so he'll actually be attached to a firm of architects. After that, he can work anywhere in Europe – the world! I think architecture's fantastic – it's really interesting, you know – and with Nikos being Greek, well, it's in his blood.

She shrugged with worldly acceptance. I nodded back.

– Indeed.

On the Guildford train she let slip that Hubert, or whatever his name was, had turned up on Symi and spoiled the end of the holiday for Clair. It accounted for the phone call on her birthday. Bloody pest! Not good enough to take out Clair's rubbish. Jess made me promise not to tell Clair that I knew and I gave my word. Shame I didn't have his telephone number, though.

Safe in Guildford, Jess brought me up a rather average cup of tea and a glass of water at nine o'clock and kissed me goodnight. It was very early for me to go to bed. Jess was disappointed because she'd made us a cheese and walnut salad for dinner but I could manage only toast and tea. Perhaps this mini-stroke business had had more of an effect than I would admit.

CLAIR

Terrible plus seven

I slept straight through till one on Saturday morning then dipped in and out of the usual scenarios. Waking fully, I was disoriented, but the hum of the air conditioning brought me to. It was just after seven. My travel gear was flung across an armchair and the rest of my stuff scrambled from the suitcase. Best not to let Connie see that. *Sod it! I've just made a sixteen-hour journey at a minute's notice and I have jet lag.* But after five uncomfortable minutes, I dragged myself out of bed with the intention of tidying. I was in the second guest room; curtains in heavy cream and coral striped brocade matched the deep pile ecru carpet and toning furniture while lilies and blush roses in a vase on the dressing table gave off sweet and musky scents. It was modest by Floridian standards, palatial by mine. Beside me lay the remote control for the TV. I love surfing American telly – the sheer choice as over-abundant as everything else; one channel showing back to back 'Murder She Wrote', another almost seamless episodes of 'The Simpsons' – and a classic film channel where you could watch 'All About Eve' at three in the morning or 'Citizen Kane' over brunch. World news was a problem, though. By doing complicated things with the satellite control you could get both Fox and CNN news, who gave varying versions of national events. Otherwise, there was only a bunch of local stations featuring identical female presenters with improbable hair and little power suits, who brandished microphones at neighbourhood disputes or gabbled the latest highway news. I never could find BBC World Service TV.

America certainly wins the gold for showers. Water froths from showerheads, pummelling and caressing by turn. In my mother's house, the guest en suites are always stocked with marvellous, fruity scented gels, shampoos and lotions. So, after a little television indulgence, I retired to shower for a full fifteen minutes. Swathed in peach coloured towels I padded back through to the bedroom to the fitted, mirrored wardrobe. Inside were clothes from trips dating back twenty-five years to soon after my Grandma Emily died. Neat plaid skirts and lacy blouses, t-shirts appliquéd with flowers and cutesy figures, dozens of day and evening dresses, several jackets in pastel shades and a collection of shorts and tailored trousers – all bought by Connie to render her daughter and granddaughter more presentable to Naples society. I wore them under sufferance, it being easier in the long run to do what Connie wanted. There was the yellow dress from the last trip that I wore to the Water Carnival. I hoped it would induce a better mood in my mother than last night. Then I remembered the dolphin tattoo. Sleeves would be a good idea. I put on a pale blue linen button-down dress (bought for neighbour Irma's Theater Benefit) and fastened the matching low-heeled sandals that my mother had insisted on. It was after eight. She would be at breakfast. I pulled the bed straight, towelled my hair a little and went through to the Florida Room.

Connie sat reading the Naples Voice, a half-eaten pancake at her elbow. The television was on, featuring the usual news bimbo with unnatural hair, power suit and minor issue.

– So you're up. Sleep?

– Thanks.

Outside the Florida room, expensive velvet green turf stretched across the back yard. Not for Connie the coarse goose grass of her neighbours. At Connie's the scene never alters. Sprinklers play in the thick heat amidst palms, hibiscus and bird of paradise flowers that flank a lawn stretching some twenty yards down to the pool, jacuzzi and gazebo. Connie and Joe retained a gardening company rather than a gardener. Most of the employees were Hispanic so, because neither Joe nor Connie knew any Spanish, instructions were given by phone to the company's office or via Antonia. It was the same with pool maintenance. There was a guy down there now, clad in blue overalls and baseball cap, fishing about with a large pole.

– Clair! Chiquita! ¡Ven aquí, cara!

– Antonia! ¿Como està?

Antonia was the one person I was always glad to see. She'd worked for my mother twenty years but she was head chicken. She decided her own hours of work, the hours Connie and Joe would keep if they wanted meals, when it was time for her next pay rise and how much it would be. It was all done discreetly and everyone was happy because Antonia ran the house like a dream. And she spoke good English. Even Connie deferred to her. Antonia was also a buffer between my mother and me when necessary. By the odd touch, word, glance she changed the whole atmosphere of the house and made it tolerable. It was Antonia who hugged my sobbing, pregnant self after Connie's first eruption of moral outrage. We hugged again, now.

– Hey, Antonia! How are you?

– Better seeing you, honey! Let me look at you… Say, you brown! Where you been?

– Greece.

– Well, you looking good! Welcome home.

She soon had me seated with my mother and enjoying a bowl of papaya, mango and pineapple with yoghourt. There was a cafetière of fresh coffee and a basket of hot croissants covered with a white linen napkin. Usually, after a day of travelling, I felt bloated with all the bland fare. But I was ready for this breakfast, savouring the fruit and managing both croissants.

Connie had spoken to the clinic and Joe was stable after a comfortable night. We would visit him around eleven, drop by the yacht club for lunch at twelve thirty, return to the clinic by three then home for a nap. We'd have a light snack at five thirty, visit Joe again sometime after six and return home for cocktails, dinner and bed. This was what Antonia had agreed. She would be gone by three that afternoon; it was her day to collect the grandchildren from school.

My mother hated driving the Rolls Royce. It was quite possible that she'd summoned me not for Joe's sake but so she could have a driver she could bully. I remembered the route to the clinic from her varicose vein surgery two years earlier. On the way there she vacillated between recounting the lead up to the heart attack and criticising my driving technique.

– I told him he shouldn't play golf in the heat, but he wouldn't listen. Watch that truck! Wouldn't even use the golf cart between shots.

She was looking older and her skin, while coarsened by the climate of the Gulf, was pasty from living in the shade. Her eyes were still her best feature, hazel with gold flecks, thick lashed and framed by well-defined eyebrows. She seldom wore eye make-up. Linking manicured hands across the apricot patent leather purse resting on her lap she talked, staring ahead, twisting her coral ring. She'd had that ring ever since I could remember. A gift from an old friend, unspecified, peach coral surrounded by seed pearls set in a thick gold band, worn on third finger, right hand. When stressed she would wind it endlessly, like now. She sighed.

– That's Joe for you. Just goes right ahead and does what he was gonna do, anyway.

I never understood the foundation of Connie and Joe's relationship. Companionship? They shared very little, not even meals except socially. Sexual attraction? Twenty-five years ago when they'd met, Joe had neither looks nor charm and Connie, although still stunning in her forties, was something of an ice maiden – with one notable exception. They both had money, so it wasn't financial security. Could it just have been social convenience? In a world designed for couples, had they decided to hook up and have an easier time of it? Well, there are worse reasons. Maybe Connie would tell me sometime. But after all these years, I doubted it. She screeched as we approached the turn off.

– Here, here, here!

The clinic was as white and squeaky as private healthcare demanded. She took my arm as we walked to the coronary wing. Maybe she wasn't so tough, after all.

Never robust, Joe looked shrunken in the hospital bed. Tubes went in and out of him, a transparent mask covered his mouth and nose and he was surrounded by an array of equipment monitoring and displaying his vital signs in lines and bleeps. He sensed we were there, opened his eyes, adjusted his mask and spoke.

– So, Jess couldn't make it?

We stayed around an hour. I held his papery hand and brought him up to date with descriptions of Symi and a heavily edited version of Jess's activities. Connie remained silent, for the most part, relating only a list of callers wishing him well. I doubted he was listening to her.

Connie took my arm again on the way back to the car. We drove through wide palm-fringed streets to the yacht club where a valet – not unlike Nikos – parked the car for us. I was beginning to feel the effects of my journey. The chill air-conditioning of the clubhouse made me shudder as we headed toward the lounge for a pre-lunch aperitif. Connie had set rules; aperitifs pre-lunch, cocktails pre-dinner. Never more than one. I ordered a white wine for myself; whisky was not acceptable, nor gin or vodka, all of them being spirits and therefore unladylike. Connie, though, always took her martini 'very dry'.

My mother held high status at the yacht club. She and Joe part-owned a 40-foot ocean-going yacht, Warsaw Concerto, and regularly employed crew to sail them down the Florida Keys or, occasionally, around the Gulf of Mexico via Jamaica as far as Cozumel. As citizens of the land of the free, they were not allowed to visit Cuba, only a short cruise away. It was absurd to waste the capability of such a superb yacht on what were, essentially, little jaunts. But, hey, who was going to argue with the Dubrowskys? Over here, money and fame were class, and they had enough money to do without the fame. Or the class.

Connie was rubbing at her palms, itchy with chronic eczema.

– You still having trouble, Mum?

– Aw, they give me injections and pills and creams. None of 'em do much good.

I stroked her palm.

– Poor hand.

Connie whipped it away, hissed.

– Not here!

Several people stopped by our table to ask after Joe, most of them coiffured matrons in expensive outfits not designed for sailing. I knew one or two of them and was introduced to the others who all said 'So glad to know you!'. A new member, Sheldon, voiced gruff concern. Connie directed his attention to me. He nodded.

– So, you're the one with the daughter?

– I'm the only daughter. With an only daughter –

Connie gave me a look that meant trouble. I pulled back.

– How do you do, Sheldon?

He nodded, told Connie to give Joe his regards and left. Connie drew breath to admonish me but I got in first.

– Yes – I know. I have thumping jet lag. He'll get over it.

We could only pick at the lavish buffet lunch. Joe was wide-awake on our return and complained about us being away so long. Connie described our time at the yacht club. He perked up.

– Did you see Fred and Sherry?

– They're in Nassau.

– How about Everard? You see him?

– Everard had a stroke last week. He's in here, too.

– Everard had a stroke? You never told me.

– I told you last week.

– You couldn't have. I'd have remembered.

Connie set her face and started on the yacht club Christmas schedule, which had just been posted. This took a merciful half hour, during which I excused myself to go to the loo. By four, all three of us were exhausted. It was nine p.m. according to my body clock. Back in the car, I stealthily reduced the temperature of the air conditioning, hoping that the shock would keep me awake. If my mother noticed, she didn't say anything – which meant that she hadn't. The ride back was silent. She operated the remote control for the electric gates and garage door; we didn't leave the car until safely locked into the concrete bunker of the garage.

I thought a swim might stimulate me. Stepping into the garden was like falling into warm soup. I swished the door shut and headed across the lawn. The kidney shaped pool was set in pale terra cotta flags to complement the colour of the house. I had never seen Connie and Joe use it or even the white recliners and wondered who did, other than Jess and me. It was part of the status package. There was a slight movement in the water, generated by the filter system; every follicle contracted with the cold as I dipped my toe. Three days since there had been cobalt and turquoise sea, dry heat, craggy landscapes and the open sky of Symi. Now, the chemical tint of pool paint, cloying humidity and encroaching foliage suffocated me. Sheldon instead of Captain Panos, the antiseptic yacht club replacing the heat and noise of Nobby's. I plunged into the chill water.

After drying off I rang Guildford. Maggie answered, her voice reaching across the miles, stroking my face.

– Oh, Maggie…

– What's the matter, darling? Is Joe worse?

– Oh no, he's stable – I just – miss you –

Connie wandered in, searching for today's paper. I adjusted quickly.

– Mum, Maggie's here – would you like a word?

Startled by the suggestion, Connie gestured 'no' and sat in her armchair to re-read the social column, inhibiting further easy conversation. I imagined Maggie at the other end equally alarmed by my question.

– Oh – sorry, Maggie – she's just um… Did you and Jess meet up OK?

Yes, they had. She was still at work. It was ten thirty-five at night there; Jess would just be finishing her waitressing job.

– I'm fine. That metaxa stuff you brought back is too like medicine for me, so that young charmer, Case, popped down for a carryout of Grouse. Bye the bye, I see what you mean about Symi. Beautiful photographs.

– I brought a couple with me, just to remind…

I chatted self-consciously until Connie coughed, indicating the phone bill was running up. Like she need worry.

We returned to the hospital for a pointless half hour, during which Joe slept, then back to the apricot mansion. Antonia had prepared a cold meat salad, which we picked at over some re-runs of 'Dad's Army' before going to bed. As I stepped into my room, Connie asked,

– Still seeing that guy? Gordon?

– Howard. No. Goodnight, Mum.

I hadn't seen Howard since a stiff farewell at Gatwick on Wednesday evening, two – or was it three? – nights ago, and had no intention of seeing him again, ever. Well, not through choice, anyway.

CHAPTER FIFTEEN

MAGGIE

Saturday 11th August

I slept lightly, exhausted myself shooing a walrus off the strand at Kilachlan, and woke early. I went down to the kitchen and made tea, intending to take it back up to bed. But the morning was bright and the garden needed a companion, so I went out onto the cracked patio and sat on a rusting metal chair. They reflected the state of the rest of the house.

By the time my great-niece surfaced, I was bathed, dressed, unpacked and on elevenses. Jess accepted a coffee and sat sleepily at the kitchen table. The day was pleasant and progressing steadily towards lunchtime. I was still a bit stiff from yesterday's journey but of the mind for a bit of urban indulgence.

– Fancy going into Guildford for a keek at the High Street and a spot of lunch?

– Oh, wow! You sure?

– I'm sure. Can you be ready for a taxi at twelve? Where d'you suggest we eat?

It had the desired effect. She was off and into the shower like a trout leaping upstream.

We weren't home until after five. I was exhausted, happy to flop in the sitting room with my feet up while Jess took her contraband upstairs. The sales were still on and she deserved a cheer-up after the holiday. Besides, she was being a good wee soul helping out with her waitressing job at the Italian restaurant. She came back down looking more like a fashion plate than a waitress. The new top was probably unsuitable for work and she wore a heavy gold necklace that looked surprisingly real. I said nothing. She brought the holiday photos for me to look at while she was out. That would take all of ten minutes. After a hug of thanks and several kisses, she left after six. I heard her exchange a few words with someone on the way out. There was a tap on the door and a beautifully sculpted young face peered into the room.

– Hi, I'm Case. And you've just got to be Maggie.

Just before seven the front door slammed, interrupting Case's self-analysis. He popped out to check and reported back to me.

– Jess. Must have forgotten something.

I told Case to help himself to another whisky and went upstairs. Thuds, bangs and startling curses came from Jess's room. I knocked.

– Bugger off, Case!

As I opened the door Jess turned, snarling on me, then stopped in surprise, face red, eye makeup streaking her cheeks. I went in and brushed a few strands back from the hot forehead.

– What's happened, pet?

– Bloody man! Said I looked like a centre page spread and sent me home to change!

– Oh, dear.

– So I told him where to stick his job!

It took a while to soothe the ruffled ego, calm the temper and encourage a face wash. By the time Jess, in rumpled t-shirt and jeans, appeared in the sitting room, Case had vanished. Fortified by a large Glenmorangie, she outlined the flare up at the pizza restaurant. I nodded sympathetically. It wasn't the time to point out that her employer had a right to his views.

– Let's sleep on it, Jessie James. Tomorrow will bring its own solutions. But now we need some supper, then I want you to tell me about the other people you met in Symi.

Jess looked at the photo folder lying next to the whisky bottle and nodded briefly. Later on, when Clair rang, she motioned secrecy. I told her mother she was still at work.

FRASER

Saturdays were half days. I spent the morning on bureaucratic bumph plus a request for a transfer to another island – Symi was too quiet, apparently. Tonight was the set at Angelina's. But the afternoon was my own – although I was always only a phone call away from duty. I wandered down to Nobby's to see whether there was a boat spare for a few hours, leaving a sullen Nikos in the office. Pan Aegean were more demanding than Aegis although less efficient at tracking down their staff. I was halfway down a beer when Nikos joined me, a cousin's dinghy being unexpectedly available for the afternoon. With a cool box of beer and a couple of towels as cargo we were soon puttering out of the harbour to find a deserted beach.

Nimos Island had served as refuge in the past. There was enough shade to spend a few hours in comfort and it was secluded enough not to bother about swimming trunks although skinny-dipping is officially a no-no in Greece. We grounded the dinghy and sloshed up the blistering pebbles where we cracked a few cans each in between the odd lazy swim. But despite the indolence and freedom I wasn't enjoying myself. Inevitably, it was Nikos who brought up the topic.

– You, too, eh Fraser?

– Me, too, what?

– You miss the mother, I miss the daughter.

– Shove it, Niko.

– You know what I think about you, Fraser?

– I have a feeling you're going to tell me.

– You think it's strong to say nothing. Yes, men should be stronger than women, but they should not be without feelings. Maybe it's because you come from such a cold place. You have snow and a lot of rain, I know. If you knew the sun of many summers, warm sea, making love on a –

I persuaded him it would be unwise to go on if he didn't want the other eye colouring in.

Late afternoon the sea roughened. We set off back for Yialos in case it turned into a storm. By the time we butted into the harbour, the waves were fairly alarming and even Nikos was feeling queasy. After tethering the dinghy, we moved on unsteady land legs to Nobby's for a soother before climbing to the apartment.

Back up there the water pressure was almost non-existent, couldn't coax more than a few tepid drops out of the showerhead. Had to sluice armpits, hair and other uncomfortably salient parts with bottled mineral water. Although my skin was fairly well weathered by now, it still felt tight with the effects of sun and brine as I started the haul up to Angelina's, 12-string over my shoulder. I tried to recall the same journey of two weeks earlier, but nothing remarkable about it sprang to mind, only the evening that followed. Something ached as I plodded behind Nikos towards this week's audience.

MAGGIE

Mid-August

There was no escaping it – Jess was a handful. And she thought I was a soft touch, feeding me vague stories about where she was and what she was doing. I knew pretty well that she was exploiting the fact that her mother was away and it worried me because I wasn't too aware of the real or supposed dangers that young people faced these days. Should I confront her or play her at her own game – fake innocence?

The solution presented itself via two young men, a young chap called Raz who'd been her boyfriend before she went to Greece. The other was the drama student, Case. I spoke to Raz when he rang the house one evening – it turned out he knew all about me and Kilachlan and the dogs, Esmeralda, the Scrymgeours et al. So we had a bit of a chat and then he said he'd tried Jess's mobile but only ever got voicemail. I felt sorry for him but I couldn't interfere. If Jess hadn't told him she'd met someone else, it wasn't my place to. He asked me if she was still working at the Italian Restaurant.

— Aye, I believe she is.

— D'you think it'd be OK if I went round there?

— To be honest, I couldn't say, Raz. But myself, I wouldn't approach someone at their place of work.

— Yeah, maybe you're right. Thanks, Maggie.

A couple of days later, young Case popped his head round the sitting room door and said —

— You got a moment, Miss Harkin?

Which surprised me because I'd introduced myself to him as Maggie. It must be important.

— It's Maggie, and yes. Come on in and sit you down.

He did but then sat tongue-tied trying to find a way into whatever was his problem. A little Whyte and Mackay eased the way.

— Look, Maggie, me and Jess used to be tight and it's not like I want to diss her, like no way. But —

— Sorry, Case, you're going to have to translate.

What he had to tell me confirmed the worst I'd imagined. Jess had not been out for coffee with a friend these past nights but at nightclubs. Case had seen her with another girl, taking drugs. He was concerned that Jess might get herself into something she couldn't get out of, with the drugs and drinking under age. I thanked him and said I would consider what he'd told me and speak to Jess when I thought best. I promised him that I wouldn't bring his name into it.

The next time Raz rang for Jess, I asked him if he knew anyone of her companion's description. He did. It turned out that she was a bit of a ringleader at school and well known as a — I don't quite recall what he said. It didn't sound too complimentary, though.

— Why? What's Jess done?

— Let us just say, Raz, that I have concerns.

— Want me to look out for her?

Case had asked exactly the same question and my response was yes, if he did it discreetly. Raz was another question. There was a certain naïvety about him that gave me less confidence.

Jess grew more and more jittery and, consequently, so did I. Her exam results were due in a few days and I sensed that she genuinely feared the worst. The day came and she went down to school to pick them up. I dithered around the house all morning, waiting for her to come back. Eventually, I rang her mobile phone. She answered in a shaky little voice that dissolved quickly into tears. All I could say was –

– Come home, pet.

She did.

CLAIR

Life in Naples, Fla.

Days fell into a pattern: breakfast, visit Joe, lunch at the yacht / golf / country club, visit Joe, home for a nap, visit Joe, home for dinner, TV and bed. Occasionally, while Connie was sleeping in the late afternoon, I managed to escape. The temptation to smoke was agonising and I needed distractions. One was the internet at the local library where I composed an email for Fraser – then saved it as a draft and wrote to Jess, instead. AS level results were imminent. *Of all times for Joe to have a dicky ticker. I should be with her, now.*

Subject: How's everything?

Hi JJ

This is your old mother sat in the Library in Naples escaping Granny for five minutes (nothing changes!). Joe seems to be getting over the worst of it, but I have to stay on because Granny can't cope with all the driving or having to eat lunch on her own in public. I've been to the art store on Tamiami Trail highway. Really got the bug from your lovely birthday present! Maggie said she'd seen the Symi photos. You obviously found them in my bedroom. I have a few with me. There's a super one of you on the jetty with the dad and little girl at Nimborio. Remember? Will try to paint it. Antonia sends lots of love and asked if you had a boyfriend. I said 'dozens'. Have you seen Raz? Hope it wasn't too difficult

I abandoned the email, afraid of the odd misplaced word. Jess was bound to have frayed nerves at the moment anyway, with exam results looming. There were twenty minutes of the internet session left. I emailed Connie's number to Sonya – even though I knew she already had it – begging her to ring. After that there were still fifteen minutes, enough for idle hands to do their worst.

Subject: (no subject)

Dear Howard

Symi was unfortunate for us with good and bad on both sides. I apologise for any unacceptable behaviour or ingratitude, it wasn't meant.

I have happy memories of our time together and hope that you do, too. Sadly, I see no future for our relationship and I doubt that you feel differently.

All that remains is to wish you great good fortune and a better chance of happiness in the future.

Clair

The warning flashed 'end of session' as the cursor hovered over 'send'. My nerve failed and I clicked 'delete'. *Howard must know it's over by now?* One email sent out of four was not a productive use of my freedom, but at least I'd avoided having a cigarette.

That evening, while Connie slept in front of the TV, I tried a pencil sketch from the Nimborio photo of Jess. The result was depressing. Frustrated by my lack of practice, I set up a still life in the kitchen but painting in artificial light was not ideal. The only thing to do was to rise early and work in natural light. So the following morning and most mornings thereafter, I rose just after six, drenched myself with insect repellent and worked in the garden painting extravagant blossoms, pool and sky. When the humidity drove me indoors, I made thumbnail sketches of Antonia going about her chores and furtive studies of Connie. While my hands were occupied my mind roamed across the Atlantic to either end of Europe, counting days backward and forward to happier situations.

Connie seldom ventured into the back yard because of sunlight, mosquitoes and other potential hazards – like Hispanics with no English. But she and Antonia, both, were keen to see what I'd been up to. I was childishly pleased by their interest, biased though it was. Antonia was overawed.

– You sure clever, cara. These are real pretty. You must put them in an art store. People will buy like crazy!

– She gets it from Jimmy. I can't draw a straight line.

At first, I couldn't think who 'Jimmy' was. Then I realised. My father. If he was mentioned at all, and I couldn't actually recall many occasions, it was 'your father' or 'he', not even 'James'. But to refer to him as 'Jimmy' was extraordinary. Especially in front of Antonia. Was Connie making a happy connection between my father and me? Or was it just that, with Joe in hospital, she could relax second marriage etiquette a little? Whatever the reason, I was touched. It also felt ridiculously good to have her approval, albeit tacit, for once. The moment was glorious but fleeting.

In the days that followed, Connie cranked up the criticism. My hair was too wild, I dressed like a hippy, I should get a decent job, I spent too long on the phone, I should have found a proper father for Jess, I drove too fast,

I had Communist ideas and I shouldn't carry that great purple satchel or wear blue nail varnish on my toes. Prudently, I still wore sleeves long enough to cover the dolphin tattoo. Antonia, on the other hand, made a point of preparing my favourite food, giving secret little winks and squeezes in passing and leaving well intentioned, if less appreciated, Catholic prayer cards on my pillow.

Nothing, however, not Joe's heart, nor my failing as a daughter could fend off The Shopping Trip, a mandatory ritual involving Connie dragging me round her favourite clothing salons and picking out 'suitable' clothing for me. Latterly, she had given up on Jess, conceding the generation gap to be unbridge-able. No such luck for me. I learned, early on, to submit to the awfulness of Connie's taste, take the clothes home and sell them. Dozens of trousers and tops in nightmare hues, shoes designed for arthritic hookers and dresses inspired by pantomime dames had accompanied me eastward across the Atlantic over the years. It was scary how many Surrey matrons shared Connie's dress sense. One horror from the early eighties went to a dress agency in Godalming and reappeared in a pub in Weybridge. A hideous polyester blouse with ectoplasm down the front re-materialised at a parents evening – on Jess's form teacher. Thereafter I confined my enterprise to eBay. Worse were the clothes that Connie insisted I keep in Florida.

This time, the best she could be beaten down to was three pairs of ankle length cotton trousers, a jacket with appliquéd flowers, a knee-length A-line skirt and a floral blouse. All a gorge of pastel shades; all had to be seen to be worn. At least I wouldn't meet anyone I knew – I hoped. We went for a cocktail at the country club with a wardrobe fit for a drag queen stowed in the trunk of the Rolls.

The morning of AS level results felt like my own day of reckoning. My attempt at capturing a hibiscus bloom on paper looked like a bad case of vaginal thrush. Antonia came to the French windows.

– Clair – Maggie on the phone for you.

Poor Maggie. Jess had left it to her to impart the news: bombing in History and Maths with two D grades, gaining C's for French, English Language, English Literature and General Studies and B's for Media Studies and Art. Half an hour later, I tried to explain SATS and the GCSE/AS level/A level system to Connie for the umpteenth time. She couldn't see the point of it all, or what was wrong with the old system. For once, we saw eye to eye. I'd had boundless sympathy for my child sitting an endless series of examinations from junior school onward. Jess's schooling was geared to getting a generation of children through a set syllabus that denied them the time to acquire general knowledge and, consequently, any real perspective on the world. It was, I argued pointlessly with her head teacher, at the cost of an education that encouraged curiosity, nurtured particular talents or interests and respected individuality and imagination.

I told myself I mustn't be too disappointed in Jess's results. The fact remained that if she couldn't better her grades by next summer university mightn't be possible. Connie was unfazed.

– Joe didn't go to college and he's done pretty well.

Implicit in the statement was my own lack of progress following higher education. She went on.

– Jess should get a proper job, train for the hotel industry, maybe. Hotels never go out of style.

The idea of Jess on a reception desk handling guests with anything approaching civility was fantasy. But Connie refused to be wrong in her own house. Or anywhere else. She made out a cheque to Jess, popped it in a greetings card from the stock she kept in her study and left it out for Antonia to mail.

The 'throw money at it' solution my mother applied to most situations did not, unfortunately, include mine. There would be a cheque to cover airfares and sundry expenses for the current trip, but just enough and no more. Though I toiled for pennies and scrimped to keep mine and Jess's lives together, I had never turned to her for financial help. Not when the sandwich business curled up and died, when the dinner party enterprise proved indigestible, nor when any of my other optimistic ventures hit brick walls. Connie and Joe were dollar millionaires many times over, but since she'd endured long working hours for very little money until she inherited it, she decided her daughter could do the same. Well, that's the only reason I could think of.

I rang Guildford immediately on our return from the hospital that afternoon, but Jess was not yet back from work. Maggie was soothing.

– I'll make sure she rings you when she gets in. She's fine. We had a wee chat and she's determined to do better. I think it's been a good warning.

– I just don't know how to play it, Maggie. I wish I was at home with you both.

We moved on to more general subjects. Jess had shown Maggie how to shop online and they'd had extravagant fun. The freezer was wedged solid, the drinks cabinet overflowing and there were enough loo rolls to entertain a Labrador puppy farm. Apart from working and the occasional lunch out with Maggie, Jess was spending most days at home watching DVDs. On the odd night after work, she went to a friend's for coffee.

– Raz?

– He's rung but she's not spoken to him.

So Raz was dumped. Even if he had been about to deflower my daughter before we went to Symi, he was a likable, intelligent young man. What a shame.

– Don't worry, lass, Case is keeping an eye on our girl. I gather he's quite a man about town – well, about Guildford.

– Case? Keeping an eye on Jess? Maggie, he's a complete rogue. Has he paid his rent, yet?

– I wouldn't know. Did he owe you?

– Three months. Is Jess still wearing a thick gold circlet round her neck?

– Yes. Why?

Jess didn't ring that night or any other, nor was she ever available to come to the phone. I emailed.

Subject: Want to be with you!

Hello Darling

I'm sorry we keep missing each other on the phone. An email seems a very cold way to tell you that I love you and I'm thinking of you. I realise your results were sort of what you expected – but I know you were still disappointed and I'm so sorry. We'll find a better way of managing schoolwork and life for you so that you can approach A levels with more confidence, I promise. Granny has sent you a card that should cheer you up! (Try and send her a 'thank you' and a 'get well' card for Joe, eh?) Please give Maggie a big hug from me. I'm sure she's passed on all the hugs and kisses I send you over the phone. Try and speak soon, JJ – I miss hearing your voice.

Love Mum x

Sonya rang one afternoon after we'd returned from seeing Joe. Connie managed a disapproving look on her way to her bedroom for a nap. Antonia whispered aside.

– I check your Mama's phone is pull out. You hear if she put in again.

Sonya had been back in Britain nearly three weeks and was bored with Brian whingeing about the unprincipled tactics of US production companies.

– I mean, what does he expect? The cast of fucking Sesame Street?

However, the Dickens project was looking promising and she was keeping that very much to herself.

– Clair – you still there?

– Sorry…

– Dreaming of Greek toy boy?

What sweet relief it was to share the libidinous pleasure and the angst of Fraser. Eclipsed for once by my sexual exploits, Sonya was magnanimous and congratulated me. And she reassured me that she'd sorted Jess's iPhone, late of octopus incident. Thereafter, we kept in touch by email and phone.

Connie didn't mind about Sonya so much, it was Maggie's calls she didn't care for. Everything was fine at home, Maggie assured me. Yes, Jess was getting on all right at the pizza place. The friend she visited after work was Sharn. I found the news unsettling; Sharn Fellowes was sullen, spoilt, oversexed and educationally dispossessed. Pretty much like Jess at the moment.

To everyone's relief, after nearly two weeks, the consultant said that Joe could come home. With his heart's walls paper-thin, its muscles tired out and Joe's general health not strong enough to consider a transplant, the prognosis was depressing. His bedroom – Connie and he each had their own – was made ready and Joe arrived in pomp, attended by nursing staff: Shiloh, Krystine, Dirk and Brandie, who visited thereafter on a rota.

In healthier times, Joe maintained a generally taciturn nature punctuated by sudden volleys of frankness. He engaged with brain, not heart. But he'd remained uncharacteristically silent over my lapse of morality in producing an illegitimate child. Given his and Connie's exalted social status in Naples his liberality was surprising until, that is, I learned of at least one similar failing in Joe's past. Thus, he and I had some common ground even though, in his eyes, my transgression was worse than his. He tolerated me as a reformed fallen woman and I accepted him as a docile dinosaur. He was, however, unashamedly fond of Jess. Once home, he traded on our fragile bond and demanded I sit with him. He didn't want conversation, just company and Connie was too much like hard work. I utilised the long, silent hours in his room trying again to translate the Nimborio photo of Jess with the man and child to canvas. This time, I made better progress. Occasionally Joe would demand a viewing and offer words of advice. He had a sharp eye and criticised constructively but he warned me –

– Don't you go painting no portraits of me all trussed up like a chicken!

Poor old bugger, he is, too – and he looks well past his 'use by' date. How long is he going to be like this? Will he ever get any better? What kind of life is he going to have? And then Mum. She's had the shock of losing one husband suddenly, now she has to watch another one die slowly. With this in mind, I tried to be more tolerant of my mother. But it wasn't easy when Connie made it clear that, as a daughter, I was a major disappointment.

With Joe back and out of imminent danger, I hankered to get on with my own life and wondered how soon would be decent to make a move. I still hadn't spoken to Jess following from the trauma of exam results. And she hadn't sent Joe a 'get well' card, a discrepancy he had mentioned. I had a feeling that all was not well, despite what Maggie said. Sonn said she'd been planning going to Guildford.

– No, Sonn, it's too much. I'm probably just being neurotic.

– Don't be daft. I want to catch up with Maggie and the devil child.

Things were about the same with Brian. Average. And the PR business was very quiet, it being August. But it looked like the Dickens project had some mileage in it, if not vast amounts of money. It would mean a foot in the American door for Brian's company and possibly some kick back on the PR side for Sonya's people. Emotionally screwed maybe, but Sonya was nothing if not commercially astute.

The following day, from two o'clock onwards, I could barely sit still. Sonya would be in Guildford by now. Joe noticed.

– You got ants in your pants, or what? Hardly painted a damn stroke today.

– Just thinking about Jess, Joe.

– Should've brought her over.

– She's not a little girl any more, Joe, she's seventeen. She makes her own decisions.

– You mean she didn't wanna come?

Joe was no fool. I wasn't sure whether Jess hadn't wanted to come because she was lovesick for Nikos or she just preferred to stay in Guildford. Either reason would upset Joe. So I endowed her with newfound academic dedication and employee loyalty knowing Joe wouldn't argue with these virtues. Whether he appreciated their taking precedence over him was doubtful. Connie put her head round the door, for once relieving a difficult situation instead of creating it – or so I thought.

– Phone.

I hurried to the kitchen, forgetting it was too early for Sonya to be ringing. As I picked up, I heard Connie replace the receiver in the Florida Room.

– Sonya, hi – how are – ?

– Sheldon Bolder, here.

Who? Aren't you a character from Dynasty?

– Connie says you're free tonight. I'll call by, pick you up around five. Taking you out to the launch.

– You're what?

– Taking you out to the launch. Wear deck shoes.

– Uh – afraid I can't make it, Sheldon, I'm waiting for a phone call.

– You can call 'em offshore. See you at five.

He hung up. He hadn't said my name once. I went through to Connie.

– Mum, what was all that about? Why did you tell him I was free tonight?

– I don't see a pile of invitations on your dresser.

– You have no right to meddle in my life like this!

There was a silence and I knew I had crossed Connie's invisible line. The tension of three weeks ruptured.

– You should get on your knees –

She did actually say that. Connie spoke – still does – in B movie clichés.

–… and thank me for putting Sheldon your way – instead of which, what do you do? Tell me not to meddle in your life? Well, I tell you, you'll regret the day I stop taking an interest in you – and that's getting closer, every stunt you pull! You're a loser like your father and like his goddamn queer sister! And you're going to end up nowhere like both of them! You didn't even plan to have a kid, just had one because you couldn't be bothered not to. The least you could do is make up for the shame you caused Joe and me!

Connie never shouted but spoke with an indomitable force and fluency remarkable for a woman of such limited conversation. As she continued, all her frustration and discontent centred on me: I was at the root of the unhappy years in England, my selfishness the cause of her humiliation, my indolence the overriding factor in Jess's recent failure. I gaped, mesmerised by my accuser, until she dealt the heaviest blow:

– I just wish I'd gotten rid of you when Mom said!

My legs gave way and I flopped suddenly on a low sofa from where I saw Connie stamp a gold-clad foot then withdraw, slamming the door behind her. I tried to control the trembling by breathing deeply. But it wouldn't stop. The intentional cruelty of it was stunning. This was my childhood again; sudden, disproportionate punishment for some small or imagined misdemeanour leaving me too shocked and wounded to retaliate. Now, just like then, there was no one close by to help.

Had Grandmother Emily really urged aborting me? Undoubtedly illegal at the time although wealthy Floridians probably had a convenient doctor who 'saw to' such indiscretions. But why? Connie was married. Did old

Emily disapprove of my parents' marriage so much? More than this, if Connie had known about my miscarriage would she still have said it? I didn't want to know the answer.

Slowly, I calmed myself and went to the second-best guest suite where I watched two whole episodes of 'Murder She Wrote' while I tried to forget that my mother regretted I was alive instead of a bloody mess in a bucket. As the piano music tinkled in over the end credits for the second time, I roused. At least Sheldon would get me out of the house for a few hours. And if I missed Sonya tonight, I would hear from her soon. I stared in the mirror and saw Maggie. It was comforting. I had other genes.

FRASER

Right to the last nanosecond with their constant 'Sorry, Fraser, think you'll find you're wrong' – the Witterings were mega PITAs. As the last ripple of ample backside disappeared beyond passport control, I felt orgasmic relief. The new Aegis crowd was agreeably innocuous and, apart from a mislaid hearing aid, were no trouble. After a couple of days I began to feel twitchy. There was very little to distract me from thoughts of a tallish bird with explosive hair. I haunted Nobby's, nurtured an interest in American football, did two extra nights at Angelina's bar. It was useless. All neural pathways and physical urges led to Clair. Annie-toned allusions to my extended adolescence taunted me until I banished her sassy phantom.

– Shut it, you weren't born for most of it.

I couldn't remember feeling like this since – well, I couldn't remember feeling like this. Calling, emailing or writing to Clair was not an option, though. The eejit words at Rhodes airport haunted me: Love you doll love you doll love – and on and on. What did they mean?

– Annie – I'm not telling you again!

I thought about going on a few strenuous hikes, but there were very few places on the island I didn't know by now – and hiking would be a solitary affair. Neither Nikos nor Nobby's idea of exercise extended to anything vaguely athletic and Panos, of course, was no help.

– Fraser – you thinking of Beautiful Buds or her mama? Think! In bed – one way, something younger, other way, something older! Pretty good, neh?

He slapped me on the back and poured me a quadruple measure of low grade Metaxa. I stifled the urge to douse him in it and light a match.

I tried taking it out on the 12-string, but the neighbours in Chorio complained – and at Angelina's, the clientèle became bored of 'Wonderwall' and 'Thank You for the Days'. I couldn't concentrate on reading, listening to the BBC World Service or watching late night porn at Nobby's. Maybe it was just time to move on from Symi. This Clair business was only a symptom of it. What was I thinking of, anyway – a fifty-year-old woman with a seventeen-year-old daughter? She was probably grey, dyed her hair. Back in Britain, in the cold and drizzle, what would she look like over breakfast? Best to let it drop. I'd bonked a tourist – happened all the time. Besides, she hadn't been in touch with me, so she couldn't be that keen. I found this rogue strand of reasoning hopeful but it was interrupted by two loud voices.

– West Wittering?

– Piss off home!

Each shout was followed by expectoration and raucous laughter.

The Meldüz brothers had just walked in to Giannis's Fish restaurant, where I was lingering over an early supper of tuna salad and red wine. They landed noisily at my table. I tried to sound remote.

– Hi, guys. How's the carpet business?

After a few ouzos the evening turned into a session and a welcome escape from depression. The following narrative is courtesy of Giannis and – well, that would spoil the story. Way after ten, it appears, I accompanied the brothers, somewhat unsteadily, back to their caïque intoning 'Flower of Scotland'. As I stepped aboard, someone called my name. By this time Metin, was firing the engine. But before Orhan could slip the mooring rope, someone else caught hold of it, someone with such an air of authority that the brothers changed their minds and took off for Datça without me. This is where I take over the chronicle.

Next morning, I remembered none of this, such is the effect of red wine and ouzo on a troubled mind. But, as the past revealed itself in terrifying glimpses, I was forced to conclude it would have been better to have woken up in Datça rather than where I was now. In Ali Mavrakakou's bed.

Ali placed a black coffee on the table beside me, managing to eat a slice of bread and twist her hair into a knot at the same time. She was nervy, shy and girly all at once.

–… very late for surgery but I am free this afternoon – I don't know if… clean towel in the shower… really have to go –

She knelt beside me, smiling in a way that struck me with dread.

– See you later Bronco Buchanan.

Then she kissed me familiarly – too familiarly – on the lips and left.

– Bronco Buchanan – no – NO…!

I lifted the sheet, looked down at the sleeping Bronco Buchanan, my childhood nickname for… I prayed I would soon stagger back through the portal from this parallel universe.

CHAPTER SIXTEEN

CLAIR

The Connie inside comes out

To while away the time until five, I washed my hair and dried it with a brush and hairdryer, taking elaborate care to tame it shining and straight, almost to my breasts. As I looked in the mirror this time, it wasn't just the hair that was so different. The features were harder, older. It was a face that revealed bitterness, disappointment. I was intrigued by the alien image, tried to read the character of the woman facing me: Connie. In there, along with Maggie. *She's you, too, Clair. And you've always been frightened of her. It's time to get to know her. Starting tonight.* Tonight, the Connie inside me would take revenge on the other Connie and her kind. I opened the wardrobe and chose maliciously. There were some of my mother's old cosmetics and costume jewellery in a drawer. I began shaping the retribution. Sheldon Bolder's date would be with Connie Dubrowsky. Applying Connie's make-up, I probed her mind.

The door chimes rang at five on the nose. Antonia came to the second-best guest suite and called softly. I was ready. She drew breath as I opened the door to her.

— Why, Clair, you look…

— I know.

My hair was heavily backcombed and swept back into a large coral clip. My eyebrows were pencilled into ginger arcs and my lips, heavily outlined, glared apricot. Heavy gilt bangles and earrings clanked and glittered against a pink and blue floral blouse and pink and lilac jacket. At my neck was an apricot chiffon scarf of Connie's. The pale green trousers completed the nauseating mélange of pastels. Plus sensible navy and brown deck shoes. If only Fraser/Jess/Sonya could see me now. Sheldon didn't bat an eyelid.

— Let's go.

Mercifully, Connie remained in dudgeon as her doppelganger left the house and climbed into Sheldon's powder blue Rolls Royce. Not so Antonia, who stood at the front door with her personal angel and devil doing battle. I imagined she would shut herself in the kitchen, pray for my soul then laugh her head off.

On the drive south to the marina, Sheldon took a large detour to loop past his house.

—… bay view, lagoon view, canal waterfront, Gulf access, four beds with walk-in closets, four bathrooms…

Is he trying to impress me or sell it to me?

−… games room, heated pool and spa, tinted windows and zoned temperature control.

It was just another pastel chunk of Florida real estate, a big chunk admittedly, even for Florida, making the palm trees look like shrubs, but what it boasted in size was diminished by its taste. Dominating the forecourt was a large fountain where several heavily bosomed water nymphs froze in suggestive frolic around a priapic King Neptune. Sheldon put his hand on my thigh.

– That's the way I like my women, high-breasted an' low on expectations. Not that I've ever been known to disappoint.

He had to be in his mid-seventies. I fought rising bile.

– Maybe you just haven't met the right woman, yet.

He was oblivious to the insult. *Sheldon, you are only in the shallows and already you are out of your depth.*

– If you're a good girl, I might bring you back here for a little nightcap.

He winked at me as the seabed beneath him gave way to an ocean trench.

We travelled south to the marina where my beau passed the keys of the Rolls to a valet and stepped into an electric buggy for the journey to the mooring.

– Get in! Save your energy.

He chuckled to himself, thinking of the fun ahead, no doubt. As I stepped in, he stamped his foot on the accelerator of the glorified milk float and we rolled along the jetty.

Normal people would have called it a yacht. Only the inverted snobbery of the wealthy would call it a launch; it was an extension of the house. Or a shag ship, like Joe E. Grey's tub in 'Some Like it Hot'. Pity Sheldon had none of his charm. I pictured the sleek mystery of 'The Hilarium', that sexy black vessel on Symi. Sheldon boarded, ungallantly leaving me behind in the buggy. A dark-haired man, presumably a crew member – or the crew – greeted him and stood talking for a few moments. I wanted nothing more than to turn the bloody buggy round and drive to the airport. But I focused on revenge even if I wasn't certain how to achieve it. Eventually, Sheldon noticed I wasn't there and yelled with some irritation:

– What are you waiting for? This one ain't good enough?

– Au contraire, it's just – titanic.

For a split second, as he peered through his aviator spectacles, I thought Sheldon might be onto me. But, no. He sat me astern on a white leather banquette with a sticky turquoise drink and took the wheel as the dark guy cast off from the jetty. The sun was well on its way to the west as we nosed into the Gulf, the engine grumbling up from Lee Marvin to an Eartha Kitt purr. The humidity was intense with no relief from the breeze on the boat. We sliced through warm broth. *Three weeks ago, I was with my young lover on a Greek Island, shivering as he touched me, laughing, drinking wine, diving deep in crystal water. Now I'm stuck on a sea of pus with a geriatric lech and a glass of blue gunk.*

Sheldon stood proudly at the helm, his grey chest hair curling stringily above the V of his shirt, his knotty hands playing the wheel back and forth like a movie actor pretending to drive. *He has no idea what he's doing. No wonder he has to bring the hired help along. What a berk. I'm going to enjoy demolishing him.* I sidled to the rail, discreetly slopped my drink downwind and remained there until the prime real estate had sunk slowly below the gelatinous horizon. The engine slowed then cut out followed by the metallic rumble of the anchor chain. I knew time was short. I felt a hand on my buttock and swivelled round into Sheldon's nostrils.

– What say you and I go get nautical?

Over his shoulder, I could see the help looking impassively ahead.

– Every nice girl loves a sailor!

Moi – camp in the face of crisis.

– Way to go!

He led me by the hand into – the upstairs cabin? The stateroom? – poured himself a large bourbon and topped up my glass with fluorescent goo. Then he sprawled back on a black leather chaise, legs akimbo in lemon slacks, one arm flung along the back. Uninvited, I sat on a black leather barstool and set my glass next to a silver tray of cocktail accessories. He contracted his eyebrows to what he must have imagined was sexy and growled.

– So, here we are, Chris.

– Clair.

– Sure you are. Drink your drink.

– Bottoms up, Sherman.

– Sheldon!

A strained pause.

– You know, Clair, for a woman of fifty, you're pretty foxy, 'specially when you smarten yourself up. Shame about your jugs, but you can't have everything.

He paused, eyes narrowed to indicate partial approval, then –

– Why don't you make yourself comfortable?

He patted the plump leather beside him and casually unzipped his fly, exposing a wirily erect penis.

I threw the nearest thing at hand. Oddly, though, the stain wasn't sticky blue. It was red. And Sheldon was howling with pain. I looked down. It wasn't a cocktail glass in my hand. It was a bottle of "ASS IN HELL" - X'TRA HOT Chilli Sauce. Sheldon was on his feet, making for his cabin, still yelling. Suddenly his henchman was there.

— Mr Bolder?! Where is he? What's happened?

I gestured the cabin door with the sauce bottle and he dashed in after Sheldon. I noticed a screwtop cap on the floor between me and the sofa. *Always check the lid before shaking the bottle.* Sounds of running water, two male voices, one high pitched and urgent:

— Get me the ice bucket!

The other empathetic —

— Oh my god, Mr Bolder — keep it under the faucet — no! Cold! Cold!

Chilli sauce! How much of it got him full on? Christ — he's going to sue! No, wait — wait — it was attempted rape. Self-defence. But he can afford platinum plated lawyers — I'll go to Sing Sing! All right, Connie, what do I do?

— You find the galley, Clair. You get some plastic bags or cling film. You put the chilli sauce bottle in one, you put the cocktail glass in another and you keep them as evidence. And you make sure where your bar stool was and where the silver tray was.

Half an hour later, as I sat on deck, snapshots on mobile phone — *How the hell do I get them onto the computer? Jess will know* — loot safely stowed in handbag, the engine started. A metallic rattle and thud and the boat swung around. I was at the rails, ready to step ashore. The electric buggy was waiting, thoughtfully pointing in the right direction. Sheldon appeared hatchet-faced and wearing swimming trunks. He walked bandy-legged.

— You're gonna regret this, you tight-assed British broad with your saggy tits!

— Saggy tits and a tight arse? I'll tell Mummy you said that.

— You ain't gonna run home to Mommy?

He actually looked scared. *Ho ho. So he's afraid of Connie.*

— And I'll also tell her I've seen bigger pricks on a pincushion.

The crewman climbed ashore to tie up the launch then returned to let down the gangway, unable to meet my eye. I took the opportunity to make for the buggy, slide in and put my foot to the floor. It tottered off at just above walking pace, leaving Sheldon bug-eyed and splay-legged on the jetty.

I took a cab from the boathouse. The spare remote control for Connie's safety gates was wedged in my handbag (with the cocktail glass and sauce bottle) so I was able to let myself in. Connie's bedroom light was on. Exhausted, I closed the front door quietly and stripped off the pastel mess as I headed for the second-best guest room. I put my evidence on the dressing table. There was a note on the bed from Antonia.

'Dear Clair, Sonya call you and call again tomorrow. Send love. Hope the crazy lady and Mr Bolder have a good time. A. x'

There was also a sealed envelope, no name on it. Inside was a cheque for $4,000 made out to 'Miss C Harkin' from Connie and Joe's joint account. Nickels and dimes to them. Recompense for my flights and lost income. It was also the nearest I'd get to an apology. If I left immediately, I might even get back in pocket. I undressed quickly, brushing out the tangle of backcombing and lacquer. Connie stared back at me from the mirror. *Thanks, you were great. No – you were terrible – but great. Or maybe it's the real me. Terrible Clair. See you again sometime.*

The next morning Joe, with the help of Shiloh and Brandie, was able to get out of bed for the first time in a month. Connie and I communicated in monosyllables. After breakfast, I rang the airline and booked my flight for Friday, two days hence. I spent them finishing the painting of Jess at Nimborio, which I gave to Joe.

MAGGIE

It was a sorry time for Jess; I concentrated on soothing her over her exam results. We went through possible causes and solutions and she resolved to do better next term. But there was the other problem that the lad Case had brought up. Just the mention of drugs scared me. Given that he and Jess lived in the same house, I couldn't let on that he was my source of information. On the other hand, I wanted to put a barrier across Jess's downward path without worrying her mum. Bless her, Clair had enough to be contending with over in that unhealthy place. What had Jess got herself into? What to do? Who to speak to? I did, of course, have many conversations with Julia in my head. But this was beyond the both of us. Then it came to me. Clair's old friend, Sonya. Getting hold of her number was another question, though. I enlisted Case. Asked him if he could get the number off Jess's mobile phone for me. It wasn't an easy mission, given that she rarely let the blessed thing loose from her hand. He rose to the challenge supremely. For my part, all I had to do was divert her when he tipped me the wink. I must say, it got the adrenalin racing but I enjoyed the test of ingenuity. This time, Grouse came to the rescue. I sent her to the kitchen for another bottle while Case was sharing a Sunday tipple with us. He had the number instantly and sent it to his own phone but with only seconds to spare before Jess returned with the bottle.

I rang Sonya and told her the whole story. I must say, she was a very good listener and it was a great relief to share the problem with someone – especially someone who cared about Clair and Jess.

– Don't worry, Maggie darling, I'll fix it with Jess and not a word to Clack.

Clack?

Sonya came down in her sports car. Somehow the three of us squeezed into it and tore off to Ye Olde Ship Inn, a favourite of Jess's where she consumed most of the alcohol and talked non-stop about Greece and Nikos. When she slalomed off to the Ladies I raised my eyebrows to Sonya.

– It's OK, Maggie. I'll have a one to one with her back at the house.

She rang me the next evening for a debriefing. How she'd done it, I don't know but Sonya had extracted enough information to make her hair stand on end. Jess got a stiff warning and an offer of help. In return, she'd promised to mend her ways. I stood down Case and Raz.

FRASER

Everything was still a blur when I reached the Leftéris café. It was Friday, the day of the walk to Mihail Perivliótis monastery. Only three weeks earlier I'd arrived for the same unhappy trek in the same painful condition. At least there weren't any teeth-gritting Witterings on my case. Neither, though, was there Richard to ease the pain. But, just as I hadn't known what lay before me then, I didn't now. I suspected it wasn't going to be as much fun. I was right. At two o'clock, my mobile rang. Ali.

– Where would you like to meet?

– Sorry, I can't – I'm working.

– You didn't say that this morning.

– Ali, I was hungover this morning.

Bad move. Silence.

– Ali, are you there?

– Are you telling me you only slept with me because you were – drunk?

– No!

Too quick and not convincing. Plus a serious virtual look from Annie.

– Look, I'll call you when I get back from Pedi.

I didn't have to stay with the group once they'd settled themselves in Pedi but hung on, anyway, joining a couple at one of the beach tavernas. I had to be careful. Ali would know through the Symi grapevine exactly where I was, what I was doing and with whom. I was desperate for some time to think things through but since I'd swapped my brain for dog meat there was fat chance of any coherent thought – or forgetting my monumental stupidity.

I sat with a psychiatrist and a GP, both of whose professional services I was in need of. The psychiatrist worked at one of the high security hospitals back in the UK. He was very skinny and kind of twitchy, bad skin. I wondered if that was a result of his day job. How could he let go of all that angst at five o'clock? I resisted probing him for any juicy anecdotes. His wife, the GP, on the other hand was plumpish, had a great sense of humour and was fascinated by everything – Symi, sea, sky, Turkey, food – me. She dominated the entire conversation and I was content to let her. She was also very direct.

– Do you have a partner, Fraser?

A difficult question because I didn't know. But I listened with interest to my own voice saying –

– Actually, I'm seeing the GP on Symi. Ali Mavrakakou. Perhaps you'd like to meet her?

Which was how the four of us ended up having dinner together. A cheap ploy to put off one to one contact with Ali for the evening. Nikos was suitably appalled by my account of the previous night's activities.

– Ali?! 'Kin 'ell, Fraser, you're crazy! You'll have to marry her or leave Symi!

– There's a third option. Castration without anaesthetic.

– But how could you be so – ?

– Blootered and still get my leg over? No idea.

– Maybe you didn't actually –

– I have reason to believe I did. She knew 'Wally'.

– Who?

And so began my unwilling, retrospective courtship of Dr Ali Mavrakakou. That first soirée was a little strained initially. Ali had obviously expected a romantic dîner à deu. But once the two GP's started swapping medical yarns the evening was safe. Even the psychiatrist loosened up and contributed a few jaw dropping tales from the institution. All featuring other shrinks. And naming no names. I was content to listen while I tried to link fragments from the previous night. It couldn't have been just red wine and ouzo; the Meldüz boys must have slipped me a Nobby's Blaster at the very least. But then I couldn't possibly have done the business – could I? I would have to rely on whatever Ali volunteered.

I walked her back to her apartment, conversation flowing like concrete. She pouted when I refused the invitation to join her.

– I am asking you in for a drink… nothing more.

– But you're so beautiful and I'm so horny, it'd end up being more. Let's take it gently.

Nauseated by my own cheesiness I sprinted home, wrestling my pet demon.

– OK, Annie, shut it!

There was no possibility of taking it gently. I was captive on the island and word of the 'liaison' had already spread, courtesy of Orhan and Metin. So Nikos said. Right. One to one avoidance tactics became my preoccupation. I manipulated punters shamelessly for dinner invitations and, when the buggers were too mean, made sure we bumped into them. But I couldn't avoid the odd night in alone with her and it was horribly obvious that we had nothing in common. Ali was an attractive woman by many people's standards, but I flinched when she touched me. And I couldn't avoid comparisons with another woman whose touch produced a quite different effect. Even the thought of it. I was too ashamed by now to contact Clair. Wondered what her excuse was.

Thankfully, there were the evenings I was occupied with Aegis activities. With Ali almost permanently on call, sometimes away for two or three hours, we hardly saw each other during the day. Nikos and I didn't share much downtime any more and when we did, Ali was bound to appear sooner or later. The Wednesday Rhodes trip became an excuse for a solitary night in my own bed. So it continued until October when the end of the season loomed.

One rare night on my own, strumming loosely, I stumbled across a song from the seventies and indulged for a few bars as the lyrics came. I was always baffled by my memory's randomness. 'Clair, the moment I met you I swear… dum de dum da di da di there…' No – then: 'Why-y-y, in spite of our age difference do I sigh?' Bit Freudian that – or coincidence? I played a duff chord and skipped to – 'Nothing means more to me than hearing you say, I'm going to marry you…' shuddered to a halt, every nerve ending sparking, my fingers splayed away from the frets. Get tae – this is Gilbert O'Sullivan's life! Then I saw Ali standing there. She looked like I'd hit her.

She didn't call by after that and I didn't contact her although I stuck to my usual routines to make it clear that I wasn't avoiding her. All the same, I managed to. Symi became an Ali-free zone. I felt a total shite – a very relieved total shite. But the sort of shite people had started avoiding. Maybe

I was being paranoid. Panos collared me a few days later. An elderly aunt of Ali's had been taken ill; she was going to Kalamata to care for her. A locum was coming from Rhodes fill in. I did the honourable thing and went to the hydrofoil when she left. She stared back at me, still the confident, assertive Ali I'd known these three years. But unsmiling.

– Look, Ali – I'm really sorry –

– No. I am sorry.

I got the message that it was a different kind of sorry she was feeling.

– Look – Aegis finishes in the next week or two and –

– It will be safe for me to come back?

Said with a slight arch of an eyebrow. We both stood awkwardly for a moment then she turned and boarded the Anes line vessel. I watched it pull away and pick up speed. Next to me, Mixailis started up the three-wheeler and headed out along the harbour to the petrol station. I went the opposite way to the office and made my homebound arrangements, then composed an email to Clair. Eight weeks and no contact. But to tell the truth I hadn't stopped thinking about her, not even for a whole hour at a time. In the message I trod a line between chatty, pithy and, well, poetic. And before I chickened out Annie made me press 'Send'.

HOWARD

The last days on Symi, the wisdom of going there at all, weighed heavily. Clair's extraordinary behaviour at the party, I accepted, was no excuse for my subsequent, appalling lapse of standards. She had every right to be angry. But the humiliation in front of that Scottish lout still smarted, and fear of her continued scorn diminished my will to contact her. Even her answer phone alarmed me. But if I overcame this irrational fear, would she want me back? And did I want her back?

The Saturday after my return, I went down to Dorset. I dialled Guildford again before I left but, as usual, put the receiver down before the first ring. At the cottage in Whitchurch Canonicorum, a tongue salad awaited me (I hate tongue, but my stepmother never remembers). Endured it, gave her a pot of Greek honey. Drove her into Lyme Regis. Dolly loves nothing more than an interesting ailment, especially if it entails inevitable demise, so the short drive to the coast was filled with graphic descriptions of suffering delivered in reverent tones; the victims all people I didn't know or couldn't remember. The sea was a bit rough. We stopped at the Fossil Shop so she could fiddle through the baskets of clinker. She never bought anything because it would be 'a waste to spend a whole pound on a bit of polished grit'. Clair, on the other hand, who was always on her uppers, would have squandered a fortune on stones that were supposed to improve artistic talent, women's health or bloody horse race predictions. I found myself missing her, even if only to tell her how absurd it all was. After dropping Dolly back, I travelled home feeling glummer than ever.

CLAIR

Bliss for a while, until...

Maggie and Jess met me at Guildford Station. I clung on to them both, afraid they'd disappear if I didn't. We took a cab – Maggie hadn't felt up to Jess's driving. Back home Jess dragged my bags away, pushed Maggie and me into the sitting room and reappeared minutes later with a tray of Buck's Fizz.

– Toast you coming home!

We drank to my arrival, then the traditional: "Here's tae us, wha's like us, damn' few and they're a' deid!" after which Jess bounced out to the kitchen while I cuddled Maggie on the sofa.

– I know, lass, you've had a rotten do. But you're home now and I'll not go 'til you've had time to tell me all about it – about Florida and whatever it was that went on in Symi at the end.

My head jerked up. Not only did Maggie have remarkable sensors, she had a tenacious memory. Symi was six weeks and two centuries ago.

– You are one spooky broad, Maggie. Is there no place to hide from your – ?

– Nosiness? Nope.

I snuggled up, luxuriating with having her in my own home. The doorbell rang and Case answered, unusually for him at the early hour of eleven a.m.. The sitting room door creaked. Through a filter of lashes I saw a tall shape looming over me. I squeezed my eyes shut until pin pricks of pointillist colours filled my head. The delirium of jet lag? No, no, no. This is me we're talking about. Everything is always real. I had to be grateful for small mercies. At least this time I was on a sofa, not on a Greek toilet. The voice followed.

– Clair – I didn't realise you'd been away. Sorry – hello, Maggie, how are you?

– Very well, thank you, Howard. Clair, darling, Howard's here.

Whereupon, my beloved, traitorous Maggie, swirled dervishly from the living room.

Next, Howard was on his knees – or one knee – descending into farce beyond even his behaviour in Symi. Thankfully, this time he wasn't sweating and dressed in shorts.

– No, Howard, don't! Please, please, don't!

But he did.

– Clair – I should have realised that this is what you want. Forgive me for taking so long to come to terms with it. Finally, I have. Marry me.

They say that expletives are the refuge of inarticulate people. Bollocks. I have always been fairly fluent when it comes to offensive language – and I gave it full rein.

– You...!

Howard changed colour and expression several times in rapid succession before he made it to his feet and out of the house. I did the Hound of Hell bit, I think. As the front door slammed I made for the kitchen. Maggie and Jess cleared as I burst through.

– Where's the whisky?

They both said –

– I take it that was a 'no', then?

FRASER

The Anes Line suspended hydrofoil services due to the weather, so I missed my plane from Rhodes. There wasn't a Glasgow flight for another week. I could have taken the first flight out to anywhere, but the company had paid for my ticket and I wasn't exactly awash with funds. Nikos was back at university and most of the other reps had left. Even Nobby had deserted his post and winged it to Brum. I spent a grim couple of days drinking and re-hearing Panos's conquests, most or all of which were undoubtedly imagined. In between times, I sat in the apartment experimenting with chords or played games on the office computer. Checked my email an embarrassing number of times. She hadn't replied. End of that story.

The landlord let me stay the extra days in the apartment for peanuts, assuming that I'd be back next season. I didn't tell him otherwise although I wasn't sure myself. Upsetting Ali the way I had was enough reason to move on. But to what? Another job with Aegis? Accountancy? Bumming around again? Out of boredom I hopped a ferry and got a deal at one of the smaller Rhodes Town hotels. Wandering round the old quarter then back along the front, I passed the bar where the three of us had raised a Mythos. Escape was a random local bus. Not so random. The bus station at Rimini Square was for eastbound travellers. Lindos was southeast on the coast. And in Lindos was Mel. I took the next bus that headed down the west coast, passing through Kritika and Ixia, resorts filled with ugly, purpose-built hotels that made me wonder if I'd left the Aegean already. On down past the airport it travelled, squeezing through the ironically named Paradissi, a narrow street of dusty houses where an ageing population dodged traffic to pop next door or visit the local shop. This was the downmarket side of the island, despite the sin bin of Faliraki that devalued the east coast.

I got off at Kremasti, a pleasant enough place given the horrors I'd just witnessed, and headed towards the beach. The bus had meandered inland imperceptibly and it took me over ten minutes to walk to the sea. By the time I found a beach bar still open I was ready for a beer. The beer tasted bland and too fizzy. The weather had turned warm again but the sea was still wild and several testosterone fuelled windsurfers bucketed about on waves churning brown with lifted sand. Beyond them the swell shifted pale green and indigo back and forth between Rhodes and Turkey. A dusting of sand caught my eyes, swirled dry wrack and food cartons around. I couldn't come back to Greece if it wasn't Symi. And not to Symi if Ali was there. Or if Clair wasn't? Tried to stop wondering why she hadn't replied.

I didn't have any more revelations on the way home. Annie and Jude were at the airport to meet me and I was painfully glad to see them. She'd borrowed a mate's car. Jude was shy until curiosity got the better of him – it took all of about twenty seconds, transparent wee bugger.

– What've you brang me, Fraser?

– Jude! 'Brought me'. And you mustn't ask questions like that. (Annie)

– Why not? (Jude)

– 'Cos your Uncle Fraser's a troll who eats gobby wee boys. (Annie)

– But it's OK for your Mammy to be a gobby wee girl? (Me)

– Aye – and it's OK for you to take the bus, mister. (Guess who?)

Outside it was cold and wet with a meat cleaver of a wind. It was great to be back.

CHAPTER SEVENTEEN

CLAIR

Terrible plus a couple of months – and then some

October. Friday morning. I hit 'Print'. Having let down the last employment agency through 'exhibiting disappointingly unprofessional behaviour' as they put it, by visiting my seriously ill stepfather in America, I was undergoing the ritual humiliation of typing and IT tests to join other agencies. Akme Assistants? Bettatemps? Who cared? Connie's money, eked out carefully, had allowed me to stay at home for the first week, luxuriating in the sheer joy of Maggie's company, and for the second, after a reluctant farewell to my darling aunt, sorting house, finances, Jess, Case, Phee, more Jess, remembering and forgetting to get the computer fixed thereby infuriating Jess, who said she needed it for homework, but more, I suspected, for cheaper email / Facebook contact with Nikos.

My apathy regarding the computer was probably its association with temping, the vile occupation that would prevent me from painting – for I was now a woman obsessed. Joe was so delighted with the painting of Jess in Symi that I couldn't wait to try again. So, back in Guildford I tried to reproduce the image. But whether it was the different light or environment, acrylics didn't suit the composition and didn't satisfy me. I hunted out my oils, and with the slower technique something more interesting started emerging. It was exhilarating and unnerving, a testament to everything I'd let slide, artistically and personally. I took a grip. Symi must have provided negative and positive effects. I would just remember selectively. *And I am, after all, daughter of James Ranald Harkin, master artist.*

Despite this cathartic experience, there was my current half-life to get on with. On the last Thursday, nearly nine weeks into my fifty-first year I cleaned my fingers with turps, dressed smartishly and hit the agencies. By the time I got home, they'd rung me with a job. Start Monday. Company of surveyors, top of the High Street. *Oh, goody.* Life looked up a little when Sonya rang on Saturday morning and suggested an evening of debauchery, chez moi. *Brian's let her down at the last minute.* Still, it was a good excuse for a last blow of extravagance by way of food and booze. Cigarettes would be a problem. So far, I'd been good. But Sonya would arrive bristling with them – could I resist? One thing about Jess dumping Raz and putting Sainsbury's, where he worked several shifts, out of bounds was that we could shop at Waitrose without feeling guilty. I revved up the Polo and hit the road to Godalming. There was a Sainsbury's there, too, but I engaged selective memory again.

After the Saturday supermarket scrum, I decided on an afternoon of indolence before the evening's dissipation. I really ought to ring Connie, but our phone calls were identically depressing. Besides if there was a problem, my mother would soon let me know. By two, wearing jeans and a sweatshirt, I'd lugged the decaying floral sun lounger to the patio and settled in the tentative warmth of early autumn with the Guardian Weekend and a long scotch. Halfway through the Travel section I heard a sound that shrivelled my mood to a pellet of dread lodged deep in my small intestine.

– Hello-o-oh! Clair?

It was Brenda from next door. The humanoid equivalent of a black hole. I was trapped.

– Have you got a moment? Only I have a problem and – well, it's difficult with no one to talk things over.

That's what happens if you turn moaning into an Olympic sport. No friends.

– Do you think you could pop over? Only Judith and Gabriel are with their father and I want to be near the phone in case they need me.

Brenda deluded herself that her children, deprived of her presence for more than half an hour, were reduced to emotional wrecks. And anyway, why couldn't they call her mobile?

– I do hope it's not too much trouble.

Yes, it is too much trouble you manipulative great lump of blubber. Just once, just once I get a whole – half – an afternoon to myself and you go and flob your clammy great tentacles over the fence and drag me down to the bottom of your abyss of self-pity. I am not talking octopus here, I'm talking Kraken.

– No – it's fine. I was only reading.

I scrawled a note hoping that Jess would find it on her return from town: 'At Brenda's – please invent emergency!'

We sat in her large drawing room. Brenda sagged into a pink leather sofa, looking like Miss Piggy riding Dumbo side-saddle. The whole room was a shrine to the children with photographs covering every surface, relieved by the odd framed certificate for one or other's excellence at some trivial pursuit. On the mantelpiece was a wedding photograph – *why?* – featuring a slightly slimmer Brenda in a long white dress designed by someone with a cruel sense of humour – and her skinny, newly-committed husband, David. Somehow, the photographer had captured Brenda's sinister leer of triumph and David's gape of unwitting, naïve pleasure.

– Look, Clair, I'll be frank…

Oh no, Brenda wants to talk about sex. Again. And how she can get some. In fact, she was never that frank. And she didn't really want sex so much as a man who would fix household appliances, drive, mow, prune, decorate, take abuse, pay for everything and look like Brad Pitt. I prepared myself for a toe-curling interlude.

– See – it's not the same for you, Clair. I was used to having a man around full-time and now –

Her eyes welled and she dabbed them with a sodden tissue.

– Now I'm all a-alone a-and it's not easy bringing up two children when your h-h-heart's broken…

Try doing it without a fat maintenance cheque every month. Now that really isn't easy.

–… s-so, you see, I haven't got the confidence you've got, Clair, to go out and meet people. I wouldn't know where to begin.

– Why don't you get a job?

That was nasty, Clair.

– Oh, but there's the children –

– They're at school all day.

– I haven't got any skills.

– Not even computer?

Bugger. Computer. Repair shop. Forgot again. Jess will go ape-shit.

– Computers frighten me.

– But you used to work for IBM –

– And anyway, there's the house.

– What about the house?

– Cleaning, repairing, things like that. And there's shopping, cooking, washing –

I saw no evidence of the cleaning with thick dust on most surfaces and a carpet that looked like a pizza. *Still, who am I to talk… ?*

– If you had a job you could get a cleaner, you could pay someone to mend things. You could get your shopping delivered or do it at weekends. And you could give the kids little jobs to do.

Now be fair, since when had Jess towed the line there?

– And you'd meet other people at work, improve your social skills –

At this, Brenda had a full-scale weep. *Fancy suggesting the idle cow should get off her arse and do something to help herself. You are a bitch, Clair.*

– I only meant a part-time job.

I made a number of suggestions to test Brenda's skills of rejection. I had to hand it to her – she was pretty sharp. I started with the old chestnut: night classes – 'too scared to go out alone at night'; then, day classes – 'all old ladies'; going to a gym – 'too embarrassed about my weight'; joining a dating agency – 'too expensive'; reading the Lonely Hearts column – 'only weirdos advertise'; getting a dog – *getting a dog?* – 'too expensive and too much bother'. The door chimes went. It was Jess, my darling saviour of a daughter.

– There's phone call for you Mum – the GUM Clinic in Farnham Road has an emergency appointment free.

Trust Jess to dream up a date with the clap clinic. Sonya loved it.

– Good old Jess! She should write scripts for EastEnders –

– Oh ha ha.

– Speaking of which, have you looked at your email recently? I sent you both this wonderful spoof soaps thing I got from a casting buddy, like if Chekov wrote Coronation Street and Harold Pinter wrote Neighbours. Didn't you get it? Jess normally emails straight back.

– No. Computer's bust and I keep forgetting to sort it. Jess bounced me round the room when I got back from Brenda's.

– She's got her new iPhone – what's wrong with that?

– Too expensive.

– Aah. What kind of a mother are you, neglecting your daughter's love life like that? By the way – you haven't mentioned your Scottish –

– Haven't heard. History.

– OK.

Case was out, so Sonya settled herself at the kitchen table facing the hall to make certain he wouldn't miss her. She smoked an occasional cigarette dangling it outside the back door in deference to me. Halfway down the second bottle of Pinot Grigio I asked –

– How's Brian?

– Don't! We were supposed to be in Paris this weekend. Eurostar booked and everything – and shithead gets a call to say his mother-in-law's broken her hip and they've got to go dashing off to –

That's why she's here. Brian let her down at the last minute.

– I dunno, one of those places on the south coast you go to die. I've told him not to leave his mobile on when he's at mine, let alone answer it – especially if it's Cellulite Woman.

– Sonn – you have a heart of flint. Anyway, why couldn't you and I have used the tickets?

— Well it was a sort of business trip of his. Besides, I wouldn't want the slimy great turd to imagine me up the Eiffel misty-eyed with longing. It really is time I got rid. Jolyon's never off the phone – wants to carry on where we left off in June. Says it's the longest foreplay he's ever known.

— You serious? But you said –

— Tell me about your American matelot.

— Sheldon?

Sonya loved a smutty story well told. Her response was gratifying.

— Christ! Why couldn't the silly arse use Tabasco like normal people? Does Mommy Dearest know?

— Well, I won't tell her and he's hardly going to.

— Could sue you for damaging his bazooka.

— I've got the evidence and photos. I'd countersue – and sue Viagra for supplying the weapon.

— Hardly a lethal one by the sound of it.

Much honking with laughter.

— How do Connie and Joe know Mr Not-so-Big, anyway?

— Yacht club. Think he's more Joe's friend.

— Not if Joe hears about it. Sorry, I haven't asked, how is Joe?

Sonya liked Joe and vice versa. They'd met just once when he and Connie stayed a few days in London before going on a Mediterranean cruise. He approved of Sonya for persevering in business, liked her forthright manner – albeit toned down considerably in deference to Connie. And Sonya admired him because he was very, very rich. Joe didn't like London, dirty, he said. He never came to Britain again.

I described the sick room. Sonya commiserated.

— God – he's not a bad old fella, but it sounds profoundly dull. Glad you're painting again, though. Shame you left the Jess painting there.

— I've started another one in oils.

— Show us!

I took her to the easel on the landing, the only place in the house with room for it that wasn't let, slept or lived-in. I lifted the cloth.

— Wow, Clack, that is so beautiful! And it has a feel of something – can't quite say, but it reminds me –

— Oh god, derivative – you mean I've copied someone.

– Oh for the love of – that is not what I meant! It's amazing. You have to do this full-time.

She was always generous in her praise. I loved that about Sonya.

– Thanks Honey, but it don't pay the rent.

Encouraged, though, I fetched my portfolio and spread out some of my stuff from Florida.

– I really mean it, Clack, serious. Forget the half-baked business schemes and the temping and the teaching. You must keep painting. You're so talented. You've got to promise me, you'll do some more and take them to a gallery – there must be some around here. Promise?

Shortly before twelve we heard someone come in. Sonya was in through the back door sans cigarette, running her hand through her hair and adjusting her bosom in a second. But it was only Jess, returning from work, feeling headachy. She kissed Sonya, refused mothering, took some mineral water from the fridge and went to her room. We two settled into maudlin mode, Sonya regretting that her womb had never fructified, me bemoaning the awful life I'd thrust on Jess. It was gone two a.m. when the victim of my fertility wandered back into the kitchen for a snack and ordered us drunks to bed.

Hungover with a pot of tea the following morning, Sonya and I agreed that men weren't worth the trouble, that the world had it in for any woman over twenty-eight and that Jess had a great future as a storm trooper. We hugged farewell, roping Jess into a communal embrace before she wriggled out the front door to her lunchtime shift at Boccaccio's. As Sonya's silver Audi turned the corner onto Epsom Road, I noticed the Polo had acquired a few bumps and scrapes since Jess had been provisionally licensed to terrorise Britain's highways. Just then, Brenda's curtains undulated and I fled into the house leaving the Polo bumped and dirty at the kerb. Instantly, I was drawn to the canvas.

HOWARD

For too long my social life had revolved around the twin centres of Clair and work. Now the first wasn't available and the second was a political quagmire. My belief that I would easily attract a younger woman had turned out to be optimistic. Frankly, attracting any female I could bear to be seen with was proving difficult. Most of them at the Education Authority were attached, not that I had a moral barrier, but I needed someone for personal and social purposes. Any covert element would defeat the object. The unattached were either young, lumpen and dull, or middle-aged to aged, lumpen and profoundly dull. There was the swathe of teaching staff to consider but little opportunity for contact with the lower ranks; the upper echelons of female head teachers were too high profile and, to a woman, partnered. And they were mostly on holiday, anyway. Fortunately, it meant there were no parties, barbecues or other enforced jollies. Even the Bridge Club was on a break, which was unfortunate because it was a Clair free zone – she detested card games. My playing partner, Annabel, was a mentor of sorts; a lawyer, of indeterminate age and brilliant, but with a decided resemblance to a Bullmastiff. Even she was unavailable, being in the Dordogne with her brother and his family.

As I reached for copies of The Sunday Times, intent on studying the Lonely Hearts column, I felt sure everyone in W H Smith's could sense my purpose. Of course, I wasn't desperate enough to advertise, myself. Internet dating was for adolescents. Yet I admit, once home, I pored over the columns with something bordering on prurient interest. There were plenty of women looking for men – but what were they like? I rang 'Gorgeous F, 35, 5'5", GSOH, looking for M with mind for country walks, wining/dining, TLC. N. London', and listened to her message. She had a very high voice – Clair's was quite low – and shared a flat in Potters Bar. I hung up. 'Are you lonesome tonight? Don't be. Caring F, 45, 5'7" …' She was 'into Tango' so unthinkable. 'Fun times w. caring, sharing M, sought by F. arts grad. 38, 5'6" … '. Three cats and didn't drive, thus a liability.

One night back in Guildford, Clair had answered her mobile to Sonya and gone down to the sitting room 'so as not to disturb you', leaving me in bed. After some time, I went down and heard her saying: "… he sounds like Howard – prefer to get a woman at a supermarket so he can return the product if it's faulty…". She laughed at Sonya's response. I assumed it was that film company chap who was 'like' me. I just poured another glass of wine and crept back upstairs.

I poured myself a glass now and sat thinking. Maybe I'd got it wrong. Maybe Clair had found me 'faulty'. So why hang around for nearly two years? Granted, she hadn't been interested in me at college. But despite her being in with the pretentious arty crowd, I found her attractive. She was slender with a mass of light brown hair. Well, to be honest, I went for Sonya to start with. She laughed at me. So I asked Clair out, but she made some excuse about not dating married men. Then I heard a rumour about her and a hairy Art lecturer and went off her rapidly. Still, we all fall into a pit occasionally. I did with my wife – or 'the one who got the house' as I call her. Amongst other things. Still, when Clair popped into my head all those years later and I looked her up she responded to me more positively. Well, I wasn't married for one thing, and she was in her late forties by then and an unmarried mother. But even then, she wasn't – I have to say it – as appreciative of my attention as I might have expected. Why? After coping alone all those years, surely it was a relief to have someone share her troubles, sort out the odd little problem with that disaster of a house? Take her out to dinner? Was I just 'better than nothing' to her? The question nagged me.

I sat in my own home like a guest in a hotel room, my glass resting on a coaster on the marble coffee table, shades of neutral everywhere. By the time the uplighters clicked on at dusk, I had decided. I certainly deserved better. Better than this. Better than her. I picked up The Times again.

CLAIR

Retribution

Monday afternoon at the surveyors' office my mobile rang. The permanent secretary at the other desk pursed her lips. Major offence taking personal calls on your first day. It was Jess's school; could Mrs Harkin come in for a chat with the head of year at four thirty? Jess was all right but it was quite important. *Christ, Jess – what have you done that they want me in this quickly?* Great start with a new employment agency.

It was bad. Jess had smoked dope on school premises. The offender waited outside, white-faced and sullen while her year head spoke to me.

– You will understand, Ms Harkin, that this is a very serious matter. Even with the downward reclassification of cannabis –

This was just before the upward re-reclassification… Normally, it would have meant exclusion but, with Jess halfway through her A level course and having ground to make up, they were lenient. Jess was suspended for two weeks and had to continue her course work at home.

– Promise you won't tell Maggie.

We were in the car. I was too furious to speak but also uncomfortably aware, following my birthday shenanigans on Symi, that I was on shaky moral ground. Apart from the suspension and obvious blot on Jess's school record, it was more than likely that I would forfeit this week's work and, perhaps, any future work with the new agency. That, in turn, meant no computer repairs. I weighed it up in silence. Back indoors, I was able to deliver judgement.

– I won't tell Maggie on the following conditions: One, not only are you on suspension for two weeks, you are grounded for a month. That includes Boccaccio's –

Jess opened her mouth to protest but thought better of it.

– Two, once the suspension is up, you keep your head down and you work until your grades are up to where they should be. Three, you promise never to be quite so unutterably brainless as to contemplate doing it again.

– What about the computer?

– Learn joined up writing!

The agency rang. The surveyors had been pleased with me up to my early departure and, provided that I guaranteed to work the proper hours consistently, were prepared to take me back. Hearing myself giving profuse thanks for a job that filled me with despair reminded me of a favourite Maggie quote: 'The mass of men lead lives of quiet desperation'. *Lucky them, they'd be bloody suicidal if they had to go out temping.* In my relief, I relented, agreed to get the computer fixed and rang the repair shop straight away. Miraculously, they were still open. First positive bloody thing all day.

As I struggled in with the equipment, the geek behind the counter smirked.

– We only need the 'box bit', not the screen.

I was too weary to care about being patronised. *Just sodding well fix it.*

Case was there as I pulled up and carried the monitor back in for me. He wasn't preparing for an acting rôle at the moment and so was being his genial, would-be-roguish, self.

– You look really pissed off, Clair. I'll put the kettle on. Offload on me.

He did, I didn't. But he did manage to cheer me up by producing a cheque for the back rent. Up to date, something that hadn't happened since he moved in.

– Are you sure you can – ?

And what was the rest of that sentence going to be? Tourette's generosity, that's what I've got.

– It's cool. Mum had a win at the bingo. Nice one, eh? So, p'raps I could have my – ?

He whistled and gestured his neck.

Jess lay on her bed reading. She froze when I asked for the gold choker.

– Shouldn't we wait until the cheque clears?

– It will. Give.

A pause.

– Um – I haven't exactly – I mean, it's not here at the moment.

– Not here? What do you mean? Where is it?

– I meant to tell you.

– Tell me what?

– I've lost it.

Another explosive session ensued. No, she didn't know where she'd lost the choker! If she did, it wouldn't be lost, would it?

– Don't be so bloody cocky! When did realise you didn't have it?

– I don't know.

– Well yesterday? A week ago? Two weeks?

Jess shrugged, eyes fixed on the bedspread.

– Look at me! When?!

– I told you! I don't fucking know!

Prolonging it was futile. If it was gone it was gone. I had to think what to do. *God knows how much it's worth. It's a helluva lot of bling, that's for sure.* The choker had sentimental value, too.

– First, we must be honest with Case. So you will come down, now, and apologise.

– No way. If he'd paid the rent in the first place –

– I don't believe I'm hearing this! You are in no position to moralise!

– Makes two of us then.

– What did you say?

The silence was jagged. I postponed the almighty retribution Jess was due; Case was waiting downstairs. His beautiful features tightened when I broke the news. He was too shocked to be angry or to acknowledge my apology or even answer the tentative question regarding compensation. Just shook his head slowly in disbelief. As an interim gesture, I tore up his rent cheque promising that, somehow, I would put things right. It was then, after an interminable pause, he told me how much it was worth. My stomach lurched. I had no doubt that he was telling the truth and equally none that it would have to be an insurance job. *Shit – insurance! Did I renew it?*

A shuffle through the wedge of window envelopes behind the bread bin revealed a renewal letter from the insurance company, five weeks old. I would have to renew immediately and then leave a decent interval before claiming. There would still be an excess to pay, a limit on recompense for a previously unspecified piece of jewellery – and the risk of voiding the policy if they found out I took lodgers. To punish Jess, I threatened that telling Maggie about the dope was in the balance. The cloud of fear on her face was satisfying. My small triumph was deflated when Connie rang half an hour later to remind me that she and Joe were still alive – just.

The remainder of the week was a glumfest. I called home frequently from the relative privacy of the loo at work, or the street at lunchtime. Jess resented being checked and avoided me at home. My refuge lay on the landing where I painted out my anger on a few other Symi-inspired scenes before returning to the Nimborio portrait. In this version, the colours were subtler, outlines muted, curves softer. But there was more. The captured moment was so significant. Because of the father figure in the family group? Or simply the perfect composition, caught by chance? And Sonya was right, there <u>was</u> something familiar about it. So long as I wasn't ripping off an old master. Damien Hirst and Tracey Emin certainly had nothing to worry about. By Saturday I had finished two more canvasses before admitting that the Jess painting was complete. I let it dry.

The computer, too, was ready by Saturday morning. As I handed over enough cash to make a supermodel get out of bed, I suspected it might have been cheaper to replace it. Jess came with me to carry it back. Not, of course, for altruistic reasons. Back home, she shot upstairs connecting cables and was soon back online, muttering about getting an Apple Mac. At least it meant she was serious about schoolwork. You can't write essays on an iPhone. *Or can you?*

Downstairs, I shifted some of the mess around, attempting to turn the place into a happier environment. Without success. The landline rang and, for once, I managed to get to it before my daughter.

– Hello, Clair? It's Richard – Mandy's husband…

HOWARD

My first tryst (Are you intelligent, articulate and easy going? F Slim, 45, blonde WLTM you. Herts.) was pleasant enough looking, if 'blonde' was borderline untrue. But our meeting, one Thursday evening at a riverside pub near Stevenage, was punctuated by calls on her mobile phone from her twin sons who, at fourteen, could not function without her constant attention. I willed my own mobile to ring, but it remained stolidly silent. After forty-five minutes, I could stand no more and invented a dog that I had to let out. She rang me twice after that, but I claimed a full diary each time and she took the hint.

CHAPTER EIGHTEEN

CLAIR

One of the sweeter raisins

Richard was coming to dinner. Without Mandy. A client had booked him into The Angel Hotel while he did two days' consultancy in Guildford. The clients claimed him for the first evening. And I claimed him for the second. What to wear? I tore through my wardrobe. Only office clothes or jeans – and my Symi gear. And one of the few times of year when there were no sales on. Even at Debenhams. Plus a significant shortage of cash. *Crisis.* Charity shops were the only hope. Not too close to home, though, bearing in mind the lesson of Connie's unwanted gifts. Maybe some wealthy old size 12 - 14 bint had offloaded a few Versace outfits. If Versace ever got as gross as 12 - 14. Probably never squeaks above size – whatever. Size zero is an unfathomable lack of woman to me.

I struck lucky in Cranleigh. Someone had tired of a grey silk Jaeger shirt that blended superbly with some other rich bitch's black crêpe trousers. *Plus my best black heels and hair up. Fantastic. Shame I can't share my excitement with Jess. That way lies derision. Or stonewall.* Jess didn't know the object of my impromptu shopping trip, nor was she going to ask. But by the time I arrived back the scowl had gone. She even made me a cup of tea. The unalloyed joy of having the computer back, no doubt. Her slight relaxation of discontent didn't extend to dinner though and she took her cauliflower cheese up to her room. I nursed my secret in solitude over a dry-ish lasagne and a glass of tepid white wine.

Sunday. I cleaned the whole house with uncharacteristic enthusiasm. The old place scrubbed up fairly well. It was almost shabby chic, heavy emphasis on the shabby. By evening, I needed a thorough cleaning myself. I would buy food, wine and flowers on Monday. I would not, however, tell Jess. Not until Tuesday evening. *And she's going to whine: Why didn't you tell me? And I'm going to say, if I can be cool enough, "Because you didn't ask".* So smug was my mood it withstood listening to Connie for half an hour. Joe was no better, she was the same and Antonia sent love. Same as last time.

Monday dawned on the second week of Jess's suspension – thirty-six hours before the dinner date with Richard. My excitement was flawed occasionally by the recollection of him bandaged up on the sofa being tended by the exceptionally loving Mandy. Had that been solely on account of the accident? Or was that how they always were with each other? Then me, sitting in the 4x4 hoping he hadn't seen me, while Fraser went back to speak to him outside the chapel. *Fraser. Who?*

Monday evening. Richard minus twenty-five hours. Jess sprinkled parmesan on her spaghetti pesto then disappeared upstairs again which left me free to peel, chop, seal and simmer for the following night; Chicken Provençal – tofu for Jess – with Garlic and Rosemary Potatoes, asparagus and courgettes. Some ready-made gourmet soup or other – with a swirl of cream, baked apple with brandy cinnamon sauce and ice cream, cheese and biscuits. Coffee. And then? Just knowing he was a mile and a half away at The Angel Hotel was exciting. I pictured him walking through the wood panelled foyer, exchanging pleasantries with the receptionist, going up to his – single? – room. Enough. Time for a long bath with red wine and facemask.

Tuesday. The nights were fading fast. I was home with the last glimmer. Two hours and he'd be here. The light was on in Jess's room. Time to tell her. And to remind her that her current status meant she was invited for the meal only, not for socialising afterwards. Tap tap.

– Jess?

– What?

I went in.

– You might like to change. We've got someone coming for dinner.

Jess swung round from the screen.

– So should you. You don't want Richard seeing you like that.

She was wearing her best jeans and underneath her cardigan, a strappy top. And make-up.

He arrived two minutes early with flowers and wine. We kissed on both cheeks. Jess waited second in line and hugged him. He responded warmly and allowed himself to be ushered into the living room and plied with wine before responding to my enquiry after Mandy.

– Blooming. Sends her love. Jess must keep you up to date with all our news.

I smiled and nodded. She hadn't, of course, just like she hadn't mentioned that she knew about Richard's visit. I wondered just how much Richard knew of life in Aborigine Road. I felt undermined and the pleasure of seeing him was spoiled. But I smiled and nodded.

The meal went well and Jess behaved as though there was nothing amiss, being positive about school and university prospects and generally as charming as she knew how. She cleared table, poured wine and fetched from the kitchen. Richard chatted happily about Symi, Leeds, music, cricket, books and cinema. About Mandy, he said little beyond that she was fine and recently obsessed with Pilates.

Every course was a success, even if the Garlic Rosemary Potatoes were slightly overdone and the baked apples more au point than necessary. After cheese and biscuits Jess, who normally didn't drink real coffee, reached for the cafetière to pour herself a second cup. All evening she had avoided my eye and was at pains to do so now. *OK, you've done very well, but it's time for all A-level-students-on-suspension to get lost.*

– Darling, we must tell Maggie about this evening.

Jess focused stolidly on her coffee cup. I addressed Richard.

– My aunt in Scotland. We adore her, tell her absolutely everything.

Recognising the coded warning, Jess stood up.

– Sorry, Richard, got homework and – stuff.

After she'd gone, I poured us both more coffee. Richard smiled, folding his arms and leaning on the table.

– What a wonderful holiday Symi was – despite my minor mishap.

– Yes – yes. It was.

– What's your best memory of it?

I couldn't possibly tell you.

– Oh, spending time with you and Mandy, swimming, tavernas – stuff.

– You'll have to do better than that.

– Pardon?

What does he know? His eyes didn't shift.

– May I tell you a story, Clair?

I nodded, dreading the worst without knowing what that might be.

– I'm significantly older than Mandy – this is where you say 'Nonsense' by the way –

– Sorry – Nonsense!

– Too late. Anyhow, I'm aware that the age difference provokes comment. People wonder if I am a sugar daddy, a father figure or just a dirty old man. What have I got that would attract a beautiful young woman like Mandy? Not a lot – unless she's heavily into electrical engineering. She's not, by the way. So, why are we together?

You need ask?

– Richard, you don't have to justify anything to –

– I know. If you'd prefer I didn't –

– No, please, go on.

— First, let me say that Mandy doesn't mind me telling you this.

So you've discussed telling me? And why? To warn me off? How humiliating. He took another sip of coffee, traced the rim of the cup then began speaking quietly.

Mandy's was a sad story of abuse within her family. Her comments on Symi started dropping into place. Richard had been her father's employer and discovered her situation by chance when her father was taken ill. I felt compassion for Mandy and respect for Richard. He truly had been that knight in shining armour, the strong – but blessedly not silent – type. *I could have done with help like that. Why didn't you meet me?* His voice faded back in over my maudlin abstraction. What he told me made sense of everything. The comment about fathers messing things up, particularly.

— …the accident on the scooter. I'd been so sensitive to her fear and insecurity, I – she – thought that we could never have a 'conventional' marriage, for want of a better term. She might well have found someone else. That was our deal, after all, that the marriage was her sanctuary from the past. But unexpectedly, wonderfully, something extraordinary happened. I let myself need her.

Richard's story was just as surprising. Went for the priesthood but dropped out of seminary, knowing it was wrong. Married, but the wrong woman, divorced and gave up on personal happiness. What followed with Mandy was pure compassion until, unlike so many, Richard and Mandy realised what they had and the love grew.

— I'm so happy for you both, Richard.

— So what I'm saying, in a roundabout way is…

He made eye contact.

— …age doesn't matter. What matters is two people who need each other finding a way to be together.

Bloody hell – he knows! He knows about Fraser.

— Don't be embarrassed. Yes, I – we, Mandy and I, became aware of you and Fraser on Symi. You were very discreet, I doubt anyone else noticed. It started with your sunburn. He was very concerned. Then your – other fellow – arrived. Fraser was extremely reluctant to take him to your apartment. After he was forced to, he went off and had a skinful at that Nobby's place. Arrived for the guided walk next morning with an almighty hangover. I stuck with him in case he keeled over. Your name came up very frequently. He knew about the surprise birthday party and how much you'd hate it. When you turned up at it –

— Don't! I was such an idiot.

Richard laughed.

– No you weren't and obviously he didn't think so. He insisted that you had a single room. Then the next night, when Jess came to Nobby's Bar alone, he was very twitchy, wouldn't join us for a meal and left as soon as he could. Seeing you both in the jeep the next day was a happy ending. Does Jess know, by the way?

– She hasn't said anything. But there isn't anything to know, now. We're not in touch.

– That's a great shame. Would it be impertinent to ask why?

– No. It's just he hasn't called – nor have I. It's nine or ten weeks now, so... Everyone has holiday flings.

He reached across, put a hand on my shoulder. Suddenly, horrifyingly, I was in tears and unloading everything since leaving Symi – the homecoming, Case's choker, Florida, Connie, Joe, Maggie, Howard, the misery of temping and, finally, Jess's most recent misbehaviour.

– No wonder you're feeling low, Clair. Sonya and Maggie sound very supportive.

– They are but I don't want to –

– Burden them? They love you. That much is obvious.

– I'm always going to them for help or advice. They have their own lives. I ought to grow up. But it's – oh, I don't know.

– A very deep chasm with no obvious way out?

We sat in silence. I felt ashamed and relieved. I remembered calling him 'Daddy' in my delirium – but still, I felt the despair lightening a little. He looked at his watch.

– Much as I'd like to stay, we both have work in the morning. I just want to say, Clair, you are an extraordinary human being, but even extraordinary human beings can't exist in a vacuum. And you are grown-up. Most women are from about the age of two. Poor Fraser is only in his late thirties – it'll be some time before he's out of his adolescence. He may need a bit of encouragement.

I called to Jess that Richard was going. As we waited for her at the bottom of the stairs, he glanced up and noticed the easel, insisted on taking a look. He stood looking at the Nimborio painting for some time. Jess joined us, regarding the canvas impassively. Finally, he said

– I think this is your way out of the chasm, Clair.

HOWARD

The second, 'Lively, sensual lady seeks tall gent for wining, dining, love and laughter, Bucks/Beds', was a nurse at Stoke Mandeville Hospital. She suggested Sunday lunch at The Oak in Aston Clinton, but I restricted it to a drink, foreseeing no immediate escape with a full roast in front of me. Trixie was short, hefty, had a slight cast in one eye and greeted me by hollering my name across the saloon bar. I cringed, glad of being nowhere near Hitchin, and made a mental note to use a false name in future. After ten minutes I excused myself to the Gents and from thence made a dash to the car and home.

CLAIR

Terrible ambition

Richard's visit was the catalyst I needed. I felt potent, empowered, talented and somehow, validated. I would cope with life. A thank you card from him arrived a few days later, eulogising about the evening and my talent, sending much love and encouragement from himself and Mandy – who signed it with two kisses and a smiley.

There were eight galleries listed in and around Guildford. I went to them all that Saturday. They were kind, mostly, explaining that Saturday wasn't a good day to hawk my wares and why didn't I join Surrey Artists? *Yes, I should. Not that organised.* I tried a couple further afield and met with success at the second, 'Cyntra'. The owner, a 1960's caricature of an art critic in pink shirt and bow tie, surveyed the three canvasses and flipped through my portfolio, unimpressed, then squinted at the signature.

– Harkin? There was a young painter in the fifties – name of Harkin. Had a show at a – my father's gallery in Chelsea.

I felt myself flush with pride.

– That was my father, James Harkin.

– Really? Well, what a… Got any of his stuff on your walls?

– Yes – but it's not for sale. It belongs to my mother.

– Pity. Well, if you ever…

He pulled out a couple of gouache studies and three of the pastel sketches.

– Get these framed and I'll see what I can do. You can leave the canvasses here.

Pleased as I was that he was taking some of my stuff, I couldn't help feeling it was his way of getting to some of my father's stuff. Even so, I raced back into Guildford, to a small framer's in the centre. They could have them ready by Thursday. My credit card cowered but took the strain. *Speculate to accumulate.* I rang Maggie with the good news. Told her about Mr Bow-Tie's comments.

– Well, well. Could be that Jim's work is becoming collectable. Perhaps he's left you a legacy after all.

– It's all Mum's though.

– Except for one or two pieces I have. The one of your mother and you as a baby. Some of his wilder stuff. But they're really all I have left of him.

– Oh Maggie – of course they are. You couldn't ever think of parting with them.

The one of Mum holding me as a baby. Something in my brain was struggling to surface.

Despite my pleasure being qualified, it gave me a bit of a boost. I was the daughter of a collectable painter. Why had this never arisen before, though? Connie. She didn't rate his work and discouraged me from going down that route. So, I'd never met his friends nor gone for the art world seriously beyond taking art history and teaching kids to daub. I'd mentioned him at college, but only to other students and none recognised his name. As far as Connie was concerned, any financial worth in my father's paintings had been eclipsed by grandma Emily's and Joe's millions.

I decided to make the most of the positive feeling at having my work accepted before I destroyed it with analysis. *Email Fraser!* I followed the impulse without question, sat at the computer and composed, recomposed – then disposed. Just couldn't do it, even on a high.

The following Saturday, I took my framed work down to Cyntra Gallery. The study of Jess at Nimborio was in the window! Inside, two other canvasses were displayed, one of the island at Aghia Marina with bathers in the foreground, and a view of Yialos from Aphrodite One terrace. A woman in a fusion of violet and lilac looked up from a book of fabric samples.

– He's out for the day. Up to you if you want to leave it.

She handed me a business card. I scrawled a message on a Post-It note and left the five framed paintings propped against a wall. Went home and stuck the card in the mirror frame in the hall. *As if I'd forget where I'd left my brainchildren.*

Jess was in the kitchen dressed to go out. She had been back at school for only a week and was still grounded socially.

– Mum – Boccaccio's rang. They said if I couldn't go in tonight they'd have to advertise my job. And I have to earn some money to help out with…

Case's gold choker.

– and I got good grades on the coursework I did while I was on – while I was home. I am working hard, I promise. And I will come straight home.

– OK.

She'd been preparing for big-time wheedling.

– What?

– I don't want a fight and everything you say is reasonable. So, OK.

She almost preened. And she was genuinely pleased to hear about the gallery. Even hugged me before getting her coat. *There – that wasn't too difficult. And it feels a lot better, doesn't it?*

HOWARD

My third date was in London at the Captain's Cabin pub off St Martin's Lane: 'Slim, attract. F 5'6", 43, seeks tall, n/s M, 30s-50s for culture, dining out, maybe more? Ldn/SE'. The centre of London would not be my choice for a rendezvous but I had to avoid the Hitchin area. My mind flickered back to a taverna on Symi. Clair again. I refocused my thoughts to the present and skimmed the crowded bar. The only woman I could see sitting alone was well past forty-three with a face like an anaemic aubergine and at least eleven stone. I bought a glass of wine and sat at a distant table, hidden behind The Times. I put The Telegraph, the agreed signal, on the seat next to me. Thus masked, I rehearsed my new greeting: "Hello, I'm Dominic". Another lone woman walked in, slim, casually dressed and carrying a rolled newspaper, banner obscured. She seemed to be looking for someone, though. With some relief, I stood and waved.

– Diana?

She didn't react, having spotted her friend. Unfortunately, the real – or equally falsely named – Diana, stood up and smiled. Yes, it was aubergine woman. She made her way across, carrying her glass, her bottle of mineral water, a large handbag, an umbrella, a mackintosh – and a copy of The Telegraph.

– You must be Dominic! I'm – oh…

We both realised instantly that we had met before and that our names were not Diana or Dominic.

CLAIR

Terrible surprise

I arrived at the surveyors' office on Monday to be met with some surprise. I was no longer required. Hadn't the agency told me?

— No. When was this decision made?

Friday night, apparently, not that I had any rights, being a temp. I went straight to the agency, trembling with rage and humiliation. They admitted guilt. Cock up. Really sorry. If I went home they'd call me as soon as anything else came in. *No wonder my moods seesaw — it's not the menopause at all. It's being a bloody arsewipe of a temp.* Back home I made a coffee and switched on the TV. Obese, tattooed and pierced, sexual incontinents yelled at each other and had DNA tests done on their offspring. I switched off, went upstairs and trawled the internet for work, spreading my areas of consideration ever wider and stretching belief in my own ability to snapping point. Welder, waitress, pensions administrator, HGV driver, recruitment adviser, sous chef... drama teacher. *Oh, why not?* I rang the education agency. Come in, they said, for an interview.

By three thirty I was sitting outside the Head Teacher's office in a middle range private school between Guildford and Dorking. Weighing it up against my politics. Feeling as though I was facing reproach, like Jess three weeks ago. The secretary opened the dark wood door.

— Head is ready for you, now. Would you like to come in, Ms Harkin?

Those half dozen, well-remembered steps to certain reprimand. *Smile — you're here about a job...* The figure behind the desk had her head bent. She looked up as the door closed, rose and came round, hand proffered.

— Ah, Ms Harkin. Thank you for coming in at such short notice.

Her brows contracted behind the gold-rimmed glasses.

— Have we met?

Glue oozed out of the floral carpet and fixed my feet to the floor. It was the 'transvestite' from the supermarket car park, the one who'd tried to run me down.

— Oh, no! I'd remember.

As it was a private school, the Head Teacher had a little more leeway. After ringing a couple of my referees, Miss Frome offered me employment until the end of term. The security check could follow.

— Better a semi-known quantity than no one at all. Not flattering, but there it is.

I was to start on Wednesday.

I agreed to baby-sit for Brenda, who was being elusive about an engagement that Tuesday night. I didn't give a toss where she was going, what she was doing or with whom. My total lack of curiosity was too much for her.

– Look – I'll tell you – but you'll have to promise not to –

– Brenda, please don't. I hate being asked to keep secrets – I'll forget and tell someone then you'll hate me.

– But it's not a secret, it's –

– Just go and have a nice time.

Once she'd gone, I settled on Dumbo the sofa to reread The Crucible and swat up on theatre games for my new post. Sonya rang. After an annoying 'guess what' game, she uploaded the news.

– Brian's moved in! We're à deux, a couple, a pair – he's left Cellulite Woman!

– But I thought his mother-in-law was – ?

– Wish us abundant joy!

– I wish you abun –

She'd rung off. It was difficult to concentrate for a while. Something like – was it envy? – weighed me down. Not envy of her and Brian, but of that elation, that belonging. For a moment the thought crossed my mind that I'd been too hard on Howard. I dismissed it. But it was to return over the next few days, more and more persistently.

Brenda arrived back after eleven, coy, furtive and with eyes gleaming. I sloped off home, too preoccupied to wonder.

FRASER

The heating had broken down at Jude's school, sabotage not ruled out – in a primary school – no shit. Anyways, we were spending some quality time together. That is, I was trying to read in front of the gas fire and Jude was bouncing on my chest. Mondays were heavy for Annie with two lectures, a seminar and today, a tutorial as well. So, Uncle Fraser was on extra duties. I was doing bar work in Glasgow city centre but it was my day off so it worked all round. I'd begun to think staying in Glasgow might not be such a bad idea due, partly, to my growing-up-and-doing-something-sensible-for-a-living debate and largely, probably, to the Ali Mavrakakou complication on Symi. On the other hand, I could work elsewhere for Aegis. If there was anywhere else needing a rep. 'If' was as far as I'd got. My mobile rang and I heaved Jude off my chest.

– Hello?

– Kalimera! Jings to mickty!

I was so involved in Annie and Jude's life right now, I thought he was a figment of my imagination.

– Niko? Mate! How are ye's?

He was coming to London for meetings and interviews in December and staying with Clair and Jess.

– I didn't know you and Jess were still – ?

There was a chuckle at the other end of the line.

– Of course.

I waited, reluctant, then just asked –

– Does – er… ?

Clair. Still the contraction and expansion of various emotions and body parts at the thought of her. Even though she'd never replied to my email. Even now. Even though… I realised I was on my feet, striding about.

– Fraser? Hello?

– Och – nothing. It'd be great to see you. Come and stay.

– I arrive at London Gatwick on fifteenth December.

– Call me when you're in Guildford and we'll sort something out.

It was a weird conversation. Nikos belonged to Symi, to Nobby's Bar, to the apartment in Chorio, Nimos Island, to too many beers and not enough sleep. I rang off feeling I'd been a bit distant. It was the connection with Clair. She really did exist. And she didn't want to know.

– Fraser!

Jude collided with my legs.

– Come and play wrestling!

– Is that choc ice round your gob?

Big eyes.

– Naw.

CLAIR

Back to school (another synonym for Terrible)

Miss Frome was not a transvestite. She was in her late fifties or early sixties and married to her career. Her BMW was at least ten years old and her dress sense firmly rooted several decades earlier – pre mini-skirts. The school, Elyots, was for eleven to eighteen-year-old girls, part day, part board. Drama classes crossed the range to GCSE and AS/A level. I had a day's induction with Ricki, an English teacher from South Africa, who had been deputising following the sudden departure of my predecessor. After a brief introduction to year eight, lots of little Alices and Emilys, a Sacha, a Soraya, two Freyas, three Ashleighs, an Autumn and a Filumena, I was left to find out what they'd been up to all term. They were quite sweet, eager to perform and, on the whole, it was a happy reintroduction to teaching. I split them into groups and they improvised scenes featuring 'a surprise', with variable success. Unfortunately, following an indigestible lunch of quiche in the staff dining room came year ten: names from Ariadne to Zinnab, all with venom coursing through their veins, bored, undisciplined and wanting to be somewhere else. And all hating their set text: The Crucible.

The last class of the day was with year thirteen, Upper Sixth in my day, and at the same stage as Jess in the A level course. Like Jess, they were allowed to wear their own choice of clothes to school and, consequently, sported a uniform of low-cut jeans and short, tight tops. Unsettled by the disruption of changing teachers so far into their course, they needed a lot of reassurance. I worked differently with the small group, sat them in a small circle, listened to them, and asked them how they thought I could help. During this, a thick gold snake choker worn by the stunning, distant, Chloe transfixed me. I worked hard to concentrate for the remainder of the lesson. I had to find out so loitered after class asking who was a boarder, who wasn't, how they were enjoying sixth form. Chloe clearly wasn't into chat. I caught her by the door.

– See you Friday, Chloe. Great choker, by the way. Unusual.

– Cheers.

– Only I've been looking for one like it ...

Chloe gave me a look that said, "You? Afford this? In your dreams, teacher", and sauntered out. Esther, stockiest of the group, shot to my side.

– Her boyfriend gave it to her, he's loaded, he owns a bar in Guildford.

She giggled and looked uncertainly at the others.

– I don't suppose I would have been to it?

My reply invited beans to be spilled. It worked. The girls were eager to gossip. The bar was called 'Booze'n'Crooze', the owner one Willo. Back at home, I threw 'Booze'n'Crooze' into mealtime conversation. Jess was too extravagantly cool. *You're nicked. Let the next conflagration ensue.* Which, of course, it did. With the force of all our combined history.

STILL CLAIR

Progressively Terrible

I hadn't been sleeping. Not just 'not sleeping well'. Not sleeping. I lay in bed each night waiting for the wave of unconsciousness to envelop me, felt it coming tantalisingly closer then ebb away, leaving me stranded on a bleak outcrop of wakefulness. Sometimes, I went down and made tea, watched TV or read a book, toes tucked under a cushion on the sofa in the cold sitting room. Mostly, too weary to move, I tried willing sleep to return but the concerns of the present would crowd my head, each vying for individual attention. No sooner had I indulged the Jess situation than loathing of teaching would jostle forward only to be hounded out by financial worries, my doubts over Howard, concern for Joe, rage at Connie and – lurking in the background all the time – my feeling of hollowness over Fraser. Invariably, sleep receded beyond the horizon. Night after night, green digits on the radio alarm counted me slowly through the turmoil until –

– Good morning, this is the Today programme – it's just coming up to seven o'clock and here's Diana Speed to read…

A pedant would point out that I did, occasionally, dip into sleep immediately prior to the radio switching on. In the few minutes of relief that came with knowing the night was nearly over I would plunge into a neap tide of terrors so real that I awoke, heart racing, drenched with dread. Having a drug-using thief for a daughter played a significant role in the nightly scenario. The scouring session that was our latest confrontation revealed more than I had expected or feared.

– Why, <u>really</u>, don't you have Chase's choker?

Long, long pause. She had sold it to Willo, owner of the Booze'n'Crooze bar. The reason? To support her growing experimentation with drugs which had progressed, if that is the right word, from dope to ecstasy and, finally, a couple of 'champagne' hits of cocaine. Thankfully, if only due to lack of funds, she hadn't sunk to crack cocaine. Sharn Fellowes, inevitably, was a name that cropped up. I sensed Jess was relieved that her secret was out. When emotions had subsided a little, we talked for a long time. Jess admitted disillusionment with her current way of life; the nightclubs bored her and made her head ache, the guys weren't Nikos and Sharn had turned out to be shallow and selfish. Drugs, at first to dull the pain of leaving Nikos in Symi, had taken over. She was no longer in control and it frightened her. She wanted her life back the way it was but didn't know how to change. Neither, I noticed, did she ask for help or say 'sorry'. Shocked as I was, I felt we'd turned a corner. The main point on which we agreed unequivocally was that she would stop, now. Dropping Sharn was a not a difficult point to win.

Jess's confession superseded all my other worries and cast a sinister shadow over my waking hours. That the new owner of Case's gold snake chain was a pupil at Elyots, added a dangerous complication. I had to return it to Case but couldn't think how without being proved a lousy parent and an unsuitable teacher. And losing my job. Ordeal though teaching was, it paid better than temping. But it was adding to the stress.

After my first day at Elyots, I'd been left pretty much on my own. The volume of work was frightening; I had to prepare classes in advance, read new texts and look out old teaching notes as well as learning the names of all my new pupils and, as a last consideration, take classes. School was not as I remembered. At first, I blamed it on the private system thinking that the children of the wealthy were more likely to be imperious with teachers. But, no. Other teachers assured me, Elyots girls were abnormally mild. State schools were far, far worse. Why else were teachers practically bidding for jobs in the private sector? Nevertheless, I had to learn to wheedle, cajole, confront and fight for respect, and then, if I was lucky, get in half an hour's teaching. As the term wore on, I became angrier and more frustrated. So you don't like The Crucible as a play? Tough. That's the set text. I didn't choose it. Refuse to work and you're the losers.

– You called us losers, Mrs Parker. I'm going to report you.

– My name is Harkin, Miss Harkin, and I said you'd be losers if you refuse to work. The choice is –

– You called us losers. I'm going to tell Miss Frome.

– Fine. Then you'll be a liar, too.

– We don't have to take abuse from teachers.

– You also think, apparently, that you don't have to take instruction.

– Why should we? You can't tell us what to do.

There was no time for any other life, not that one was on offer. Sonya was permanently unavailable these days, busy building a nest with Brian. But I spoke to Maggie regularly. There wasn't any point in holding back; Maggie always knew when something was wrong. Besides, I had no reserves. I needed to lean a little, guilty though it made me feel. All promises to Jess were revoked. Maggie was predictably surprising.

– Listen, lass, it takes a lot more to shock me. I got wind of what Jess was up to when you were in Florida and we did have words. Obviously not the right ones. She promised it would stop if I said nothing. It's been a difficult secret to keep. Maybe I shouldn't have. You mustn't think that you've failed her, not unless you think I've failed both of you. Jess knows right from wrong – and she's chosen wrong, for the moment. What we have to do is nudge her in the right direction, pretty firmly if necessary.

Maggie also provided a possible solution to the choker problem.

— Let Jess work it out. Allowing her the waitressing job is positive. It means that she can start making inroads into what she owes. And there's another thing, but I won't say until I have your word that you won't argue.

Oh god, she's going to pay for Case's choker. I can't – But I promised and Maggie laid out her plan.

— I had it in mind to give Jess a start with her first car. Maybe that money should go to get the young man's necklace back. Then Jess would have to pay the money back to herself.

There was a storm when Maggie's cheque arrived, made out to me. Jess raged about betrayal and told me to fuck off out of her life. After she'd slammed out, I curled on the floor, face buried in a cushion, howling until the tears dried up and I was tired out. My face felt like a rubber mask hanging on the bones of my skull. My head thumped, my body ached and my spirit coiled around itself. So low did I feel, I imagined how comforting it would be to have a solid old bore like Howard to lean on. It was just after six thirty, he wouldn't be home, yet. But his mobile would be on. I projected the awkward conversation and resisted, then crawled across the floor and lifted the receiver, hesitated until the high pitched 'off the hook' siren cut in and replaced it, ashamed of my weakness. Then I actually fell asleep, full length on the floor.

I woke just before nine. The room looked the same, curtains drawn, table lamps on, but sounds outside came from the distance of night. Inside there was quiet, save for the complaints of an old house. I rose stiffly, rubbing joints, massaging my numb arm to life. I'd been dreaming about painting. It was Friday. Tomorrow I would go to the Cyntra Gallery and check on sales. I washed and went to bed, waiting until two when Jess slammed in. Once more, the clock's green glow accompanied my night on its grudging journey to morning.

CHAPTER NINETEEN

STILL CLAIR

Terrible disappointment

The study of Jess in Symi had gone. The shock was both pleasant and alarming. Did I really want to sell it? *Well, yes. But…* There was no sign of lavender woman. Mr Bow-Tie was in the back and came through scowling, it was obviously too early in the day for him. Didn't recognise me, but had obviously decided I wasn't a customer – or not a rich enough one.

– Yes?

– I've come about my paintings. Clair Harkin. The one of Symi was in the window.

He remained hostile for a moment, then remembered.

– Ah, yes. Yes. Went last weekend.

He sorted through a small box file and handed me a card with a cheque attached. I thanked him. The week's grimy discord dissolved. But when I looked at the cheque I was staggered.

– Thirty-five pounds?

– Yes?

– The materials cost that!

– And your point is?

– Nothing – I'm just surprised. I –

– You're unknown and very few people remember your father. No one's going to pay hundreds. And there's commission. But in the future, who knows?

I fought my disappointment.

– The others? Has there been any – ?

– No. Leave them if you want. Up to you.

His sympathy was finite. *They won't sell stacked on the landing at Aborigine Road. And there's the framing to pay for.*

– OK. Yes. Thank you. Sorry if –

– No problem. Thanks for coming in.

He was already making his way to the back of the gallery. I walked slowly back to the car and started the engine. The heater had only just got up to speed after the journey from Guildford. I moved off, noticing the decorations zig zagging the street. Shit – Christmas. That's all I need.

Back at Aborigine Road, David, Brenda's ex, leant against his car waiting for his children. He smiled weakly baring tiny teeth in a large amount of gum, made more obvious by the recent addition of a gingery moustache. He was friendly in the submissive, eager way of a small dog, the sort that came back for more punishment. Here he was again, waiting outside in the cold, not allowed into the house he'd bought. Brenda often kept him half an hour or more over the agreed pick up time because the children weren't ready. Her mantra was:

– He doesn't know how hard it is to bring up two children all alone.

Of course, he only pays for everything. Her constant carping would have turned Mahatma Ghandi into an axe-wielding maniac. But David submitted to it all, being one of the 'anything-for-a-quiet-life' brigade. I felt helplessly angry on his behalf.

– Hi, David. How are you?

– Oh, Clair. Yes, fine, thanks. You? Jess?

– We're OK, thanks. Where are you taking the kids today?

– Oh – er – Christmas shopping, TGI Fridays, then the Odeon.

– Sounds expensive. Do you want to come in while you're waiting?

– Thanks but –

And he nodded towards the house, nervously. As I headed for the front door, I heard Brenda usher a sullen Judith and Gabriel out.

– I don't want them back before seven!

– Right-oh!

He fumbled with the car door as the children plodded down the path. I peered through the dried leaves of the beech hedge dividing us and saw Brenda framed in her doorway. She was wearing jeans! *Walrus dressed as shrimp.* And she'd had her hair restyled and highlighted. *Good grief. Maybe she took my advice about dating. What on earth will she attract dressed like that?*

Jess was in the bathroom. I made coffee, desperately formulating plans for the unexpected festive season; I just hadn't noticed December creeping in. And I had to make contact with this Willo at Booze'n'Crooze to discuss the gold choker problem. *Can't cope. Christmas first?*

I bought stamps, Christmas cards and stuff for the States: a gauze wrap for Connie, a talking book for Joe and the traditional bulk order of English Countryside Calendars for distribution around Naples plus a few rolls of cheap wrapping paper from the market. I wrapped everything in Waterstone's coffee shop, stretching out a skinny latte, then I queued for centuries at the Post Office and posted the lot. Walking back downhill towards the car park, I looked up at the little stars and long silvery fringes shimmering across the High Street and the 17th century clock over the Guildhall. The lovely old cobbled street falling towards to the backdrop of the North Downs provided a charming foil for the whole display. Intent on the illuminations I blundered into the path of a couple walking arm in arm in the opposite direction. I stepped back, making an automatic apology without registering their faces until –

– Hello, Clair.

– Howard!

I could hardly have been more astounded – this was the seamiest surprise, including the toilet episode in Symi and the proposal fiasco – because Howard's companion was… Brenda. Brenda from next door.

STILL CLAIR

Merrily Terrible

I spluttered outrage on the phone to Maggie until even I thought I sounded a bit dog-in-a-manger. She cut across it.

– Now, lass, Christmas.

– But –

– Christmas?

– Yes, please.

– Through Hogmanay, I hope?

– Certainly. I'll bring stuff. Email your shopping list.

Willo was understandably chary when I announced myself on the phone as a customer's mother. It could only be a complaint. Having caught his attention, I was as frank as I could be about the choker without being accusatory. My daughter had made some bad decisions, I said and I understood how difficult this might be for him, but I had to return the goods on my daughter's behalf and would, naturally, reimburse him. There was a slight pause and then he replied that it wouldn't be possible because the goods were no longer in his hands.

– Oh, that's unfortunate, Willo.

– Meaning?

– Meaning I hoped we could settle this quietly. I'm as keen as you not to involve the police.

It was enough. He named his price.

– Don't make me laugh. It's not worth half that.

Probably unwise, but it was too late, I'd confronted him.

– You'd shop your own daughter over a couple of hundred quid?

– Her and you. You paid three hundred. Asking for fifteen hundred is greedy.

– Price of gold is going up every day, you know. I have to think of my own interests.

– Five hundred. Your choice.

We settled on six fifty. It was worth nearer a thousand. For a second time that year, I recognised Connie's genes in me.

I arranged for Jess to meet him in a pub. At first, she refused to go. Connie's genes helped me out again.

– So I go? And Chloe's there? What happens to my job? And our income?

I pulled on a furry hat, drove Jess to the pub and waited outside. I could see Willo sitting at the bar, exquisitely rumpled hair, two-day stubble, leather jacket easily worth Case's gold choker. He was fit, that much was clear. Together, he and the stunning Chloe would be the epitome of cool.

We were all players in a parody of television cop shows. Willo feigned not recognising Jess, made it hard work for her. Eventually they both came outside. I lurked, pretending to be transfixed by the Christmas display in the shop window next door. Jess went to pull out the bundle of notes.

– Here it is.

Willo hissed at her.

– Oh, subtle. Not like there's CCTV round here or anything.

Willo linked Jess's arm and they started along the road. I followed. Without little change of pace they turned and started walking back. The transaction had taken place. Willo nodded towards me.

– This your Mum, then?

I stood aside prattishly. Jess glared. Willo slid away.

– OK, I've got it. All right?

– It's the same one?

– Yes!

I was not going to be intimidated.

– Show me.

At home, Case was gracious. But there might be a problem with the back rent I'd repaid him, he shook his head apologetically, college expenses – and with Christmas coming up – you know? I nodded, in no position to argue. Jess melted away. There was still enough of Maggie's cheque to put a deposit on a car.

In school, Chloe wore a platinum and diamond pendant.

Part of my deal with Jess was that she did something constructive about her drugs problem. It didn't extend to her doing any research on it. Guess who that was left to? There was a six to nine month waiting list for drugs counselling. The only options to bring it forward were going private or OD. The helpline volunteer explained the acronym patiently.

– Overdose – kicks in NHS drug care – if you're lucky.

We had to find the money somehow. Question was, how? We were only scraping by at the moment and all Jess's earnings were going on paying back the £650 into her car fund. There was nothing for it, she would have to use the remainder of her car money to pay for counselling. It was a question of priorities and –

– You're right, Mum. I'll do it. And I will pay it back.

– That's something you'll have to tell Maggie.

She chose to see a counsellor in Reigate, a couple of stops away on the Gatwick train, and insisted on going alone. Returning from her first session, she was preoccupied. I was anxious to know how it had gone but didn't want to put pressure on her. Or me. Eventually, she brought it up.

– D'you know, sometimes they put rat poison in Ecstasy? Puts you off, knowing that, huh?

Oh my god! Don't look too surprised. Nod your head sadly. Jess smiled.

– She's great, Mary, doesn't make a fuss. Just – listens.

Just listens. At £50 an hour. Who wouldn't?

Jess had made an appointment for the following week. I was glad she was keen to continue. Was it enough to make me feel any happier? No. I needed selfish comfort. I needed someone to be looking out for me in a very instant and positive way. I was fed up with coping. Yes, Maggie coped, Sonya coped. But they didn't have the daily, unremitting problem of Jess.

Images of a walk under the pines and a small seashell of a room came back to haunt me, the feel of body contact, skin to skin. Full length.

HOWARD

It was bound to happen sooner or later and I was glad that it was sooner. Wouldn't have wanted to bump into her outside her own house. Christmas may not have been the most auspicious of times but Clair had made her own bed – without room for me – so she would have to get used to lying in it.

Things were moving fairly fast with Brenda. I'd been invited for Christmas Day. I assumed, perhaps, that it was their father's turn to have the children this year and that there would be a hole in her life at a time for families. Turned out not to be the case. He never had them at Christmas.

– I have all the hard and difficult times so I deserve to have the happy times, too.

– But doesn't he ever – ?

– He can have them at Easter – if he does everything as agreed.

That was that. I was going to have a family Christmas. With children, apparently. I rang Dolly to say I wouldn't be in Dorset.

CLAIR

Jess finds out the meaning of Terrible

Normally, Jess didn't get up until about lunchtime at weekends but she went out early that Saturday. I was too busy with the approaching festive chaos to think it odd. Around two, I was on the phone hearing about the Yacht/Golf/Country Club festivities that Connie and Joe were missing due to Joe's damaged heart. Connie, of course, knew nothing of my traumas with Jess and work since leaving Florida. The only positive development I could report was the school job.

– Well, at least you're back on the tracks you were on twenty years ago.

Yes, Mother, and I'm just as depressed about it, only more able to cope with the depression. The calendars had arrived, Connie continued, they weren't the same quality as last year but it was too late to do anything about it now, she'd just have to give them out. I studied a cobweb in the corner above the television and projected my mind up to it until Connie was reduced to a white noise hissing in the receiver.

The sitting room door opened and Jess's excited babble dragged me back. I waved her to be quiet.

– Sssh! I'm talking to Granny. Sorry, Mum, I was talking to Jess –

– Mum! Look who it is!

– Jess – will you be –! Please give him mine Mum – and Jess's. Speak soon. Bye.

I put the phone down.

– Hello, Clair.

It was another of those Greek thunderbolts.

– Niko!

Two hours later the three of us sat in the kitchen over the remains of take away Chinese. I had contained my anger with Jess rather than embarrass Nikos. But Jess's moment was coming. I was punch drunk with Jess-related dramas and well on the way to lashing out with fury. I reached that point when Jess, eyes sparkling with lust and alcohol, took Nikos by the hand and said:

– Hey – you look knackered. Let's go to bed.

– No, Nikos. You go on to the sitting room. I need to speak with Jess.

If Jess was too immature and irresponsible to let me know that Nikos was arriving, he was astute enough to unhand Jess and do as he was told. The moment he'd gone –

– OK, lady, how long have you known he was coming?

– Not long.

– How long?

– Couple of days.

– You bloody little liar. Now you talk straight or he's on the street. You, too if necessary!

There was nothing else left with which I could threaten her. Jess, assuming eviction impossible, was defiantly silent, even smirked slightly in triumph. Provoked by such insolence, I moved decisively, slamming the kitchen door behind me and wrenching round the huge Gothic key that, unbelievably, clicked shut.

Nikos greeted me uncertainly. I was direct.

– Niko – I didn't know you were coming.

– But Jess said you knew.

– Jess has had… Jess and I have had some problems since Symi.

Despite the hollering from the kitchen, despite the slamming of the back door, the banging on the front door, Nikos and I talked. He was a different man outside the island. He had not come all this way just for love. There were professional and academic contacts to visit in London. I was heartened rather than alarmed by his pragmatism. We came to a deal. He could stay, but he and Jess did not sleep in the same room. No sex at Aborigine Road. He understood the directive was in response to Jess's behaviour, not a judgement on him. I said that when we went to Scotland, he could –

– You are going to Scotland? But Fraser didn't say that you were –

– I'm half-Scottish and my aunt lives there, Fraser has nothing to do with it.

– That's sad. Fraser is in Glasgow. I know he would like to see you.

I will stay calm. But I felt the heat rising in me. *Jesus – don't know if I'm blushing or flushing.*

– Perhaps, if you are going to Scotland, I could travel with you?

Spoken softly. Pragmatism was certainly his thing.

During his time in Guildford, Nikos and I became friends, much to Jess's initial chagrin. Sleeping arrangements were an issue only with her and this, ironically, flagged up her immaturity to Nikos. He had some introductions to firms of London architects, set up by his tutor at Aristotle University in Thessaloniki. Jess travelled up after school a couple of times to go on brief trips around the tourist sights. But it was clear that the relationship had changed. He behaved more like a big brother and, surprisingly, became a confidant over her drug problem. I remembered with some embarrassment that it was Nikos who had checked the apartment for signs of dope on my birthday in Symi. I wondered whether he held me accountable for Jess's current habit.

– Niko – about Symi, when you went back to our apartment to –

– No problem, forget it. Holidays. But in Greece, the consequences are significant.

He was convinced that Jess's danger was past. And it did appear that she was clear. *Counselling? Or the male influence she's always needed?* Over the course of his stay, I found myself thinking he could be just the man for my difficult daughter.

There was a little bit of squaring up between our guest and Case who, hitherto, had seen himself as the alpha male of the house. I used it shamelessly, including a mention of outstanding rent, which caused Nikos to raise an eyebrow at his competitor. There was a cheque on the table before nightfall. This time, I showed no delicacy in pocketing it and despatching Jess to pay it in the next day. Nikos was an asset in other ways, too. I was satisfied to see Brenda's curtain twitching feverishly each time I left the house. *If Brenda had an imagination she might think we were having a mènage a trois – and pass it on to 'our mutual friend'.* Soon, though - gratifyingly,

Howard's TVR turned up, parked outside next door. Nikos was impressed by the car at first then astonished to learn to whom it belonged.

– Gluefeatures? How come?

Jess was happy to fill in the details and communal hilarity helped me over my illogical resentment of the situation. Then it spilled over into ribaldry that got a bit close to home.

– Enough!

Nikos did a quick mime of all three wise monkeys and suggested a trip to the pub. It was my last day of term and time to slough off the residue of hormonal angst from Elyots. Jess had a couple of days to go. Nikos linked arms between us and started it –

– Biddly diddly diddly diddly dee!

We launched into 'Two Ladies', Nikos announcing with hubris to Brenda's front window –

– Und I'm the only man – jah!

Blimey – if he's like this on the way to the pub, what will he be like on the way back? Disappointingly, Howard's car was gone by then.

Having Nikos around underlined the absence of Fraser and our lack of contact since Symi. I felt humiliated that my daughter's beau, the one over whom I'd had such doubts, had proved to be the more constant, even though I knew there to be some ulterior motives. Even more difficult was the fact that Fraser had invited Nikos to spend Christmas. Could we stop in or near Glasgow? I agreed, not wanting to appear affected by the chance of meeting him. But my intention was to avoid it. No point in expecting Nikos to understand that. I tried to remain cool, busied myself with doing piles of shopping to take north and packing the quart of bags into the pint-size Polo.

STILL CLAIR

Merrily Terribly in denial

We set off from Guildford on 23rd December with a scowling Jess wedged into a corner of the back seat and clamped in headphones. Nikos took over driving at Keele Services. It had seemed reasonable to put him on the insurance, as it would save me doing the whole drive. He had a few trips to the supermarket and one spin on the A3 under his belt – hardly preparation for the high-speed slalom that was the pre-Christmas M6. Being used to Greek driving habits, Nikos had no fear. I sat back knowing I was safe to snooze until Carlisle where I would have to start navigating. I woke at the Penrith and Keswick exit. It was sleeting. Nikos assured me he was

OK, that he remembered the directions and I should try to get more sleep. But the diminishing distance before Fraser tormented me. Carlisle 20m – Moffat 60m – Fraser 100m-ish. *How am I going to deal with seeing him? Talking to him?* Despite which, the next I knew, we'd stopped at Hamilton Services, a dozen miles or so from our meeting point. It had taken seven and a half hours, so far. Not bad in a battered Polo so near Christmas. Jess and I scrambled out and made for the Ladies through the dark afternoon. Nikos strolled to the restaurant, speaking on his mobile. Reapplying mascara in the cruel light over the wash hand basin, Jess emerged slowly from her ill humour.

– Be strange seeing Fraser again.

– Mmm.

I was in my best jeans and a new, dusky pink sweater, not my usual 'long drive' jogging pants and comfy jumper. Fraser liked me in pink. I still didn't know whether I would be able to face him. On the other hand, I couldn't remain childishly in the car. For one thing, Jess would wonder why and, for another, it would embarrass all of us. But how to handle it?

– Come on, Mum – we've got another hundred miles after Glasgow.

– You go on ahead. I'll meet you back at the car.

Shocked at how aged and tired I looked in the fluorescent lighting, I needed a few moments to myself, I decided. I strode back to the Polo and got into the driving seat.

I knew the West End of Glasgow. Arty and student-friendly, it was where, during the long summer holidays thirty years or thereabouts since, Sonya and I had accumulated many a creditable hangover. Sailing past Hillhead Station, I realised I'd gone too far so pulled up a side street and found my way back to roughly the right spot, parallel to the main road. Terrible Clair emerged.

– Sorry, I'll have to drop you here, Nikos. I can't leave the car full of stuff. Asking for trouble.

Jess groaned.

– Oh, Mum, it'll be all right for a few minutes.

I gave her a look. It was enough. She went with Nikos to the café, promising to be back at the car in ten minutes. I called after them.

– Say hello to Fraser for me. Maybe see him some other time!

But as Jess and Nikos turned the corner, the struggle began again. *'Some other time?' 'Can't leave the luggage in the car'? So why the pink sweater and the best jeans? In case! In case what? Just in case I didn't chicken out at the last minute like I just have. Why's that? Luggage in my head. Coward! Yup.*

The hundred miles ahead were a short hop after the miles we'd already covered and I felt refreshed by the stop at Hamilton. Shame not to take a break on the Byres Road but there it was. I got out of the car, leaned against it, savouring the air, the insidious wetness of Glasgow. Glad I was on my way home, my other home. The sleet was suddenly dense and I stood up quickly, opening the car door. As I did, someone walked past and a small voice piped up.

– Fraser! I need a streamy!

– OK, Jude –

Fraser? Jude?

– Fraser?

I could never rely on my mouth to stay shut.

– Who – Clair?!

A pause then we spoke together, stopped, laughed. Jude broke the moment. He needed to pee. Now. He wasn't interested in Fraser's friend. Couldn't wait.

– Och…! Clair – are you coming for pizza?

– Can't leave the Christmas gear in the car. Jess and Nikos are there.

– Fraser! I really need –!

Fraser was torn.

– Just a minute – c'mere, Jude! Excuse us, Clair.

He took Jude behind the car. I heard everything that went on.

– Sorry about that. Clair, this is Jude. Jude, this is Clair. Normally, he'd shake hands – but under the circumstances…

– Hello, Jude.

– 'Lo.

We all waited in the drenching sleet.

– It's good to see you.

I don't remember who said it. I just saw in his face that it was true. Jude tugged and whined. Fraser took him by the shoulders.

– Jude, Clair and I are going to do some grown up stuff. OK?

– OK…

Jude's esteem for his uncle was wavering by the look of it.

– Count to twenty – slowly – without looking and you get pizza.

No remorse over Jude's innocence or our hidden agenda. This time there was none of the romantic delicacy of the first kiss in Symi. We were hungry for each other. Before Jude counted two, lips, teeth and tongues were fully engaged, by five we were grappling. By ten, we couldn't let go. Peeking early, Jude was disgusted and demanded instant gratification pizza-wise. The old biro-on-hand technique for phone numbers was all the little tyke would allow before we were torn asunder in the Glasgow hinterland.

The Polo wrapped me in chill while every bit of me that wasn't molten with desire fizzed and glittered. *So Symi was – ? So why didn't he – ? And why didn't I – ? And when will – ?*

Continuing the journey, Jess was more talkative, glad to be in the front seat, sorry to leave Nikos, pleased to have seen Fraser and enchanted by Jude. In fact, much of her conversation was about Fraser, which suited me. But I was on my guard. *After all 'a kiss is just a kiss'. Yeah – but what a kiss.* Despite caution, I was pretty sure I was a gonner. At my age. And I wasn't just in lust.

CHAPTER TWENTY

STILL CLAIR

Christmas bliss

Three hours later we were in Kilachlan. Maggie was a good hugger. Didn't let go until you did. According to Julia, no mean hugger herself, it hadn't always been the case. Brought up by a strict father and kindly but remote housekeeper, Maggie didn't acquire the art of hugging until Julia and I came along. She soon made up for years of Presbyterian repression and then nobody could stop her. My dad also had the innate ability, she said, but never really got going because Connie wasn't the hugging type. He was restricted to his little daughter, me. This late, late evening she hugged us out of the cold and into the parlour. The only light came from the fire and from the Christmas tree, festooned with decorations as old as me. Bulbs with glass cones and Chinese lanterns the colours of boiled sweets.

– D'you remember, Maggie – you and Julia and me putting the lights on the tree?

A smile that said 'yes'.

With all the outrageous fortune recently, I felt as though I hadn't set eyes on Maggie for years, though in reality, it was only two months. Something was different, though. I sensed a weariness. *I'm so selfish; I forget how old she is.*

– Maggie darling, it's been a long day – let me tuck you up in bed. I'll sort Jack and Tatty.

– After the drive you've had? You will not!

– Indeed I will.

I won; another disconcerting change. Leaving Maggie in the bathroom, I went to the room I was sharing with Jess. The terriers curled blissfully on the sleeping Jess's bed and resolutely ignored my whispered commands, even managed little growls as I lifted them to the floor. Tatty was straight back up while Jack, the realist, trotted to the back door. Minutes later, letting them into Maggie's room, I was concerned to see her sitting motionless on the bed as though too tired to get undressed. Maggie looked up, blew a kiss and bade me goodnight as much in command as in blessing.

Despite the joy of being back with Maggie in Harkin Croft and all that it meant, I'd been looking forward to being alone with my thoughts. Thoughts of Fraser. That strange little interlude in the sleet had buoyed me to a ridiculous high. But now my mind was laced with concern at the change in Maggie. Ironically, sleep came instantly, depriving me of all unease – and of any romantic or raunchy fantasies.

Christmas Eve. The day got off to a rocky start when I remembered that none of the food had been unpacked from the car the night before. Jess slept on 'til after ten to avoid doing anything useful. Nessie and Wally Scrymgeour arrived in the van as I was unloading and gave me a hand. Luckily, the cold night meant that nothing had suffered. Nessie and Wally's visit was a social one to exchange Christmas gifts with Maggie. They brought a box full of Nessie's preserves and a home-baked Christmas cake, complete with snowman. It was laced, Nessie winked, with something to keep the cold out. Wally received the predictable but nonetheless welcome glugging, tubular package and Nessie her accustomed choice of hand cream, soap and talcum powder and there was a Christmas card that clearly contained generosity of another kind. They stopped for their traditional dram and sherry then set off for Gallanach. They were spending Christmas with their daughter on Kerrera, the island that shields Oban from the sea's excesses. Wally would have stayed on for another but Nessie, anxious to catch the last ferry, twitched and fiddled until Maggie shooed them on their way.

Once they'd gone, Maggie declared it Christmas. Easy. No more work, simply indulgence. Jess peered sleepily in at the doorway, clad in a Hunting Stewart dressing gown that had belonged to her great grandfather, and giant panda slippers. Seeing Maggie and me on the booze came as no surprise to her. She mumbled something about breakfast and shuffled off. Maggie drained her glass.

– About time the we'ans had their walk. What's the weather doing?

I tackled the jumble of carrier bags in the kitchen. It was quicker and less stressful not to ask for Jess's help but to move around her. Maggie joined after a few minutes and soon everything was away. Then she and I muffled up and braved the damp air. Going down the lane, she took my arm. Nothing unusual in that, but she leaned a little more as if needing physical support, not just the comfort of linking arms. Fear of Maggie's mortality had haunted me down the years since Julia died. With that terrible loss, some of the brightness had gone from Maggie's face. When her sense of humour had eventually started creeping back it had lost its dry edge. Julia's death was a wound from which she would never fully recover. And now she seemed so drained. It frightened me. Then came the guilt. If I'd cared more about Maggie instead of always letting her look after me, she'd be stronger now. She interrupted my flow of remorse.

– Mind when Jess was a baby and you were staying here?

– Oh, yes. It was a special time.

– Aye. Happy days.

She's doing it again, reading my mind – trying to make me feel better, telling me that I've given as much to her. But it's not true.

— So — tell.

Maggie whacked the seventh post for luck.

— Tell what?

— What's cheered you up? Does it or he have a name?

I had just pulled up off Byres Road in my story when Isobel Mudie's dog, Jasper, cannoned past us in pursuit of Jack and Tatty. Isobel was Kilachlan's nearest to a lady of the manor. Like another aristocratic matriarch, she found her family an endless source of exasperation. Maggie squeezed my arm.

— We've been hunted down. Have to save it for later, pet. Isobel! Has the family arrived, yet?

— Indeed not, nor Archie's not back from Aberdeen. And on Christmas Eve. Hello, Clair.

— Mrs Mudie. How are you?

— Well enough. Christmas is a lovely time isn't it, though?

After ten minutes of Isobel's platitudes, we managed a brief skirmish down to the surf. Strolling back along the lane, I shared as much of the Fraser story as I comfortably could. Maggie was well able to fill in the gaps. I could tell she was pleased for me, not least because it was an end of Howard, about whom she'd never commented — which was comment in itself. Jess was still in her dressing gown, talking on her iPhone and sipping Glenmorangie as we entered the croft. The blissfully drenched Westies were wrapped in towels, nose and whiskers peeping out. Maggie observed loudly that it was time to be dressed so that the festivities could begin and Jess sloped off out, still murmuring into the phone. After she'd gone, Maggie finished ruffling Tatty and set her down.

— Would that be Nikos she's talking to?

— Don't know.

I was unsure of Nikos's status with Jess, now.

— Maybe, maybe not.

Maggie folded the muddy towel.

— D'you know what they're doing over the holiday?

— Who?

— Both your young men.

I felt my mouth twitch and looked down.

— Oh — they're with Fraser's family, I suppose.

— Why don't you ring and find out? They might enjoy the ceilidh.

The Kilachlan ceilidh was a Hogmanay essential. I needed little persuasion and retreated to the wreckage of our bedroom, already dialling. Fraser picked up.

— Clair! I was just — I wanted to give you time… aw, shit — Hello. How was the drive up?

— Good, just on three hours.

— You must have been buggered.

— A bit.

A pause. Who next? What next? Ah — the old choices, the old dilemmas.

— I missed you last night.

Him. Spoken seriously. I stuttered.

— Me, too — you. Um, Maggie wondered about — New Year — sure you have stuff arranged, but if you —

— Cancelling it as we speak —

Jess was pleased, not ecstatic, but very pleased. The gut-churning thrill was mine. Fraser was coming to Kilachlan for Hogmanay.

Christmas Day dawned pearl grey. Pale sun, fingered through mist, touched the light frost and illuminated a fairy tale landscape. Maggie roused Jess to help her milk Esmeralda in the small outhouse. I had the porridge oats in a saucepan when Jess arrived back, eyes bright and cheeks pink with the cold, carrying the pail of warm milk.

— Let's have English porridge!

At the croft, this meant dousing the oats in milk and serving the porridge with honey. Delicious. While Jess sent and received copious text messages, Maggie and I went to the Christmas Day service.

The Mudies were in their family pew. Archie Mudie gave me a mildly lecherous once over while Isobel nodded 'hello'. Beside them the twins, Donald and Fiona, in their thirties and both unmarried, stared blankly. They reminded me of George Bernard Shaw's response to Isadora Duncan when she imagined their joint offspring — 'But what if it had my body and your brains?'. Poor Fiona had inherited her father's rotund build and bulbous eyes and her mother's stupidity. She did some minor admin job in Edinburgh. Donald, however, was an Adonis with the perfect features of his mother and the amoral cunning of his father — and doubtless the same immoral proclivities. He was 'something in the City', lived in Dockside and travelled up from London in a Porsche or a Lotus — whichever didn't need cleaning, no doubt.

The service went on. And on. Maggie shushed me to silence over the warden's boozer's nose and the minister's razor rash. Several centuries later, she whisked me through the handshaking in the porch and back to the croft. The tree, our pagan symbol of Winter Solstice, lit the corner by the fireplace, its tub buried in extravagantly wrapped gifts. Maggie had spirited two bulging stockings to hooks either side of the fire. It must have been after breakfast and before kirk. Jess's stocking, amidst sweeties, clementines and nuts, contained a diamante banana bar for her navel (procured by the Scrymgeours' granddaughter who was fast outgrowing Kerrera), a miniature framed photo of Jack, Tatty and Esmeralda, enamelled side combs, a tiny bottle of heather honey cologne, sparkly tights, socks with toes in them and a book of William McGonagall's direst poetic gems. I had some exquisite Celtic silver earrings, sable paintbrushes, my favourite foundation, lipstick and mascara, a long pale smoky blue chiffon scarf, the colour of my eyes, and an anklet –

– For sunnier days. Just in case the Greek experience got into your blood.

Maggie knew how to touch a nerve.

Equally furtively, we southern Harkins had concealed Maggie's stocking behind the curtains. In it were finger mitts, leg warmers, an 'evil eye' from Symi to hang outside the door, ginger in dark chocolate, a citrine crystal set in silver, a monkey on a stick and four gob stoppers.

Maggie also gave us a cheque each. She silenced our protests.

– That's enough! Who and what else am I to spend it on?

But our reactions and thanks were appreciated. Our large gifts to her seemed modest by comparison. Jess had attached mementos to a framed mirror: some of her infant drawings reduced on a photocopier and glued on, postcards from Maggie to us, a transcript of 'Wee Willie Winkie' (a favourite of baby Jess repeated endlessly by Maggie), photographs of Maggie, herself and me, shells and driftwood from Kilachlan's shore and several whisky labels – all varnished into place. It embodied the love and shared memories between us all. Maggie stared at it for a long while. Jess looked anxiously at me. I smiled back. If Jess can do this, she's the marvellous human being I always suspected. Finally, Maggie said:

– What a waste! All these beautiful thoughts and this aul heid looking back at me in the middle of them!

Our turn to protest while Maggie hugged Jess. My gift was portraits of the three of us painted as a triptych, Greek style with Maggie in the centre. She was enchanted.

– What did I ever do to deserve you two?

– Dunno, but it must have been pretty wicked.

Maggie smacked Jess's bottom and the moment escaped bathos by a hair. There were chews for the dogs and a new bell with her name on it for Esmeralda.

— Can't she come into the kitchen, Maggie, just for Christmas?

— No, lass, because she'd have to go out to the bothy again and that would make her miserable.

So we took Esmeralda some hot bran mixed with potato peelings. She butted Jess gently, rubbed up against Maggie and licked greedily at the little heap of salt in my hand before burying her head in her food tin. Jess tied the bell as she fed.

— Could we take her for a walk? On a tether?

— When the weather's warmer.

— You always say that.

Television was banned on Christmas Day (the ban circumvented by selective recording). Smoked salmon sandwiches, vegetarian goodies and a steady flow of alcohol kept us going before dinner. Jess took the terriers down to the beach while Maggie and I, coordination happily shot, messed about with food in the kitchen. Dinner would arrive eventually. By three, we flopped by the fire accompanied by two never-ending drams and the Queen on Radio Scotland. The magical time of gathering darkness was upon us. Jess arrived back with two wet dogs and adopted her usual sprawl on the hearthrug, nuzzling their little bodies, a glass resting on the granite slab before the flames. We were home.

We had dinner in the tiny dining room, decked for the occasion with pine branches, holly and tartan ribbons, candles on table and windowsill. There was game pâté for Maggie and me, garlic toast for Jess, then Aberdeen Angus beef for the carnivores, nut roast for the veggie and ridiculously over-catered roast potatoes and vegetables. No one had room for pudding and we retired, slightly on the far side of comfort, to the fireside.

I felt a sudden urge for a cigarette, a need I hadn't felt for weeks. Luckily, I no longer had my safety valve packet so there was no danger of succumbing. I took a turn around the garden in the crystal air, musing on relativity. From Christmas Day to New Year's Eve is six days real time, half an hour of spending-time-with-Maggie time, and five years of waiting-to-see-Fraser time. Then the mobile in my coat pocket bleeped a text message. What it said made me smile.

HOWARD

Thus far, I had avoided meeting Brenda's children. So, while I was invited for Christmas Eve, I chose to drive down the following morning in an effort to limit the first encounter. Staying until Boxing Day felt excessive as it was. I arrived in Guildford around noon. Brenda was waiting at the front door with a smile that struck me as somewhat less than spontaneous. I soon learned she'd kept the children waiting for me to arrive before they could open their presents. Not a propitious start.

Clair's car was not there. North of the border with the redoubtable Maggie, no doubt.

Naturally, I went bearing gifts: some kind of general knowledge board game for the children and a set of crystal glasses for Brenda. I didn't want, at this point, to give anything too personal. Good heavens, we hadn't even been to bed together. Oddly, it wasn't something that troubled me too much. I wondered what sleeping arrangements Brenda would have organised.

The children were polite and barely spoke apart from thanking me for the gift. I doubted they actually liked it. Brenda seemed pleased with her goblets and reset the dining table with them. She gave me a silk tie, a bottle of cologne, a guide to boutique hotels (why?) and two tickets for a concert in London – some male singer.

At lunch she asked me to carve the turkey. I felt awkward A) because I'd never carved a turkey before and B) because it was a sort of 'head of household' role. Made a bit of a hash of it and managed to cut my thumb, necessitating a lot of fuss with a first aid box and the separation of bloodied turkey to a separate plate. The children made ill concealed vomiting gestures, frowned at by Brenda. Got past it and on to Christmas Pudding served with cream. I prefer brandy sauce. Then the children were excused while Brenda and I had port. One thing led to another and, well, to cut a long story (I imagine) short, I fell asleep. Woke up round about five-ish lolling on the rather lumpen pink leather sofa. The children were in their rooms, Brenda was smiling thinly and the table was spread with the inevitable turkey sandwiches, Christmas Cake et al. What to do but eat more?

After an evening of television, the children were sent to bed. More port, more swinish stupor and, somehow, arrival in the bedchamber where we awoke, in the same bed, the following morning. Brenda rose and appeared a while later in wafting nightwear and mellow aspect, with breakfast on a tray.

Clair's car was still absent when I left to drive down to Dorset. Dolly was cool with me having been, in my absence, forced to spend Christmas with a Women's Institute friend. Not a season to remember.

CLAIR

Raisins soaked in alcohol

Though Christmas was a minor event in comparison to Hogmanay, Boxing Day drinks with the Mudies was a Kilachlan tradition. We arrived at noon. Several of the neighbours were in, most of whom knew Jess and me, so the hour passed tolerably well for all except Fiona Mudie, who sat miserably in a Hunting Stewart frock on the sofa. Her brother Donald cast an appraising eye over Jess, stayed long enough to appease Isobel then sauntered out. Archie, on the other hand, ogled Jess openly, plying her with an inferior malt and invading her body space until she'd backed the length of the room to avoid him. Maggie broke away from her cluster and whispered to him. He barked with laughter, after which they chatted amicably until it was time to leave. However unlikely it seemed that Maggie and Archie would have anything in common, they had undoubted rapport.

Back at Harkin Croft, we spent a relaxing day allowing our distended bellies to recover. Looking in to say goodnight to Maggie, I found her sitting up in bed with the blue shoebox open and a jumbled photographic record of her twenty-two years with Julia scattered across the quilt. I apologised, not wanting to intrude on reminiscence.

– No, no, come in, lass. She was your friend, too.

– Of course she was.

She patted the bed. I sat next to her and for a while we relived the time all three of us had shared. There was the Westminster flat, St James's Park, Battersea Gardens and Funfair, days by the seaside and on the river. I'd often wondered why there were no photos of Julia around the house. The moment to ask had never been right before but, for some reason, the question was out. Maggie thought for a few moments and shook her head.

– I don't know. We were so used to – not…

– Not making things too obvious?

– I suppose, yes. And then, when she… I couldn't look at a photograph. It was easier just to keep her in my head and my heart. A photograph would have made it – made <u>her</u> too real.

It was the first time Maggie had referred to Julia's death.

– How long did it take before you could?

Maggie nodded towards the dressing table. On it was a picture of me holding the newborn Jess, taken minutes after her birth.

– 'til you gave me something else to think about.

How could I be so dense? All that love — Jess didn't just bring it with her — she got Julia's share, too.

— Maggie? Tell me.

Maggie leaned against me, silent for a few moments, deciding. Then she spoke, fluently and steadily as though she'd been waiting for this moment.

MAGGIE

— You and Sonya had just moved into your flat in Ealing, the one with the long corridor from the front door. You'd invited us to dinner. I came straight from work and Julia had already arrived. The three of you were into the second bottle of wine and giggly, especially Julia. It's always the same when one person is a bit behind on the alcohol, the others seem to be in a secret club — and that evening I never really caught up. When we arrived home, Julia and I had a bit of a tiff — which very seldom happened. I put it down to the wine… if only it had been. Being Julia, she hadn't told me that there was anything wrong. It wasn't until next evening that we sat down and talked. She'd been to see a specialist, you see, a consultant oncologist. There was a lump in her breast. She hadn't told me. She'd come to you straight from getting the results of the biopsy.

— People are so aware of cancer now, but we weren't then, didn't do breast checks. She had a mastectomy but there were shadows on the X-rays. By the time it was diagnosed, you see, it had already invaded the lymph glands. Then it was her lungs, her bones. It was soon clear that it wasn't a question of being cured, but how long she could stave it off. The chemotherapy made her so sick that she stopped it. If life was going to be short, she said, she wanted it to be glorious.

— She had a list of 'things to do'. Tea at The Ritz was one of them and she wanted you there. Remember that posh afternoon with tea and cakes, everyone staring at us for laughing? She always said that you were really our child. Odd that, she was so much ahead of her time in her thinking. But however close to you she felt, she wouldn't put you through her dying. Very clear about that, said you'd lost enough already. Julia knew when she kissed you goodbye on Piccadilly it was forever.

— She'd been all over the world working for the airline, so the 'glorious' she wanted was just for us to be together and enjoy what time we had left. We came up to the croft. As for those last months, I'll always be grateful to Hugo Benfleet. He was a good employer and a generous man. He said to take whatever time I needed and there'd be a job for me if and when I wanted to go back. But the real surprise was our local rogue. Archie Mudie.

– He'd tried a pop at both of us, Julia and me, the first time we came up on our own together. We thought it was hilarious. Then, once he discovered our situation, it became a personal challenge; he arrived one night with a magnum of champagne and a glint in his eye. Naturally, we patted him on the head and sent him back to Isobel. But if ever he was in London he insisted on taking us out to dinner. He was great company and very amusing; we had some marvellous evenings. For him, being seen with two ladies suited his image and, of course, with my connections I was able to introduce him to some useful people. Isobel, of course, never knew. Archie loves her to bits, by the way, always has, but he needs a lot more. He was a good friend to us when we needed one, and discreet. Yes, difficult to believe, isn't it? He gave me the loan of his pied à terre in Kelvinside whenever Julia was in Glasgow Infirmary.

– At the drinks party today, I told him he'd have as much chance with Jess as he did with Julia and me. You heard the reaction. It put me in mind of other times, happy and sad. He was there at my best and at my worst. Kept me company or left me alone as I wished. He had a very soggy Harris Tweed shoulder sometimes, and he provided practical help when I really needed it.

– Julia wouldn't let me contact her family when we got the diagnosis, she was afraid they'd make her stay with them. It was when she was at her lowest that Hugo Benfleet's wife, Felicity, got involved. Hugo had kept in touch while I was nursing Julia, at first here in Kilachlan, then in Glasgow, sent flowers for her – Johnnie Walker Black Label for me. Kept me afloat, you might say. One day Felicity looked in Hugo's diary, found a Glasgow address against mine and Julia's names and jumped to a devastating conclusion. She thought that Julia, Hugo and I were a ménage à trois and the flat was our love nest. It was Archie's little flat, of course. Ironic, really, considering Archie's fantasies. Felicity confronted Hugo. He explained the situation quite candidly, but she wasn't convinced. She wanted revenge on him for years of infidelity. So, she went to the Chief Whip and offloaded her suspicions.

– Parliamentary circles are very incestuous. Felicity didn't foresee the consequences of her actions. Remember, I met Julia at a Benfleet end of session party at their house in Sussex? Julia's parents were neighbours of the Benfleets but Julia's father and Hugo were business associates, too, board members of an American investment bank. It was an Oklahoma bank, founded on oil, right wing and very 'Christian', didn't want anything ungodly defiling its money. Somehow, details of a potential scandal reached the Chairman. Hugo and Julia's father were asked to resign. It all happened within about twenty-four hours. Julia's parents came straight to Glasgow, to

Archie's flat – I found them on the doorstep when I arrived back from seeing her in the Infirmary.

– They yelled abuse, refused to come into the flat, said they didn't want to be contaminated by filth like me. Everyone in the close heard and someone called the police. They managed to contain things. A policewoman stayed with us while I told Julia's parents that their daughter was dying.

– The next morning, the Blumenbergs had Julia moved to a private hospital. They refused to let me see her. There was nothing I could do. For the last ten days of her life Julia was in a strange room with only her parents to visit her. I don't know what they said to her or how they treated her. She died on my fiftieth birthday. I wasn't allowed to go to her funeral.

– I was living in a sordid nightmare. Remember this was the nineteen seventies; things were on the way to being liberal but nothing like today. Hugo was very apologetic, very loyal to me and kept me on as his secretary until I retired. Somehow, Felicity and I managed to avoid each other all that time.

CLAIR

No more denial

As Maggie related this history of love, prejudice and loss I recalled fragments of scenes: Maggie and Julia, so merry on that day at the Ritz, the telephoned news that Julia had died and Maggie saying, "No, lass, don't come to the funeral – she wouldn't want you to". On this Boxing Day in Kilachlan I shared the depth of Maggie's sorrow that she, too, wasn't at Julia's funeral. What would she have done without Archie's practical kindness? Or, indeed, the loyalty of Hugo Benfleet – Ben? How else could she have survived? Ben's influence on the Harkin women had so many facets.

Jess looked in early the next morning. I put my finger to my lips and moved carefully from under the quilt, crept from the room.

– What's the matter, Mum? Is Maggie ill?

Her face was taut with concern.

– She was feeling sad last night and we had a long talk.

Jess let Jack and Tatty out and made some tea. I took Maggie in a brew and found her sitting up, looking rested.

– How are you feeling?

– Quite, quite well. Thank you for last night.

– I only listened, Maggie. I'm so sorry I wasn't there for you when –

– Oh, you were there, in my heart. Now, give me that tea and let's get the day started.

I volunteered to milk Esmeralda. Jess and I negotiated with our bête blanc for a goodly while to no avail. Maggie was drawn by the shrieks of exasperated laughter but refused our pleas for help on the grounds of entertainment. Fifteen minutes later, we amateur dairy technicians emerged bruised and with half the usual measure of milk. Maggie took the lid off a bucket of bran and propped it in a corner. Esmeralda, unable to forgive Maggie her treachery, retreated with narrowed eyes and refused to budge. We left her in caprine dudgeon and went back into the house.

Jess was first to notice as we entered the parlour with mugs of coffee.

– That's new. Who is it, Maggie?

On the dresser was a framed photograph of Julia wearing her airline uniform, smiling in an uncharacteristically restrained manner, her hair swept up under a pillbox hat. There was another of her with Maggie. *Yes – it's the sea front at Brighton – I took it! I'd just finished A levels – we went to a Berni Inn for lunch, then we went paddling by the pier in the rain.* And there she was with me sitting on her lap with my Andy Pandy doll. *I must have been about three. That was the flat in Westminster.* There were photos of Julia everywhere. Framed. Waiting all these years.

– Maggie? Who's the lady in all these photographs?

Maggie looked over and I smiled. It was time Jess knew about Julia.

– That's Julia, Jess. Julia Jessica Blumenberg. She was a very special friend of mine.

I put a match to the fire, set providently the night before, and Maggie began with the Benfleet party, fifty years earlier. Jess cuddled up to Maggie for an edited version. After a while, she asked –

– Julia Jessica – is that why you called me Jessica, Mum? After Julia?

– Yes.

– So she was sort of my great aunt, really, wasn't she?

– She would have thought so.

– Maggie, you're just so cool and Julia sounds just so – I dunno – fun.

Encouraged by Jess, Maggie brought out the blue shoebox and we three Harkins went through twenty-two years of snapshots. For Jess, learning that there had been a gay relationship in the family was like finding a precious heirloom. And discovering that she was named after Julia thrilled her.

– Did Granny know – you know – about you and Julia?

— Yes and no. When we grew up, Jess, everything 'out of the usual' was suppressed. So, like Queen Victoria, your grandmother preferred not to acknowledge that lesbians existed.

She's said it! The 'L' word. She's actually said it. And Jess hasn't batted an eyelid.

— But she felt awkward around us. Not so awkward that she stopped us from looking after your Mum when she was little. Connie didn't have any option, though, after your Granddad died. Poor woman.

I remembered. Mum was always tense when they were around. And when she came to pick me up from the flat in Westminster, she never stayed. I don't think she ever sat down there. She'd be angry with them if they'd fed me and critical if they hadn't. She never wanted to hear what I'd been doing, never let me bring any paintings or drawings home and told me not to mention my Auntie Maggie at school. And yet here was Maggie being generous about her. Jess was fascinated, probing.

— What did Granny do to earn money?

— She took a waitressing job in London when she and your Mum were living with us. Then she moved to Guildford and we didn't see them so much.

Maggie had talked herself to a standstill.

— Enough! What say we go out for lunch today?

Jess wanted to hear more but greed overcame her curiosity.

— Great! Can we go to The Wide Mouthed Frog at Dunstaffnage?

CHAPTER TWENTY-ONE

STILL CLAIR

Getting fruitier

Wherever there was a wall or a horizontal surface, there was Julia. Harkin Croft was a happier place for it and Maggie's weariness seemed to have lifted. An end to denying Julia was her perfect Christmas gift. A few photos disappeared over the week, as though Maggie had enjoyed the indulgence and was getting back to normal. Enough remained, though, to proclaim Julia's importance in her life. And in mine.

The aftermath of Christmas followed an easy pattern of late breakfast, walking dogs, back for a snifter, lunch then a choice of snoozing, reading, painting, revising or preparing for class, depending on which of the Harkins we were. One afternoon, as I made a discreet study of Maggie, dozing with Jack on her lap, Tatty at her feet, I had a revelation. There on the wall behind her was the inspiration behind the Nimborio study of Jess – my father's study of Connie holding my infant self! It was <u>his</u> influence. That fluidity, that softness – <u>he</u> was my muse. I told Maggie. She hadn't seen my painting.

– I'd love to have a version of it, if you can bear to paint it again.

Of course I could. Knowing his style was my influence felt strange and moving. I wanted to explore it further. It was a link, a very profound one, to the man behind the door whom I could never reach.

Evenings comprised the slow preparation and enjoyment of dinner, perhaps TV and inevitably, a phone call to Connie – at Maggie's insistence. Penance was due for not being in Naples. I had used Jess as the excuse for avoiding Florida this year. Too many pleasures and distractions to compete with homework I lied, knowing the distractions in Kilachlan to be at least as enticing. But it was true up to a point. Jess was more likely to study at Harkin Croft than in Naples where sun and sea made escape from the jagged atmosphere of the house irresistible. As it was, she avoided the majority of calls to her grandparents on the grounds that each conversation was indistinguishable from the last. No such release for me.

– Hello Mum. How are you both?

– We're the same.

– What have you done today?

Connie would list the callers who'd paid respects to the Dubrowsky millions from which Jess and I were intended to infer that A) we didn't know how much fun we were missing and B) some people bothered about Connie and Joe at Christmas. Sheldon Bolder's name never came up nor had it since my departure, which was odd since Connie had made such a big deal of my 'date' with him. On the other hand, it was reassuring to think that no lawsuit for assault with a deadly sauce had been filed. Still, I was curious and, braced by distance and Jura Malt, asked after him. Connie was vague.

– Well now, he seems to have dropped out of things. Went on vacation back in the fall. Haven't seen him since then. Some talk at the yacht club, don't know what.

– Maybe he's got the hots for someone.

I enjoyed it even if it was lost on Connie. I told her about my insight into the Nimborio painting (that Joe now had framed on his wall) and my father's study of her and me at the croft.

– You could be right. I guess it's logical.

Yes, Mum, I knew you'd be as thrilled about it as I am.

Fraser and Nikos were due around three New Year's Eve. It approached so achingly slowly that time all but congealed. Early on the 31st, Jess and I prepared for a late lunch of salmon and pasta with dill and a winter salad. Back in our room, Jess's clothes had exploded from a drawer leaving no surface uncovered. I dug out my new pink sweater and cleared a corner of the dressing table for my make-up, peering into a triangle of mirror. *There she is again, old bag. Follow me up to Scotland, would you? Yeah, well, you can bugger off. Go and haunt Brenda.*

I stayed in the kitchen so I couldn't be the first out to meet the car. Maggie and Jess waited, unabashed, at the parlour window, peering through the bare hedgerow, competing for a first glimpse. Jess suddenly yelped and bounded out, Maggie went second and I was last. *I can be cool when I want.* Fraser was second out of the car. Our greeting was low key even diffident, I hoped, given that I wanted to climb inside him. For Jess and Nikos the time apart had filtered out any platonic elements. They met anew and both liked what they saw. Maggie ushered her girls and their boys into the house, Jack and Tatty circling us all excitedly.

Lunch over, five gregarious people sat around the fire, conversation out-crackling the flames. Four of us sipped the sweet, smoky Oban Malt that Maggie had been saving for 'an occasion'. Fraser disgraced his heritage by admitting a preference for vodka. Unperturbed, Tatty had fallen in love with him and nuzzled under his arm shamelessly. *That's my place, kid.* Overwhelmed by the influx of visitors, Jack stayed with Maggie. Nikos didn't appear to be enjoying the malt as much as he claimed; we three women had finished ours before he'd drunk a third of his. Jess passed him a cognac.

– Hey, Niko – try this! You'll never want to drink Metaxa again.

– I never wanted to after the first time.

Maggie had used her influence to get the boys into the Hogmanay ceilidh at the village hall. I anticipated revenge on Fraser and Nikos for the 'Two Ladies' incident in Symi. We set off near nine, well wrapped and fuelled. Jess and Nikos led the way as Fraser and I chummed Maggie. We leaned into the wind, stung by needles of ice. Despite the threat of snow there was only a net of white lace on the ground, but it was brittle and shattered underfoot. Strains of accordion, fiddle and drums carried through the dark, drawing us to the warm heart of frozen Kilachlan.

Inside, balloons and paper chains bobbed in the heat generated by band and dancers. We thawed rapidly and settled at a table next to the Mudies. Isobel's eyes popped at the sight of the two young men and she sat up a little straighter. *My god, she's actually thrusting her tired old bosom.* Donald had returned to London, but Fiona sat between Isobel and Archie, in the same frock and mood as Boxing Day. As Fraser and Nikos were introduced I caught a sideways glance between Maggie and Archie. Knowing now of the link in their past I found every little look and gesture significant. Isobel almost simpered as Nikos lifted her hand to his lips. Archie squared up to him.

– Since you appear to have mesmerised my wife, I'll make myself useful with milady, here.

And he dragged a protesting Jess into the middle of a set.

Supper was at ten, so there was plenty of time for 'stripping the willow' and swinging partners. The old wooden floor had faded to brownish-grey from years of ceilidhs, jumble sales, mothers' and scouts' meetings. Fraser and Nikos vied for a first dance with Maggie, but she declined saying that she wanted to catch up with Isobel and Fiona. She loved to dance and the Mudie women bored her sideways; the same shadow of concern crossed my thoughts and re-awoke my fears. But Fraser lugged me into the Dashing White Sergeant and I put my unease on hold. Nikos was more than happy staying at the table surrounded by three women, even if his eyes seldom left Jess. As soon as she was able to slither away from Archie, she claimed him on the dance floor. Watching, I realised vengeance on him was not so certain. He was a natural dancer and hardly faltered under Jess's instruction. She was a veteran of many Kilachlan ceilidhs and, away from her cool Southern acquaintances, was an enthusiastic Scottish country dancer. Fraser, too, was no mean shakes and admitted sheepishly to having taken lessons as a child.

– Fling and sword dance?

– Don't get any ideas, Harkin.

Maggie acceded to a ladies' 'excuse me' picking Nikos first, then Archie and finally Fraser in a waltz. Fiona Mudie watched bleakly from the door of the

Ladies as the Harkin women monopolised the best looking men, Archie aside.

As supper appeared, band and dancers retired to the sides. The buffet offered venison pâté for starters, haggis, mashed neeps and clooty dumpling for the main. Fraser explained the constituents of each dish to a hesitant Nikos.

– Neeps are – god knows what the Greek is – anyway turnips, root vegetables boiled and mashed. But clooty dumpling, that's really special. Dried fruit and spices and suet and flour and a few other bits, boiled in a muslin bag for about a week then served in slices with butter – or fried with eggs and bacon.

Nikos looked queasy. Cannily, Jess had brought a bag of leftovers from her lunch, padded out with cheese and crackers. Copious spirits of one kind went down making other spirits rise exponentially. Soon, the vocal level in the hall was louder than the music had been. Wally and Nessie Scrymgeour, back from Kerrera, worked the bar and buffet. If not strictly Caledonian, Nessie's angelic Pavlova was a Kilachlan legend. Wally took a few minutes off to come across to the Harkin party, eyes alight at seeing Jess. Kilachlan was good for Jess. There were people who loved her, had watched her grow up – people she respected and admired. Nikos would see a different side of her.

Fraser arrived back, plate piled high with the ethnic goodies and a look of rapture on his face.

– I haven't had clooty dumpling since I was about eight. My granny in Broughty Ferry used to make it.

Nikos looked as though he'd seen a slug in a sandwich. Maggie took pity and led him over to Nessie who gave him tasters of everything. Wally took Nikos's place next to Jess, updating her on local gossip until, tormented by curiosity, he launched into what he imagined to be a subtle line of enquiry.

– So, Jess, you and your Mum have found yourselves a pair of sweethearts. Which is whose?

Fraser inhaled a mouthful of haggis.

Next came the raffle in which Fiona won a Puma sports bag, Nessie a pair of driving gloves and Nikos a 'Scenic Argyll' tea towel. But the moment of truth, the real test of head and legs versus intemperance could be postponed no longer: the Eightsome Reel. *See if you can handle this, you jammy Greek git.*

Mêlée commenced with Jess, me and aforesaid sweethearts in the same eight. As the first male dancer took his turn at the Highland Fling in the centre I watched realisation dawn on Nikos and felt a frisson of schadenfreud. But come his turn he outfaced all doubters by adapting the Syrtaki, Zorba's dance, to a Highland lilt. It had the desired effect – laughter from our set got the idlers on their feet and clapping. Fraser joined Nikos in the centre, displaying somewhat less expertise but raising the fun factor. The other sets, overcome by curiosity, abandoned the reel and crowded round the Greek sector. Refreshed by a whiff of the Aegean in the programme, the band improvised around the Zorba theme, prompting strings of inept but enthusiastic dancers to thread around the room. It was a surprise when the strains of Big Ben boomed out across the din. Our human granny knot unravelled in chaos and regrouped for Auld Lang Syne. Nikos was caught between the scheming Isobel and Kilachlan's sub-post office mistress, Miss Dowd, liberated from her glassed-in prison and enjoying cosying up to an exotic young man.

But the fun wasn't over. As the uneven but lusty strains of Auld Lang Syne halted, Jess was whispering to the accordion player who nodded and consulted his colleagues. Once thirsts had been slaked, he made an announcement. A novelty number, apparently. Before the boys could gather their wits, Jess had dragged Fraser to the stage where a guitar was thrust at him. She passed a headscarf to Nikos and tied another round the head of a puzzled Archie Mudie. Biddly diddly diddly diddly dee. One way of getting back, eh Archie?

HOWARD

New Year's Eve. I patted a little of the cologne on my neck and sprayed a couple of puffs of gel over my hair. It wasn't exactly a 'comb over', but it did have a tendency to fall the wrong way and expose more scalp than was comfortable. Clair had always urged me to have my hair cut short, not try to hide advancing baldness, but I didn't want to look like some media leftie of ambiguous sexuality. Funny how fashions change. Short hair used to be the badge of conservatism. Or skinheads. I checked my watch. Two fifty. There was just time.

I poured a gin and tonic and went to the window, peering through the blinds. Not that I was anxious for Brenda to arrive. Clair was always late, rushing in in a flurry of apology and explanation. And yet, exasperating though it was, I was always glad to see her. No, not just glad… Still, that was all past. Clair was definitely history.

Brenda was the present and she was – compatible. Never made me feel superfluous. Or fat. And she enjoyed my comfortable lifestyle, unlike the resolutely independent Clair. Had I used the coincidence of meeting Brenda to make Clair jealous? Initially, I suppose. She certainly looked put out that Saturday before Christmas in Guildford High Street. It didn't give me any satisfaction, though, just made me feel I may have burnt my boats. Then that young chap turned up singing outside the house in Aborigine Road, arm-in-arm with Clair and Jess, as if they were making fun of me. He looked familiar, but I couldn't place him.

I had tried to engage my bridge partner, Annabel, in conversation over the Clair / Brenda situation but she was oddly reluctant. I was perplexed. She'd always been willing to talk over Education Office business, dissect bridge opponents and tactics and even advise on minor legal matters – without charge. But she'd cried off the last few games, which was annoying because I had to ring round to find another partner. Maybe it was just pressure of work. Or maybe she wasn't the friend I thought she was. No, Brenda was perfectly adequate. For now. So why did I feel so morose? Why could I not shed the foreboding that in a long series of mistakes, this liaison could be the most profound?

Her car turned into the cul de sac. It was two minutes to three. After a journey of about sixty miles involving two motorways, she was on time. I knocked back my gin, put the glass in the dishwasher and sprayed some breath freshener before going to the door. Brenda didn't approve of drinking during the day.

I wondered if the Italian Restaurant I'd booked would be up to the mark for New Year. They certainly charged up to the mark prices.

CLAIR

New Year sleeping arrangements

Snow fell steadily on our walk back to Harkin Croft. No one in Kilachlan thought of driving tonight. The breathalyser was a friend to none, even if wielded by a closely related officer of the law. When we reached the door of the croft, I produced a first footing kit from the purple shoulder bag – a nugget of coal (wrapped in clingfilm), a whisky miniature, a slice of bread and an airline packet of salt – and passed it to our dark-haired man, Nikos, with instructions. He seemed baffled at having to go in first and then give them all to Maggie but did as he was told.

Ritual over, Maggie went to her room while Jess made hot drinks for everyone. Fraser and Nikos were bedding down in the parlour, one on the sofa, the other on cushions on the floor. Around two, Jess and I, reluctantly, repaired to our own room. *Why can't I be more liberal? More honest? Can't use Maggie as an excuse.*

– Jess… if you want to stay with Nikos tonight, I – well, it's OK by me. I'll sleep in the parlour. Fraser won't mind, I'm sure.

Duplicity, thy name is Clair. Jess was too opportunistic to question.

– Cool, Mum – thanks.

In the parlour, Fraser and I put all the sofa cushions on the floor, nervy as burglars. I turned a cautious key in the door and made for the sheets that Fraser held open.

– Welcome back.

– Glad to be back.

Maggie could not have been unaware – of that I am sure.

Our lovemaking picked up where it had left off that afternoon in Symi with no sense of interlude and no shyness, just a wonderful reunion of hearts, minds and bodies. Mainly bodies, sure. I loved the smell of his skin, his hair and the feel of his firm flesh; he remembered every detail of my sensitivity. He <u>had</u> been thinking of me, he <u>had</u> remembered me, in every way. And I him.

Fraser and I cooked breakfast together, me on eggs – in more ways than one – Fraser on toast, tea and coffee. Our moves synchronised as though choreographed. Having talked and made love for what was left of the night it was, I suppose, reasonable. *I'd forgotten this. It's unnerving – so physical. It's like my chest is wide open with bliss. The emotional breast, that's what they used to call it. Yep. True. And my legs can barely hold me up. I'd forgotten what that felt like, too.*

– So you really didn't get my emails?

– Promise. There was a blip with the computer. I had to get it fixed.

– That shouldn't matter on web-based email. They should still be there.

– Don't intimidate me with IT jargon.

Why would I lie?

– Has anyone else used your computer? Or know your password? Apart from… ?

He looked at me for a moment. The answer thudded uncomfortably hard. *But why? Why would Jess… ? Hang on – when she was grounded? Does this mean she's known all along?*

– I'm so sorry Fraser – I think we know the answer.

– Jess? All this time we could have –

– Darling, look – we've had some serious problems, Jess and I. I can't believe she could do this but she – well, she hasn't been herself. What she's done is unforgivable – but I really don't want to deal with it now. I don't want to spoil this time.

By way of answer he put his arms round me, held me tight, tousled my slept-in hair.

– Enough said. Not my place. I'm here now and it'll take more than the we'an to get rid of me.

I took a tray in for Maggie then rapped on Jess and Nikos's door.

– Breakfast, dining room, five minutes – ready or not.

It wouldn't be easy biting my tongue for the rest of the time at Kilachlan – or indeed, on the journey south.

By twelve, everyone was more or less dressed. After the large breakfast, no one was particularly hungry. Maggie presided over snifters from an armchair by the window then insisted that she wanted to be left alone with Radio Scotland, a bottle of malt and a good book 'til teatime. Milking of Esmeralda was delegated to Jess and Nikos – who claimed it was in his blood – and dog-walking to Fraser and me. *She is so blindingly astute.* Outside, the snow was a good three inches, considerable for this part with its mild winds from the west. Gloved and scarfed, we walked the tartan clad Westies to the strand. Fraser was duly impressed.

– You're more Scot than I am if you grew up with this.

– More fortunate, maybe, not more Scot.

Jack and Tatty nosed around half-heartedly preferring to spend their New Year's Day in front of a fire, not schlepping around sub-zero shores, despite their sporty little coats. Fraser and I strolled arm in arm. He spoke steadily, looking ahead.

– I adore you, you know. I know I should be cool, but I absolutely fucking adore you.

Not love, then? Cynical bitch. Give him something back.

– I keep thinking I'm going to wake up and find I've dreamt you.

Is that the best you can manage? Give him something more. I can't. Why not? Fear?

Exchange of the past four months' activities was subject to some censorship. I didn't go into the entire history of Jess's illegal drug activity, theft and other unpleasantries. Joe and Connie featured, but Sheldon and Richard lay side by side on the editing suite floor. Fraser related his triumphant return to Glasgow. There must have been more to the last four months than that? He interrupted my suspicious little rankle.

– What do we do now, Clair?

– How do you mean?

– Us. What next? Not just today and tomorrow – I suppose I mean from now on.

Saying it seemed to surprise him as much as it did me. This need for a decision was a new twist. We stopped walking, both studying the iron cold beach. Jack and Tatty huddled miserably around my legs. My words whipped away, white vapour in the clear air.

– You mean the logistics? You and me, Glasgow, Guildford and Symi?

– Well – yes.

It was an angular moment. Fortunately, it was shattered by the Mudies' dog, Jasper, who rammed into Fraser knocking him full length. Man and dog rolled over in a clumsy tango. It took both of them a moment to gather their wits. I teetered between concern and laughter, hand clamped firmly over mouth, as Jasper scrabbled up and galloped on.

– Sad indication of waning impotence when even a man's dog doesn't obey him. No injuries, I hope, my friend? Apart from pride?

It was Archie – sans last night's headscarf – looking florid from his struggle up the gentle incline. Fraser put his hands behind his head.

– No, no. I'm just taking a wee rest. Join me.

Archie insisted we accompany him back for a dram, by way of an apology. Isobel and Fiona were out, so we had the large drawing room to ourselves. Jasper, usually exiled to the kitchen, bounded into an armchair with unbridled delight. Tatty snuggled against Fraser while Jack glanced uncertainly at Jasper then at his faithless partner. Archie excused himself to fetch 'a special drop'.

– As I was saying before I was mugged by Archie's dog, what next?

I stood at the bay window studying the strand.

– I don't know. It's a little soon to make any decisions about our – relationship.

– There can't be one, not with you down there and me up here – or over there.

– I can't commute to Glasgow or Symi and you can't do the opposite.

– Looks like one of us is going to have to move, then.

– You're the gentleman. It should be you.

Archie delivered the last comment conversationally from the doorway.

– And what better way to seal it than with The Mudie Malt? Never was a great believer in sealing with a kiss. Too easily forgotten.

He brandished a Ribena bottle half full of clear liquid. He didn't faze me.

– Before I punch you, Archie, is that what I think it is?

– What do you think it is?

– Not Ribena.

– Correct! Home brew. The finest.

He took out three liqueur glasses and passed the brimming thimbles with a grim twinkle. Shit! Archie's not stingy with his measures. That stuff must be bloody rocket fuel.

— Lang may your lum reek wi' other folks' coal!

Archie knocked it back. Fraser raised his glass, a condemned man.

— Clair, I want you to know that my life's ambition was to see Guildford. And Archie, I forgive you.

He puckered up and sipped, stopped breathing for ten seconds, then made a long, ragged intake. Archie faked innocence.

— What d'you think?

Fraser's eyes watered.

— An aggressive little brew — aromas of tanning factory and dead badger, flavour of dirty nappies… aftertaste of toxic waste.

— Knew you'd like it. Clair?

Oh, well, at least I'll have last night to remember. If this doesn't dissolve my brain. I knocked half of it back. It was surprisingly smooth to start with, but —

— Jesus, Archie!

— Ho ho. Now, where will you both stay? Guildford?

Walking back along the lane we dissected the interlude laughing, but self-consciously. I stopped by the five-bar gate.

— Are you sure, Fraser?

— Are you, Clair?

— It's not difficult for me. I want you in my life. But I'm not being asked to move or change.

— To be frank, I'd sort of decided I wasn't going back to Symi. Time to grow up. But are you really sure? I mean, there's Jess.

— Why should it affect Jess?

— Well, given her email sabotage, plus she's bound to notice another person at the breakfast table.

Hang on — this isn't what we're talking about, is it? Moving in together? Of course — he needs somewhere to live! How stupid am I? What do I say, now?

— We could always eat at your place.

— Sorry?

Of course — men don't do subtlety.

— You'll need somewhere in Guildford. We could eat there.

The moments fell in slow thuds at our feet. I watched him, he watched me. He grinned.

– I'm a terrible cook. What say we do the noisy stuff at my place and eat at yours?

Right answer. Maybe it was an honest mistake.

– Sounds good to me.

I yelled our 'hello', breezing into the croft.

– Sorry we're late! Been drinking moonshine with Archie Mudie!

We were met by varied reactions on five faces, the more astonished of them Isobel's and Fiona's. Mother and daughter had swapped Crachan House for Harkin Croft and another glimpse of the hunky young Greek. Jess was oblivious to the fragility of the moment.

– Wow! D'you think he'd let me try some?

Isobel moved swiftly from surprise to annoyance.

– Oh, for Heaven's sake, not that old stuff again. He promised he'd given it up.

Nikos looked puzzled. Fiona launched into an excited account of illicit stills and Customs men after which he was keen to know whether Archie had any of his illegal brew left.

The Mudie women didn't seem inclined to rush home and scold Archie. We sat on awkwardly until I excused myself to start dinner. Even then, Isobel and Fiona were slow at taking the hint and didn't leave 'til nearly five. Fraser exploded into the kitchen.

– This has to be one of the most bizarre days of my life!

– Stick around, kid. For me, it's fairly routine.

– I look forward to it.

STILL CLAIR

The leaving of Kilachlan

I was firm. We could not all leave together and abandon Maggie to the debris of the festivities. Nikos and Fraser must go on ahead. Jess and I would leave the following day, pick up Nikos in Easterhouse and take him on down to Heathrow. So, the boys left at lunchtime on 2nd January. Maggie parted from them fondly, wished Nikos a safe journey home and hoped to see him again before long, invited Fraser to bring his sister and nephew up any time. That evening, Maggie, Jess and I had a quiet dinner at home. We were comfortable and happy, as though it was usual to be together as a family. Jess voiced it.

– I wish we could always eat like this, just the three of us.

Then spoilt it with –

– Well, not always, of course – but, you know…

The leave-taking next morning was swift. Maggie never showed her reluctance to see us go but, this time, she seemed almost light-hearted. I attributed it to the new openness about Julia. Intrigued by the number of photos around the house, Fraser had asked me who the wee stunner was.

– A close family friend. She died some years ago.

– I'm sorry. She looks like she was a very special friend.

– She was.

Now, as Maggie stood on the doorstep, Westies at her feet, it was as if she had just left Julia in the parlour for a moment and would return to her as the car drove off. And, in a sense, she will. She's allowed to visit her memories again. But my heart still ached with shock and sorrow at the cruelty of Maggie's bereavement, the taint of shame that she had lived through in silence.

I let Jess drive as far as the outskirts of Glasgow for the practice. The snow had melted partly and a dank haze shrouded the journey south. There had been plenty of opportunity for her to mention the New Year sleeping arrangements at the croft but she waited 'til now. As the dim impression of Loch Etive faded away to the left she blurted –

– Mum – I know about you and Fraser! Nikos said he's daft about you. It's mutual, isn't it?

Quite the actress. She improvised on her theme.

– Vast improvement on Gluefeatures. He coming to live with us?

The living together bit wasn't an issue between Fraser and me yet, so it was hardly something I would discuss with my daughter. I decided that neither were the lost emails, not while she was driving.

– He's getting himself a place in Guildford. We'll see how it goes.

She didn't ask any more about when or where it had all come about, which I would have thought odd had I not known about the emails. My story in Symi about the night in Aphrodite Two must have sounded fishier than Billingsgate once she'd seen his emails. I was burning to talk about Fraser, the future and my renewed energy for life, but I was too pissed off with her to share it. At least she'd be spared the horror of hearing about my sex life.

Would I want to hear about sultry nights of passion between Connie and Joe? *Maybe she deserves to hear about mine as punishment.*

We were in Glasgow by eleven. A satnav was way bottom of my must-have list and Jess was a fair map-reader. We made only a couple of wrong turns before pulling up outside Annie's flat. Fraser was at the front door and scooped us both into his arms. Annie waited at the top of the stairs, a brown-haired, brown-eyed girl with pale skin. She invited us in for a cup of tea. Jude clung to her shyly, sidled around her as we went in. Even at five, he showed signs of towering over her in the next few years.

– Och, Jude – you're being a pain. You've met Clair and Jess before!

As we adults greeted one another – Jess and Nikos like they'd been apart for years – Jude made a bid for the attention that was rightfully his.

– I can speak Geek – mee leneh Jude! That means my name's Jude! And I can say 'kali-mary' that means good morning and 'ef-harris-too' that means thank you and – I can speak Swaleelee, too!

– Swahili, Jude.

– Swaleehee. Listen – Jambo! That means hello.

He shook hands with the five adults, each of us repeating 'jambo'.

– OK, pal, we've got the gist!

Fraser whisked the mini multi-linguist upside down and dangled him, delighted and squealing, in mid-air.

– Och, Fraser! He's just had a smoothie –

We stayed about half an hour. Knowing how fond Fraser was of Annie, I wanted to create a positive impression. She was so obviously young enough to be my daughter I felt the age gap between him and me yawn cavernously. But she dispelled my anxiety as she hugged me goodbye.

– Cannae tell you what it's been like here – three male egos, six smelly feet and non-stop football. You wouldnae take another one off my hands while you're at it? Not Jude, by the way.

Fraser smiled thinly.

– Cheers Annie. Subtle as a welder's crack.

Nikos made his thanks and his farewells, leaving Fraser with –

– See you in Symi?

My lover gave a Marcel Marceau shrug before embracing his friend.

Three on the pavement waved off the three in the car, heading towards the motorway. I drove as far as Carlisle where Nikos took over. It was largely a silent journey, all of us had a lot to think about. Jess was due for counselling the following day.

I should let these two have some time alone together before the airport. Does Jess deserve it? After trying to wreck Fraser and me? Still, I think this relationship could turn out to be an important one for her. And there he is, about to fly over a thousand miles away. I hope it doesn't louse up her A levels. And I hope I can keep my mind on her and on work instead of mooning over Fraser – when all I want is to have him with me, all the time. Why are these feelings so strong? And how come I'm so fickle? First it was Richard, then Fraser, and then Richard again – now back to Fraser. Can I trust myself to behave? At least I've been sensible about the moving-in thing. But I want him with me. I want to know what the possibilities of 'us' are.

Must ring Maggie. As soon as we stop. See how she is. How wonderful that she's opened up about Julia at last. If I'd known then that she was so ill could I have changed anything? Possibly not. What a sad bitch Ben's wife was, blowing their lives apart to get at him. And Julia's parents. The bloody bigots. They should have been proud that a woman like Maggie loved their daughter. They should have loved Julia enough to let her spend her last days with Maggie – with her lover.

I did, of course, realise that I was making no concession to the age nor to the circumstances of that time. Even so, I could feel only anger and compassion on Maggie's behalf. *What a terrible, terrible time she's been through. She must have been crying inside for years. Or was she just numb? How could she keep it locked away? And she never let on to us, always put Jess and me first.*

We were making good time and stopped at Hilton Services outside Birmingham for coffee. Nikos didn't need to check in for another four hours. I stayed in the car while they ran through the rain to the cafeteria.

– Hi Maggie.

– Hello lass – how's the journey? Where are you?

– Fine – we're at the services near Birmingham. How are you?

– Oh, I'm very, very well. Missing you already, of course. But I'll be down soon.

– Good. Your room's always ready.

– Liar – it'll be a bloody tip at the moment.

We talked for a few more minutes then I locked the car and followed Jess and Nikos.

The last leg of the journey was slower, although we still arrived at the airport in good time. I gave Nikos a quick hug at the drop-off point, told him he was welcome back in Guildford any time. He thanked me over and over until I pushed him off towards Departures with Jess. Waiting for her, I reflected on the day last summer when I'd dropped her off at Heathrow.

Life had certainly changed radically since then. This time, she returned in fifteen minutes and, although a bit teary, was in positive mood.

    – I think this is my first really grown up relationship, Mum.

    – Could be. I hope it's going to make you happy.

    – I'll make sure it does.

Oh – what glorious, youthful certainty. And oh what retribution you're about to get!

CHAPTER TWENTY-TWO

STILL CLAIR

New Year, new baby

The house was cold. Case would still be in Swindon with his mum; Phee was in Northampton, probably. Quelling my usual fear of intruders, I did a swift check round the house. Nothing amiss. In an hour, the boiler was fired up again, central heating gurgling, washing machine churning and frozen meal in the microwave. Jess sat at the kitchen table with a mug of tea, going through the post, wincing or huffing over the imbalance of reciprocal Christmas cards. There was one postmarked Leeds, from Richard and Mandy. Mandy was pregnant.

The news penetrated like a metal spike. *Why am I having this reaction? You know why, Clair. No, I don't. I really don't. Did he know when he was here? Does it matter if he did? Would I want a baby, now? Richard's? Fraser's? No. So why am I having this reaction? You know why, Clair.*

Jess was delighted and rang them instantly, bringing the phone into the kitchen.

– It's just so fab! Are you going to call it Symi because of where –

– Jess!

– Richard, here's Mum.

I took the leaden receiver. *What is it about bloody telephones these days? Always someone you don't want to hear or something you don't want to know. Come on, grow up. Be pleased for them.* Richard sounded years younger, a little bashful and absolutely delighted. The baby, he said, was due late May. *So he knew when he was here.* All during our conversation. He knew. I tried to concentrate on what he was saying. Mandy was in bed, still experiencing some tiredness and discomfort. I sent sympathy, love, congratulations and promised to ring again soon, managing to get away without mentioning Fraser and New Year. *Why? What's the problem? Nothing. Jess can tell all by email soon enough.* No sooner had I turned off the 'talk' button, it rang again.

– Clair – Brian's left me.

STILL CLAIR

Rotten fruit

Sonya drove down to Guildford. There was no time to deliver my thunderbolt to Jess re. the emails, besides which, she had school and counselling the next day. She dived into bed before Sonya arrived. I mentored my friend until three a.m. as she see-sawed between fury and despair over Brian's desertion. The festive season, it transpired, had been bad timing for his change of accommodation and lifestyle. He was used to opening his presents on Christmas Eve whereas Sonya preferred Christmas morning, he'd complained about pre-packed Christmas fare and refused to watch the Queen's speech from bed. More generally, he hated clearing up after himself, demanded her attention twenty-four seven, was childish, boring and a lousy shag. The truth was, he actually missed his saggy wife, his ghastly kids and even his mother-in-law.

I needed to share Maggie's account of Julia's death for my own ease of mind and because it might have moved Sonya beyond her current distress. I wanted to tell her how pissed off I was with Jess. But the stream of vitriol could not be dammed. My news would have to wait. By the evening of the next day I'd lost track of time, reeling from Sonya's constant analytic loop. It was only when, at seven, Jess ran in from the rain that I remembered where she had been and realised how late it was. Annoyed at Sonya for grabbing my attention and me for letting her, Jess spat out the news that she had terminated her counselling.

– But, Jess, you've been doing so well –

– Exactly. That's why I don't need to go any more. Anyway, since you actually forgot I was going you obviously don't think it's such a big deal.

After a twelve-hour drive followed by Sonya full on? Be fair.

– What did your counsellor say?

– Anything that passes between me and Mary is confidential.

No amount of reasoning could mollify her. Easy to be so self-focused when you're young. Or Brenda next door.

Sonya decided to stay for a couple of days to avoid Brian. With her iPhone and access to our computer, she was able to keep work ticking over. Much as I loved her she was a pressure I could have done without. I snapped at Fraser the first time he rang, called back straight away to apologise and got Annie; he'd gone to work and left his mobile at the flat. He didn't call me for two days after that and, between Sonya's manipulative need and my efforts to prepare for term starting, I couldn't find private time to call him. Nor was I able to confront Jess over deleting my emails.

Maggie rang to tell me about a Buchanan family jaunt up to Kilachlan. Annie and Jude were due to stay with a pal in Oban for a couple of days and Fraser had rung Maggie to suggest they meet. So they were coming for lunch the day after tomorrow – same day I was starting back at Elyots. It struck me as rather presumptuous of Fraser to impose them on Maggie and while I recognised that she would enjoy the company and the unexpected nature of it, pangs of envy were sharp enough to make me reach for a paper hanky. Ridiculous, I knew, because this was a positive development, the families meeting. But it had all been done without reference to me. I rang him that night but got his voicemail.

The first session on the first day back at Elyots was a double period with the poisonous Year Ten, all of whom saw the return to school as a personal affront. The lesson embodied all my horrors of teaching, exploiting my imagined lack of preparation and exposing me to the hormone-induced anarchy of the upper school. That night, I drove home dispirited, my mind zigzagging between all my other pits of despair, then at home I walked into another emotional rout with Sonya. Too tired to cook, I rang out for an Indian meal. Sonya toyed with a few grains of rice and burst into tears. Jess declared the vegetarian biryani bland and disgusting, made Marmite toast and went up to her room. I shovelled the rejected meals into the bin, sat Sonya in the sitting room with a bottle of red wine and tried to work on the next day's lessons, head bulging with the unpleasant intricacies of life. My mobile rang. It was Maggie.

– Hello Aborigine Road. Harkin Croft calling.

– Maggie! Hello, darling. How did it go today?

– Ah. A bit unexpected –

– Something's wrong –!

Indeed, something was wrong. Jude had come down with chicken pox, discovering his first itchy spot at lunch after the sausage and mash and before the ice cream.

– Och – he's a couple more spots but he's fine. It's going around the school. He and Annie are going to stay with me for a couple of days 'til he's over the worst. He's tucked up in bed with the dogs. Annie and I are just enjoying a dram.

– So long as you're all right, darling.

– And why wouldn't I be? Away and ring that man of yours.

I did as I was told. We talked until his battery ran low and then I stayed up 'til two kidding myself I was working on lesson plans.

For five days Sonya revisited her brief period of domesticity endlessly, vacillating between forensic and pathological moods. She developed the dementia of a caged animal. Each morning Jess and I left a wild-eyed, chain-smoking madwoman who, by night, had become a drunken, wild-eyed, chain-smoking madwoman. I rang Kilachlan daily and enquired after Jude's health while beating down the green-eyed monster that lurked inside me.

Annie answered the phone a couple of times, which tested my possessiveness even more. Maggie was quite obviously enjoying their stay.

– Ach the we'an's fine. Spots have nearly gone and he's having a ball. The dogs spend half the night with him then sneak in to me. And Annie's great company.

– Don't let them tire you out, darling.

– Clair, it's doing me good. There's no need for you to worry – about anything.

She'd seen right through little old insecure me. Naturally.

To Case, Sonya was both fascinating and a challenge. He had tried a bit of amateur counselling and a magic mushroom cure to ease her pain. Finally, he struck gold, sexual healing, and got her into bed. Or she him, more like. Arriving back one day after school, I caught sight of her fleeing semi-clad from his room. I headed for the drinks cupboard. Tea would not do after the week I'd had. Fifteen minutes later an unfocused snapshot of Sonya entered the kitchen.

– Don't say anything, Clack, desperate times require desperate measures.

I poured another whisky.

– Trust you to trump me on the age gap thing. Just do me a favour and spare me the details.

Fortified by sexual conquest, she decided to return home and get her revenge on Brian. She'd come up with a plan that would piss him off royally. I urged her not to do anything illegal.

– 'Course not, darling, just damaging.

She'd gone within the hour. I went up to air the office immediately, knowing it would stink of cigarettes. It did. Half a packet of Dunhill was on the desk – *don't, Clair* – and a pair of silk knickers underneath it – you didn't do it in here, too? The stairs creaked as Case tiptoed his way down. *And how am I going to deal with that one? Do I maintain silence or ask politely if my friend was a good shag? Life just gets better and better.* The phone rang.

– Hello Harkin.

– Hello – it's so good to hear your voice.

– How would you feel if I said "I'll be down Monday"?

I wavered over confronting Jess about Fraser's emails but reasoned it was better to get it out of the way before he arrived. I knocked on her door Saturday morning and went in uninvited.

– What?

She was still in bed.

– Jess, Fraser's coming down on Monday.

– Nice.

– It's time you explained to me why you deleted his emails.

– Don't know what you're talking about.

Standard liar's response. I waited, standing just inside the door. She waited, face averted.

– Could you shut the door, please? It's getting cold.

Ignoring the issue. Classic tactic of the guilty.

– I'm talking about you using my password and deleting Fraser's emails to me. I'm also talking about an explanation and an apology.

Silence. *OK, see how this fits.*

– And letting Nikos know just how mature you really are.

That worked. She was out of bed and eyeballing me.

– If you hadn't been such a –

– Be very, very careful what you say, Jess. I have quite a long fuse but it's been burning for a while. So far, everything, everything in this house has been about you, your needs, your feelings. And in return, not only did you attempt to destroy the one good thing that's happened to me in a very long time, but you wheeled in your Greek boyfriend without the courtesy of asking, mentioning it even. I lose sight of who you are sometimes. You used to be such a loving little girl but now you've become the sort of prima donna I have to teach at Elyots. When will you learn that no one, no one in the world loves you more than I do, and yet I'm the one you attack, yell at and punish? If you're afraid that anyone else will get the love due you, you couldn't be more wrong. But you are testing me to my limit.

Jess held my stare but was breathing deeply. Her eyes filled but the tears didn't fall. She bit her lip hard.

– Sorry.

– Is that it? Sorry?

– I don't know why I did it. I was just angry. And I thought if he really liked you he'd email again.

– At that stage of a relationship, if one person ignores – or appears to ignore the other – it can end before it's really begun. That holds for people of our age as much as for people of yours.

More silence. I didn't have the will to take it any further.

– Look, as it happens Fraser and I are OK, now and we're going to be seeing a lot of each other from now on. Life will be more comfortable if you square it with him yourself. You're an adult, you should take that responsibility.

More silence then she mumbled –

– OK.

I left it there.

At school on Monday, Chloe was particularly vile. How much did the Year Twelve siren know about the thick gold choker her boyfriend Willo had given or any connection with me? Something, it seemed. Maybe it would be wise to ignore the rudeness and concentrate on the other girls. Difficult, though, because of the awkward atmosphere and because Chloe felt able simply to walk out of class at any time she chose. Ricki, the English teacher who'd helped me initially, took me aside. Caught lounging in the Common Room during a drama period, Chloe had claimed that Miss Harkin let anyone skive off if they wanted, and besides, drama classes were boring. Chloe's behaviour had always been a problem and Ricki was sympathetic, but emphasised how important it was to be unequivocally in control. That lunchtime I sat on my own in the staff room trying to ignore the smell of macaroni cheese while two emotions battled for supremacy. The first, depression over my poor showing as a teacher lost out to the second, nervous excitement. Fraser was arriving tonight.

I took my time showering and changing. I would wear the pink sweater, of course – *and? Maybe those trousers I bought when Richard came to dinner.* The panic to find the right thing to wear was so different, though. *Why? Does the fact that we've already had euphorically good sex come into it?* Wandering downstairs in my old dressing gown, hair in a towel, I noticed a light on in the living room. Must've left it on when I came in. I put my head round the door.

– Clair? Is that you?

It was Fraser. Caught an earlier train. Very amused. Hugged me hugely. An hour later, both of us curled on the sofa, he said:

– Look, I'd better go and check in at this B & B. They'll think I'm not coming.

I sat up, stunned.

– What do you mean?

– Well we agreed, didn't we? I'd get my own place.

– Not first night, neep head! Ring them. Tell them you can't make it.

Before he could, Connie called.

– Joe's had another heart attack, it's touch and go.

Fraser found me a flight on the internet. Soonest one out was to Miami. I could hire a car at the airport and take Interstate 75 – Alligator Alley – across the Everglades to Naples. I called Connie with the travel plans. Wrong, of course. I should have taken a different route. And why wasn't Jess coming? I gabbled at Fraser.

– Should I take her? No – school's too important. And we don't know if he's really going to… God, that's awful – if we thought he was going to die, I'd…

Fraser reasoned, soothed, then suggested –

– Why don't you ring and get my name on your car insurance? Then I can drive you to Heathrow. And you'd better ring Jess.

Jess had gone to the cinema with friends. I texted her to get home asap then went up to email Elyots and pack while Fraser explored the kitchen and improvised a supper. We were just sitting down to eat when Jess rang. She was upset and on her way home. After I put the phone down –

– What do I do about her? She needs someone here.

Fraser cleared his throat.

– Look, I've made the move down here. I have to find work, I have to find somewhere to live –

I followed his thought process.

– It makes sense for you to stay here and keep an eye on Jess for me. If you don't mind?

It was decided. Jess arrived home and knew better than to kick up.

In bed, Fraser held me gently, kissing my eyelids, bidding me sleep. Which I did, until the alarm rang at four a.m.. Unusually, I managed to sleep on the plane, too. Not wholesome, deep sleep, but sleep enough, peppered with fitful mini-nightmares that deserted me only an hour and a half before landing. Over the remains of the airline meal I reflected that, however bad the reason for the journey, it had been a new and deeply pleasing experience to have someone help me sort arrangements, be there for Jess and look after the house. Was that what it was like to live with someone? That sharing? I'd forgotten. *Maybe I should think again about having him to live with me. He's not a user. He really does care – and don't I deserve that luxury?*

In Miami, I got through Immigration in under an hour and was even more surprised to hear my name over the speakers. I went to the information point to discover that Fraser had booked my car hire. There was a Toyota Auris hybrid – with satnav – waiting for me. Not just a great moral choice but anticipating my panic over getting lost. Incredible! This was the right man for me. My spirits lifted as I passed through the muggy

Florida atmosphere to the waiting car where the air conditioning blasted a welcome chill. I left Miami International and, on the advice of my Neverlost Navigation treacle-voiced hunk, took the Palmetto expressway. By the time we reached the Interstate 75 intersection, I was ready to thump the patronising git. Fortunately, there were very few choices to make for the next hundred and four miles. I stopped at the first Amoco station on I-75 and rang the house at Naples. It was around two thirty in the afternoon. Antonia picked up. Connie was at the hospital.

– Better get here soon as you can, cara. But you drive safe, now, hear?

– Sure, Antonia.

Unlike many US Highways, Interstate 75, that appalling environmental scar across the Everglades, had a decent speed limit. 70 mph. It didn't mean edging up to 80 with no fear of a ticket. It meant 70 mph. Three and a half hours later I pulled up to the electric gates at the Dubrowsky mansion. Antonia was waiting at the front door, in tears. Joe was dead.

I rang the hospital, claimed kinship.

– Sorry for your loss, Miss Dubrowsky. Mrs Dubrowsky has just left.

Connie arrived in a cab a few minutes later and suffered herself to be hugged. She dropped her apricot leather purse on the hall table.

– Well, that's that I guess.

And she went to her room. Antonia and I exchanged looks.

– Thanks for staying on, Antonia. You go home and I'll see you in the morning.

Antonia kissed me goodnight and squeezed me tight.

– Help you all I can, cara.

– I know.

I called Jess to break the news. It was near midnight at home. She was very sad, but distance and forewarning softened the blow. She wanted to know about coming to the funeral. I deferred the discussion until a date had been set. On a practical level, she'd rung Elyots on my behalf and spoken to the school secretary to make sure that they'd read the email. No, there was no response. Home news was that Fraser had oiled the door hinges, put new screws through the handles so they didn't fall off and fixed the tap in the bathroom. Oh, and he'd got bar work, started this evening and wasn't back yet. *Wow – he doesn't let the grass grow.*

– And Mum, I did what you asked. I told him I was sorry about – you know. He said to forget it. Didn't even tell me I'd made a tit of myself.

Somehow, we both managed a small laugh. I fell into bed without eating but, in spite of immense weariness, didn't sleep.

The next day, I dropped off the hire car in Naples. By the time I arrived back at the house some ninety minutes later, Joe's funeral was already set for a week later. It would be quite a social event in Naples. Connie most certainly wanted Jess there, called the travel agent right away and had them find flights. The funeral directors arranged everything from interment to paper napkins, which was convenient in one way, but left Connie with very little to occupy her aside from the lawyer and the order of service. She and Joe had already bought two adjoining mausoleum spaces in Naples Memorial Garden Cemetery. Dying was very big business on the Gulf.

One thing my mother could always do was shop. She was probably only a British size 16 and could have shopped anywhere but found herself a dress and jacket at Salon Z, the outsize department at Saks. In her circle, black was de rigueur, still, for funerals. I had a problem finding anything black that didn't feature trousers and bought the first black skirt suit that fitted me. The horror didn't end there because the issue of hats, also de rigueur, arose. Eventually, Connie settled on a sort of inverted black gerbera. I found a pillbox with a netting trim. How would we kit out Jess? Internet. I emailed her to choose a suitable outfit from Burdine Macy's website, I would check it out, Connie would pay for it and it would be sent straight to the house in Naples.

Fraser rang.

– All I ever say is 'Missing you'. Will I ever get the chance to say I'm fed up with you?

– Be careful what you wish for.

– Sonya's here, by the way. She's quite a gal.

My stomach tightened. Sonya in the house with Fraser? *Get a grip, she's there for Case.* Which, indeed, proved to be – the case – for the Swindon stud was at that minute being bundled into Sonya's Audi Sports, Richmond-bound. *What? To get back at Brian? And what about the rent he owes me?* Clearly this was a fund farewell... Annie and Jude were back in Glasgow, more or less a spot free zone. And Maggie was fine, just fine.

– By the way I've been having a wee keek at your paintings.

– Oh?

– They're fantastic. We have to talk seriously when you get back.

Talk seriously? The pleasure of impressing him cheered me immeasurably.

Once the clothes shopping was done, there was nothing to do but lounge around the house. Connie allowed me to drive her to the lawyers but otherwise refused to be seen in public until the funeral. I had nothing to distract me but TV, the occasional foray to the supermarket and a quiet swim when Connie was in bed. I didn't have the heart or concentration to draw or paint. Jess was to arrive the day before the funeral and would stay for four days; school was too important for her to miss much at the moment. I rang Elyots. The secretary put me straight through to Miss Frome. Not good.

– Ah, Clair. Thank you for calling. At last.

– I'm so sorry, Miss Frome. It was all very sudden. I hope you –

– Don't worry. We've coped. In fact, we have found a permanent replacement for the drama post.

– Oh – so –

– Thank you for all your help. My condolences.

The line went dead before I could reply. Like Connie said, "Well, that's that I guess". Although I wondered whether they really had found a replacement or the Chloe business had come to light.

Connie decided she would come up to Florida South Western Airport to meet Jess, insisting that we leave early. Far too early. My suspicion that she was dying to get out for lunch was confirmed when she suggested we go on into Fort Myers itself. We stopped on McGregor Boulevard, conveniently near the 'Prawnbrokers and Fish Market' restaurant. It was busy. The set-up was confirmed when Connie whispered to the maître d' and we were shown to a table for two straightaway. *Maybe she wants to talk. It'll be easier for her in here with all this eating and socialising going on. She can't get emotional. More to the point, nor can I.* But all my mother said was –

– I think I'll have the crab.

Jess's plane was on time. She'd had a tight turn around in Cincinnati because of a delay at Gatwick. She was gritty and dishevelled but otherwise fine. Connie allowed Jess to hug her a little longer than usual.

– How are you, Gran? Poor you.

– Oh, I'm OK.

Connie was actually smiling as they parted. It occurred to me, somewhat belatedly, that we were all Connie had, now. *What are the implications of that? Will she want to come and live in England again? No, surely not? Christ – she won't want us to come and live here? Mind you, Jess could be tempted, if she didn't have to live with her grandmother.* Jess loved riding in the Rolls, despite her budding socialist principles. I didn't enjoy driving it precisely because of my own and because of the way it drank fuel. Try telling that to Connie. Jess chattered to her grandmother from the back seat all the way to Naples. It was over a year since they'd seen each other. Jess had changed a great deal in that time, not all of it visible. Naturally, Connie knew nothing about the drug situation. *Long may it remain so.*

Antonia had waited specially to see Jess. She'd prepared a black cherry ice cream milkshake, Jess's long-time favourite and ritual beverage on arrival. For Connie and me there was rum punch made with Mount Gay and full of tropical fruit. We sipped it in the garden room while Jess and Antonia had a long chinwag in the kitchen. Antonia stayed way over her time, as she had every day since Joe's death. Before leaving she whispered briefly to me.

– Young man – Freezer? – call for you. He knew my name! Say to give you his love and he call again pretty soon. You have un'enamorado and you don't tell Antonia?

We all went to bed early. Jess had chosen an entirely suitable short-sleeved wrap over from Burdine Macy's and was gracious about my having opened her parcel and ironed the dress. The black shoes she'd bought in Guildford were not quite as sober as Connie would have liked but would have to do. Her 'hat' was a black velvet Alice band with a black flower attached which, also, would have to do. It was a relief not to have a fight on my hands for once.

The Dubrowsky family were originally Polish Catholic but Joe had only ever set foot in a church for occasions such as this. The funeral directors had tactfully suggested a non-denominational church service followed by a 'family only' interment. Guests could go straight from the church to the yacht club for the funeral breakfast, have a drink or two until Connie, Jess and I arrived. As for hymns at the service, all Connie could think of was the battle song of the Republic and 'Nearer my God to Thee', so that was what we had along with 'My Country 'tis of Thee'. Joe had been proud to be an American. The night before the funeral, Jess asked if she might say a few words about him at the church. Connie was concerned that it wasn't included in the printed order of service but touched that Jess wanted to and said 'yes'.

The service was mercifully short and the church predictably full. I noticed Connie scanning around, ticking off a mental checklist of attendees. There was a hush of expectancy when the 'departure from program' was announced. Connie's coral ring rotated overtime. Jess walked with great poise to the pulpit and opened a sheet of paper.

– Joe was the closest to a dad I ever had. Living in England, I didn't see him that often. But I knew he cared for me and that I was often in his thoughts. He believed that family doesn't mean just blood-ties, it means people who love each other looking out for one another. He never said so, but I knew that, too. When Joe had a heart attack in the summer, I didn't come across to see him and I wish I had. Now I have to say 'Do widzenia,

Joe' and hope that, wherever he is, he'll hear me and know how sorry I am. And if he does, he'll understand and he'll forgive me, because that's what dads do...

All around, the hankies were coming out. Even Connie had dissolved. I was numb. Jess had never shown signs of being that close to Joe – and it was the first time that she had ever spoken in such heartfelt terms about having a father. She finished with the poem 'Death is nothing at all', by which time there were audible sobs. She folded her paper and walked back to the pew. As she sat, I put a hand on hers only to have it removed. *Bless. She's so near the brink. Sympathy's the one thing she can't take.*

We three generations sat in silence in the black limousine, gazing anywhere but at one another, following Joe's hearse to the Memorial Gardens Cemetery until Connie said:

– I thought his lousy son could have turned up. He'll be getting enough.

Jess spun around from the window.

– Yes, honey, Joe had a son. Hasn't seen him in years. But you're right, he did think of you as his little girl.

The interment was simple and dignified, took no more than sliding in the coffin and saying the prayer of committal. We retired to the Yacht Club and stood inside the door of the Americas Suite in a presentation line. The mourners, were, by now, well-oiled and deeply emotional. Expressions of sadness and compliments on Jess's eulogy were profuse. I rose from my torpor at a handshake that was too firm and too long.

– Sorry for your loss. This is my wife Soo Lin. We're just back from our round-the-world honeymoon.

It was Sheldon Bolder. Beside him stood a tiny Oriental woman. Girl.

– So sorry – so sorry.

She intoned, as though she had been schooled, glancing nervously up at Sheldon who put a possessive arm round her shoulders.

– OK – that's fine, honey.

I felt both pity and disgust as he steered his child bride to the buffet.

Connie came into her own once formal duties were over. With Joe at rest so was the coral ring. She held court from a deep leather sofa while Jess and I found a side room and a bottle of Johnny Walker to ourselves.

– Before you say anything, Mum, all that about Joe – I thought Granny would like it. I don't mind if he had a son. And I don't know if he thought of me as his little girl. I was quite fond of him, though.

She swirled the ice around in her glass, took a swig and said casually –

– Perhaps, one day, you'll tell me whose little girl I am?

It was so much the wrong time, the wrong place. She was immediately contrite.

– Oh Christ – I'm sorry, Mum – sorry, sorry, sorry! I didn't mean that. Forget I asked!

– Darling, it's OK. You have every right to know –

– No! I don't want to! I just... look, please, can we talk about something else?

– All right – let's give it some time and space.

At last, the question was out but instead of bringing us closer it increased any space between us. Next time, and it should be soon, I would bring up the subject. We sat in silence for a while and, gradually, started talking trivialities then joined Connie in the salon.

Fraser rang that night. It must have been the early hours of the morning in Guildford. I related the day's events leaving aside Jess's question.

– Sounds gruesome, doll. I know you'll have to stay on for a bit, but –

– I'll have to stay on for a week at least after Jess.

– Aye. Well – don't forget I'm loving you in Guildford.

He's said it again. Try to give him something.

– That makes me very happy.

Oh, what? That your best, Harkin?

Next day, Connie decided to clear Joe's belongings.

– Isn't it a bit soon, Mum?

– There's a good time?

Antonia shook her head quietly at me and the three of us got on with it. Jess stayed in the best guest room, watching TV. His clothes went to the Salvation Army. I suggested that Oxfam America might want his spectacles and Antonia put them all in a box. Connie hung on to his jewellery. His son might want a watch and a set of cufflinks, if he ever turned up, but the wedding ring and everything else she would keep. It could always be refashioned for her. His golf clubs could be sold. I was about to ring the golf club when Connie stopped me, irritated.

– You want the golf club to think I'm short of a buck? We'll put a box number ad. in the paper.

Joe had very few other personal possessions and, by mid-afternoon, most of them were packed in bags and boxes and awaiting collection by a local 'man and van' outfit. Jess and I went for a swim, then helped Antonia with dinner. While we were eating that night, Connie announced that she'd booked a hotel up the coast at Charlotte Harbour for the following night –

– So you can have a little vacation before you go back, Jess.

In truth, my mother wanted out of her current situation. We agreed without argument. I rang Guildford and left Fraser a message about the change of plan.

The next morning, Jess gave Antonia a long hug and promised to come back soon.

– You bet, chiquita – or Antonia come get you!

It was another balmy Gulf day, lacking perspective or relief. We arrived at the hotel after the short stretch north on Highway 75 and Jess took off for the pool. I located internet access and let Fraser and Maggie know where we were, then headed for the water myself. Connie waited at the poolside bar. A table for three was laid. Resting in Jess's place was an envelope. Connie nodded her permission to open it.

– That's from Joe. You don't have to wait for all the legal hoo ha.

As she pulled out a cheque, Jess put a hand to her mouth. I looked first at my daughter, then my mother. Neither of them cared to enlighten me. Jess leapt up and flung her arms around Connie.

– Thanks, Gran.

My throat constricted with anger at being excluded and I stared hard at the menu as the blood rushed to my face. Connie patted her affectionately.

– Thank Joe. That was a good address you gave.

The list of appetisers swam before my eyes while Jess chattered excitedly about how much easier her life would be from now on. University would be a doddle. No problem with fees or a student loan for her. *How bloody much was it? All the years I could really have done with a helping hand!* It was insufferable. I excused myself from the table, went into the hotel and headed for the bar. Jess found me there twenty minutes later. Before she had a chance to lecture me, I cut in.

– I don't mind about you having the money, Jess. I mind about my mother excluding me from decisions about my own daughter. I mind about my own mother punishing me in any way she can for even being alive! And don't disagree with me. You don't understand. You couldn't understand. You're too young and you've been too spoilt. So just leave me alone and let me get over it. Tell Connie I've been sick.

– But, Mum, you're –

I gave a look that dried the words on her lips and made her scurry back to her generous grandmother. An hour later, I hauled up to my room and lay on the bed watching the ceiling lurch. I woke after six, head thumping. There was a note under the door. Connie and Jess had gone shopping. They'd see me back in time for cocktails at six thirty.

We met in the lounge bar. Connie asked if my head was better, but hardly waited for a reply, going on to enthuse over the shopping she and Jess had done at the Bell Tower Shops in Fort Myers. They must have taken a cab early on to have got that much shopping in. Perhaps Connie and Jess were more akin through skipping a generation.

– By the way, got you these.

Connie casually pushed a box across. In it were a collar and earrings in silver and abalone shell. A sweetener. Jess had had a hand in this. *They've got you. Go on, play along – just to get through the evening.* I felt the weight of Maggie's Celtic earrings in my lobes.

– How lovely. Thank you. I'll look forward to wearing them.

So pleased were both of them with their generosity and with all their other purchases, they didn't detect any flatness in my voice. Or chose not to.

As we ate dinner in the hotel restaurant, Jess enthused over Nikos, architecture and her plans for the future and Connie listed the ills, divorces and demises of her peer group at the yacht, golf and country clubs. Neither really listened to the other, just waited for a convenient gap to dive in. I noticed that Connie wasn't worrying her hands. Strange that the eczema should leave off at a time of such emotional stress. We all went to bed around ten thirty. Jess had to be at the airport by seven a.m. for her flight to Atlanta, where she would change planes.

After a clinging farewell between grandmother and granddaughter at Passport Control next day, Connie and I were driving back to the hotel when Connie stunned me by saying:

– All this has been a kind of strain on you, too. Wanna stay on here or head back to Naples?

It was decided by a message at reception from Fraser to ring him urgently – on his mobile.

– Fraser? It's me – what's the matter?

– Clair – I'm so sorry, love – Maggie's had a stroke.

CHAPTER TWENTY-THREE

STILL CLAIR

Terrible decision

I drove Connie back to Naples. She was incredulous.

— You mean you're going to her? When I've just buried Joe?

— She needs me.

— So do I.

— Come with me.

— The hell I will.

— Sorry, Mum. I have to go.

She stood by, pointedly, while I phoned and found a flight via Philadelphia to Glasgow and a hire car to drive back to Fort Myers. The usual cheque to cover fares hadn't appeared. It was hardly a diplomatic request at that moment and while I was alarmed at the strain on my credit card with no job to return to, I couldn't ask.

I took leave of Antonia that night. It was a very early start the next morning.

— I feel so bad about going. But I have to.

Antonia was a little unsure. She had never met Maggie, of course.

— Clair, if your aunt needs you…

— I wouldn't go if it wasn't really serious.

— Sure, cara. Don't worry, I'll make sure your Mommy's OK.

As I left, Connie came to my bedroom door, but no further, and said goodbye. *No 'thank you' for my support? You're welcome, anyway. No, don't worry that I lost my job. So long as Jess has enough.*

Concern for Maggie and bitterness over Connie's behaviour contrived to make me miss the airport turn off. Senses jolting to the present, I made a circuit of Fort Myers, trying to find my way back. Time was very tight indeed. I dropped the car off and ran to check-in. The flight had already been called and it was uncertain whether my bag would be accepted for loading. I was uncharacteristically in luck. On board the plane at last, I sank into my seat waiting for the physical payback. It didn't come instantly, but as the plane taxied I started shaking, prompting the businessman next to me to summon a flight attendant.

— It's OK. I'm always like this leaving Florida.

It was dark in Glasgow, near midnight, and horribly cold. I hadn't packed for this kind of extreme. I rang home from my mobile, pulling my jacket close. Sonya answered. Bugger – misdialled.

– No – you're OK – I'm in Guildford, darling. Fraser asked me to come down to stay with Jess.

– Where is he?

– With Maggie. Didn't he say?

Fraser had flown up to Glasgow then driven up to Oban with Annie. They were both with Maggie, who was still in intensive care. *Both with Maggie? Am I redundant in all my relationships?* Instant remorse tripped my mind to 'grateful'. Of course, it was marvellous of Fraser and Annie to be so supportive. They were there for me as much as for Maggie, sharing the worry, giving practical help. Fraser would have had to sort his job – maybe lost it, like me – and Annie would have had to find someone to look after Jude. They'd have had to arrange to meet each other, find the hospital and explain their relationship to Maggie to the staff. All this disruption to their lives because they cared. *Consider yourself well slapped.*

– Clair – you still there?

– Yes. What about Jess?

– She wanted to go up but I managed to talk her out of it.

Luckily, I was in time for the last airport bus. On the ride into Glasgow, I texted Fraser to let him know I'd landed. Buchanan Street bus station was only a short walk from a Travelodge. More damage to the credit card. He rang as I was letting myself into the room.

– Poor sweetheart, you must be shattered. I should've come down to –

– No – I'm really glad you're with Maggie. How is she?

– Conscious. She knows you're on your way.

– Is she going to be all right?

– The consultant wants to talk to you.

There was a train after eight the next morning. After a night of ruthless insomnia and mindless television, I took a cab the mile to Queen Street Station and managed to grab a baguette as I ran for the train. The journey to Oban was just under three hours. Luckily the train was warm and Oban was the end of the line so I could doze for a while. Some chance. I stared into miles of winter mist, my mind groping through its own haze backward to Florida, forward to Maggie and to the immediate future.

Fraser was on the platform at Oban. I allowed myself to lean into his arms before he hurried me into to the waiting car. On the way to the hospital he told me Maggie was sitting up, but warned –

– Be prepared, love, she has paralysis of her right side – and problems talking.

– You said she knows I'm coming?

His voice was gentle.

– Well, I think she does. We've kept telling her.

I set face and mind into coping mode. Too much sadness, too many hospitals.

Maggie was in a small side ward with one other lady. I was stunned that I couldn't, at first, make out which one was Maggie. They were two old ladies with grey hair and sunken faces. Then I saw Annie sitting at the bedside. Fraser squeezed my hand. Annie sensed us and came over and kissed me before leaving quietly with Fraser.

I didn't know the best way to approach her. As I touched the poor, cold right hand and looked into her face, I saw the recognition, the attempt to smile.

– Hello Maggie, darling. I can't leave you for five minutes…

A sound came from her mouth; a rising inflection at the end was all that was distinguishable. It would be a long while before she was back to the old Maggie, if ever.

The bed was surrounded by cards. Maggie had more friends than she knew. I stayed three hours, despite Annie and Fraser cajoling me to take a break. I was obliged, finally, to leave the bedside when the geriatrics consultant did her rounds. I spoke to her by the nurses' station and was shocked by what she said.

– Since your aunt had a minor ischaemic incident – a mini stroke – back in August –

– No! This is the first time she's had –

– Miss Harkin, she was my patient then, too. Her GP, Dr Sharma, has been attending her since.

Why didn't she tell me? Bloody hell, Maggie! I need to know if you're not well! While I was getting pissed and stoned in Symi you were – Oh God, I KNEW there was something wrong and I never bloody phoned! I NEVER BLOODY PHONED!

The consultant looked at her watch, but spoke kindly.

– I'm sorry you didn't know. People like to keep their independence. Maybe she was trying to stop you worrying. Your aunt has had a left-brain stroke. There is some paralysis of the right side of her body and significant speech impairment. We can't tell how severe the incident was, as yet, but we'll organise another CT scan in the next couple of days, an MRI if she's up to it. We'll have a good indication then.

– Can she understand me?

– Talk to her, keep her mind stimulated. Give her time to answer. Massage her right hand and arm gently.

Maggie drifted in and out of sleep, exhausted simply by the effort of remaining awake. I, too, finally succumbed to drowsiness. Feeling a hand on my shoulder, I realised I'd nodded off.

– C'mon, Clair. Fraser's taking you back to the croft.

It was Annie, speaking with such kind firmness, it was impossible to refuse. He was in the car outside, engine running, heater on. The cold was fierce, the few yards from reception to the waiting car seemed miles. I shuddered all the way to Harkin Croft. It was strange to go through the yellow door and not feel Maggie's embrace nor hear the welcoming yelps of the Westies. Fraser reassured me over Jack and Tatty.

– They're with Mr and Mrs Scrymgeour. So's Esmeralda.

Nessie had set the fire and left a broth – her broths were a main meal. I could manage only a few mouths full before my eyes drooped again. Fraser made me have a warm shower then tucked me into bed with a hot water bottle.

– Poor substitute, I know, but I'm away to fetch Annie. Now, go to sleep, you. That's an order. OK?

– OK.

I slept as soon as I heard the car turn the bend in the lane, didn't wake even when Fraser got into bed beside me sometime later.

Waking next morning was a confusing experience. The room was still dark. Nothing filtered through the curtains. That slow, regular breathing, the warmth of another body next to me was my imagination, surely? A lucid dream. A great one, but – hang on… By degrees, I accepted that I was conscious, I was not alone, the person next to me was Fraser and I was in Scotland. And Maggie was in hospital. I sat up, knuckling my eyes and mind to clarity. Fraser stirred as the cover moved, exposing his back to the bedroom's chill. The bedroom. We're in Maggie's bedroom.

Fraser followed me to the kitchen, put his arms around me.

– Come back to bed, doll.

– I've got to go to Maggie. I'm just –

– Clair, you're more use to Maggie rested.

He made tea. I went back to bed and took in familiar sights: a seascape of my father's, Lautrec's study of Yvette Guilbert in a green dress, the silver dressing table set, the sprigged wallpaper, the blue satin quilt and Julia, Julia, Julia. Such a haphazard mix of sights and memories, such a strange jumble of feelings. Fear of losing Maggie, disbelief at finding such a caring partner, guilt, resentment and anger at Connie – and Jess? I'm losing track of Jess. Fraser came in with a tray of tea and toast.

– Well done, Harkin. Stay there and be spoilt.

Maggie had had a better night. Her eyes were brighter, she tried to say 'Clair' when I walked in. But the tears welled to her eyes. My turn to counsel and soothe.

– Don't get upset, darling, we're going to get you well again.

Later she was able, almost, to say 'Jack and Tatty'.

– They're with Wally and Nessie. So's Esmeralda. See? You're doing so well, Maggie. And tell you what, we'll bring Jude to see you at the weekend.

Annie came to say 'goodbye'. Fraser dropped her at the station and returned to sit with me while our patient slept. I leaned against him accepting togetherness, too tired, too grateful to question it, neither of us aware of Maggie rising to consciousness until she said, quite clearly,

– That's good. Stay like that.

We both smiled, didn't shift, apart from Fraser nodding.

– Right you are.

On the way back to Kilachlan Fraser pulled up at a pub. I didn't want to go in, sure I looked a fright. Not unreasonable after the past few days and my odd mixture of clothing. Fraser took my face between his hands.

– You look bloody gorgeous. And my guts are digesting themselves. C'mon!

Over baked spuds, he told me about Guildford. The job was in a pub at the back of the High Street that had live music a couple of nights a week. He'd jammed with one of the bands one night, covered for three malingering staff and driven another to A&E following a particularly lively domestic. Due to that and appearing to be handy with his fists –

– It's the accent, not the muscles – to which you, sweetheart, can bear testament.

He'd even been headhunted for manager at another bar. A place called Booze'n'Crooze. He patted my back as I choked on a baked bean.

– You know it?

– Mmm hmm. Wouldn't recommend it.

As it was, the landlord of the pub was sufficiently glad of him to let him have time off for a family crisis.

– Hope you don't mind me saying 'family'?

– I'm glad you did.

Later, as we lay in bed, I was disappointed that he did not turn to me. I felt for his hand, kissed his fingers, stroked his chest then down across his stomach.

– Are you sure you want to?

Our lovemaking was reassuring, affirmative – and surprisingly energetic. Afterwards, I said:

– That's good. Stay like that.

Maggie's progress was erratic. Sometimes her speech would be clear, her thought coherent. Then she would disappear into a vale of confusion. A CT scan was scheduled for Monday morning. Nothing could be certain until then. On the phone to Sonya, I admitted my fear for Maggie, for myself – and for the future. She was reassuringly pragmatic.

– Whatever's going to happen, darling, worrying won't change it. One step at a time.

Jess was behaving impeccably going to school, coming straight home, doing homework – in all, being a model of diligence and modesty. It didn't sound like Jess, but I hadn't the energy to question it. Sonya was, however, gleeful over a recent coup in the 'Brian/revenge' campaign.

– Remember Jolyon?

– 'Dogging in front of the telly', Jolyon?

– Don't be unkind. Property developer, Jolyon. He's a gem. Persuaded a few of his friends – like, super wealthy friends – to come in. We're a production company! We're going to do it ourselves!

– Do what?

– The film – the female director? Who Brian's company wanted to back? I've nicked her!

My friend, the movie mogul.

Next afternoon, I bumped into Archie Mudie at the hospital. His manner was diffident. Didn't want to be in the way, he said, just wanted to know how Margaret was faring and wish her the best.

– Why don't you go in and tell her yourself?

– Good lord, no. Wouldn't want to embarrass the lass.

He couldn't be persuaded and hurried off. A staff nurse came over.

– He's been here every day. Won't go in. Just asks after her, then disappears. Is he friend or family?

– He's an old friend, a very good old friend.

Nessie and Wally came in later that day. Nessie brought Maggie some scones. Archie carried a winter bouquet of rose hips, berries, holly and dried teasels that the sister wouldn't let them leave. Infection control. They felt awkward, talked to me rather than Maggie and left after twenty minutes.

Maggie improved steadily and could soon concentrate long enough to hold a conversation, battling to find the words and to enunciate carefully. The will to get better was almost too intense and, at times, she had to be forced to rest. On Saturday, Annie and Jude came up by train. Maggie was having a good day and when the two of them burst in she became almost animated. Jude was extraordinary; Annie must have primed him well because he chattered to Maggie about anything and everything, apparently unaffected by her changed appearance. He'd brought her a painting he'd done of Jack, Tatty and Esmeralda on holiday in Africa, a colourful abstract of unidentifiable splodges. When Maggie failed to take it from him, he had a moment of uncertainty. But Annie motioned him towards the bed and he understood, placing the painting in Maggie's good hand. She gave a lopsided smile and slurred a 'thank you'. This was rather too much for Jude who backed away to his mother. Annie took him to the cafeteria. When I tried to reassure Maggie, she signified that his reaction was understandable and had not upset her. She was delighted with Jude's painting and wanted it fixed to her locker.

Later that afternoon Annie offered to read to her while Fraser, Jude and I dived out to a supermarket. Back at Harkin Croft that night, we three adults glutted on microwaved curry while Jude dug into fish fingers and chips. After he was in bed, we stared at Saturday night tosh on TV, each dozing off at different times and waking to a change of programme. At eleven, I rang the ward to check on Maggie and send her a 'goodnight'. Fraser and Annie sat back almost guiltily as I came back from phoning.

– What is it? What's the matter?

Annie was direct.

– We were talking about the logistics problem you have with Maggie.

Fraser took over.

– It's your business, love. But if we can help –

I knew I had to confront the truth, was glad to admit it.

– I just don't know what to do.

The Buchanan family's devotion to Maggie was understandable; she had shown them great kindness. Helping me was helping Maggie and vice versa they reasoned. Annie had listed a few immediate options for Maggie:

1. a nursing home near Kilachlan – limited choice

2. live-in help – super expensive and possibly not an option given Kilachlan's remoteness

3. nursing home in or near Guildford – but M probably wouldn't want to leave her home

4. live with Clair and Jess – M would miss home, the sea, Esmeralda and wouldn't want to impose

5. Clair move to Kilachlan – reduce earning potential and leave Jess alone for A levels OR

6. Annie and Jude move in with M

Number six must have been a maverick leaping the fence because Fraser turned to Annie, startled. She faced him brightly.

– What do you think?

– Say that last one again? That wasn't –

– Jude and I could move in. Jude could go to the local school, I could convert to distance learning. Nessie Scrymgeour could cover if I needed to be away for a day. It would be easier than –

I stared deep into my whisky. Fraser cut her off.

– Annie! That's well out of order!

Annie was ready for him. She and Maggie got on well, she said, she didn't have the same commitment to earning as me, well, not at the moment, Maggie loved Jude and he loved Maggie. It was a practical solution to a difficult problem. Fraser looked at me, struggling to penetrate a labyrinth of complex emotions.

– But we don't know how Maggie would –

Annie was direct.

– Maggie suggested it. Before she had the stroke. Maybe she saw it coming.

I rose and left the room before I caved in.

In the bedroom, I lay face down on the quilt. *I've lost Maggie.* Fraser followed me after a few seconds. He touched me and I flinched.

– OK – I'll let you be.

He went back to the parlour and I heard raised voices. I felt for my mobile.

– Sonn?

I poured out my hurt. Sonya was equally shocked when I told her it was Maggie who'd suggested the arrangement, then said:

– If it's true.

– It's true.

– But Maggie hardly knows this – this –

– Annie. Remember I said she looks a bit like Julia?

– Maybe – but do you really think – ?

We talked until my credit ran out, then Sonya rang me back.

– Just occurred to me, Clack. New Year with you and Jess being all lovey dovey with the boys – ?

– Yes?

– Maggie needs to be a part of that extended family. What better way?

A banquet for thought. New Year had come straight after Maggie allowing Julia back into her life, remembering all the love and loss. However discreet I'd imagined my relationship with Fraser to be, new couples always made their attraction obvious. Jess and Nikos hadn't bothered to restrain their feelings. It must have accentuated Maggie's lone state. *And yet she celebrated everyone's happiness with us. Sonya's right, though. Why shouldn't Maggie have some of that? Because I'm jealous – and I'm suspicious. They hardly know each other. Is Annie gay? Is it a lesbian relationship? Is it any of my business if it is? But Annie's young enough to be her granddaughter! How would that make Jess feel? The age thing again. What was it Richard said about age – when people need each other they must find the way to be together? Am I just afraid that I won't be important to Maggie any more?*

There was a soft tap at the door.

– Clair – your mother's on the phone.

I went through to the now empty parlour. Connie, surprisingly, was mild, enquiring after Maggie's health, reporting on her own, nothing more. No criticism, no accusations. She even said 'Take care, now', before she hung up. Annie had gone to bed and Fraser tried to persuade me to join him, but I preferred to sit alone by the weakening embers with the last of the Oban malt. Eventually I crawled in beside him and spent a sleepless night feeling both surrounded and usurped by Buchanans, vacillating between acceptance and intense resentment of Annie's solution.

CHAPTER TWENTY-FOUR

CLAIR

Too much to bear

Next morning, I was on the beach while the light was still grey, wretched through fatigue and heartache. Blades of north wind sliced through my coat. The internal question/answer session riled on. *Why didn't Maggie mention the idea of Annie moving in? Because I was at Joe's funeral, staying with my bitch-mother. How could she ask someone she barely knows to live with her? Because Maggie is intuitive, because Annie is intriguing and bright, because Jude would be another child to cherish. What reason could Annie have to bury herself in Kilachlan, unless – ? Unless what? She wants to exploit Maggie?* The wind carried away all but the nearest of sounds, so it wasn't until she was nearly beside me that I heard Annie. She was dwarfed by Fraser's cagoule.

– Clair, I'm really sorry. That was a rotten way to tell you last night. It's not what you think.

– And what do I think?

– A lot of negative things. I don't blame you. I would in your place. But I don't want to take Maggie from you. I couldn't.

She touched my fear so accurately that I couldn't respond.

– Look

Annie pulled out a vacuum flask from the folds of the jacket.

– Coffee.

The CT scan was encouraging. The damage to Maggie's brain was not as bad as feared. She could come home by midweek. Already she had appointments booked with the speech and physiotherapists. The ward sister explained that the Stroke Nurse and GP would monitor her. She might also be entitled to home help. Maggie sat in an armchair beside her hospital bed. She wanted to discuss her future. I was ready.

– Annie told me what you discussed about her and Jude moving in. She still wants to.

Maggie shook her head, waved her left hand in dismissal.

– Too mush.

– Annie doesn't think so. And you'd be helping her, too.

I'd had a change of heart over Annie. The conversation we started on the beach had continued long after the cold drove us indoors. There was reason to trust her and I understood how she and Maggie could help one another.

– Darling, Annie and I have talked. She doesn't want to stay in Glasgow just for her parents – they have each other. And she'd love Jude to go to a school up here. She adores you and you're obviously fond of her. She's spoken to her tutor and he thinks distance learning could work. Plus, who knows, she could be seconded up here after her degree. The short-term options for you are a nursing home, coming to Guildford – or staying at home with Annie and Jude. And Jack and Tatty. I'd love to have you – but I don't think you want to leave Scotland… do you?

Maggie faced me for a few moments then slowly shook her head. It was settled.

I spoke to Jess that night but didn't mention the new living arrangements, just told her that Fraser would be coming back with me after the weekend. She sounded relieved.

– Good. Sonya sends love – she has to get back on Monday, anyway. This film she's doing – there might be a part for Case. He's got this permanent grin on his face. He's back here, by the way – 'cos Sonya's flat will be her office from now on. Hey, I'm glad Maggie's feeling better. Did she get my flowers?

Jess had sent an extravagant bouquet to Maggie, making me wonder if Connie's cheque would get her as far as university. Maybe it wasn't extravagant. Who could tell without knowing just how rich Jess was, now? I didn't tell her we'd had to take the flowers back to Harkin Croft.

STILL CLAIR

Fermenting fruit

We stayed until Maggie, Annie and Jude and, essential to everyone's happiness, Jack and Tatty, were installed at Harkin Croft. Esmeralda stayed with the Scrymgeours for the time being. It was hard leaving, but both Maggie's confidence and her affection for Annie and Jude were so evident that I had only the smallest of pangs to quell. *I am only human, not a flaming saint – even the holy blessed martyrs must've had off moments.* As we drove down to Glasgow, I suggested stopping at Rest and Be Thankful. Fraser was not enthusiastic. One step into the icy drizzle persuaded us back to the car but I intended to have my moment. It was inspired by Maggie and Annie's domestic plans.

– You and your bright ideas, Harkin.

– I've got another one.

– I don't know if I can stand hearing it.

– You can. Remember what Maggie said – at the hospital – when we thought she was asleep?

– You mean "That's good – stay like that"?

– Yes. Well, let's. I mean – really stay like that… move in with me?

There was a brief pause before he spoke. *Oh no, done it wrong again – thought that was what he wanted –*

– Right you are.

– Right you are?

– If you fancy – all right, YES! Yes, yes, yes – just stop hitting me!

We dropped the car off with his parents, Rosemary and George, and stayed briefly for tea. Much as I had been curious to meet his parents, I felt let down. They were a pleasant, middle class couple. I hadn't expected anything else from what Fraser had said – which wasn't much. I just wanted them to be more – like him, I suppose. Rosemary Buchanan was polite, as though I were a slight friend of Fraser's. George said very little, even as he ran us to Glasgow Central Station. *Hasn't Fraser told them about us?* On the train, he confessed he hadn't.

– They wouldn't be that interested. Annie moving away with Jude is too major a crisis.

He said it glibly but it was underscored with exasperation.

We read, dozed, held hands and talked over the new arrangements at Kilachlan. I was careful to skirt round my talk with Annie on the beach. Fraser didn't probe. Such was his faith in Annie's counselling skills, he wasn't curious about my sudden acceptance of her moving in with Maggie. It was just as well because Annie wasn't ready for him or her parents to know the truth about her life in London. She'd had the courage to tell me, though, and it was enough to make me reconsider. And she would tell him everything, in time.

Rolling south we made plans for Guildford.

– You, Harkin, are going to do a whole load more painting.

– If there's time.

– We'll make time. That stuff of yours is amazing.

We'll make time – 'We' – I like that.

The house was empty. I was still dressed in a mixture of Florida clothing and borrowed woollies. Before anything else, I wanted to change into my own winter clothes. We hefted cases upstairs to – *'Our' room now, I suppose. But I don't remember leaving it this tidy –*

– This doesn't look like Sonya's doing.

– I did some sorting – it was a bit of a cowp.

Ouch. The kitchen was tolerable. There was note from Jess saying she was working at the library. *Wow. Maybe Nikos had a bigger effect on her than we all realised.* Also, there was an answer phone message from Connie saying that she had rung Kilachlan, spoken to a stranger and was everything OK? *My mother actually concerned about Maggie – or me? The earth must be shifting on its axis.* It was too late to cook, so we rang for a pizza. Fraser was starting at the pub again next day on the lunchtime session. I would have to hit the agency trail once more, if there were any left that would have me. Fraser was sympathetic.

– God – your talent and you have to go out typing and filing for a bunch of morons.

– No one wants to buy my talent. Well, not for more than thirty-five quid, they don't.

– We need to have that talk.

Just then, the pizza arrived and with it, telepathically, Jess. We caught up with each other's news over the dinner table. For expediency's sake, I described Maggie's new living arrangement simply as Annie moving in 'for the time being'. I didn't want Fraser to witness Jess flaring up over anything more than an octopus – just yet. But it was open season on the Nimborio painting and the frugal payment I'd received. Her voice rose in pitch and decibels as she invented new and incrementally abusive terms for the fraudster. I promised I'd seek justice but pointed out that getting some kind of paid work was a priority. Then artfully, almost as an afterthought, I brought up Fraser's live-in status. She was very laid back.

– Cool, be good to have someone who knows about electrics.

She was keener to talk about Sonya who had found a co-producer and was talking megastars. Jess thought hi-jacking the film project and poaching his contacts was an awesome way of dissing Brian.

– Couldn't agree more, JJ. On the other hand, casting Case in the movie isn't way up there with her brightest ideas.

Jess crowed with triumph.

– She made him cough up his back rent, first. I paid it into your bank account.

I was more impressed by Jess finding the paying-in book than by Case finally paying out. It was seriously good news, though. The few hundred quid plus Phee's rent might keep us afloat until the next job, whatever that might be. I'd get onto the Guardian jobs website and have a look for something seriously worthy.

Fraser and I spoke to Annie, later. Maggie was in bed. Jude would start at the local school next week. Nessie was coming in to assess how she could help. All was well, everyone was happy. As Fraser put the phone down, I said,

– Except your Mum and Dad?

– Aye. But Annie has to make her own life.

As we lay on the brink of sleep, he cleared his throat a couple of times then spoke seriously.

– Case paying his back rent got you out of a hole, didn't it?

– It gave me a foothold on the sheer wall of the hole.

– Look, you need money, I need somewhere to live. I'd pay rent anywhere else, so I'll pay it here.

– Fraser, there's no –

– That's on top of my share of housekeeping and bills and stuff. OK?

– But –

– That eases things a bit for you to start painting. This is not up for discussion. And they say Scots are mean…

– I'm half Scot. You don't know what I charge, yet.

CHAPTER TWENTY-FIVE

FRASER

I lay awake for over an hour, watching her breathe, not wanting to disturb her. When she moved away naturally in sleep, I spooned around her, realising what I felt was, probably, 'happy'.

HOWARD

We barely knew each other. Even with Christmas. I say 'even with Christmas' – she said we'd done the deed – couldn't remember us doing it but I wasn't going to argue. Certainly nothing happened at New Year, but then it was very late and the Prosecco had flowed. And ever since then, anything physical had been 'inconvenient', by which I supposed she meant the female cycle. She hadn't put pressure on me emotionally. It was more a sort of "You're on your own, I'm on my own, we both watch The Apprentice and vote Conservative; we make a good couple, don't we?". Oddly enough, I thought she had a point, although I wasn't so keen on her "We're not getting any younger" remark.

It all came to a head one morning when I had one of those ghastly moments looking in the mirror and seeing an old man looking back. When had my lower lids started to sag? How did the lines either side of my nose get so deep? The top button on my shirt looked (and felt) uncomfortably tight. I had a jowl and diminishing hair. Was it a sign of desperation to cling onto those ever-decreasing strands? Ye gods. I patted on a little of Brenda's Christmas cologne and left for work. Traffic was heavy. The Today programme was presented by Sarah Montague and Carolyn Quinn. It didn't sound right, two women. I switched off. I felt unsettled enough. The face in the mirror was a wakeup call.

The TES was on my desk when I arrived and in it was advertised my ideal post. The juxtaposition of events made me start thinking seriously. In the Education sector it's good to present a youthful, family image. I was coming up to fifty-seven, I should be realistic. She was forty-six, acceptably younger. There was a ready-made family, which would give me more credibility as an Education Director. She had her own house to sell, so she wouldn't be a financial burden – and she could get a little job – there must be something she could do. Besides, it would be a change to have someone to come home to, to supervise laundry and cleaning, think of meals in advance, be available as an escort for dinners and other social events. Why not? She wasn't what I would choose in an ideal world. Someone slimmer, slightly more – personable – would have suited. I ignored the alternative that nagged my subconscious. That option had ceased to be six months ago.

Apart from turning me down, she'd made her preference for younger men quite apparent. I took comfort that the age gap made her look ridiculous. Enough! As I mulled it over, it seemed viable. The future could be Brenda. And if it made – the other one – regret her foolishness, so much the better. Why not, I thought?

The morning was taken up by a meeting with Deputy Head Teachers discussing strategies to deal with truancy. They were a dispirited lot; custodians stripped of authority and denied any deference by pupils and government alike. At the close I hurried back to my office, startling Pat. She shoved a paperback into a drawer and swung to face her computer. The afternoon was set aside to clear correspondence and paperwork. By three, I dropped two Dictaphone tapes – heavens forefend that we should go digital – in Pat's in-tray and invented an emergency dental appointment. Felt like a truant myself as I escaped to the car park. I clicked the TVR into sports mode, accelerated down the A1M then cut across from Hatfield to St Albans. It was unlikely that Dame Fiona's spies would catch me skiving off there.

I worked fast. First, a hairdressers – unisex, for something more up to date, and came out scalped. It was the sort of haircut Clair had urged. Her again. I resolved not to let her influence the clothes. As my style guide, I went back through the last few months, trying to remember every comment and observation of Brenda's but none of them went much beyond 'very smart, Howard'. The shop assistant urged greens, browns and khakis. What Clair had said. It had sounded dull at the time but I had to admit now that I looked better in them. I hoped Brenda would approve. The leather jacket looked horribly new. It was also hideously expensive. The shoes were more casual than I would have chosen but the shop assistant assured me they would go with chinos. At five thirty, I ran out of time. A reluctant manager allowed me to change after closing and in a few minutes the 'new me' appeared. Not so much an emergent butterfly as a mole blinking its way into the sunlight. I was quite pleased with my new image and even wondered why I'd waited so long. Maybe I'd take a look at The Guardian online dating. No, no! A decision had been made. By me. That was it.

Throwing my old clothes in the boot, I turned the TVR for the M25. It would be an abysmal journey at this time of night, I knew, but worth it. I wanted to see Brenda's reaction to my metamorphosis. It might even persuade her to swap those too-tight jeans for something more appropriate. And if I bumped into anyone else in Aborigine Road, so be it. She would have to learn sometime about my change of perspective and about Brenda's and my change of status. I fast-dialled the prospective Mrs Bunce on the hands free. Waiting for her to pick up, I decided it was time I looked at going to the gym; lose some of that excess poundage. Brenda, too, maybe.

CLAIR

Domestic harmony

Jess had left for school, Phee for university and Case for college by the time we got up. It was just after ten. A familiar white window envelope propped against the hallstand made me wince. With all the airfares, I'd be right up to my credit limit, if not beyond. Fraser came out of the shower, smelling floral.

– I nicked your shampoo. Hope you don't mind.

He kissed the back of my neck. *On the other hand, I've had worse starts to the day.* He had to be at work by eleven.

– I'll run you.

– It's no distance. The walk'll wake me up. Get painting, you.

After he'd gone, instead of picking up a brush, I decided to drum up some more immediate income. This turned out, after an hour ringing round agencies, to be futile. Some of the rates being offered were so derisory I could already feel the contempt of the client. But there was the scratchy problem of the credit card. I would have to approach Connie.

To delay the moment, I rang Sonya and left a message, then I loaded the washing machine, cleared the kitchen, vacuumed right through the house, stopped for a coffee – and finally decided to get down to it. Painting. If Richard, Fraser, Sonya and the one purchaser at Cyntra Gallery thought I could do it, so might someone else. Mid-afternoon. I'd just set up easel and paints when the front door slammed. It was Fraser.

– Ah – you're busy, carry on, I won't disturb you.

– Haven't really got going, yet. Disturb me.

– Fair enough. I've got two hours off and nothing to do.

He massaged my right buttock. Jess would be at the library again until late so between us, we thought of something to do.

Fraser catapulted out of bed when the alarm went off at four thirty, rousing me from a comfortable doze. For a moment, I was disoriented.

– Sorry, doll. I have to get back to work.

I sat up.

– When will you be home?

– Half eleven – if I'm lucky.

He searched for his underpants.

– What about eating?

– I'll grab something there. Why don't you come for a drink, later?

– I may well do.

I still hadn't rung Connie. And there was food shopping to do. I chose the least upsetting. The car was as temperamental as my mother and, having been left idle in the cold for so long, refused to start. I walked to the supermarket at the top of the High Street. Raz was in there stacking shelves.

– Hi, Raz. When did you move to this store?

– Before Christmas.

– How are you?

– Good, thanks.

Despite the brief replies, his attitude was friendly. I wondered if he knew about Jess and Nikos – or anything at all about Jess, for that matter. Meeting him again, I was sorry they'd lost touch. But to be honest, there was no contest between him and his Greek rival.

Jess opened the front door and helped me with carrier bags. I was struck again at the change in her. We made a pasta sauce together and sat down to conghiglie Napolitano and salad. As we ate, I mentioned meeting Raz and she expressed some regret at upsetting him. This was a kinder Jess; I was glad to see her. She also admitted to feeling more confident, now she'd got into the groove of working and revising as she went along. I decided to reward the compassion and diligence.

– I'm going along to have a drink at Fraser's pub later. Want to come?

– Well – I'd like to, but… OK. Just one, though.

– Great. I'll give Maggie and Annie a call before we go.

How natural it sounds 'Maggie and Annie'. What about calling Florida? Stop nagging.

Jess was thoughtful as she cleared the plates.

– Mum? What is it with Annie and Maggie?

I dumped the plates in the sink. Sooner was probably better than later. We went to the sitting room for privacy, sat together on the sofa with our coffees.

The more sordid details of Annie's story were out of bounds to her parents and Fraser but she hadn't mentioned Jess. In my heart, I knew that it was only oversight on Annie's part but my decision was, I felt, for the best. Annie's history was an important element in Jess understanding the mutual needs and benefits of the domestic change at Kilachlan. What Annie had told me was sad and shocking; her flight from overprotective parents at sixteen had led to sleeping rough, the squalor of underclass London, drugs and, finally, prostitution. Truth told so impassively made it sound even harsher. Nearing eighteen, Annie thought her periods had stopped because of the drugs and the way of life. By the time she discovered she was pregnant, it was too late for an abortion. Where pride had stopped her from returning to Glasgow, concern for her unborn baby overcame it. So she hitched her way back home, let her parents help while she had her baby, started studying and was accepted at university. When she wanted independence again, they were reluctant for her to move out. She'd had to be very firm.

I wondered if Jess would light on the drugs aspect. But, while having profound sympathy for Annie's earlier life, Jess was concerned about her coping with nursing Maggie, bringing up Jude and trying to study at the same time. It was worth discussing. I explained the sequence of decisions made by Maggie and Annie to justify the situation, perhaps to myself once more as much as to Jess.

– Annie's happier in the company of women. She doesn't know if she's gay, straight or bi. She's too damaged by that couple of years. Maggie was the first person she wanted to tell and who listened and understood without judging. Jess, you must remember that only Maggie, you and I know what really happened to Annie.

Jess was earnest in promising discretion. The story touched her, especially since Annie at the lowest point had been a similar age to her, now.

We linked arms down Aborigine Road. As we crossed the main road, a sports car turned in past us. Howard's. Unfortunately, it wasn't possible to see whether he was alone. *Although I really, really don't give a toss.* We sniggered over Howard/Brenda scenarios all the way to the pub, bowling in flushed with cold and laughter. Fraser was pleased to see us, treated us to a red wine and a Coke.

– I thought you weren't coming.

– We were having a girl talk.

– Enough said.

It was a music night that night with a passable singer songwriter duo. Fraser took time off serving to sing 'Midnight train to Georgia' and 'Losing my Religion'. Brilliantly. Not that I was biased. I fell asleep quickly that night, head resting on Fraser's chest.

FRASER

Ron told me one of the evening staff had quit and did I know of anyone? Thought of Clair immediately. She's an independent sort of bird. It would give her some spare cash and still give her time to paint. And it would be a way of spending a bit more time together. At the moment I was only catching glimpses of her morning, mid-afternoon and late night. What to do? Decided to go for it – in a boyish, diffident manner.

CLAIR

Another reinvention

When Fraser got back after the lunchtime session next day, I was at work on the wintry scene outside the landing window. He stood behind me as I painted, didn't speak until I stopped to clean a brush.

– Ah – I don't know how you'd feel about this, but I thought I'd run it by you –

– What?

– Only I thought – well – it'd bring in some money and give you time to paint – and we could –

– What?

– I need another person behind the bar, evenings. How would you feel about it?

As it happened, it sounded like the perfect solution – apart from my inability to do mental arithmetic.

– That's OK, there's a computerised till.

– I'll have to watch all the soaps and learn how it's done.

– Actually, you start tonight.

It was a fairly laid-back pub, so smart jeans were acceptable. I put on slightly more make-up than usual, piled up my hair and boobs. Fraser whistled.

– What you doing afterwards, sweetheart?

Jess was home earlier from school. Me working behind a bar was a great idea as far as she was concerned, possibly on the off chance of some under-age drinking. Before leaving, I rang for the day's update on Maggie and managed a short conversation with her. She was glad that Jack and Tatty were back but missed Esmeralda. When Annie came on the line she dismissed her role in Maggie's improvement, putting it down to the will to get better. Jude had started his new school and already had an invite for a party at the weekend. All was well. As I put the phone down it struck me how seamlessly the Buchanans and Harkins had shaped themselves into an extended family. And how comfortable I felt about it. I felt less comfortable about Connie who was due a phone call – and equally due a request for funds from her financially beleaguered daughter.

Fraser tinkered with the car and teased a rumble from the engine, saving us a dreary trudge in the drizzle. Walking into an empty pub made the task ahead seem more achievable. *Here goes, reinvention number – whatever.* The landlord, Ron, came in to give me the once over. He was thin with a boozer's nose and rheumy eyes, a man of few words and a huge capacity for gin. Why he encouraged music in the pub was mystifying. He nodded his approval to Fraser as he took his place on the other side of the bar. Fraser gave me the thumbs up.

– That's it, you're in.

– Wish all interviews were that simple.

– That was never an interview. That was judging my taste in birds.

He moved to a customer before I could make a put down.

It was very, very hard work, no time for standing and handing out worldly knowledge. But the customers were good natured and patient while I fumbled with the till. My colleague was supportive, too, winking suggestively now and again and helping out with large rounds. Fortunately, it wasn't a music night, so I could actually hear what the customers were saying. At closing, Ron asked Fraser if we'd like to stay on for a drink. It being my first night, I felt obliged but Fraser excused us.

– Maybe tomorrow, pal. Clair's not used to bar work – look at her. Wee thing's shattered.

As we tortured the car into action, I remarked on our employer's shyness.

– Och, Ron's not shy. He just doesn't do women.

– He's never gay?

– No way. Women have a place in his life, but not a happy one.

I still had Connie to ring. Conscience and bank balance inflicted equal anguish on the five-minute journey home. By the time we arrived I'd granted myself a reprieve on the grounds that I was too tired. I tried Sonya's number, though – and left another message.

Despite the still novel pleasure of sharing a bed with Fraser, economic angst gained ascendancy during the wee small hours. I resolved to ring Connie as soon as decently possible. Nine o'clock Naples time would be two p.m. Guildford time. Looking at the green digits I calculated – *three forty-eight – say four o'clock, that makes it ten hours plus – forty-eight from sixty's… a bloody long time to get myself into a state.*

Next day, I grasped the nettle and dialled. Antonia picked up.

– Clair – is very good you call your mama now. She real sad.

Connie told me in a small voice that the house felt empty. I sympathised that it was natural, once the flurry of arrangements and condolences was over, for life to seem like a vacuum. It was no time to ask her for money.

– I'm sorry, Mum – it's a very lonely and difficult time for you.

– Oh yeah, I didn't give you a cheque for the flights. That is why you're ringing?

Her accuracy was disconcerting.

– The flights? No – but goodness – I think it was around…

I am fooling no one.

A couple of days later, Fraser and I were leaving for the evening shift, just shutting the gate as a tallish figure approached. I felt a sudden shock – Howard – or was it? I nudged Fraser and nodded towards the figure.

– What?

– Ssshh! Look who it is!

– Who?

Too late.

– Hello Clair – and – er – hello – um…

He'd forgotten Fraser's name, or pretended to. Fraser was equal to it.

– Fraser. And you'd be the one with a taste for Oz backpackers?

I glared at Fraser then forced a smile for Howard.

– Hello Howard. You look – different.

– Well – time for a change. Been working out at the gym and – er –

Fraser was relentless.

– Clair tells me you're with fat bird next door, now?

Howard was icy by return.

– I see you've lost none of your innate charm. Clair, hope you're keeping well?

I nodded. He was looking good – well, much better than I could ever have imagined. I witnessed a slight tinge of – well – *Why didn't you do this before, Howard?* I was gaping, I suppose, as he turned and walked up next door's path. Fraser barely waited for him to be out of earshot.

– What a tosser! D'you see the jacket? And the number two cut?

He opened the car door.

– C'mon, get yer arse in the car, we're going to be late.

It was unsettling, I admit, not because I wanted to abandon my handsome-ish, young, sexy, loving, appreciative, new squeeze, no. It was just that if, and it was a significant 'if' – if Howard had made that sort of change sooner, while we'd been together, would I be in this situation now? And yes, Howard was still the same person and it's the person inside that counts – but would I have been shallow enough to go along with his new image? Would I have taken him to Symi with us? Would my life be very different, now? Could I have been that superficial? Lucky he'd hidden his modest light under a comb-over. *Face it, you had a very narrow squeak.*

Fraser said very little apart from a few guffaws about the haircut. He didn't ask what I thought or felt about it. He must have felt totally secure that I was with him, now, and not with the old guy. That's the difference with blokes. Not given to introspection, analysis or generally disappearing up their own sphincters.

Soon after the Howard episode, I demonstrated the flaw in my female ego by – well – making a complete tit of myself. A letter with the Aegis logo arrived for Fraser. I feigned lack of interest, but then couldn't resist a series of pointed references and barbed comments. So he told me; Aegis had asked him to reconsider joining their Symi operation in the summer. Even his openness was not enough. I needed reassurance, over and over, that he wanted me, that our relationship meant more to him than Symi. My lack of confidence made me whittle away at him until he snapped.

– I've told you a million bloody times, Clair. If you don't trust me…

– I do – I do – sorry-sorry-sorry-sorry-sorry… it's just – me.

It was our first difficult moment. I withdrew into shame. Unexpectedly, this great young guy had walked into my life, apparently wanted to stay, and I wanted to ruin it all. It was the typical female 'let's end it now and I'll take the pain that's inevitably waiting for me'. I felt instantly ashamed. For once, everything else was on the up, too: Maggie improved daily, flourishing in the company of Annie and Jude; Jess continued to behave well, even through her re-sits; Connie had transferred the flight money into my account so I could breathe again; I had a job I rather liked that gave me time to paint; Case had paid the rent this month and, with Fraser augmenting my income, finances as well as life, were definitely improving. *And so Clair decides to self-destruct.* In Sonya's continued absence, I gave myself a good mental slapping.

There was still THE issue, though, to address. Jess's father. I had rehearsed it innumerable times since her birth; what to emphasise, what to omit and mostly, to let her know how much I had wanted her. Since that moment in the side room at Joe's funeral, I'd known it should happen soon and would have done it by now but for Maggie's stroke. My daughter had shown the courage that I should have. One Sunday, while Fraser was on a lunchtime session, I seized the opportunity. As Jess loafed on the sofa listening to her iPod, I put down a mug of tea beside her and sat in the armchair. Our front room was more of a confessional, these days. Jess took an earpiece out.

— Cheers, Mum.

— Jess, can we talk?

She sighed.

— What have I done, now?

— Nothing, darling. I want to talk about that time back in Florida at Joe's funeral. You asked about your father.

She looked startled, as though it was the first time the subject had been broached. Indeed, that moment at the funeral seemed light years in the past. So much had happened in the interim. She began by suggesting another time. I was firm.

— I didn't bring it up before because I thought that if you wanted to know you'd ask. That was wrong of me.

— Look, Mum, you really don't need —

Worked up to a pitch, I continued.

— You may have heard the name Adam mentioned?

Jess nodded slightly.

— Adam was my one, long relationship. I met him when he took a room here, after your Gran moved back to Florida. He was a teacher — he played in a band. I was twenty-two, he was about twenty-six. Anyhow, we were together seven years and I always assumed that we would get married but, well, things didn't go according to my plan and we split up. I was devastated, just couldn't make sense of the world or anything in it. Then I —

— You discovered you were pregnant by him? He was my father?

— No, no. Your father was the one who comforted me and made me believe that I was worthy of being loved.

Jess sat up, intent. The predictable questions came. I responded with rehearsed semi-truths.

— I couldn't tell your Gran who he was because I didn't want her holding a shotgun to his head. And I couldn't tell Maggie because it wouldn't have been fair to make her keep that secret. He was a lot older than me, thirty years or more, and quite well known, successful. I will tell you his name, one day. But right now, for your sake — and theirs, I can't.

— Not until Gran and Maggie have died? You're afraid I might let it out?

319

That stung because it was true.

– I don't want you to have that responsibility. He's a father to be proud of, Jess; intelligent, cultured, fun – and very handsome. You look a lot like him when he was younger.

By the time we made Jess he was over sixty, had white hair. Like Richard. Jess hugged her knees, trying to take it all in then, inevitably, wanted to know where he was, now. My eyes filled with unpredicted tears.

– He died, darling, when you were four.

That day, hearing it on the news. Heart attack – on holiday in France with his family. Having to ring Maggie to say how sorry I was – calling Mum, making sure Joe was out, breaking the news about her ex-lover. My ex-lover. Little Jess, asking why Mummy was crying. Sonn – coming down with wine, listening, sharing. And I wasn't sure why I was crying. Because he meant so much or because he didn't mean enough? Or was it a release? For him and for me?

– Did he ever know about me?

Jess was plaintive.

– I didn't tell him. I didn't want to complicate his life or compromise him.

It was a sidestep Jess didn't pick up. The truth was, I didn't know. But I always felt sure he would have wanted to see her, would have insisted on helping me out, had he known. We talked on, mainly about how I had coped with the pregnancy, the contrasting reactions of Connie and Maggie to the news. I hoped I had tailored my story so that Jess heard nothing she couldn't repeat.

– JJ – can I ask you something now, darling?

– Sure.

– You never asked about him, not until Joe's funeral. Why was that?

– I don't know, really. It was like – I never needed a dad. I had you and Maggie and Sonya. It's like I almost didn't notice – well no, of course I noticed. But it was sort of – irrelevant. There were lots of other kids at school living just with their mum. We were normal. Of course, now I know we're <u>not</u> –

I must have looked surprised because she poked me and laughed. Wherever her sense of humour came from, she used it to her advantage.

Later, I rang Sonya.

– You told her about Ben?

– Not exactly. Not his name.

– So what, really, was the point?

Jess was quieter than usual for a day or so, stayed out a little later after the library closed. But otherwise, seemed to be fairly positive – would occasionally prod me and say 'Normal?' then ape around. Somehow, it all seemed too easy after the build up I'd given it in my head.

After two weeks at the pub, I felt like I'd been a barmaid for years. The music nights were a lot of fun and very hard work. Fraser was popular, made it clear I was his lady and we worked well as a team. The regulars liked us and the weekend staff deferred to us; to all intents and purposes, it was our pub. Ron didn't mind. Less trouble for him. I developed a routine. I painted in daylight, what there was of it, and started a study of St Catherine's Lock, about a mile the other side out of Guildford. My style was developing, relating a rhythm of movement to environment, empathy between person and place. My life was beginning to fit me, too. At the rare times Sonya was available for conversation I was unable to rein in my happiness. I tried to be sensitive to her situation but I must have exuded smugness. Sonya was generous if somewhat too candid.

– Don't apologise, Clack, it's been long enough coming. Grab it.

Fraser upgraded the household to 'happy home'. He and Jess had an easy, jokey relationship with Nikos as a reference point as well as me. Case no longer took liberties with the rent. Fraser's singular moments were expressed in music, up in our bedroom, sometimes flowing, sometimes strident chords, over and over again until the sequence was right. Occasionally I intruded, made brief studies of him bent over the frets in concentration or head back, exulting in the perfect progression. Hungry for a history to bind us, we reminisced over Symi and Kilachlan as though years separated the experiences. Lovemaking became slower, deeper, as minds and bodies moulded into one another, made unspoken promises and commitments.

I should have known things were going too well.

Something else we shared was Monday night off. This particular Monday, the first after Easter, we went to Boccaccio's for dinner. Jess worked there Friday and Saturday nights, so there was no clash. I'd met the manager, Mario, a couple of times. At the end of the evening, complimentary glasses of Amaretto arrived at the table, Mario joined us and we stayed chatting until gone eleven. Mario was interested in Fraser playing for the customers if ever he was free. As we walked home, we imagined a family concern like Boccaccio's with Jess waitressing, Fraser playing guitar and me covering the walls with artwork. We elaborated on the fantasy, ridiculous under our present circumstances, but pleasant enough. A stylish music and art kafeneion – no, hotel – in Symi, of course. Maggie would have her own suite of rooms; Jack, Tatty and Esmeralda would have run of the spacious courtyard. The word 'souvlaki' would be banned out of respect for Esmeralda. Annie would be appointed Chief Psychologist for the Dodecanese and Jude would graduate from school on Symi to study architecture under Nikos who would be a Professor of Architecture and married to Jess who would be a famous – Fraser was still searching for the word as he put the key in the lock. The door swung open and hit an obstruction.

– Suitcases – bugger me! Don't tell me you're letting out the lavvy, now?

As I followed him in I recognised the luggage – and the world started spinning in reverse.

CHAPTER TWENTY-SIX

STILL CLAIR

Terrible with socking great rancid raisins

I peered, tortoise-like, round the door. She inclined regally and took advantage of my astonishment to get in first.

– Well? Aren't you pleased to see me?

Jess laughed nervously.

– Look, Mum – Gran's here!

Connie sat in state in the sitting room, the remains of a light meal on the coffee table. My mouth and throat froze. Fraser pushed me gently forward. Connie surveyed him coolly and turned to Jess.

– Jess, aren't you going to introduce me to your boyfriend?

Fraser held out his hand.

– Fraser Buchanan. Clair's boyfriend. Pleased to meet you, Mrs Dubrowsky.

Connie allowed him a touch of her fingertips.

– Very civil of you to walk her home, now –

I found a voice.

– Mum – why didn't you tell me you –

– Don't I get a kiss from my daughter these days?

Duty done, I stepped back and looked askance at Jess, by now a very small rodent mesmerised by two queen cobras. Connie smiled at me.

– Jess tells me that you let out two rooms. Looks like you and she better share so I can have one of yours.

Jess entertained her benefactress while I went upstairs and sorted my – Fraser's and my – room for Connie. Fraser was incredulous.

– You aren't seriously telling me that we have to sleep separately because your mother wouldn't like it? Forgive me for being indelicate, but you're fifty – not fifteen!

The tables had turned. Fraser was miffed not just by the sleeping arrangements but because I hadn't told my mother about him. I continued tearing off sheets and pillowslips.

– Look, just give me a hand. We'll talk when she's gone to bed.

– Where? Either side of a locked door? Christ! You said she was difficult, but –

– And you're not making it any easier – hold this –

I shoved the end of the duvet into his hands and yanked at the cover. Inevitably he let go and I reeled back against the wardrobe, catching my spine on the handle. He ignored it, thumping down the mattress.

– So where am I supposed to sleep?

– I dunno – I'll make you up a bed on the sofa.

– This is unreal!

He stomped to the kitchen leaving me to face the interloper alone. She was spiked saccharine.

– You didn't tell me you were 'involved'.

– It's all quite recent. It didn't seem the right time when I saw you last.

– When you saw me last? So it's not that recent?

Jess studied the floor awkwardly as Connie rode a wave of jet-lagged malevolence.

– Jess tells me he's moved in here. You didn't feel I should know?

– I didn't think it –

– Was my business? That my daughter was cohabiting with her toy boy in my house? Wrong, lady!

She held out her hand for assistance. Jess helped her past me, and upstairs.

Up in Jess's room she told me the first she'd known of Connie's visit was a call from a limousine on its way from Heathrow.

– But why didn't you ring me?

– You were having a night out with Fraser, I didn't want to spoil it. You found out soon enough.

Thank you for that, Jess. Quite right.

Unsurprisingly, my night was ghoulishly conscious, save for the usual lucid door knocking dream. I struggled from half-sleep around eight and went down to the sitting room. The bedclothes were strewn aside. Fraser was in the kitchen, hunched over a coffee opposite Case. I touched him tentatively. He wrapped his hand round mine, but briefly. The three of us moved round each other in an awkward morning ritual. Jess joined, shortly, ready for school.

– Anyone taken Gran a cup of coffee?

Our silence persuaded her to volunteer.

Fraser and Case both left earlier than was necessary. Instead of bringing a ray of Florida sunshine, Connie had descended on the house like smog, infecting everyone with gloom. Now, in the harsh light of mid-morning, she arrived for breakfast. I was blitzing the kitchen and not yet dressed.

– Why aren't you at school, Clair? I thought you'd gotten yourself established again?

– No – it was only supply teaching 'til they could get someone full-time.

– Didn't you apply for it?

I was speechless at the irony, given it was my swift departure for Florida that lost me the job. Probably. Connie closed her eyes and shook her head as though inertia was what she'd come to expect. She changed tack.

– I forget how cold it gets here. I'd better go shop for something warm. How soon can you be ready?

I spent the day as shopping-wallah for Memsaab Dubrowsky. My dodgy finances meant I usually only ventured into House of Fraser as a shortcut from North Street to the High Street. Today, Connie seemed to be launching a takeover bid for the store. I stood about long enough almost to have a sales tag stuck on me. Around four, I called a cab and deposited Connie and excess baggage back at Aborigine Road then set off for the pub on foot. Fraser and I exchanged barely a dozen words all evening and he despatched me home early, with depressing coincidence, in the same cab I'd shared with Connie earlier. I arrived back in time for a cool 'goodnight' from my mother. She didn't actually say 'A daughter of mine? Working in a bar?!'. But it was in her every nuance. How conveniently she forgot her own past.

Lying on the new blow-up mattress in Jess's room, I was raw with impotent rage. The house was Connie's, of that I had been reminded firmly and frequently since her arrival. She didn't like the number or character of its inhabitants and wasn't damn well going to hide it. In fact, I wouldn't have put it past her to evict the lot of them. Why the flaming, sodding hell should it matter to her, living in that block of flesh-coloured sorbet in Florida? My nerve endings were a billion incandescent points. If only the mattress had been filled with combustible gas I could have sparked a gigantic explosion followed by a raging pyre that swallowed the house and everyone in it. Except Connie was probably fireproof – asbestos, no doubt.

Then there was my fledgling relationship with Fraser. Now my mother was in the house, the only time we could be alone was outside it, which somewhat defeated the object of living together. We worked together, sure, but had no privacy. What irked was he'd been pretty glad to share my pram before she arrived; flinging his toys out now was not a helpful reaction. Where was his support, his sympathy? Was he just a bloke, after all?

FRASER

Me:

— She suddenly breaks out in orange pustules that can only be lanced in Florida.

— One to Mac.

That was Ron, to whom all Scotsmen were Mac. Next, Case:

— The next bitchy remark she makes turns into a mad bat and bites her in the jugular.

— One to Casey.

Ron wasn't good on names. Case didn't take it personally. Ron:

— Mac?

— The Nice Police lock her up and give her lessons in being a human being.

— No, not painful enough.

This, I thought, was unjust.

— You haven't met her, Ron. It'd have her pleading for death —

— I know the type. Casey?

— How about we fling her into a concrete mixer and — and —

— Still not enough.

Ron was a mean umpire, whichever woman had turned him this way would be a match for Clair's mother.

— One more go, Mac — and it's a forfeit.

My relationship with Case had graduated beyond the defensive camaraderie of two frightened men in a predominantly female household. Traumatised by eleven long days of the American matriarch's presence we'd joined forces in the campaign to rid Aborigine Road of Constance Dubrowsky. So far it had resulted in a couple of after-hours drinking sessions courtesy of Ron. From Ron's point of view, the benefit was twofold, providing not only drinking companions but the opportunity to destroy one of the planet's 'monstrous regiment of women', if only metaphorically. On the rebound from Sonya and missing the luxury flat in Richmond, Case was an easy convert to Ron's misogyny. Mrs D's bullying intensified his bias.

— Time's up, Mac.

— I'd like to explore the poison theme — I think the rules allow it?

— Not very original — go on, Mac.

—Yesss! I'm playing the Rasputin gambit: poison the old bag, then shoot her, then drown her under the ice.

Case conceded victory, gracious and admiring in defeat.

— My man! Sweet! If only...

— Game, set and match to Mac!

I got another vodka – and Case had to down the Guildford equivalent of a Nobby's Blaster – mercifully minus the absinthe.

CLAIR

Terrible Clair

A few evenings later I went home from the pub a little early, my head thumping, leaving Fraser to clear up. I took a couple of pills and flopped on the sofa waiting for the waves of pain to recede. The house seemed deserted. Connie must have gone to bed and Jess and Case would be out. Phee was mouse-like, anyway. After a while, I noticed a piece of paper stuck between the seat cushions. It was an empty envelope, addressed to Fraser and postmarked Northampton. Northampton was the Aegis UK base, but the envelope didn't bear the Aegis logo. *Has he asked them to use an unmarked envelope so I wouldn't know they were sending him a contract for this season?*

Desperate and low on sources of comfort, I sank into an exhausted doze. I was woken abruptly by a sharp crash. I vaulted to the hall to find Fraser and Case who, having fallen through the front door and knocked it against the wall were trying, absurdly, to close it silently while scolding each other to be quiet. Another time, I would have laughed. But tonight Connie's genes won over. Terrible Clair emerged.

Case staggered upstairs as my lover slumped at the bottom, eyes bulbous and bleary from drink. I marched to the kitchen, filled a tumbler with water, marched back, jerked his head up by his hair and threw it full in his face. He blinked, puzzled, wiped his eyes with his coat sleeve and acknowledged me, vaguely.

— Wha' wuzz tha' for?

— Get up!

I yanked him by the collar, pulling him to unsteady feet so that he grasped for me. After a lopsided tango to the sitting room, I dropped him in a heap. His head banged on the side table, bringing his scuzzy world into focus.

— You bitch! You fuckin' bitch!

Enough. It was not just my turn, but my right to abuse him.

– You bloody child! Grow up! Don't you have any imagination in that bladder of a brain? Can't you see I need some help here? And all you can do is get wasted with your pathetic little male clique. That bloody piss-head Ron egging you on? Or can't you cope with an adult relationship?

– Sorry, I'm sorry. Won't do it again, promise.

He held a hand against his battered head.

– I'm not your bloody mother! I'm trying to hold the house together, provide a stable home for Jess and cope with her problems. I'm on call to my flaming mother back and forth across the Atlantic and now she's invaded the only space I had. Maggie's ill and I'm worried sick about her. I want to be there and I feel guilty as hell that I'm not. Your bloody sister is, though. My professional life is going nowhere. I'm fifty and I'm not ready to be thirty, yet. I don't need you behaving like a knob. I need your support. And this is what I fucking get!

I waggled the envelope in front of him, too shocked at myself, too angry and disappointed to explain. He blinked at it with incomprehension, but had definitely sobered. He breathed deeply a few times and sat up, spoke quietly.

– OK, OK, I hear you. I'm not going to do this to you again.

I must have slept, because I was beating at that same door, hoping to get some attention from my Daddy. I didn't, of course. Then, as Fraser checked my driving licence and said *'How old?'*, I saw Maggie watching from across the harbour. And halfway between us, standing on the ferry's deck, was Julia – only it wasn't her. It was Annie.

Next morning I went to the sitting room and found no sign of Fraser or that he'd even slept there. I trawled my aching mind for some residue of last night's conclusion but caught only a sour haze of regret or foreboding – or both. Connie was in the kitchen, dressed and at breakfast. Just seeing her eat, her once beautiful eyes narrow over sagging, powdered cheeks that undulated as she chewed, repelled me.

– You look a little the worse for wear, Clair.

– Yeah – well…

– Best get dressed, the designer's due at eleven.

– The what?

– Interior designer, coming at eleven. Didn't I tell you?

– No, you didn't.

– Well, the house needs fancying up if I'm going to sell it.

Before I could recover from this, the door opened. It was Fraser, wearing his leather jacket, carrying a grip – and his guitar case.

– 'Morning, Mrs Dubrowsky. Clair, can I have a word?

We faced one another in the hall. I braced myself for the next blow. I could barely whisper.

– Where did you sleep last night?

– It doesn't matter – look, this isn't easy…

The envelope was from Aegis, he said, thanking him for the last three seasons. The job in Symi had gone. He really had turned it down despite which, he was leaving for Gatwick, catching the next available flight for Rhodes and thence to the island. He knew enough people there – Nobby, Panos, plenty of shopkeepers and taverna owners – to find some kind of work. He'd spoken to Ron, made sure that the bar was covered. My job was still there if I wanted… He touched my cheek.

– Sorry, doll. It's just, well, I'm too far down your list.

I stood on the same spot for some time after he'd gone. I had a sudden flash of Jess perched on a chair arm nine months ago, scolding me for smoking, lecturing me for thinking of returning Maggie's cheque. Pre-Symi, pre-Fraser, pre-Jess and drugs, pre-Joe dying, pre-Maggie's stroke, pre-Annie and Jude – and pre-Connie in residence.

After a while, realised I'd missed out Howard. It took my attention from despair for a moment. *Wonder where he is, now? Next door?* I went into the living room and peered through the curtains. His car wasn't there. *Of course not, it's Tuesday – he'll be at work – sixty miles away.* As if I needed banality to distract me from the present. Fraser was gone. It was over. I went upstairs, took an extravagantly long shower and allowed myself to cry, tears mingling with the soap and spray, streaming down my body. *Sorrow washing over me.* When I emerged I heard Connie talking to someone.

– I don't want anything glitzy, just dicky it up to sell.

It was the interior designer. I had to get out, if only to prevent my hands from closing around Connie's throat. I blasted my hair dry, planning to drive up to Richmond. If Sonya wasn't there, or not available – well, at least I would have had a journey with a purpose. As I stood in what was now my mother's bedroom, sifting rapidly through what was now my 'section' of the wardrobe, I heard the front door slam and glimpsed a pastel blur exiting the front gate to a Volvo Estate. She was certainly into the violet range, whoever she was. Something seemed familiar, so familiar that everything from Jingle

Bells to Big Ben jangled in my head, but recognition wouldn't surface. *Who is she?* Fraser's exit had wiped my memory of all lesser topics. As the Volvo left, I grabbed a top and went back to dress in the room Jess and I now shared.

Connie caught me coming down the stairs.

– Going out?

– Yes.

– Anywhere special?

– Erm – something for work.

– For that run-down bar? You're doing something for them? You let people walk all over you, Clair.

I left the irony hanging in the air between us.

– See you later.

Connie passed me a cardboard tube.

– This came for you. I signed for it.

A cylindrical package with the Aegis logo on it.

– Thanks. See you later.

I lobbed it against the hallstand and went out.

In Richmond, I fed the meter enough to build an extension on Aborigine Road. Sonya was in. As soon as I hit her front room I started to unload. She stopped me mid-sentence.

– Look, Clair. I'm really, really sorry that you're in this situation. But now isn't too good a time for me.

Of course it wasn't. Sonya was my friend but she was busy and I had gate-crashed her working day. I was so blinded, though, by my own problems I wasn't able to see the situation for what it was. I turned and sloped towards the door.

– Sorry to be an inconvenience. I'll get out of your way.

Sonya stamped in annoyance.

– Don't you dare do that to me! I am always there for you. Too bloody often. Perhaps if I wasn't you'd grow a fucking backbone!

My face must have been a tragedy mask. She went on rapidly.

– Tell you what, though – your squeeze has done what you should have done years ago – buggered off and left Connie alone to count her money.

This was so blindingly true there was little more to say. I left. There were still a couple of hours on the meter, so I bought a packet of Silk Cut and headed for the river, sat on a seat shuddering with cold and chain smoking. I was an abandoned lover, inadequate daughter, failed mother, neglectful niece, professional friend-in-need and a sodding-well smoker again. I was also bloody freezing so went into the town, had a miserable, overpriced coffee then drove back to Guildford. On the way, Sonya's 'tour de grief' over Brian and temporary residence in Aborigine Road went through my mind. *That wasn't a brilliant time for me, but I certainly didn't show her the door. I even provided a beautiful lodger for her to shag.*

I got to the pub and realised I had no recollection of my journey there. Ron let me in and went back to the phone where he continued a muttered conversation. I put out ashtrays and beer mats, bottled up soft drinks and mixers, checked the ice machine, fetched crisps and nuts from the storeroom, sliced lemon. Ron finished his call and checked the till, normally Fraser's job, then went upstairs. On impulse, I measured a large whisky, downed it neat and regretted it instantly. Not only was it unprofessional, but also very unwise on an empty stomach. I took a bag of crisps, rang it up and paid then scoffed the lot, not even noticing the flavour. Ron didn't want me there on my own. Nor did I want to be there – or at Aborigine Road. My mobile rang. Jess.

– Are you at the pub, Mum?

– Yes.

– Case said Fraser's gone. And Gran says she's selling the house.

– I'm afraid it's true about Fraser, darling. But don't worry about the house. Gran wouldn't leave us homeless.

Wouldn't leave Jess homeless, maybe. Silence.

– Jess – you there?

Shit – she could do without all this, just when she's been doing so well.

– Yeah.

She sounded very young.

– You OK, Mum?

– Don't worry, darling. Everything's fine.

Required response from mother to insecure daughter. *Didn't learn it at _my_ mother's knee.* Another silence, then,

– OK, Mum. See you later.

– All right, darling.

As I put my phone back in my bag I saw Ron watching me. He must have heard some of it. All he said was:

– Opening time.

He flipped my empty crisp packet into the bin then shoved back the bolts on the doors.

Fraser's absence was a force field round every optic, pump and glass and Sonya's outburst revolved in my head. From the first few regulars and through the evening's rush, enquiries after Fraser were frequent. Ron and I took turns to field them. I didn't hear what reason he was giving. For my own sense of pride, I stuck to 'an urgent call from Greece' and assured everyone that things were fine between us, knowing that comparisons between stories would be made. I'd just have to face it out. Ron and I worked efficiently despite barest communication. *Perhaps he misses Fraser, too, and feels some sympathy for me? No. Ron has only alcohol and cynicism in his soul.* However, at closing time he took his turn clearing and cleaning, even asked if I'd be all right getting home.

– Thanks, Ron, I have the car.

He nodded goodnight then, as I reached the door, said:

– She staying long, your Mum?

I met the unexpected interest as frankly as I could.

– Don't know. Longer than her welcome.

He nodded again, thoughtfully this time.

– OK. Can you do lunchtime tomorrow?

– Um – yes, I suppose –

– G'night, Clair.

It was the first time he had ever said my name.

Connie was in bed when I got back, so I didn't have the opportunity to take Sonya's advice and send her packing. Or me packing. My mobile hadn't rung since Jess and there were no messages recorded on the phone. Jess was in the living room watching a comedy rerun on TV.

– Hi, Mum.

Her earlier anxiety had evaporated.

– You OK, JJ?

– Fine.

– Only I thought you were…

She didn't respond, lost in the sitcom.

– Any phone calls?

Jess looked at me sadly and shook her head, then went back to the telly. I went to bed, pretended to sleep as she later, rather noisily, joined me.

Next morning there was a text from Sonya: 'Sorry Clack hope UR OK speak soon x'. Connie was up and out with no word of where. Jess was still in bed. I left early for the lunchtime shift, juggling food and drinks orders, after which I mooched around The Friary Centre and Waterstone's between sessions, hoping I wouldn't bump into anyone I knew. My wish was granted.

FRASER

Walking down North Street to the station, I knew I was a total shite. "Too far down your list". Just how far up my own arse was I? It was true, though, Connie was the main reason I was going. Comfortably absolved, I queued for a ticket, already picturing stepping off the ferry in Symi. Annie banged at my skull trying to get in. Nothing that a beer in Departures wouldn't soothe. I'd ring her from the airport. Once I got there though, I figured it would be better to wait until I was in Greece. Annie could be very persuasive. And she was bound to give me a row.

It was my habit to fall asleep instantly on planes, but this time I stayed awake for the whole four hours. Read NME and the airline magazine, cover to cover. The in-flight video was mega-dreary and we flew above cloud most of the way. I had plenty of time to think, never a happy situation. Considered the pros and cons of my current headlong escape. On the pro side: 1. Escaping the Apricot Monster, 2. Being back on Symi. On the con side: 1. Leaving Clair, 2. On a plane without a job to go to, 3. Almost no money to live on when I get there, 4. Nowhere to live and… 5. Leaving Clair. Then another con hit me. 6. Ali Mavrakakou.

HOWARD

She said yes. Applied for the post. Shortlisted. Interview Thursday.

CHAPTER TWENTY-SEVEN

CLAIR

The raisin ferments

Raz came into the pub just after evening opening time. I confirmed his age to Ron and passed him a beer. I was pleased to see him. Mutual, apparently.

– Wish I'd known you worked here, Clair. I'm in the library most nights so I come past on my way home.

– Really? Jess works at the library a lot.

– Oh? Haven't seen her.

Raz hadn't thought before speaking, too busy getting his money out. Knew by my face it he'd ballsed up.

– Well, she might've been… I mean, on a night I wasn't –

– Please don't pretend. It's important.

He admitted he'd never seen her there and stared hard at the towelling mat on the bar, looking like he wanted to commit suicide by smacking himself round the head. I felt sorry for him. After all this time he still liked Jess. I had to continue serving. Ron, as ever, sat morosely silent. So the poor young guy drank his pint in mortified isolation. If he could have crawled out, he probably would. I caught him as he drained his glass and turned to go.

– Raz, I won't tell Jess how I know, promise.

He smiled shyly, mumbled something and hunched out into the cold spring night.

As the mediocre Everly Brothers tribute failed to harmonise, I had thinking time. On one level I ricocheted from pump to optic to till and round again, honing memory skills on drinks orders and churning customer small talk. Underneath that, I was running through possible explanations for Jess lying to me. Top candidate was she was back on drugs. Next, she was having an affair with someone she shouldn't – how would I deal with that one? Third she was living a life of indolence on her new wealth. There had been new clothes, an iPod and an iPad but no mention of buying a car or driving lessons. Perhaps she really was saving the money for university. In which case, why was she lying about studying? My approach would have to be low key, straightforward and preferably out of Connie's earshot – if something this big could be concealed from her sonar system. She was guaranteed to blame Jess's misdemeanours on my poor parenting skills. On the other hand, if Jess was on a drugs spending spree, Connie was funding it.

Ron wasn't around most of the evening. He reappeared about ten and, shortly after, one of the casual staff sauntered in and started serving. It wasn't his usual night but Ron nodded to me.

— Better get off, sort out your domestic.

I'd underestimated his capacity for fellow feeling. *Whatever you do, don't argue with him. Go.*

— Cheers Ron — appreciate it.

He lifted his glass.

— Make it up sometime.

Connie was still up, surprisingly, and didn't argue when I asked her to switch the TV off. Neither did Jess when I asked her to come downstairs for a talk with Gran. The household was in a state of flux. She would assume that was the topic. I wondered, given Raz's revelation, what the next body blow would be. Three generations, each with her own agenda, balanced on the edge of the arena. Older and younger looked to the middle for a lead. It was clearly unexpected when it came.

— How was the library today, Jess?

Surprised by the mildness of it, she failed to detect danger.

— Er — fine. Why?

Connie was less equable.

— That's why you called this summit? To ask about the library?

I ignored her.

— What were you revising, Jess?

— Erm — English.

— See anyone you knew?

Connie caught a thread of interest and turned to her granddaughter. Jess was intuitive enough to realise she was walking a razor wire tightrope with the spotlight full on her. She took a step, a little unbalanced, now.

— Few others from school. Why?

— Because, in all the time you have — supposedly — been working at the library, no one has seen you.

— Who said? They're liars if —

Connie looked me uncertainly.

— Where have you been, Jess?

The silence was charged. Jess made a break for the door but I moved, blocking her path.

– Get out of my way! I don't have to answer to you!

Connie rose. *She's not wearing her ring – at a time like this, I notice that –*

– That's enough, Jess!

But Jess struggled to get past me. For the first time in my daughter's life, I raised my hand and slapped her. It was enough. Jess backed off, holding her face.

– You bitch! You bloody bitch!

Bitch, I'm a bitch again. She moved to her grandmother.

– Gran – did you see that?

But Connie wasn't providing refuge.

– Just tell me what the hell is going on!

– Tell her, Jess, tell her about drug abuse. About drug counselling. And tell her what you're spending her money on.

Jess gave me a look of hatred.

– Jess – honey – you haven't taken drugs, have you?

Connie's voice had lost its vigour.

– No, Gran – she's lying. She's just jealous because –

This wasn't Jess, not even Jess at her worst. It was someone I didn't know. Was this the way drugs changed personalities?

– You said you were off them.

I could hear the exhaustion in my own voice. Connie cut in.

– Jess, whatever the truth is, you better tell it.

But Jess wasn't going to volunteer anything. I tried to remain steady.

– January, when we got back from Scotland, you stopped your counselling. You told Mary you didn't want to see her any more. Why did you start using again? Was it getting all that money from Gran?

Connie paled. *If she's beginning to feel uncomfortable, good, she deserves it.* She faced Jess.

– Mary? That the Mary who called tonight? You got mad at her.

Jess found her voice.

– I'm completely off drugs. That's the truth.

It was a waiting game, now. Connie and I had the time and Jess knew it. She sank into the sofa.

– Yeah, OK. Mary is my counsellor. But it wasn't about me. I really haven't started again. I promised Nikos I wouldn't. It was about – someone else.

With a little more prompting, the story came out. Jess, being typically idealistic and hopelessly misguided, had befriended a young ex-soldier she'd met through drug counselling. She'd been spending her inheritance from Joe in a naïve bid to 'cure' him with gifts and meals out if he stayed clean, cash when he needed it. It was a testament to her compassion and a tragedy of sorts. But there was more and it proved a chilling coincidence.

– He lives in Sussex. Mary's the nearest counsellor for both of us. Well, the nearest private counsellor who had a vacancy for me. So, when I... when I knew I'd stopped, I thought I ought to try and help someone else. And that's where I've been. With Piers –

And then she said his surname. It struck forcefully from an already stormy sky. Connie and I repeated it in unison and Jess echoed back.

– Yeah, Benfleet, Piers Benfleet. D'you know him? Mum? Gran?

'Benfleet'. 'Army'. The words resonated around us. Connie spoke, in a voice so strange it came from another existence.

– Jess, has this Piers ever mentioned anyone else? In his family?

Jess frowned.

– No, not really. His parents are divorced. Um – his gran's got Alzheimer's.

The information meant nothing to us, but past and present collided in Jess's next recollection.

– Oh – and his grandfather was in the army, too, and then he was an MP. But he's dead, now.

I retreated to the far end of the room, as though distance could change what I'd just heard. *Jess and – My god! Jess and –* then I caught Connie's look. Jess spun between us both.

– What? What!?

Connie and I, eyes locked, were having the biggest conversation of our lives. She <u>knew</u>. My mother knew about Ben and me – *and about Jess.* And finally, I was admitting it. Jess was on her feet, voice edging on hysteria.

– Tell me! Tell me what's happening!

– Sit down, Jess.

Jess stood, defiant. Connie looked at me, her voice was shaky.

– You have to ask her.

I nodded. Jess yelled at both of us.

    — Ask what?

    — Jess — is Piers just a friend? Or is he anything more to you?

    — What's going on?!

    — Just tell me if —

Jess gave me that imperious look.

    — No. Piers and I haven't fucked, if that's what you mean.

Connie flopped back in her chair, her relief palpable.

    — Shit! That _is_ what you mean! What the fuck business —

    — Jess, just shut your foul mouth for once!

There was silence for a few moments until Connie sighed, pushed herself back up.

    — It's too late for all this. Clair, you should talk to your daughter — and tomorrow, I need to have a long talk with mine. Help me up.

Jess was there for her. But at the door, Connie stopped her.

    — I'm fine. You stay here with your Mom. It's time you did some listening, honey.

She drew Jess towards her, kissed her lightly on the forehead then left the room.

    That night Jess heard the full soap opera that was my life, her life — who her father was, what he was to me, to Maggie and to her grandmother.

    — Oh my god — you mean Piers is my… what?

    — Half nephew, I suppose.

At one point she said,

    — It explains a lot.

    — How do you mean?

    — The way Gran is with you — like you're a naughty child — no, not just that — she behaves like you're defying her all the time — except you're not.

    Then, later —

    — Does Maggie know?

How would I know? But if Connie knew all along —

    — I suppose so. If your Gran knows, odds are she does.

    — God, you've all been keeping the same secret, all these years?

And when the anger kicked in —

– So my father was a dirty old man?! I mean, he practically raped you!

– No, JJ, no he didn't. I <u>wanted</u> to be with him.

– But he took advantage of you being so sad.

– Maybe he did, I can't say. I took what I wanted from him – you.

– But you couldn't know – you couldn't know you'd get pregnant –

– I gave it every opportunity. I think I would have gone on until I did.

And there, as I said it I realised it was true. I had used Ben.

I persuaded Jess we should sleep on it and, reluctantly, she went up to bed. She deserved space and time to reflect. It was getting light when we parted, eyes swollen with shared tears, both of us aching with fatigue. Jess trudged upstairs in grey light while I sat and watched the cobalt awaken in Blue Period 1, J Harkin, 1951.

Before bedding down on the sofa, I fetched a glass of water from the kitchen. The light through the open door caught the cardboard tube propped up against the hallstand. I picked it up as I went past, not really curious. Nonetheless, I ran my thumbnail through the tape. There was a roll of paper spiralled tight inside. I shucked off a few clothes, crawled under the throw and lay there wiggling the contents from the container. It was a calendar, printed on glossy paper. The back of it had the months in Greek and English and Aegis contact details. I turned it over and straightened the curling page.

On the front cover was my painting, my painting of Jess on Symi.

CHAPTER TWENTY-EIGHT

STILL CLAIR

Connie in my bosom

My mind was so much rubble after the last few hours and now this fresh quake. My painting on the calendar. Mr Bow-Tie at the gallery – thirty-five quid?! Did artists retain copyright? I wasn't sure. It was a hazy area, and I hadn't signed anything – had I? The coincidence of Aegis buying it! Or <u>was</u> it? There was no one I could tell at this hour, not even Sonya, so I may as well get some sleep. Unsurprisingly, my mental disaster zone insisted on hours of aftershocks. Finally, it subsided into a few minutes of virtual door knocking, but this time the door flew open. There stood Jess and behind her a queue of students holding library books that exploded as they tried to open the covers.

Connie was up first, I recognised her tread on the stair and waited until she was in the kitchen before fleeing to the shower. By the time I was dressed and down again she had the table laid for breakfast. The room looked formal compared to the regular makeshift morning. We behaved as though nothing unusual had happened the night before although we were over polite, too solicitous. Jess didn't surface. The two of us grimaced through grapefruit and charred toast, drank bitter coffee. I wanted to share the heist of my painting but weighed against everything else it seemed inconsequential. Connie pierced the fragile truce.

– Guess we oughta decide what to do about the house and so on. You happy here? Wanna stay? Wanna come to Naples? Your choice.

Sensitive as a rhino charge.

– Jess and I need to talk. It's not a decision we can make just like that.

– I hear you. So, how about we redecorate anyway? Fix up a few things. Then if you wanna stay, fine, if you don't you can sell it, or rent it out.

I was quick to spot the: 'You can sell it'. Did that mean she recognised it as our house? Mine and Jess's? My name wasn't on the deeds, of course. That would be something to get around.

– I got someone in to look at it. We could use her to do what you want. Save you having to shop.

I recalled the lavender phantom Connie had entertained.

– You mean the woman yesterday? Who was she?

– I thought you knew her. Her business card was tucked into the hall mirror.

Her answer didn't make any sense. I didn't know any interior designers.

– Do you still have it?

– Sure.

Connie reached for her wallet, flipped through and passed a card across, pale violet in colour. I didn't recognise the name, turned it over and saw 'Cyntra', the gallery that had taken my paintings – Jess on Symi in particular.

– What is it, honey?

'Honey' – she called me 'Honey'. I went and got the calendar from the living room.

– See this painting, Mum? I did this – it was Jess on Symi. Cyntra is the gallery I took it to. They gave me thirty-five quid for it – said it wasn't worth any more.

– But this is Joe's painting. How… ? You did another one? It's beautiful! Thirty-five?!

I went up to Jess. She was dressed and putting on make-up.

– How are you, JJ?

She swivelled and reached for me. I stroked that beautiful hair, overwhelmed by what she made me feel.

– I think I'm OK, now, Mum.

Her voice was thick with tears. Her body pulsed. I held on. A huge sniff.

– Going to have to put my make-up on again –

And the floodgates opened again. I held on, rocked her like she was a baby. On and on, on and on until we calmed, aching like lovers, wounded like fighters, being mother and daughter.

Connie kept herself busy. It was the only way she could deal with things. She'd been on the phone to Aegis, asked about the painting on the front of their calendar and got the answers she needed. In the car en route to Cyntra, though, she took on the bigger issue. Ben. Maybe that was easier for her that way, she didn't have to look at me.

– I knew soon as Jess's eyes changed colour. Knew she was his.

– But you never asked, not even to make sure.

– Maggie told me how you and she met up with Ben at the restaurant that time.

It sounded like Connie didn't know about the miscarriage, nor about how I'd tried to… *Bless Maggie for not telling.*

– So you and Maggie worked it out between you?

– Not as such.

– You mean you both drew your own conclusions?

I drove on for nearly a mile.

– Mum – do you hate me?

There was a disconcerting pause, then –

– No, Clair, I don't hate you.

Another pause and a long sigh from her.

– What happened – you, Ben, Jess – is in many ways my fault… I just never knew how to… be a good Mom I suppose.

I pulled off the road to a meadow gate. Leaves were just bursting in the hedgerow and the mud was mottled with fallen catkins. My throat was tight, eyelids hot. I heard her bag snap open, felt her push a tissue into my hands. We sat in taut silence. Connie cleared her throat.

– I – I didn't have too good a time with your Grandma, Emily. She – had – her own problems. Your grandfather was away a good deal of the time, none too easy when he was home. No rows, but it was like living in a block of ice. I raised myself, mostly…

While we sat at the side of the road the sky changed from pale brightness to ragged clouds across blue and on to flat grey. Passing cars punctuated her story, whipping the words away almost before I understood them.

CONNIE

– We lived in Coral Gables, the City Beautiful of Miami-Dade County. It was your Grandma Emily's fiftieth birthday party. I didn't want to be there but, of course, I had to. I remember my dress, it was apricot glazed-cotton with a swing skirt and button-down bodice. As I walked into the room, my mother turned to all the guests and said, "Ah, here's Constance, twenty-two. Still unmarried. Anybody game?". Like I was warm meat. In fact, she was doing me a favour. Two days later, I was on a train heading northeast, making my escape. Took a cab from Penn Station to West 76th Street where my old school friend, Ruthie Wilborough – née Gweilch – lived with her husband, Swift. Ruthie put her arms round me at the door and said, "So, you finally ditched the Fitch bitch! Come on in, honey!".

– Staying with Ruthie and Swift was fun at first. I felt more at home there than I'd ever felt anywhere. There were parties and dinners and theatre visits – Helen Hayes in Mrs McThing, the Beatrice Lillie revue at the Booth Theater. Best of all, there were guys standing in line for a date. I went on a few but nothing serious. By late summer my money was running out and I had to think about getting a job. Couldn't think what, though, I wasn't trained for anything. The only possibilities were shop assistant or waitress –

and Ruthie wouldn't hear of either. Swift had an art dealer friend who was a little sweet on me. But married. Anyhow, this dealer friend knew of a gallery in the Village looking for someone. Ruthie decided 'gallery assistant' had more cachet than 'shop girl'. I didn't know anything about Art or Greenwich Village but I took a bus down to Bleecker Street for the interview, anyway. Think it was my blonde hair and my figure got me the job. Sure wasn't anything I said.

– By November New York was getting cold. Ruthie and Swift were happy for me to stay, Swift a little too happy, if you know what I mean? So I moved into an apartment on the Lower East Side, sharing with a woman painter who exhibited at the gallery. It was fun. More parties, we ate at Pfaff's and the Village Drugstore. But the money at the gallery didn't support that kind of lifestyle so I did the unthinkable, a little waitressing and bar work on the side. Yeah, I know. Sometimes I accepted the kind of dinner invitation that meant fighting off unwanted attention after the dessert. I sort of got used to being a lot harder – more calculating.

– Greenwich Village was a different planet to Coral Gables. The Villagers were writers, artists, poets and musicians. They stayed up all night, they smoked hashish, drank brandy from the bottle and they slept with each other. I was shocked and fascinated at the same time and, to be honest, more than a little envious. I dipped my toe in the water but I didn't take the plunge. I was too much Mrs Fitch's daughter. Too chicken. Then there were the painters and sculptors who wanted me to model for them. Of course, I always said no. I said no, no, no until I met James – Jimmy. He was over to visit a friend. I liked his Scottish brogue. I liked his eyes. I liked him.

– Jimmy taught me the difference between Scotch and Scottish. And he told me I wasn't being modest refusing to model, I was being prudish. So I sat for him. And then I did a lot of other things with him… and there we have it. When it was time for him to go back to the UK, I wanted to go with him. It was his turn to turn chicken. "Sweetheart, we hardly know each other". I just took his words at face value. "But how can we get to know each other from opposite sides of the Atlantic?". Was I naïve! Next thing, he was gone and I had a problem. My painter friend knew someone who could 'help'. But I didn't want help, I wanted Jimmy. I rang Miami. I said, "Mother, I'm getting married. His name is James Ranald Harkin. He's a painter". And she said, "You marry a damned Commie bohemian and you needn't show your face here again, lady!".

– So I cashed in my bonds and sailed on the Queen Elizabeth. Ruthie and Swift came to wave me off. On the voyage I told the other passengers I was seasick, but it wasn't the sea making me sick. I took a train from Southampton to London. I didn't know anyone except for James. And I didn't even know where he lived. He'd mentioned a café on Old Compton

Street so I just took a cab there from the train station. I hadn't guessed on the odds against bumping into him there. I genuinely thought London was just a large village. It didn't matter, though, because I actually found him there. I walked in and caught him eating a sandwich. There was a girl at the table, pretty. Another blonde. I said, "Hello, Jimmy. Guess who?". You can imagine his face. The blonde got up and left.

– I sat down and the first thing he said was that he didn't have anywhere for me to stay. He rented a tiny room, not big enough for two. So I just laughed and said we'd better find another place because if it wasn't big enough for two, it sure as hell wouldn't be big enough for three. I can't believe how stupid I was, thinking it would all be OK, that we'd have a future together. He soon put me straight. The worst part was, he wasn't even angry just – I don't know – just pitying and a little disgusted. Then I cried and he got impatient because I was embarrassing him in front of his friends. I just sat there and sobbed in that poky little Soho coffee bar. Then I got up to go, dragging that great suitcase, I felt nauseous and dizzy and then I passed out. Someone called an ambulance and I remember them lifting me into it. But before the ambulance reached Middlesex Hospital – it would have been quicker walking – one of my problems was solved. I was only ten weeks gone. That wasn't the end of it, of course. I still got taken into the maternity ward with the mothers and their new babies, just to make my life a little sweeter. Things were different in the fifties. The house doctor called me 'Mrs Fitch' out of politeness; he could see I wasn't wearing a ring. When I was allowed out, James took me back to his room and nursed me. He made chicken broth, toasted teacakes, worked hard to make me smile. I think he genuinely came to care for me. Guess he'd never had anyone dependent on him before. Not even Maggie. She was eighteen when your grandfather died in an air raid on Glasgow, still young but not a child.

– I took a long time to get over losing my baby. 'Cos you see, that baby was the only… Anyhow, Jimmy did the best thing he could think of. He told me not to worry, we would get married, we would have another baby. It was like the sun coming out again. He told me he'd forgotten how beautiful I was. And we both thought maybe it would be all right.

– It was time for James to tell Maggie. He hadn't seen her in a month. I only heard Jimmy's side of the conversation, " – getting married… Long story. Will you be a witness?… Chelsea Registry Office. Tomorrow". Probably a good thing I didn't hear the rest.

– After the ceremony, we went for lunch at the Chelsea Arts Club. I knew that Jimmy's sister worked for a Member of Parliament but I was pretty uninformed on the difference between the British and American systems. I thought MPs belonged to the Royal Family and I asked Maggie if she had to curtsey a lot at the office. I thought James would explode – well he did explode. I knew he was a republican, you see, but I thought it meant the same as in the States – you know, Mom and apple pie and all that. He was so antsy to me that Maggie had to remind him it was my wedding day and brides weren't supposed to cry.

– We honeymooned in Scotland at the croft. James and Maggie had sold the family house; it would just have been sitting empty with them both in London. Maggie used her share to put a deposit on a flat in London. James went through his share – with things like trips to the States and Europe and partying in general. There wasn't much left. But they'd kept the damned croft so that's where we went after the wedding. There was no electricity or hot water. We had to keep warm with log fires and sex. But we were careful. The doctor said I needed time before trying for another baby. I wrote my mother about the wedding but she never replied.

– Back in London, Jimmy used the last of his inheritance on renting a small apartment near Clapham Common and buying a motorbike. He said he needed it to get him to the odd jobs and teaching he could pick up. We lived and slept in one room and he used the other as his studio. I took a waitressing job near Clapham Common subway and I did quite well on tips. People liked the American accent.

– By November I fell pregnant again – with you. I sent a Christmas card to Coral Gables, but I didn't tell Emily she'd have a grandchild come August. I wanted to make sure everything was fine. So I said we were happy, asked her please to write and sent my love. Again, no reply.

– I gave up waitressing in the spring, when I began to show. Stuck in the apartment all day, I got very down what with James being away all day, no money and the goddamned weather. I felt fairly certain that things were going well, so I wrote to Coral Gables again to say I was expecting a baby. I didn't say when, still too superstitious. Emily did write this time, I remember it word for word: 'Dear Constance, You have a choice. Go ahead and have the baby, ruin your life with that loser and never come home again, or call me collect. I can arrange for you to get out of this mess. Mother'. I tore it up.

– Jimmy was offered an exhibition and worked so hard on it I never saw him. I behaved badly at the opening, seeing all the slim young women laughing and drinking wine. There I was, a fat old Zeppelin with swollen ankles and a husband who left me on my own all evening. I sulked and wouldn't speak to anyone. James put me in a cab and didn't come home 'til after four the next morning.

– When you were born, life got better for a while. Your father adored you and I was so happy to be a mother. He rented a studio to work in so we'd have more space in the apartment, even though money was a stretch. But after two years of it, I was going crazy. I wanted to go back to New

York but Jimmy wouldn't hear of it. He said he was too close to getting established in London, his star was on the ascendant and everything would work out. So we stayed. We ate at Maggie's most Sundays. Sometimes I brought you up to meet her and we'd feed the ducks in St James' Park in her lunch break. But otherwise, I felt completely isolated with no friends and I couldn't work because of having a child. I heard from Ruthie, occasionally, but I was too ashamed of my life to write back and we lost touch. Jimmy and I argued more, and then the arguments turned into fights.

– After one really bad one, he got on his bike and rode off into the night. We couldn't afford a telephone so I had to wait to the morning and call Maggie from a phone booth. She hadn't heard from him. She told me to pack an overnight bag for you and me, to leave a note for Jimmy saying where we were but not to come for us until the next day. Maggie took the afternoon off and met us at the subway. We dropped the case at her place and went for tea at Lyons Corner House. Later, when you were in bed, I poured out everything. Sometime after ten, the front door opened. Naturally, I was afraid it was Jimmy. But a young woman wearing an airline uniform walked in. She was as surprised to see me as I was her. Maggie said, "Connie, this is Julia, a friend of mine". Julia was very polite, asked after Jimmy. Maggie jumped in and said he'd been called away unexpectedly. I was puzzled that a friend should have a key to Maggie's flat, but reckoned it was maybe just a temporary arrangement and if she worked for an airline, she might arrive back sometimes after Maggie had gone to bed. So, having a key would make sense.

– That night, you and I shared Maggie's double bed while Maggie and Julia used the sofa and a camp bed. I couldn't understand why Maggie had a double bed, after all, she wasn't married. Then it occurred to me that maybe Maggie was having an affair and I suddenly felt uncomfortable, wondering who else had slept in the bed. What with that and the row with Jimmy, I didn't get much sleep that night.

– Jimmy was full of remorse when he came next morning. Maggie was already at work. Julia gave you breakfast, played with you while he and I talked. We went back to Clapham on the subway. I mentioned Julia coming in late the night before and asked him where she lived. He just gave me a very strange look and then he said, "There, of course. With Maggie". I said I didn't understand, what with there being only the one bedroom. He sort of rolled his eyes and said, "They're lovers, you know – lesbians". I felt my face burning with shame that he could even say a word like that to me – and in front of you – in public! I said, "Oh my god, I left Clair alone with her!". He looked right at me and said, "Shut up!". He was so angry.

– I was just horrified. Remember, it was the nineteen fifties and I was from middle America, things are different now. For months, I refused to visit Maggie until your father put his foot down and said he was taking you to see your aunt and I could come with you and behave like a civilised human being or stay at home like the lonely bigot I was. He reminded me how kind Maggie had been to us and said I should be ashamed for stopping you seeing your own family. Eventually, I agreed, but I didn't speak during lunch or for the remainder of the afternoon. Back home, your father was just one tower of rage and made both me and you cry. You were three at the time. The things he said, the names he called me.

– I tried to come to terms with the situation. After all, I'd met lesbian women in the Village although I didn't know it at first. Everyone was friendly in the bohemian quarter, I just thought some were a little friendlier than others. Then my roommate put me straight and I made sure I was always in mixed company. But this situation was different. I was actually related to one – even if it was only by marriage. I wondered if it was hereditary and whether you would have Maggie's genes. You already had her crazy hair.

– In the early summer of that year, Maggie treated us to tea on the terrace at the Houses of Parliament. It was just before Parliament broke for the summer vacation. She introduced Jimmy and me to her employer, the MP. He was tall and very handsome with black hair. He shook hands with me and I felt myself blush as those amazing eyes looked right into mine. He stopped a little while, chatted to Jimmy about Jackson Pollock and gave you a ten-shilling note to buy candy. Ten shillings! One fifth of a week's rent to Jimmy and me. Two weeks later, Jimmy's motorcycle slid under a truck in the damn rain. I wanted to die, too.

– Without him to provide I had nowhere to turn – except for Maggie. She took us in with her and her – with Julia. Jimmy hadn't left a will, of course, so she helped sort that out. I didn't want to live off her, of course, so I took a job in a restaurant off Whitehall where Maggie knew the head waiter. One evening, as a couple came in, I recognised the man. Hugo Benfleet, Maggie's boss. They sat at a corner table, away from the crowd. She was young, red-haired and it was obviously not a business meeting. I noticed her left hand while I served another table. No wedding ring. Then Hugo glanced across and I scooted. I managed to trade sections with another waitress so I could avoid him for the rest of the sitting. But as the second sitting diners started to arrive, the wine waiter passed me a note. It said: 'So sorry to hear of your tragic loss. I would like to help, if I can. Do, if you feel able, call me on my private line.' – then there was a Whitehall number – not Maggie's – and it was signed: 'Sincerely, Hugo Benfleet'. It might as well have said: 'This way to escape!'. I had Maggie to thank for that, I suppose, indirectly.

– It was very sudden, very passionate. I didn't know if it was love but I was willing to go with the flow. Hugo had the house in Guildford and he moved you and me into it within a few weeks. And that's how it was for nearly seventeen years. Not in actual time, taking away the weekends and the summer holidays, the sixteen Christmases he spent with his family. There were a lot of lonely nights, sure, but occasional days or weeks when you were with Maggie and Ben and I could be alone together. So, we managed about half of the seventeen years, if that. But half of Hugo – Ben – was worth having. No one but Ben could have scooped me up out of that dark place I'd gone and set me on a pedestal. He made me feel beautiful, important, valued. And he gave us security when he signed over the house to me.

– That's why it was too much to take coming back this time, like the years with Joe were imaginary. I walked in and Ben was everywhere. The strangest part was when I thought about Jimmy I confused his face with Ben's. Sometimes, I think if I could have picked the best of each, they would have made one exceptional man. Your father was unpredictable, talented and, I think, completely faithful. But his first love was painting. Ben worshipped me as a woman; he was witty, made me laugh. But our life together was a secret. And he strayed often.

– That's why I wanted to move on, away from the house. A new start for you and Jess, an end to the memories for me. I was only thinking about myself, though. I see now that our relationship has ended up like mine with my mother. I'm not sure how it happened, or why. Maybe you came along before Jimmy and I really knew each other. Or maybe he and I were never meant for the long story, shouldn't have had a baby.

– As for you, Ben and Jess, I don't even know where to start. You and Ben together. It was like incest. Part of me thought, "If he can't have me he'll take my daughter", and that was a strange kind of, I don't know, 'compliment' wouldn't be the right word. But it told me that he either missed me so much he had to have you – or he had you to punish me for going away. So… that's when you and I really hit the skids. My fault.

– Strange thing was, last night, before everything came out with Jess, this funny little guy with a purple nose came to the door. As I opened it he said "I knew it was you!". I didn't know who he was but he said Ben used to go to his pub in Guildford and took me in there a few times. I don't remember. They'd been drinking buddies before I came on the scene. Guildford was Ben's refuge from that witch of a wife, I suppose. Turns out he'd helped this little guy put his life back together after <u>his</u> wife ran off with the children. Same guy you're working for. Said he'd figured out who I was from what Fraser said. Anyhow, he told me to give you and Fraser a break. I didn't let him into the house, of course. But he said you'd be home soon and to wait up and put things right. Didn't pull any punches.

CLAIR

Justice

I sat silently while everything that had been churning inside that apricot carapace for years poured out. *Did she resent me for being too like my father? Too like Maggie? For getting in the way of her relationship with Ben? For being the free spirit she would have liked to have been? For betraying her with Ben? And did she dote on Jess for being like him? Or simply for being her granddaughter – with the generation gap that eased the conflict? Or was Jess getting all the love I should have had?*

Bizarrely, Ron was the biggest surprise. Connie hadn't finished.

– So I guess I'm saying sorry – sorry for not knowing you, for not knowing –

A sharp breath in. Her hands went up to her face. It was turning into a very tearful day. I waited a while.

– Shall we go home, Mum?

Connie blew her nose.

– Yes – after we've nailed this shyster at the gallery. Then we go back and celebrate.

At least Connie's priorities were watertight.

As we walked into Cyntra Gallery some Rubik's cube in my head clicked and swivelled to resolution. There, in another multi-purpled get up, sat the interior designer I'd seen leaving the house. Of course, she'd been there when I dropped off the last canvasses – obviously had some connection to Mr Bow-Tie. She'd given me the business card. Connie spoke for me.

– You? You own this joint?

Where my mother had picked up the Bronx twang was anybody's guess. Mixing with bit part actors in the Village? Too much daytime television? Lavender Lou turned a few shades paler than her pashmina. Connie was marvellously uncompromising.

– You have some explaining to do. 'Egress' mean anything to you?

– Aegis, Mum –

– Whatever. This broad knows what I'm talking about! How come you charge nearly a grand for my daughter's painting and shove her a handful of small change? Huh?

This was the first time I'd heard anything about money. Nearly a grand? And the cheating bastard paid me thirty-five quid? Go Connie!

– Um – I'll just see if Mr –

The interior designer streaked to the back room, trailing organza.

– How much, Mum?

– Nine-hundred-and-thirty-five-pounds.

Connie had a head for figures. Urgent whispering from the interior. Mr Bow-Tie appeared, wiping crumbs from his mouth.

– I gather there's been a bit of a –

– You bet there has!

We emerged, twenty minutes later with a cheque for fifteen hundred. Two of the other canvasses had sold, the others were under my arm. Mr Bow-Tie was left in no doubt as to the consequences of failing to honour the cheque; a phone call – on my mobile – to Connie's lawyer in Florida guaranteed it. My phone bill would make a pretty large dent in the money. Nonetheless, we returned home glorious.

CHAPTER TWENTY-NINE

STILL CLAIR

Raisin' hopes (oi!)

Jess plunged down through the front door to greet us, anxious for news. She whooped at the victory and wanted to ring Maggie. I discouraged the idea. There was too much else to share with Maggie before a minor victory over a sleazy art dealer. I took the pressure off by claiming it was my turn to be expansive and suggesting a meal at Ye Olde Ship Inn. Doubter that I was, I still feared the possibility of the Cyntra cheque bouncing but I wasn't going to let it spoil a glorious bout of excess. What a rare pleasure it was to be so extravagantly generous.

Over dinner, Connie produced her next stunner by suggesting that she and I visit Maggie. Her treat. We would fly to Glasgow, hire a car and stay in Oban. She'd obviously been mulling over the implications of recent revelations. It was time to exorcise a few demons. Jess was crestfallen at being excluded but Connie was firm. She had to catch up with her schooling. Maybe she could go for a longer break when her exams were over. I didn't mind my authority being usurped in such a positive way. Connie was getting the hang of supporting me and that had to be good. There was, however, the matter of Annie and Jude staying with Maggie. Connie would find it unconventional to say the least and I wasn't about to land her with the full background. I'd have to devise an edited version. As for time off from the pub, I knew I could deal with Ron.

Despite the emotional turmoil of the previous twenty-four hours, I was beginning to feel that my feet were touching firm ground for the first time in many years – possibly in my life. There was still, though, an ache that was the absence of Fraser. I didn't know whom to blame for him going, my mother, him or me. Recent events needed to settle before I could give that particular bereavement the time and space it needed. Meantime, I explored it like a tongue in a broken tooth.

Not to be left out, Jess had a proposition to make. She wanted us to meet Piers. He needn't know about the family connection but she thought it was important for Connie and me to be sure about the innocence of her relationship with him.

– Darling, it really isn't necessary. We trust what you say.

Connie arched her eyebrows at me.

– Aren't you a little curious? It is one hell of a coincidence.

Jess's eyes implored. From somewhere in me – Connie's genes? – came the cynical thought that at least if this Piers met us matriarchs he might be less likely to exploit my daughter's good nature. And bank balance.

Late afternoon, two days later, he arrived at Aborigine Road. Jess must have employed some subterfuge because he seemed surprised to meet us. He was nothing like his grandfather apart from black hair and, perhaps, a streak of arrogance. He was heavier and had neither the looks nor the charm. It was like the Mudie twins; Jess had inherited everything positive that Piers had not. He did, however, have the courtesy to come over and shake hands. He walked with a stick. Jess had mentioned that he had an artificial leg. I felt a rush of sympathy. Connie was constructed of sterner stuff.

– How did you lose your leg?

– Iraq.

– That's where, not how.

He was taken aback by her directness. Not unreasonably.

– Aah – shrapnel. Had three ops but it wasn't healing so they had to –

– I see. So what now?

– How d'you mean?

– Rest of your life. What now? Desk job? Retrain? Live off Jess?

Piers reacted like he'd been slapped. Jess was astounded.

– Hey! That's not – !

One look from Connie silenced her and the interrogation continued.

It became clear that Piers lacked his grandfather's imagination, too. His anger over his disability was obvious, leaving him with no positive thoughts about the future. Such negativity could also be due to post-traumatic stress and I felt some empathy with Jess's response to him. This young man had been left with very little to sustain him other than family status. On the other hand, most young veterans didn't even have that. I wondered how Ben had would have felt about his grandson. The question that faced me was: Do we owe it to Ben to help him?

After Piers left we three sat quiet for a while. It seemed Jess knew she'd bitten off too much. The solution was clear but I thought it had to be her decision. Connie drove a truck through that one.

– Honey, whatever the connection, that boy is bad news. You don't owe him anything. Cut him loose.

– Gra-a-an... !

I left them to slug it out while I rang Maggie. She would enjoy anticipating my arrival and appreciate forewarning of Connie's. Annie answered, of course. Maggie was OK but a bit wheezy. She was delighted I was coming up. Then I called Sonya and got voicemail. Didn't leave a message.

FRASER

How could I have forgotten Ali? She must be back on Symi by now. Even at thirty thousand feet the idea of skydiving seemed hideously attractive. By the time we landed at Rhodes I was up for boarding the next plane back. Fat chance with my bank balance. If I couldn't get across to Symi that night, it meant escalating the credit card and generating bankruptcy. The season hadn't started, so there were no coaches going into Rhodes town. A taxi, even, was beyond my Euro supply, so I trekked off to find a bus stop. After an hour waiting with my bags and guitar, it started to rain. Everything colluded to convince me I'd done a stupid thing. Being in Rhodes, home of the fabled Colossus, I should say it was a colossally stupid thing. Even I groaned at that one.

Predictably, given my luck over the past couple of weeks, there were no more crossings to Symi that evening. Stood on Mandrakis Harbour and swore into the wind then traipsed into the town. Found a bed for the night in a tall, narrow mausoleum of a place with reduced rate for going without breakfast and a room the sort of hole where prisoners would hang from the walls in manacles. Only the thought of arriving on Symi – in disguise? – Kept my spirits above sea level.

The first Symi departure was the Anes hydrofoil, slightly more expensive than the ferry, but worth it to escape Rhodes. Without thinking I sat on the left, seaward side, missing the view of Turkey. The window was white with spray, anyway, the sky was grey and the water more the colour of the Clyde than the Aegean. Unfortunately, it wasn't as calm as the Clyde; in fact, the size of the swell made it borderline whether the hydrofoil would set out at all. The captain's personal god must have been Poseidon because off we lurched, but after a tentative raising onto its legs the vessel sank back down and rolled like a lazy whale, all the way to Symi. An obese kid a bit younger than Jude sat next to me on her granny's lap, sucking a dummy and kicking me as she swung her podgy feet. After ten minutes of the hydrofoil heaving and the kid kicking, I remembered all about rough sea on an empty stomach. Had to scramble across the fat kid and her yia yia and make dash for the loo at the back. Made it just in time, to the amusement of a couple of the crew who I knew by sight. Afterwards, I just slid down the bulkhead to the floor, sweating, and resigned myself to being the main joke in the tavernas this evening. The 'doing a stupid thing' charge was accruing evidence.

Sheltered from the western winds, Yialos is always a few degrees warmer. As I stepped off the hydrofoil wing, the clutter of houses up the hillside was a welcome sight. But I didn't have the usual feeling of coming home. The landlord of my old apartment was very surprised when I rang, believing I wasn't coming back this season. One room had already been let to the new Aegis rep who was here early to do some research before the season began. Nikos, it appeared, had gone to Samos for the summer so I could have the other room. First I'd heard of it. Felt even lower. But I took on the room. Another Aegis guy had to be fairly reasonable, if it was a guy. If not… As we haggled terms, I looked around for a friendly face. A couple of taverna owners were taking the transparent plastic wind shields down but there were few others about and The Giorgios was not moored in its usual place. The way my life was going, the first person I bumped into had to be Ali Mavrakakou.

Despite the sour taste in my mouth, I was beginning to feel hungry. At the baker's my usual favourite, the little cheese pies, looked too greasy. I spent a precious Euro on a couple of rolls and ate them dry, standing at the edge of the water by the Customs House. Threw the last bits to the ducks then hefted my bags and guitar and trudged off in search of Nobby's rough comfort. I was not disappointed.

– 'Ope yer've finished barfing – just spring cleaned the fookin' place.

The first beer was on the house. Nobby had been back a couple of weeks already. He, too, thought I'd moved on, word having got around as it always did on the island. There wasn't enough business yet to offer me any bar work and all he could suggest was odd jobbing until things warmed up. The Giorgios was north in Kalymnos where Panos's wife Marina had family. Hotel Acropolis had a convention on next week and might need help. As for other news, none of any great significance. Except that there was a replacement GP. I tried to appear casual.

– Och, that's a shame. What's the new one like?

– Should ask more what the old one's like. Come back from Kalamata up the friggin' duff.

I must have turned several different shades of horror-struck because Nobby fell about.

– Nah! She's gorra new job. I just wanted to see yer life flash past yer eyes!

– Nobby, I hope you get abducted by bollock-eating aliens.

Nobby honked into another fit of adenoidal amusement.

CLAIR

Who knows?

Two days later, Connie and I flew to Glasgow, picked up a hire car and arrived in Oban by three. She wanted to rest so I drove up to Kilachlan for an hour or so on my own. If I couldn't have Maggie to myself at least I could limit the number of people sharing her. Crossing the Connel Bridge lifted me. *Not long now.* I opened the window to catch a last whiff of salt air. It was a cloudy day and the lights were on in Harkin Croft. The door opened as I pulled up. *Please let it be Maggie.* It was. Not striding out with the dogs but still framed in the rectangle of light with Jack and Tatty bouncing ahead of her. I was home. As I hugged her I sensed her straining – she was looking beyond me.

– Wh-where – ?

– Connie's coming over tomorrow.

– Nah – nah – erm –

– Jess? She didn't come, darling, she's at home, revising.

Maggie huffed and rolled her eyes.

– B – b – nah! Fer… ach!

– Fraser? He's working.

Annie couldn't have told her he'd gone and I wouldn't – just yet.

We had tea and cupcakes in the parlour. Annie and Jude had been baking in honour of our visit and despite it being so near to supper time wanted to show off the results. After half an hour, Annie took Jude out for his bath and left me with Maggie. I was disappointed that her speech wasn't more improved. Progress must be erratic.

– S-o-o-o-oh Connie's in… ach!

– We're staying at The Queen's in Oban. I'll bring her up tomorrow. Would you like to go out for lunch?

Maggie gestured herself and shook her head dejectedly.

– No – no –… fi-fit!

– How about we bring in a parlour picnic?

This met with approval. Later, Annie brought Jude in in his dressing gown to kiss Maggie goodnight, clearly a ritual. I didn't stay long, not wanting to tire Maggie. It wasn't the right time to discuss Jess and Ben or his grandson.

That night over dinner I gave Connie a diplomatic version of Annie and Jude's presence at Harkin Croft. She listened without apparent interest then commented –

– This Annie – she know her brother's taken a hike?

Ouufff! Straight to the solar plexus.

– I don't know. She didn't mention it last night.

– Hope for Maggie's sake she has more staying power than he does.

– Thanks for highlighting it, Mum.

– You know what I mean.

Connie made no more comment. I was surprised and relieved she'd accepted the Annie situation so easily.

Next day we went to the supermarket and loaded up with goodies for lunch: smoked salmon, cream cheese, fresh rolls, salad, fruit, wine. Jude would be at school so I put a few treats in the basket for him to have later. Connie enjoyed the drive up. It was many years since she'd seen the croft. She was surprised at how neat and picturesque it was.

– It was a dump first time I was here. Hope she has an indoor bathroom, now.

I wondered, not for the first time, if this was where I'd been conceived.

There was a note from Annie saying to let ourselves in with my key. That worried me. Maggie was obviously having a bad day. Jack and Tatty were very vocal, scratching the back of the door and toppling out with excitement to see me. They charmed Connie. We went through to the parlour where Maggie was resting in her armchair, eyes closed, a blanket over her legs. Connie and I exchanged a look. I knelt beside Maggie, took her hand, spoke to her gently. She opened her eyes.

– Hello, lass.

I wilted with relief. Connie moved round to the other chair and touched her arm.

– Hi, Maggie. Longtime no see.

Maggie smiled with half her mouth, a result of the stroke not a reaction to Connie.

– Aye – aye – so you've come to talk? About Jess and her father?

After the faltering speech of the night before her clarity heartened me. Connie answered.

– Well, there's not much to discuss, is there?

– Not a lot.

I felt left out to say the least.

– Hey – I come into this, too.

They both looked at me, their perspectives different but their message the same. Nothing to discuss. Quite an anti-climax after all the years of agonising over just how much either of them knew. Now I wanted answers from them. Connie had mentioned Jess's eyes that time – but had that really convinced her? Maggie remained non-committal, whether deliberately or because of her condition I couldn't tell. Connie ended it.

– We all know what we know. When we knew it and how we knew it doesn't help anyone and it doesn't change anything. It just is.

She was right. It was too simple, too elegant but typically forthright. Jess was Ben's child and that was all.

After lunch, we swaddled Maggie in tartan rugs and took her for a bumpy walk in her wheelchair along to the strand with the dogs. Connie and she stayed at the top while I whizzed Jack and Tatty down to the water's edge and back. Fortunately, Isobel, Archie and Jasper were elsewhere. The wind was chill but Maggie relished it and returned to the croft with some much-needed colour in her cheeks.

Around four, Jude erupted into the parlour, a small hurricane trailing a debris of dogs, school bag and lunch box and followed by Annie. Seeing Connie, he stopped short, clutching to him some crumpled artwork. Connie inclined towards him, proffering her hand.

– You must be Jude. I'm Clair's Mom. My name is Mrs Dubrowsky.

For god's sake Mum! Wouldn't 'Connie' do? Jude stared at her for a moment, then said:

– You're very wide.

Annie looked mortified but any scolding was cut short by a hoot of laughter from Maggie, egging on the rest of us, including Jude who wasn't sure why he was laughing. He showed us all his latest drawing of Jack and Tatty, his pride obvious. Maggie was suitably awed, asked if she might put it on the wall in her bedroom. Jude considered it for a while then, with innate tact and a small nod from Annie, offered it to Connie.

– I'll do another one for you Maggie.

As we drove back to Oban that evening, Connie was surprisingly mellow, given the rigours of the day. Her pinkish blonde hair was a bizarre asymmetric sculpture and her rouge was streaked with tears from the wind. She turned in early while I lingered in the bar for a drink. There was a message on my mobile to call Jess. Reception was sometimes patchy at Kilachlan. I called.

– Hey, Mum! Aegis was on the answerphone when I got in from the library. They want you to call them at their office in Northampton. Wonder what it is?

We conjectured for a while then conceded it was probably the mundane offer of a minor discount on another holiday.

– Still, better than a slap round the ear with a dead octopus.

Her, not me.

I went to bed in a state of bi-polar overload. From the misery of Connie arriving and Fraser leaving and the shock of learning about Jess and Piers, to the sudden release of my guilty secret, selling some paintings and thoughts of Greece again. It probably had something to do with the bucket-sized malt I'd just downed. But life was definitely on the up escalator after lurking in the basement for too long.

Blessedly asleep that night, I met a new person who was neither male nor female and who drove a luxury horse drawn coach in which I reclined in a bath. We flashed past several places we should have stopped at, but sped on until we arrived in a large dining hall where I stepped out in full eighteenth century finery onto a table covered with candelabra, fruit and sweetmeats – whatever they look like, I just knew that's what they were. It didn't bother me that my breasts were bare because they were firm and round and white with rosy nipples. I walked in golden mules along the sumptuous table to a large triptych of a window that opened onto a sunset seascape. Everyone applauded as I had a devastatingly wonderful orgasm.

When I have a good dream it's worth waiting for.

CHAPTER THIRTY

CONNIE

Trust a damn Scot to call this wind bracing. It's a Beaufort scale storm. I'm going to look like something out of the Muppets by the time we get back inside. Just so's the dogs can take a leak on the beach. OK for Maggie, she's all wrapped up in blankets in her wheelchair. I don't mind Oban, but it gets wilder by the mile coming north. At least the cottage has a bathroom, now.

This girl living with Maggie. Clair explained and all but it still seems a pretty weird set-up. Seems to work out, though. At least it means Clair isn't up here squandering what time she has left to make a life for herself.

So, the big moment came. The moment all of us have been kidding ourselves would never happen. The one about Jess being Ben's child. I don't know how I felt about it at the time or now. What can I say?

Generally, I never had much contact with Maggie. A year or so before Jess was born, she wrote me to say Clair had been really sick and was staying for a while up here in Magillicuddy, or whatever this place is called. It was on account of Clair's boyfriend, Adam. I met him a couple of times when we were over, once with Joe and once when I was over on a solo trip. Don't know what messed things up but I do know he went off and married someone else and Clair took it badly. That's how she ended up with Maggie, always Maggie, never me. I wrote back to ask if there was anything I could do but she said Clair was getting better. Said they'd bumped into her old boss, Hugo Benfleet, and that he'd remembered Clair from all those years ago when we had tea on the Terrace. Said just that, no hint of anything. All the years Ben and I were together, Maggie said nothing. I chose to believe she didn't know.

Given the timing of Jess's arrival, I guessed Clair must've met someone on the rebound from her boyfriend. I was pretty angry with her for getting herself knocked up in the first place. Explanations made life uncomfortable for Joe and me with our friends. Joe, of course, didn't take it quite so hard but then Clair wasn't his daughter – and, of course, he'd made at least the one mistake I knew of before we met.

The first time Clair came over with her baby, I had a feeling. Jess's eyes weren't that incredible colour then so I can't say what it was. Maybe it was the way Clair behaved, sort of almost apologetic – which was not characteristic of my daughter – the way she looked at me when she gave me the baby to hold, I could tell something was behind it. Next time they came, Jess only had to give me a flash of those peepers and it was like the light coming on. All the pennies dropped. I just knew she was Ben's.

And like I said, the strange thing about it all was, I didn't know how to feel. Part of me was disgusted, like it was incest, what with Ben being around so much while Clair was growing up. But another part of me reckoned – well, if it had to be anyone… I can't even finish that thought. There was another reaction, though, one I wasn't ready for. We never talked about it, Ben and I – I just knew that us having a kid was way off the score sheet, so I didn't allow myself to speculate. Then my daughter goes ahead and does what I never allowed myself to think about. I have to admit, I know what I felt about that. It was envy. Envy and resentment. I never got beyond it, not really. As for the whole picture, I didn't have a rule book to look at and there sure wasn't anyone I could tell. Talking to Clair about it was out of the question. That would have made it real, even though stuff couldn't get much more real.

The result of that was I didn't want Clair around. She had no place in my life, apart from being a nuisance attached to Jess and more of an inconvenience than she'd ever been. I was sure she was the only reason James wanted me. She looked too like her queer aunt. And she was the reason I could never go back to the States, not until my own mother died.

I let Clair carry that load. They say people who abuse have usually been abused themselves. Did I really repeat what my own mother did to me without thinking? Or did I know I was doing it? As far as Joe was concerned, I was making a fuss of my little granddaughter and punishing my daughter for being irresponsible. He suggested once I should cool it a little. He never said it again.

She's very unsure of herself, Clair. I know a lot of it's down to me. I let it go on so long I didn't know how to go back or how to explain – or apologise. What she has done is raise a beautiful girl, and whatever scrapes Jess gets into, part of it's down to me and part of it's down to her arrogant, handsome damn father.

Money can smooth over a lot of things. If it can't buy you happiness you can sure be miserable in comfort. I'm pretty informed in that area, at least. When Mother died, she left me very comfortable, enough to buy Ben anything he goddamn wanted. But I met Joe. He was at the funeral; a widower, lonely and so rich it made my eyes water. He wanted a companion and I wanted some stability. I still had my looks and I was rich, too, so he knew I wasn't a gold-digger. I guess we got married alongside our money. That's how I got over Ben. I put myself out of his reach and out of his league. He'd signed over the house in Guildford some years before, but now I could pay him for it and let Clair stay on there. It made me feel good. Maybe Jess might never have happened if I hadn't done that. Maybe he felt I threw his gift back at him and he got even through Clair. Won't ever know, now.

One thing – Clair and Jess will always appreciate how hard it is to earn a buck. I went a little overboard with Jess after Joe died. Way too much money for a kid her age. I'm trying to put things right with Clair, now, that crook at the art gallery is just one way. And I'm taking care of Jess by getting something bad out of her life. Not the drugs, she has to do that herself and she pretty much has done. No, I mean that leech Piers Benfleet. He's completely out of the picture. Legally. I had a contract set up in Florida and he jumped at the money despite that wooden leg of his. He contacts her again or goes anywhere near her and his allowance stops. No one else need ever know. If Jess thinks he's just dropped her, so much the better. Painful but better in the long run.

I have other ways in mind to help. Clair and I should talk about it. Not just yet. She needs to get over this Scottish bastard, I mean her recently departed beau. At least <u>he</u> doesn't look like anyone else we know, Scottish or otherwise.

It's always been difficult having a conversation with Maggie, even in the early days, before I knew she was a… Just about impossible now she's had a stroke and we're waiting here in a major storm while my daughter fools around with a couple of dogs.

I'll just tuck her rug in. She's looking old – old and very, very tired. And I owe her, too. I couldn't help my prejudice then but it's payback time. Have to sort something out to help her. Maybe one of those motorised scooters or something. Get that Annie to tell me what would help.

MAGGIE

Clair and Connie have brought the dogs and me for a walk. Clair went down on the strand with Jack and – the other one – and left me with Connie on the crest. It's cold but – ach – nice.

Today, Connie and I told Clair we knew about Jess. We knew who the father was. Hugo – Hugo Benfleet. My employer for many… I knew he owned a house in Guildford. Deeds in his private file in the office – saw them when he asked me to find some – insurance papers of his. Surprise when Connie and Clair moved there to 'get Clair out of London'. Didn't have a clue where Guildford was. Obvious he was Connie's lover. Told Julia, no one else. Clair came to us – often as possible. If she ever said 'Ben' she – looked guilty – scared. 'Ben' – what they called Hugo. Had to make some pretence. There was wife Felicity and family. If Clair made a slip with his name, Julia and I would – would – not – not – it was too big a secret for a little girl. But bless Hugo, made sure we Harkin women had roofs over our heads.

After Connie's mother died – left her all that money – when she went to America – married Joe D – Du – Joe. Difficult to clear my head. Difficult – let me see – let me see – Connie was rich, Joe was rich. They lived in – that place. Clair stayed in Guildford – then that terrible time – her baby – gone and Adam – Adam left her – married someone else. That's when she – she did – that – couldn't believe it. Poor bairn, what grief. Her friend – her friend Sonya – she – I – looked after Clair. That day, back in London, Clair and I meeting Hugo. Just by chance. Saw the way he looked at her. I didn't think – I mean, he and Connie were... were... Then – how long after? I don't know. Clair was having a baby. I – I – got to Hugo, through his club. Met in Glasgow. Said 'I know about you and Clair'. Wasn't sure, but his – face – it was true. Told him about the baby. He wanted to see her. Made him promise not to. 'Haven't you done enough to our family?'. Clair and Connie, what – the wife did to – to – Julia – and me. So he helped. Little bit here and there, money, through me. Never asked about Connie. Died – Hugo – while Jess was very little. Holiday in France. Left me something in his will, not much. An – an – apology? All gone to help Clair and Jess. And Jess, Jess is so like him. So like her grandfather, too – a streak of Connie. But we're in her heart, Clair and me, we're in Jess's heart.

Clair has a good man, now. F – F –... Young man who will make her heart glad. They'll have a stormy time. But they're good together. Fraser. There! Fraser and Clair. Clair and Fraser.

Annie. His sister. Annie. Annie and her boy – little boy. Make me happy. Jude. Jude. Annie's little boy and his daddy was black. Annie can't remember who he was. Annie is studying. Studying to be a – a – something, something in the mind. Got a thing about Bill – Bill someone. Actor. Annie. Annie reminds me. She reminds me of...

At the top of the strand. With Connie. It's windy and Connie tucked in my rug. Kind thing. Kindest. Kindest thing she's done.

Julia. That's who she – who Annie reminds me of. Julia.

CLAIR

The raisin turns

I was on the phone to Aegis by nine thirty next morning and got put straight through to the MD. That surprised me. She started with an apology over the Mr Bow-Tie incident. He had approached them because the painting had 'Jess in Symi' written on the back and he'd Googled travel companies that went to Symi. Aegis was the first of the A's. Enterprising of him. Connie had discussed it with her, she said, and Aegis was keen to make reparation, albeit they had been misled. *Get on with it!*

– We offer specialist holidays, generally Arts or Cooking based. Sadly, I had news a couple of days ago that our art tutor had passed away.

– Not Marjorie?

– You know her?

– No – but I know of her. I've been to her little hut on Symi.

Suddenly my cheeks were burning.

– Yes, Symi was her favourite of all the islands.

A pause.

– Well – as much as I want to apologise to you, it would really help us if you would consider stepping in and taking her classes. I gather you have considerable experience of teaching – and your own work is exceptionally beautiful.

How did she know I'm a teacher? Connie.

– Er – thanks. Um – Symi? It would mean teaching on Symi?

– Yes, Symi but quite a few other islands, too. Would you be able to come for a chat about it?

We visited Maggie twice more before returning to Guildford. She seemed to gain strength from the visit and Connie even managed to peck her on the cheek when we left mid-morning on the last day. Back home, Jess's behaviour had been exemplary. She had most definitely been studying but, not only that, the house was relatively tidy and she had bought in the basics of survival – a loaf of bread, half a dozen eggs and a bottle of whisky. I didn't ask how she'd swung the last, just cocked an eyebrow and was rewarded with a grin and a shrug.

There was something else surprising in Aborigine Road. A 'For Sale' sign next door.

– How strong are you, Mum?

– Herculean. What's up?

– Brenda and Howard are getting married.

Ha. Ha ha ha. Ha ha ha ha ha ha ha...

CHAPTER THIRTY-ONE

FRASER

I dumped my stuff at the apartment that first day back. My flatmate, whoever he / she was, seemed hopeful. The bed was unmade and the fridge stocked with beer. Must be a guy. I decided to pay him a visit before going job hunting. I saw him unlocking the office door. He was small, in his late fifties or early sixties probably, wearing ageing, knee-length shorts and a battered sun hat. He looked vaguely familiar, but I couldn't place him.

– Hi, you must be the new Aegis rep. I'm –

– Fraser!

He grabbed my hand and pumped away. It was Timothy Stone, sorry spouse of Arsey Purple and kidnapee of the brothers Meldüz. We repaired to Nobby's where Timothy, his face glowing with happiness, told us about his escape from thirty odd years of married misery. Inspired by last year's holiday and Aegis's timely advertisement he had opted for a new life. I congratulated him. Timothy frowned.

– What about you, though, old boy? I've put you out of a job –

– No way. That was my decision. You've made a great move. You're going to love it here.

Timothy was delighted to hear we'd be sharing the apartment. I promised to help him through the first arrivals, who were about a week away.

I left him with a warning about Nobby's Blaster cocktail and went across to the Hotel Acropolis. The island tom toms being what they were, Theo was expecting me. Redecoration was woefully behind and the convention due in five days, so there would be plenty of odd jobs, after which, there could be some waitering and bar work. With my immediate practical problems solved, I did a little shopping and made my way back to the apartment, passing Vaporis cyber café. The computer screen in the corner glared at me. I swung a left and carried on. Conscience made me check my mobile. A message alert flashed instantly. 'Ring me. A x'. I switched my phone off. Then, worried that Annie might have a problem in Kilachlan, I went back to Vaporis and bought half an hour of internet time.

Subject: Fess up time

Just got yr text & hope everything OK w you, Jude & Maggie. Difficult 2 call back at moment as credit v low & – U-ll hate me 4 this – think I hate myself but. Here goes. I'm not in Guildford – in fact I'm not in Britain – I'm back in Symi. Things got v difficult w Clair. Her mother came back from America she's a cross between Joan Rivers and the Hannibal Lecter. Life excruciating. I did a runner.

Think I've fucked up oh sister of mine. Am sharing flat with new Aegis rep so U cn get in touch on the office landline if there's a problem.

Time was running out so I signed off and sent it. Then felt a total bastard. I raced to the kiosk on the bridge before it shut and bought a phone card. Outside the bar by the taxi rank, I dialled Kilachlan. Annie was abrupt.

– Yes! We're all fine.

– Look, Annie, I can't talk now. Read your email will you?

– I just did.

– Oh… OK, then.

Long pause, then she hung up.

I went back to Vaporis next morning to check my email. Nothing from Annie, but there was one from Nikos confirming he was spending the summer on Samos helping sister and brother-in-law at their new hotel. Leaving me Billy No Mates on Symi. If I'd've known that… Great timing, pal.

CLAIR

The real Clair stands up

Still no contact with Sonya. I drove to Northampton, portfolio in the boot, revamped CV in a plastic wallet. While my expectations nudged me towards euphoria, common sense anchored me to earth. For instance, how soon would they want me to go and how would that impact on Jess? Jess had been very stern the night before about me accepting any dates they offered. I was, on no account, to hang around for her exams. What did I imagine doing? Sitting outside the exam room biting my nails? Her grandmother would be an adequate chaperone and confidante. She would join me after exams and we'd bum around the Aegean until it was time for her to go university – all being well. I decided to trust my daughter's judgement.

And working on Symi? How would I cope with the awkwardness of Fraser being around? And what about being so far from Maggie? Not necessarily in that order of priority. But somewhere inside I had a minder telling me everything would be all right. Who was my minder? Me.

The fraudulent behaviour of Mr Bow-Tie had an interesting twist. He had passed off my painting as one of my father's and, as a consequence, bumped up the price. I took a look at my original and saw that it had been re-stretched onto an older frame, the fabric of the canvas had been aged, probably with cold tea or burnt sugar my memory dredged up from somewhere, along with the oil surface which had been slightly distressed and discoloured with glass paper and wood stain perhaps? And then there was the signature. J Harkin. Badly done. The Aegis MD, Estelle, offered me the painting back and suggested reporting Cyntra's boss to the Art and Antiques squad. I thanked her but the painting was indeed now hers. And as for art fraud, I'd be quite happy for her to pursue it and sure that my mother would be a willing co-accuser. I had something much more pleasant to pursue.

I returned to Guildford with a contract tucked into my portfolio. I would be leaving in ten days. The schedule started in Samos then week on, week off, during which I would travel to and research the next island. The grand tour took in Ikaria, Patmos, Lipsi, Leros, Kalymnos – skipping Kos – then on to Nisyros, Tilos, Halki, a break in Rhodes and finally, in September, Symi. Time enough to get my emotional act together.

And everything was all right. Connie was actually pleased for me. Said it was time for me to enjoy life a little more and handed me an American Express Platinum Card.

– That's for you to use and for me to pay the bills. It'll help you enjoy life in a little more style. There'll be more when you finally decide what to do. You going to catch up with that guy of yours?

– Maybe.

– Well, don't rule it out.

It was another way of saying 'sorry', and I let her. She decided to stay on in Guildford for a while, oversee the house being 'dickied up' – to Jess's and my instructions – and be around for Jess.

Jess was ecstatic at the thought of our Greek adventure. Nikos was working in his sister's hotel on Samos this season so, for the first leg of the trip, she wanted me to check him out. I wasn't so sure about that one but, hell, it would be good to see him and have an intro to the local life. After Jess came to Greece, Connie would probably go back to Naples for a while. A European package for my mobile ensured Maggie and Annie could contact me at any time. Phee would look after the house in everyone else's absence. Case? Well, nothing's ever perfect. He would have a series of minders. Question was, would Sonya provide blanket cover for other emergencies – when she wasn't in the States? I rang and this time left a message. She got straight back.

She and I picked up again as though there hadn't been a blip. We managed to fit in an overnight in London before I departed for Samos, Sonya for LA. Dinner at Veeraswamy and a boutique hotel in Kensington, my treat. For once, we were both on a high – she over her new film career and I for the transformation my life had undergone. We drank to one another copiously, eventually running out of coherent speech to invent any further toasts. She was gobsmacked that Maggie and Connie knew about Ben being Jess's father.

– So they just went, 'Yeah – you shagged my lover slash employer and had a child but that's cool'? Bloody hell!

– I know, I just don't get it. I mean, Connie could hardly tar and feather me over that, but she's torn lumps out of me over everything else. And Maggie – well, I suppose she has that Scots thing, you know, stoical, remote. Except she's not remote, not – not – remotely… remote.

Sonya knocked back her glass.

– No – far from remote – couldn't be further off. Not within a million miles of –

– Shut up.

On the day before I left, there was a tap at the front door and a smug Brenda proffered me an envelope. She was no longer dressed in jeans but in a pink tailored shift dress and heels so high that her calf muscles bulged like massive goitres.

– Clair – hello – how are you?

She cooed it as though I had some terminal disease. I didn't know whether to smack her for being annoying or laugh at her for looking so like her pink leather sofa.

– Fine thank you, Brenda. How are you?

– Oh fine, thank you – I –

– And Gabriel?

– Oh, he's fine –

– And Judith?

– Yes, yes, she's fine. I just –

– And David? How's David?

– David? Er, well I –

– And Howard? How is he? Still bald?

– Er – er – yes. No! He's – er – we –

– Getting married! You must be delighted! Now you'll <u>never</u> have to go to work.

Her smile had been fading throughout the exchange until now it lapsed into her habitual scowl.

– You needn't start being so – so – snarky and – and – sour grapes. We – Howard and I – don't have any hard feelings, which is why we're inviting you to our wedding.

– And you didn't feel able to pop the invitation through the letterbox? You felt you had to give it to me in person. How sweet of you!

– Look, Clair, you had your chance with Howard –

– You're quite right, I did. He proposed and I turned him down. Last September. Ever heard of the word rebound, Brenda? Congratulations on being second best! Kalinichta kai avrio!

Goodnight and goodbye! Terrible Clair shut the door.

Coda. Someone is missing from all this: Ron, my erstwhile employer. It was only fair that I give him notice. Knowing what I did about his visit to Connie, I approached it with ambivalence. He had provided me with some of my more enjoyable employment in recent times, despite his surliness. But weighed against a summer of art and hedonism he came a poor second. Credit where it's due, though. I'd been glad of any purveyor of port in a storm. He was typically terse.

– Saw it coming.

– Well, thank you, Ron, for – for –

– She still there?

– My mother? Yes, but –

– You're right to leg it. Good bloke, Major Benfleet. Looked after me. Looked after your Mum. And you. Well-good bloke.

There was clearly a lot more to Ron's story and I wondered how much he knew about mine. But I didn't stay to hear it. Just thanked him and wished him well.

FRASER

Annie was royally hacked off and could barely speak to me. Emailed, though, to say it made life uncomfortable with Maggie knowing I'd hurt Clair so much. I'd have phoned Maggie, but I knew Annie would pick up. And even if I did get Maggie, the stroke would make it difficult to have a conversation. Nobby and Panos, respectively, were up for selling or sharing copious amounts of alcohol while endorsing my 'stupid thing' theory. The only person to give me any sympathy was Timothy.

– A stupid thing? Listen old chap, I've just escaped from doing a stupid thing that lasted thirty years. Yours is nothing by comparison. If I could put that right, surely you can change matters for the better? Hmm? She sounds a nice woman, this Clair. And she was quite a looker, I seem to remember, apart from the day she was sick on the jetty at Nanou. Don't throw away an opportunity like that because you can't be bothered to do anything about it.

It was good advice, but I wasn't up to taking it. Besides, according to Annie, I was a slime ball from the stinkiest pit of infantile hell. Clair had to be of the same mind.

I checked out Marjorie's little hut in the hills where Clair and I had shared an afternoon... Marjorie was due any day, in fact was usually here by now. She always came to Symi for a little break before taking off teaching painting round the Aegean for the summer. The little place was fine, of course, but it made me feel worse. I did bits and bobs of work at the hotel, got a few music bookings there and a couple of gigs on Rhodes, avoiding Lindos and Mel naturally. Then one of the hotel chains on Rhodes offered me work across the season as full-time host for incoming American groups plus the odd trip out and a few nights playing in the bar. It seemed fair enough so I waved goodbye to Symi for a while, even though I knew I'd be escorting a good few trips there. It wouldn't be the same, though. I called in at the Aegis office to let Timothy know. He was snoozing with his feet up on the desk, the picture of bliss. I woke him gently, told him my news.

— Fraser, dear fellow! I shall miss you. But, of course, you must follow the work. Will you be keeping on your half of the apartment?

— Honest to god, Stoney, I have no idea what to do. Let's just wait and see if Stavros notices he's only got half the rent. If there's any hassle, I'll cough up.

— Sounds reasonable. Your departure wouldn't be connected to the arrival of a certain Ms Harkin, would it?

— What?

— Yes, I wondered if you knew. She's taking over the painting holiday interest. Seems it was a bit of a coincidence, eh? After our conversation? She's scheduled to be here September. Kismet, old fellow! Seize the day!

Would I ever have the courage to face Clair again? Something more suited to digesting in a quiet moment, not that I was to get many of those. Clair! Clair on Symi! I wondered why Marjorie wouldn't be back and reasoned it was probably an age thing. Then it was back to Clair. Clair on Symi...

It was a strange feeling being away from Symi. Even though I was back there on a regular basis, it was as a guide on the ferries that clogged Panormitis and Yialos harbours. I headed platoons of tourists across my beloved island while they pitted the walls of the pastel villas with their nasal twang and cleansed the tavernas of steak and fries. Once I got into it, I made some reasonable tips and the shops and tavernas on Symi recognised my recommendations generously. I felt unbelievably cheap.

I was worked a lot harder by the hotel chain than by Aegis. Never got long enough off to get to Symi for an evening and overnight so I didn't see any of my old friends for a beer and commiseration. One sweltering August day, as I trudged ahead of the Idaho chapter of the American Society of Upholsterers and Soft Furnishing Manufacturers, Nobby fell into step beside me.

– You gorra job on wi' these fookers. Bring 'em in the bar – soon sort 'em for yer.

I was ridiculously pleased to see him.

– Don't think I could afford the legal suits afterwards.

– Wha'rever. 'Ere, stick insect 'oo's doing your job said to give yer this.

He passed me an official looking envelope posted from London, a company of solicitors. My stomach turned over. Solicitors never sent good news. I thanked Nobby, tucked it away for later – much to his disappointment – and opened it back on Rhodes. The words blurred on first reading. Second time was no easier. It was Marjorie. Marjorie had died. I wondered when – and why it hadn't occurred to me. Why hadn't someone let me know? Or had she died suddenly? Much later, when I read it a third time, I took in the last paragraph. She'd left me her hut.

If anything could convince me what to do it was that. Just about the happiest moment in my life was spent in that hut – with Clair, that is. And here was Marjorie giving me her blessing.

Got on the phone to Timothy that night to check the painting holiday dates. Clair would be on Symi in two weeks. In that case, so would I.

HOWARD

I didn't get the job. Brenda and I were married the day after I got the letter. Judith was a flower girl and Gabriel fainted in the Registry Office. Brenda is staying on in Guildford until we can find a house nearer my work in Hitchin. Meanwhile, I stay up here during the week. Clair sent us a small painting of Symi as a wedding gift. Brenda accidentally put the hoover nozzle through the canvas. Don't know how – I've never seen her do any bloody hoovering.

CLAIR

No more Terrible

This is when I remembered I'd left my American Express Platinum Card and spare glasses on the dressing table and had that blissful dimitte diem moment of: *Can't do anything about it, so let it go.*

Oh, it was a blissful summer of gipsying around. First, Samos, where Nikos and his sister and brother-in-law treated me like a member of the family. When I wasn't teaching, I was whisked to family meals, nights in tavernas and trips to secret beaches. I started learning Greek, seriously. There was hardly any evidence of the disastrous fires of 2000. The island was spectacularly beautiful, greener and much, much larger than Symi. The students were aged from early thirties to mid-eighties. Their passion for art was heartening and teaching them very rewarding. I made some good friends. Then, a sad leave-taking from Nikos and family with promises to return and an invitation from me to visit Guildford anytime – although I had some misgivings about their reaction to Surrey's cosy suburbs after the grandeur of the Aegean.

The islands were a world apart and wonderfully timeless – they would always be there for me. Jess flew out as soon as she finished her exams, joining me on the comparatively flat little island of Lipsi. I hopped up and down on the quayside waiting to meet my beautiful school-leaver from the hydrofoil. That evening, I learned that Mandy and Richard had had a little boy, Edward. He'd been premature and in intensive care for some weeks, but was home now with his ecstatic parents. I felt nothing but pure joy for them and wrote a long letter of congratulation that very night. Next, we went to Leros, a gem of an island shaped like a jigsaw piece, where Jess had her eighteenth birthday. Aptly, we stayed in Studios Happiness. We celebrated the coming-of-age at a restaurant jutting into the sea near Aghia Marina and went on to a wonderfully laid-back cocktail bar on the fishing harbour at Panteli. Jess bought the drinks just because she could. Nikos rang as we sank our second champagne cocktail and invited her to join him in Samos for a holiday. Great joy and celebration and another round!

Oddly, she didn't bounce away like a cat off a trampoline but chose to tag along with me for a bit. She wanted to see Symi, she said. I wasn't so sure.

– Darling, there's no need to look after me. I can handle Symi – and Fraser. Just do what suits you the best.

– I definitely need to be with you when I get my results.

– That won't be long. Well before Symi. Then you could go?

– You trying to get rid of me?

I thought about it.

    — As far as Symi's concerned, yes. Maybe I am.

    — Cool. I'll give Symi a miss.

We were comfortable travelling companions, she spending her time swimming, sunning, reading and occasionally helping out in the Aegis office wherever we were while I was teaching. It earned her a little pocket money and gave her time a focus. Now and again she would join one of my classes but soon lost interest preferring to be a model for those who wanted a little practice at drawing people. Life drawing, though, was strictly out and her micro bikini remained firmly attached at all times.

Nothing had been properly resolved about the house in Guildford, about Connie's and my relationship or what our individual or joint futures might be. I deliberately distanced myself from it all with a mixture of happiness and strength. It was clear, now, that Connie had never intended to leave us homeless.

My fifty-first birthday was on Kalymnos. Jess had a special edition of Dorothy Parker's short stories and essays for me and a bookmark with a picture of Symi marking 'The Middle or Blue Period'.

    — I found your old copy up the garden by the shed. It must have been there for yonks – all mildewed and chewed. But it was open at that page.

I was glad to have it again and looked forward to re-reading it that night, But before that, we spent the evening at a taverna with a bunch of Canadian students we'd picked up in Lipsi and who'd followed us with the random devotion of youth for several weeks. Addresses were exchanged and undying friendship sworn. Aleixandre from Montreal fell hopelessly for Jess. Hopelessly, because Jess had Samos and Nikos in her sights. There was one from Vancouver who might have stolen my heart had he been just a few years older, but I knew better. And my interest was distracted by an inhabitant of Symi. I tested myself for pain, found it was still there and was glad, in a way. Healing it gave me another goal.

Jess got her A level results while we were still on Kalymnos. Not too bad – an A, two B's and a D. But not good enough to do Psychology (the fourth of her last-minute switches) at her chosen university, Sussex. We talked it over and she decided that she would take advantage of her 'inheritance' from Joe and use the coming year as part gap year, part resits. It seemed reasonable. Then she decided it was time to head for Samos and Nikos. I watched her depart on the northbound ferry with mixed feelings. We were both off into the unknown, in a way.

Come September I found myself heading toward 'that familiar headland rising from fabled depths', this time alone. I remembered approaching the

Byres Road in Glasgow nine months earlier feeling pretty much the same uncertainty. That had turned out well – to start with. But there was no Connie to blight things on Symi. We would have space to ourselves, alone – if he was here. If he was single. If he still wanted… If I still wanted…

As we headed into the spectacular harbour, I prickled with anticipation, dread, elation – before being rounded up into the customary cattle drive. Creaking down the gangway I saw the green three-wheeler parked randomly on the quayside, a bulky figure at the wheel. Then came the sound of a familiar voice. One, as it turned out, I was very glad to hear –

– How're you doin', Harkin? Kalos eelthate stin Symi.

ACKNOWLEDGMENTS

Quotation from <u>THE MIDDLE OR BLUE PERIOD, Dorothy Parker</u>, reproduced by permission of Pollinger Limited and the NAACP.

Lyrics from CLAIR (written by Gilbert O'Sullivan) QuoSony/ATV Music Publishing / Grand Upright Music Ltd.

Lyrics from CABARET (written by John Kander, Fred Ebb and Joe Masteroff (c) 1966) used by permission.

THANKS

Terrible With Raisins was a long time in the writing and, consequently, there are many friends along the way whom I thank for their interest and encouragement. Naturally, I am beholden to the people and the island of Symi for such happy inspiration.

My special thanks go to my late mother, Barbara McVernon and to my husband, Martyn Stead. Without their love and support this novel could not have been written.

Thank you to my friend and fellow writer, Mark Arnold, for his literary advice and practical help. Also, thanks to the Varnas family in Leros for an hilarious evening of coaching in Greek profanities.

Last, but of course not least, immense gratitude to my stepdaughter, Sarah Braine (nee Stead), who gave of her time, patience, knowledge and expertise to edit Terrible With Raisins – from the other side of the world.

ABOUT THE AUTHOR

Lynne McVernon has worked as a theatre director throughout the UK. She has written for the stage and adapted plays for radio and also written a number of prize-winning short stories. Website: lynnemcvernon.com

COMING SOON

JIGSAW ISLAND, the sequel to TERRIBLE WITH RAISINS, is due to be published in 2019 by UNBOUND. You can pledge for an advance copy on: unbound.com/books/jigsaw-island

Free eBook of TERRIBLE WITH RAISINS with each pledge

47396670R00210

Printed in Poland
by Amazon Fulfillment
Poland Sp. z o.o., Wrocław